WAYS TO FIND YOURSELF

OTHER TITLES BY ANGELA BROWN

Olivia Strauss Is Running Out of Time

Some Other Time

PRAISE FOR *WAYS TO FIND YOURSELF*

"Upon closing this novel, I feel as though I've just come home from actually spending time at its beach-town setting, and I'm so sad to have left that magical place. Insightful and intriguing, surreal and yet firmly grounded in all too relatable feelings and situations, Ways to Find Yourself is a book to return to again and again, like a special beach house."

—Suzy Krause, bestselling author of *I Think We've Been Here Before* and *Sorry I Missed You*

"Ways to Find Yourself is, at its core, a love story between a mother and daughter, and a moving portrait of the ways grief binds and transforms us. Angela Brown writes with tenderness and wonder about the ways love can reach across time, memory, and loss to guide us home. A beautiful meditation on who we were and who we might still become. I loved every page."

—Rachel Del Grosso, author of *Eleanor & Sam*

WAYS TO FIND YOURSELF

a novel

ANGELA BROWN

Little a

This is a work of fiction. Names, characters, organizations, places, events, and incidents are either products of the author's imagination or are used fictitiously. Otherwise, any resemblance to actual persons, living or dead, is purely coincidental.

Published by Little A, New York

www.apub.com

EU Product Safety contact:
Amazon Media EU S. à r.l.
38, avenue John F. Kennedy, L-1855 Luxembourg
amazonpublishing-gpsr@amazon.com

ISBN-13: 9781662533679 (hardcover)
ISBN-13: 9781662533662 (paperback)
ISBN-13: 9781662530869 (digital)

Cover design by Emily Mahar
Cover image: © Tessa Hadley / Bridgeman Images

Printed in the United States of America

First edition

For my twenty-five-year-old self:
You should have splurged on the good sunglasses.
You had no idea how many bright days were up ahead.

I am out with lanterns, looking for myself.

—Emily Dickinson, a letter to a friend

BEFORE

PROLOGUE

Someone always asks.

People word it differently. They shuffle phrases, tweak diction, add their own spin. In the end, the syntax never matters; the meaning stays the same. Regardless of the city, the venue, or the size of the event, everyone—everywhere—wants to know one thing.

What advice would you give your younger self?

Tonight, a woman—early twenties, wire-rimmed glasses, her insecurities hanging from her like a too-big dress—approaches the microphone. "Hi." She flinches, pulls back her head. "S-sorry. Hello." Even from a distance, it's clear she's uncomfortable hearing her voice amplified, like it's a recording and she's wondering if this is how she really sounds. It's common. At times, it feels unnatural to listen to yourself. "My question is . . ." Her words tremble, while her cheeks flush pink. "Now that you know how life turned out, if you could go back . . ."

Grace Whittaker, two days shy of thirty-three, sits at the front of the packed bookshop. She wears stylish sandals, a loose maxi dress, and a sweater draped over her shoulders. Her mother, Birdie, taught her this trick. *Always bring a light layer, Cece. Even in August.*

It's come in handy.

The last eight weeks, she's lived in Ubers, on planes, and in every Marriott known to man. In each new setting, the temperature fluctuated as much as her hormones.

Like Grace, they've been all over the map.

This season, rather than lounge at the beach with a cold beer and a good paperback like she once loved—once practically *lived*—to do, Grace has zipped back and forth across the country. The jet lag has been terrible, but worth it. For years, she poured herself into her debut novel, now a bestseller and the reason for all the travel. Lately, she's lucky to sit beside a window in a hotel lobby and feel the glow of daylight on her face. Her hair—once long, wild, and sun-bleached this close to Labor Day—is shoulder length, neatly trimmed, and dyed a rich medium brown. The bottom of her bag is free of sand. No freckles or tan lines graffiti her skin.

Things change. People change.

She feels exhausted, a little nauseous, and grateful for all of it.

Five years earlier, Grace was a different person. Different apartment. Different job. Different hopes. Different fears. Different wardrobe. Different dreams. Different friends.

Five years before that? She'd been someone else entirely.

It kept stretching back.

Over time, it was as if she'd been a hundred different people, all housed inside the same body. Each one searching, asking the same questions: *Who am I? Where am I going? What do I want? When will I figure things out?*

But that was a long time ago.

After years of looking, Grace has found herself.

Today, she understands not only who she is but also where she belongs.

In the morning, Grace will fly away from this Midwestern city and back to the East Coast. Adam—solid, dependable Adam—will meet her at JFK. Together, they'll drive to their new home in the New York suburbs, their apartment on the Upper West Side already a memory. Birdie, having made the two-hour drive from Grace's hometown in Pennsylvania, will already be there, unpacking boxes, putting away groceries, finding other small but meaningful ways to help welcome her daughter into this bright new chapter of her life.

What *would* Grace say if she had the chance to see her younger self again now? Since June, she's been asked this question dozens of times and thus has compiled a mental list of stock answers. *Have patience. Keep going. You're almost there.* But tonight—this last night of her inaugural tour—a new, more truthful thought bubbles in her mind.

"To be honest," Grace finally says, leaning forward on her wooden stool and allowing herself to be a touch more vulnerable than she has been at previous events, "I don't have a single clue what I'd tell her."

A wave of quiet laughter ripples through the crowd. The audience members understand. Despite their respective ages, they were all young—*younger*—once, too.

"It'd probably depend on which version of her I got to see." She twists her wedding band, which she first slipped on last autumn, grounding herself in this moment—in the person she is right now. "They all needed such different things."

For a beat, Grace pauses while her words hang in the air like stars. She looks—*really* looks—at the girl at the microphone. They don't resemble each other. Still, it's like staring into a mirror. Not in terms of appearance, but in energy. The quiet longing. The uncertainty. The unspoken hope that someone else's story might light the path to her own.

"But maybe it wouldn't matter." Grace's hand drifts to her collarbone, her fingers brushing against her old nameplate necklace—the one she's worn forever, that's seen dozens of incarnations of her. "Really, I'm not sure it's advice I'd give my younger self at all."

In the aisle, the woman clings to every word.

"I'd make her a promise."

Time folds in on itself. It's as if Grace is both there at the microphone and here at the front of the room, her present and her past coexisting in this space.

"I'd swear that one day, it'll all make sense—every wrong turn, every what-if, every night spent staring at the ceiling, wondering what is next. It'll all add up to something." As Grace speaks, her fingers loop through her necklace chain and then, as if by instinct, glide over the charm and trace the letters of her name. "I'd vow that even when it feels impossible, a better version of her waits up ahead." Her peach-glossed lips lift into a soft smile as she lowers her hand and touches her wedding band one more time. "If she just trusts herself, really listens and pays attention to all the signs—even when she's scared and doesn't know where she's going—eventually, she'll find her way," she concludes, her voice brimming with conviction she doesn't know is misplaced.

Because there is one thing *this* Grace—so poised, so pleased, so polished, so full of belief, and so sure of her footing—doesn't yet fully comprehend.

In life, nothing is certain.

Things once found can still go missing.

Despite our best efforts to hold on to them, they can become lost all over again.

PART ONE

Today

ONE

Five Years Later . . .

Friday

If someone had asked Grace Elizabeth Whittaker (née Porter) five years earlier to predict what her life would look like at thirty-seven, she'd have replied with ease.

She'd be married, obviously. A mother, too—the suburban type who baked banana bread and hosted a book club but still knew how to navigate Grand Central when the occasion called. She'd be a novelist, of course, with an ever-growing list of back titles and more on the way. Most important? She'd have prophesized that she'd be happy. More than happy. Fulfilled. Settled—the good kind, when it feels like you've finally exhaled after spending far too long holding your breath.

But that was all in her head.

In real life, things don't always go according to plan.

Breathe, Grace reminds herself. Not for the first time today. This hour. This minute.

Lately, it's what everyone tells her to do—the whole world newly invested in her oxygen intake. There's her therapist, Dr. Anne. The women in her grief group. The authors of the self-help books currently cluttering up her nightstand like a confused shrine. Even her phone sends her daily reminders to pause, *inhale*, and reflect.

It's no use. Her voice, like so many things she thought she'd have forever, is gone.

"Come on, Grace," she says aloud, as if her creativity just requires some gentle coaxing. "You've done this before. You can do it again," she whispers, but her tone sounds thin.

She shifts her gaze away from the blinking cursor on her computer screen, its electronic pulse a depressing metronome, and over to the collection of wilting houseplants on the corner of her desk. A podcast she listened to falsely promised that they'd expedite her healing. She flicks a brittle leaf. Just like all the others this morning, it soundlessly falls.

With a quiet sigh, she sweeps the debris into her hand and tosses it into the wastebasket—a brief moment of productivity before she drags her attention back to her nearly blank document.

"You have until mid-September," she says. "Four weeks to write a book practically from scratch." Her fingers hover over the keyboard. They wait like a row of sprinters eager to hear a starting gun. "One last chance to prove you're still yourself."

Like always, this is where her pep talk ends. The thought of beginning—of trying again—seems insurmountable. Burdensome. Impossible. Like being handed a boulder and then told to swim upstream.

Once upon a time, writing came organically to Grace. The whole process was fluid. Easy. Most days, the words poured from her mind and onto the page before she could even process them. Back in her late twenties, she wrote the first draft of her debut novel, *The Tides*, in a series of sprints. On weekend mornings—free from the rigmarole of her full-time copywriting job on Forty-Second Street—she'd peel open her laptop, start to type, and then suddenly find the moon pasted in the sky. Hours vanished in a blink. Characters appeared. Both in her story and her life, problems were solved.

Now Grace lifts her hands. She adjusts the blanket draped over her shoulders while, inside her mind, a memory stirs.

"You were made for this, Cece," her mother, a longtime English teacher, used to say. "You're a natural." Birdie was always Grace's first reader, whether Grace was thirteen or eighteen or twenty-two. "You have something important to say, my love," she'd add, her voice certain and warm. "Promise me you won't stop until you've said it."

Those days feel like a long time ago.

Her knee tucked against her chest, Grace looks up at the window. Outside, the world is a postcard of August. Golden sunlight. Blue sky. Green trees. Children coasting on bikes, their laughter audible even through the glass. It's the type of day that, in a past life, Grace would have darted outside, determined not to waste a second of it. Presently, her body remains still, as if she's physically tethered to these feelings—to this whole room.

"So what do you think?" she asks the air. "Any chance I can get a sign?" A strand of hair comes loose from her ponytail. "I'll take anything. A gust of wind. A flickering light. Just give me *something* so I know where to take this story." She blows the unruly piece away, but it falls again. "Or maybe my entire life."

Grace grew up in a house where signs mattered. Seeing a cardinal on the windowsill. Randomly waking up at 3:00 a.m. Hearing certain songs play. Walking through the surf and discovering whole sand dollars washing up at your feet. They meant someone was watching over you. Helping to guide you. That you weren't alone, even when you felt like it.

"Well?" she presses. "Anything?"

One minute passes. Then two.

She's met with silence.

Resigned, Grace peers down, as if a blueprint for her future might appear amid the mess that's taken over her once tidy workspace.

Crumpled pages. Balled-up sticky notes. Empty mugs. Her monthly planner flipped open to a grid of scribbled-out goals.

"Try not to take that thing so seriously, Cece," Birdie often reminded Grace when she caught her plotting out her life like it was a book she planned to write. "You know what they say, sweetheart," she'd add through her signature red-stained lips, as if she were out on a perpetual date with life. "We make plans and the universe laughs." She'd give her daughter's hand a knowing squeeze. "Leave some space for surprises."

Back in her small home office, Grace pulls off her blue-light glasses. Nothing productive will come from her today. Maybe not ever again. She closes her document and clicks open her email, only to find a wealth of junk. Newsletters from other authors with better momentum (*Big Announcement!*). Bank statements she'd rather not see. Promo codes for end-of-season sales, like she has anything to dress up for these days. Foolishly, she opens one anyway. Gauzy dresses. Rattan bags. Models smiling from sunny locales. A curated vision of the summer she's missed.

For an instant, she closes her eyes and lets herself picture it. The chance for an escape. A break in this awful routine. Warm sun on her skin. An ice-cold soda in her grip. The distant sound of waves. A fantasy. Even so, when her lids lift, she can't help what comes next. It's automatic. Something she's done so often these last few months she's lost count.

A few keystrokes later, the listing appears. 116 Surf Street. Sea Drift. Her and Birdie's favorite place on the Jersey Shore. The house looks the same. No surprise. Cedar shingles. Turquoise door. Pea gravel driveway. She scrolls through the rental calendar, plugging in dates for the solidly booked property, just to *see*, as if she's planning a joy-filled trip and not daydreaming about better times. It's silly, this habit, like searching online for a profile of an ex. It's not like she intends to book anything. If forced, she could provide a list of reasons to never go back. Even so, she needs to see that it's still there. Something—somewhere—to keep her anchored. Proof that at least certain parts of her past were real.

Ding.

Her inbox. A new email.

Instantly, her stomach tightens. Her pulse quickens. Every part of her body thrums with dread. Without the need to look, she's certain what new message awaits.

> Subject: Checking in!
> Sender: Mollie Grey, Chapter One Literary Agency
> Hey Grace,
> Hope you're doing well since we last spoke! Wanted to see if you have any new pages for me to look at yet. No pressure! But considering how things went with your last draft, might be a good idea for me to take a fast peek? I'm heading out of town later today and will have limited access to email for the next week, so feel free to send soon! Would love to read them on the drive!
> Should we plan a lunch in the city for when I get back? Something to toast your anticipated success? September 15th will be here before we know it. ☺
> xx,
> M

A nauseous taste fills Grace's mouth as she skims back through the message. Four exclamation points (five if she counted the subject) *and* a smiley face. Professional urgency disguised as cheer.

During their lunch in June, at an airy Italian restaurant in lower Manhattan, Grace assured Mollie—her literary agent of nearly a decade—that her new manuscript was progressing smoothly. No issues!

No worries! No stress! She *swore* this new version of her next book was *the one*, then assured her she'd pass along chapters once they were ready. Weeks later, they're not.

At that meeting, despite the breeziness of their conversation, there was something neither party explicitly stated but both privately understood: that this final round of edits was Grace's last chance. Her first book? A huge success. Her second? A flop. Her third? Still unfinished.

She'd submitted the original draft for it in January. Grace knew it wasn't her best. The months she'd spent writing it were weighed down by such heavy things. Even so, she hoped that with some finessing, it could work. Her editor sent a note a few days later, expressing that she *didn't love the direction*. Publishing speak for *Start again*. She was assigned a new deadline, which had since been bumped back three times. The September delivery date was the final straw.

Her hands shaking, Grace exhales and types a fast reply.

> Subject: Re: Checking in!
> Sender: Grace Whittaker, Grace Whittaker Books
> Hi Mollie,
> You must have read my mind! Happy to send along some pages when you're back (hopefully from somewhere with fun cocktails and water views). Just polishing a few last bits!
> Thanks for reaching out! Should be a-okay for next month's updated deadline. Exciting!
> xx,
> Grace

There. Four exclamation points. Enough to sound enthusiastic but not unhinged.

She presses send. The lie hangs heavy in her chest. Why is she pretending? Acting as if everything's fine? Like she's in control? Grace doesn't want to be this person. Overpromising. Underdelivering. Adrift, both creatively and personally. A woman who's stuck.

Outside, a car door slams.

"Shoot," she mumbles, as if whispering might make them—this whole situation—go away. "They're early." A minute passes. The thud of her heart blends with the sound of their voices. She leans across her desk to look. Beyond the window, the white moving truck is parked in the driveway next to Birdie's old green Jeep. "Great." A sigh—long and sad, like the final balloon deflated at the conclusion of a party no one wanted to end. "So this is really happening."

She rises slowly. Her limbs feel like lead. As she moves toward the door to go change out of her pajamas, her gaze drifts to a framed photograph on a bookshelf. Birdie. Early thirties. Standing on the sandy crest of a dune. A straw bucket hat and classic one-piece. Her long hair, which had just begun to turn from blond to a premature gray, blowing in the breeze. Three-year-old Grace expertly perched on her hip. They're both smiling.

The doorbell rings.

Grace turns. A glimpse of herself in the hallway mirror catches her off guard. The person in the reflection—messy, visibly tired, her brightness dulled—hardly resembles her. She looks like someone who wandered off the set of her own story and then got lost on her way back.

"Oh, one other thing," Grace says out loud. "I miss you, Mom. Even more than I can describe." She glances over her shoulder, like someone might be there. Waiting. Listening. Ready to offer advice. "I don't even know who I am anymore without you here," she says.

For a long moment, she waits—breath held—as if an answer will arrive.

There's only quiet.

Finally, Grace pulls in an inhalation, even though it doesn't change anything.

Then, not wanting to face this day but knowing she doesn't have a choice, she takes a step forward. Into a future she never planned. Toward a life she didn't choose.

Unsure what comes next, she leaves the room.

TWO

The house, like everything else, is a mess.

For the last hour, Grace has stood at the kitchen island, unable to move. Her eyes remain fixed on the steady procession of boxes being carried through her front door. Three hulking strangers, their shirts damp, continue to file in and out, hauling the contents of their moving truck inside. Silently, they stack the cardboard cubes against the living room wall. Birdie's boxes. The last of them. Her final possessions, now here in her daughter's home, because she is gone.

"Good morning."

Adam steps past the movers and through the doorframe, holding a to-go beverage tray. He wears shorts and a T-shirt, a departure from his usual work attire—button-downs, golf shirts, khakis. Clothes that suggest he's reliable. Dependable. Trustworthy. Professionally, at least.

Grace's throat tightens. "Hi," she says, surprised to see him—Adam, her husband of more than five years—standing in the entryway. "I didn't know you were stopping by." Her voice is level, stripped of the sharp edges that shaped it earlier this summer. She's out of energy for arguments. Questions. Verbal explosions. All that remains are facts. "What are you doing here?" She sets down the dry toast she was nibbling. Her almost ex-husband. Her mother's last belongings. The sights in this space are too unsettling for her to eat.

"I brought you an iced coffee." He lifts a cup from the carrier and smiles in his easy, charming way—the one that once made Grace feel like happy endings were real, achievable things. "Figured you'd need it. I remembered you said the movers were bringing your mother's things today."

If you remembered, then why didn't you offer to be here in the first place? she thinks.

"And," he adds, shifting on his feet, "I need to grab a few more things from upstairs."

The truth.

He hesitates, unsure if he should enter this space that was once theirs. Still *is* theirs, at least in some lingering, legal way. Finally, he moves inside, hands her the drink like it's an olive branch. As if a beverage could fix all that he's broken. All the ways that life has gone wrong.

She accepts it anyway and sees it's not right. Black. Likely bitter. She digs deep, summons a happy face. It's like slipping on a sweater from her childhood; try as she might, the expression no longer fits. "Thanks."

"I forgot your coconut milk," Adam notes, following her gaze. It's a small, silly indulgence, but still, it's one she likes. The old Adam—the one who'd memorized how she preferred her tea (splash of cream), which blanket she needed to sleep with (the weighted one), and how she liked her sandwiches (no condiments)—wouldn't have forgotten. "I should also mention that it's decaf." He shrugs. "Sorry. Old habits, I guess."

Nine years earlier, when their story was still on its opening pages, Adam remembered everything. Important dates. Her favorite flowers. At some point, that all changed. Lately, Grace has tried to pinpoint the moment. A square on the calendar. A specific exchange. But she can't. All she's concluded is that one day, they were solid—the future they believed they were carving out together a few smooth paces ahead. The next? The picture they had in mind was erased, like someone giving an Etch A Sketch a good, firm shake.

They met at twenty-nine while living in Manhattan. One autumn night, while getting dressed for a colleague's wedding, Grace had a meltdown on the phone with Birdie. About her job. (*I don't even like what I'm doing.*) About her recently finished novel. (*I haven't heard back from a single agent.*) About New York. (*I feel so claustrophobic here some days.*) About an ex she missed. (*Did I make a mistake?*) Like always, Birdie talked her through it (*It'll come together, Cece. Just look for the signs.*), then encouraged her to put on something sparkly to lift her mood.

Forty minutes later, dressed in a sequined shift, Grace dashed through the hotel lobby, racing to catch the elevator up to the rooftop reception. Nothing about the ride was out of the ordinary—not until the small brass box jolted to a stop.

"Looks like you're stuck with me," the tuxedo-clad stranger beside her said. "I like your dress, by the way," he added, his eyes straight ahead. "Shiny."

They talked. Adam was nice. Charming. He was from Massachusetts and undeniably attractive—blue eyes, broad shoulders. He worked for an insurance company in Midtown. ("I help people prepare for a secure future," he joked. "I'm like a fortune teller, only with a 401K.") He was a grown-up in a way her ex had never been. Grace liked that.

When the elevator screeched back to life, Adam reached over and touched Grace's shoulder. "Huh. Look at that. A ladybug. In an elevator. In autumn." He held out a finger to show her. Grace's breath caught in her throat. "That's . . . strange."

They scheduled a date for the next week. One day before it, Grace received an email from Mollie, expressing interest in representing *The Tides*. One year later, and with a book contract in hand, she left her day job, broke the lease on her downtown studio, and moved into Adam's doorman apartment on the Upper West Side. One year after that, he proposed.

Now, back in the kitchen, they stare at each other, their silence like its own language.

"So." Adam's voice cuts through the quiet. He leans against the island, no longer comfortable enough in this space to sit. When he does, Grace notices his T-shirt—the one he bought last August on their trip to Maine, the memory of that weekend like a punch to the chest. "Coffee aside, I come bearing good news."

"Oh, yeah?" Grace pulls the coconut milk from the fridge. She shakes the carton. All that remains in it are a few pathetic drips. "What's that?"

"They're making good progress with your mom's stuff out there." He sips his drink, accented by a perfect, creamy swirl. "Looks like they've already brought most of it inside. Shouldn't be much longer before the truck is emptied out and they have this all wrapped up."

She tosses the carton into the recycling bin, sighs. "I guess in the end," she says and gives him a sidelong glance, "it doesn't take all that long to dismantle a whole life."

It's been six months since Birdie died. One hundred and eighty-four long, gut-wrenching days. *An aneurysm,* the doctors had explained in the too-bright hospital hallway near Grace's hometown in Bucks County, Pennsylvania. It didn't make sense. How did a vibrant sixty-eight-year-old woman go to sleep and then not wake up? Apparently, it happened more often than people cared to admit. That February afternoon, Grace left the hospital a different person than the one who'd entered it. She walked through the slushy parking lot, feeling like a tree that'd been cut off at its roots. She didn't understand how she was still standing.

In the months since, Grace's grief had become like a second job, one that paid only in heartache. The paperwork. The endless calls. The logistics of disassembling another person's existence. Her father, James, had been killed in an accident when she was a toddler. Neither of her parents had siblings. Their parents were already gone. It all fell on her. Packing up Birdie's house—the cozy townhome she'd rented since Grace was five—was the hardest part.

For months, Grace stalled. On the first of every month, she sent a check to Birdie's longtime landlord—a man she still, despite her age, called Mr. Sam—explaining that she needed more time. But math was math. The money added up. At the start of August, she gave Mr. Sam a hug and a final check. In September, a new tenant would move in.

There were parts of death that felt like a surprise to Grace. The mind-numbing finality. The way it made her ache for the past and dread the future—the present an unfamiliar landscape she longed to escape.

But the biggest surprise? The world didn't just stop. Flowers bloomed. Seasons changed. Relationships ended. Life moved forward, whether you wanted it to or not.

Adam made his announcement in early May, the shock of Birdie's passing still fresh.

"I'm not sure I want to be married anymore," he said. They were on opposite ends of the sofa, picking through takeout and half watching a documentary about a cult on Netflix.

"Because it feels like a tiny cult?" She thought he was kidding.

"No." His eyes remained on the TV. "Because I'm not sure it's making me happy."

Adam's proclamation was a surprise but not a shock. They'd been drifting apart for ages, well before Birdie was gone. Still, the timing felt cruel.

Despite his professional love of planning for the future, Adam had zero post-announcement plans in place. No bachelor pad. No bags packed. For a little over a month, he just *stayed.* Grace had every right to demand he leave, but she didn't. And maybe that was the saddest part. Despite everything, she preferred he was there. It was better than being alone.

They engaged in a strange dance, like people who once regularly waltzed but had begun to step on each other's feet. One minute, they were shouting about how they'd lost their way from one another. The next, they were trying to retrace their steps and find their way back. They oscillated between holding on and letting go, like a twisted game of tug-of-war they played with their hearts. At night, Adam slept on the couch, while Grace lay in their bed and studied the walls. A few times, he tiptoed upstairs, and they tumbled around in the sheets, as if their bodies could fix all that was broken. But by morning, the sun always shone light on their circumstances.

In mid-June, the day after Grace's lunch with Mollie, she and Adam engaged in one last romantic rendezvous, followed by one last blowout argument. The next day, he signed a lease on a nearby apartment, packed up as many of his belongings as he could fit in his car, and moved out. They'd been stuck in a sort of separation limbo ever since.

Back in the kitchen, a knock at the door interrupts them.

"Sorry." One of the movers appears in the room. "Wanted to let you know we're at the tail end. Just need to clean up some trash, have you sign a few papers, then we'll be on our way."

"Thanks." Grace finally sips her not-right beverage and instantly smacks her lips, even though it's only partially to blame for the new sour taste on her tongue. "I'll be out in a minute."

The man steps outside, leaving Grace and Adam to themselves again.

"I'd better run upstairs," Adam states, as if this next part is natural. Normal. "Okay with you if I pop into the spare bedroom? There's some stuff I forgot to take last time. I'm going up to the lake house this weekend."

"Sure," she says, her peripheral vision consumed by the most recently assembled tower of boxes, the ones that'd been in the townhome's attic for years. Her mother's cursive handwriting marks their sides. *Baby years—Don't Toss! Elementary—Art Projects! Journals & Notebooks—Important!* The sight of Birdie's looping penmanship is almost enough to bring Grace to her knees. In search of something steady, her fingers find the chain of her old nameplate necklace—the one she hardly takes off, not even to sleep. Despite all she's lost this year, it's one thing that still feels like her. "Take your time."

Adam takes a few steps backward, bumping into the kitchen table in the process. A flurry of loose papers that'd been precariously set on its edge—those Grace brought downstairs earlier in the naive hope that she'd tackle some work while the movers were here—fall to the floor.

"Sorry," Adam says, already bending to gather everything up. In the process, his eyes slide over their content. "Wait." He shuffles the papers into a pile—old printouts of Grace's early writing, her notes and annotations scribbled in the margins—but not before giving them another glance. His brows knit. "Is this an old version of *The Tides*?"

Grace nods, noting the way his expression has changed, like he's caught her doing something illicit by skimming back over a narrative from her past. "A *very* early one," she says. "It's nothing like the story that actually went to print."

"Why are you reading through that?" Adam sets them back on the table, a hint of accusation carrying his tone.

"Just looking through some old drafts," Grace says, trying to ignore it. Wishing she could just ignore him. Ignore everything. "Trying to remember that they all used to be blank pages."

Adam gently bites his lip, some thought occupying his mind. "Well, I don't want to keep you from your work, then," he says and heads for the stairs.

Grace listens to the sound of his footsteps, followed by the creak of doors opening, first in the primary bedroom, then in the smaller one beside it. When they first saw that room at the open house, Grace imagined painting it a soft pink, putting a plush glider in the corner. Now it's a hodgepodge. An old dresser. Piles of items never returned. So many forgotten things.

We've lost our way from each other, Grace, Adam said the night of his announcement.

Of course they had. If their marriage were a book, *loss* would have been its theme.

The day they moved into this home—fresh off Grace's first book tour—they pulled into the driveway only to learn that the moving company had lost half their boxes. The next week, they were forced to smash a window because they'd lost their only key. One month later, Grace's doctor informed her that the baby—the one that'd been growing inside her all summer—was lost, too.

Six more losses over the next four years. Each one left them a little more hollow. Still, every time, they told themselves it would eventually work out. Doctors poked and prodded Grace, testing her for countless issues, only to inform her that nothing was clinically wrong. Fertility, it turned out, was a sort of game. One ruled by odds. Timing. Chance. They kept trying. By the third loss, they stopped buying the baby books. By the fifth, they stopped looking at the spare bedroom entirely. The last loss occurred shortly before their trip to Maine. When the ultrasound tech delivered the news, they were both so drained that they just shrugged.

"So you're heading up to the lake house?" Grace asks Adam once they're out on the porch watching the moving truck pull away. The home in question, a vacation spot in New Hampshire, belongs to his parents. Despite the property's undeniable beauty and picturesque views, she'd never gotten past the thought of the insects and snakes swimming beneath the water's dark surface. All the small things she feared but couldn't see. He could keep it.

"For a few days. Work's quiet. It'll be good to get away." Adam adjusts the duffel bag's strap on his shoulder. "What about you? Any big plans for the weekend?"

"Pffft." She laughs. It sounds like she's a raft someone squeezed too hard. "I have a book due in a few weeks, which I haven't quite written." She looks back at the house, thinking of everything else that waits for her inside it. "Among other things."

Adam waits, like he has something else to say. Whatever it is, he clearly thinks better of it. Instead, he steps closer, puts his arms out for an awkward hug. It's clumsy, like they're teenagers faced with a first embrace, neither of them sure how to angle their heads or what to do with their hands. Thankfully, it only lasts a moment before he pulls away.

"Tell the eels and slugs I said hi," Grace calls out, forcing lightness into her tone as he walks to the curb.

"Will do." Adam opens his car door, then stops. "Oh, I almost forgot." He meets her gaze, pauses. "Happy early birthday, Grace."

"Oh." Her head jerks. The words land heavier than they should. "Um . . . thanks."

Adam looks at her for a second too long, as if he's debating something.

"I may have forgotten your coffee order." His voice is softer, now that there's distance between them, and touched by an emotion Grace can't quite name. "But contrary to what you might think, I haven't forgotten everything."

THREE

"I'm drowning," Grace announces, and falls backward onto the couch, like someone auditioning for a melodrama. A small wooden trinket box—once perched on her girlhood dresser—jabs her in the spine. "Maybe not literally, seeing as I'm on dry land." She sets it beside her phone, currently on speaker. "But *definitely* emotionally."

"You opened them, didn't you?" Jenny asks, employing her signature nurturing, yet exasperated, tone. Jenny has been Grace's best friend since the first day of sixth grade, when they walked into homeroom wearing the same purple shirt and scrunchie. They've remained inseparable—or as much as life allows—ever since. "I *told* you not to go through them alone."

"It didn't seem this bad in my mind," Grace mumbles, surveying the chaos she's unpacked. Her old retainer. Teenage diaries. Floppy disks. Birthday cards. College essays. Rolled-up posters. Souvenirs from every era of her life. It's like a strange pop-up museum exhibit. *Grace: A Retrospective*. "I also forgot my mother saved every shred of paper I ever touched. She was like a hoarder, but only with my memories."

Once Adam left, Grace did everything to avoid the boxes. Scrubbed the sink. Checked the mail. Cleaned the fridge. Brought her laptop downstairs, hoping—then failing—to craft a single page. Still, the stacks loomed. She started with Birdie's belongings—the boxes Grace packed up herself a few weeks earlier—before moving on to the others. The ones her mother had been privately packing up for years.

"Stop what you're doing," Jenny says, her backdrop a cacophony of joyful mayhem. Kids shouting. Something crashing. The baby crying. "I'm coming over. We'll schlep everything to the basement, which is what you *should* have had the movers do in the first place when—"

"You don't need to come here," Grace interrupts, flipping through an old journal filled with her adolescent attempts at poetry. "I live two hours away. You have three children."

In high school, Jenny—a preppy soccer star—went through a brief rebellious phase. Blue hair. A longing to head west. For a year, she made everyone call her "Niffer"—an unnatural abbreviation of her first name, Jennifer. Today? She lives ten minutes from their hometown in Bucks County with her husband, Eric. Her school-age kids carry Pottery Barn backpacks. During the holidays, she sends photo cards of her family in matching tartan. People change.

"Fine. Plan B. You come here for a few days. Stay in the spare room. Swim. Work on your book. See the kids. They miss you, and—Charlie! Stop hitting your sister with the dinosaur!" Jenny exclaims, then pulls back. "Plus, we can celebrate your birthday on Wednesday. I'll make pancakes. You *love* my pancakes."

"It's true." Grace tears open the packaging tape on a new box, this one labeled *Miscellaneous*. No category. No date. Just memories. "You really do make the best breakfasts."

"What was that noise?" Jenny asks, instantly suspicious. "Did you open another one?"

"I sneezed," she says, reaching for a joke.

"Grace."

"Look, I appreciate the offer—*all* your offers. But I'm not great company right now. It's better that I'm alone."

"Haven't you basically been alone all summer?"

"Not if you count when Adam still lived here. Or when I visited my therapist. Or grief group." Grace tries for a sarcastic smile. It hurts, like lifting weights after months of skipping the gym. "Plus, I saw *you* when you helped me pack up Mom's house. I'm basically a socialite."

"Grace, come on. It's me. You don't have to pretend. I'm not a stranger." Jenny stops herself. "You can fall apart with me."

Grace's phone dings. She checks the screen and finds a notification from an affirmation app. *Feel what you're feeling. You're not the same person you were yesterday*. She swipes it away. "I'll think about it."

"Liar."

"Probably."

As Jenny wrangles her children, Grace lifts something new from the box. It's heavy and wrapped in tissue. Whatever it is, Birdie apparently believed it was worth protecting. Piece by piece, Grace removes the paper, half expecting to find an old snow globe or figurine. Instead, she discovers a large mason jar full of sun-bleached shells. A lump forms in her throat. Every summer, on the last day of vacation, they made one together before heading home.

"Dear God, Birdie," Grace whispers through a sad gasp of a laugh. "You kept this?"

"I knew it!" Jenny proclaims, then pauses. "So? What is it?"

"It's . . . nothing." Grace traces the lid with a fingertip. "Just old beach memories."

Everyone has a place. For years, Sea Drift was theirs. A stretch of barrier island off the southernmost tip of New Jersey. Twelve miles long. A half mile wide. Close enough to Delaware to touch. On a map, it was so small it looked like a mistake—a smudge of ink versus a place.

It wasn't the Jersey Shore most people probably pictured. Everyone had Atlantic City crime dramas and bad reality TV to thank for that. Sea Drift wasn't glamorous. No old New England money. No wild horses. But it was quiet. Timeless. Saltwater taffy shops. Rickety boardwalk rides. Decades-old bungalows that leaned from the wind.

Every August, beginning the summer after James died, Birdie rented the same two-bedroom house the week of Grace's birthday. It never changed. Not the springy mattresses. Not the dusty beach decor. Not the terrible plumbing. Each time they arrived, Birdie—dressed in a floppy hat and bright, breezy dress—dropped her bag, looked around, then proclaimed, "Well, Cece, looks like the only thing that's changed since last summer is us!"

When she was young, Birdie's parents brought her to Sea Drift on day trips. She fell in love with it. The fudge stores. The specific way the ocean sparkled. The fact that it was an actual island, like something from the adventure books she liked to read.

When Birdie married James, they couldn't afford a faraway honeymoon. Upon her suggestion, they booked three nights at a Sea Drift motel instead. Though they grew up in the same Pennsylvania town, James had never been to the island. During that trip, he fell in love with it, too. When they returned home, they put a jar on the dresser in their first apartment and dropped loose change into it every night. Little by little, they promised to save for the life they wanted. A home. A child. A family vacation by the sea.

Birdie kept her word.

As time passed, Grace's visits dwindled. Something always got in the way. Jobs. Adam. The lake house. Book deadlines. Pregnancy losses. Just *life*. For a while, Birdie kept renting it, even when Grace only came for a few days. Eventually, she got the memo. The year Grace set out on her first book tour, Birdie simply let the tradition go.

"Grace," Jenny says now, "you can't sit there staring at your old things. Come here for a few days. You need air. And sun. And—"

"You're making me sound like a houseplant," Grace says, wishing she could reclaim those last few summers with her mom. "Which isn't great, considering my track record."

"I'm serious," Jenny laughs. "You've spent all season packing up Birdie's house, dealing with Adam, and beating yourself up about your book. You need a fresh perspective. A reset."

"Maybe," Grace murmurs, setting down the jar and deciding to leave it at that.

Seconds pass before either of them speaks again.

"So other than your old orthodontics, find anything good in there?" Jenny asks.

"Only if you count a shoebox of notes we passed senior year."

"I'm sure *that's* full of literary masterpieces to inspire you," Jenny deadpans.

"You have no idea." Grace continues to pick through the box's contents—mix tapes, a knot of friendship bracelets—not sure what she hopes to find. Maybe an instruction manual Birdie wrote on how to live once she was gone. Instead, she pulls out her old Magic 8 Ball. "Deliberating about prom dresses consumed months of our time."

"That sounds like an actual vacation to me right now."

"Tell me about it." Grace sets the toy aside, continues to sift. A moment later, her fingers curl around the edges of a department-store gift box, the kind Birdie used to get from the local Macy's. She opens it, certain she'll find a pair of her flared teenage jeans. Instead, her hands go cold. "Oh, God."

"What now?"

But Grace can't speak. All she can do is stare at the photo album, and the title, *Summer Memories*, written in Birdie's familiar handwriting. Her grip tightens on the cover. She flips and is greeted by photo after photo of summers past. Birdie and toddler Grace eating swirl cones on the boardwalk. Birdie and middle-school Grace reading paperbacks in the sand. Birdie and preteen Grace on the Ferris wheel, arms raised. She turns the page again and finds her sixteen-year-old self—hair kissed golden, skin gorgeously tan, that faded-blue tank she practically lived in that season—staring back at her.

"Grace?"

"I should've gone back. To Sea Drift." Her voice cracks. "I was so stupid. So selfish."

"There were reasons," Jenny says gently. "A lot of them. Birdie knew that."

Grace doesn't respond. She shuts the album. When she does, something slips loose from the pages. A sand dollar. Fragile. Perfectly intact.

Without warning, a memory washes in.

The night of their third date, Grace explained her fixation with signs to Adam. They'd just left a restaurant in the West Village and were stopped at a corner, the neighborhood's cafés spilling light onto the sidewalk as they waited to cross. That was the moment Adam abruptly interrupted their conversation, took Grace's face in his hands, and kissed her for the first time.

"We should keep doing this." He pulled back. The rest of the city kept moving, even though to Grace it felt as if everything had stopped. "Spending time together, I mean."

The light changed. They took a step. And that's when Grace saw it: a shiny penny, planted at her feet. Her heart did a somersault as she instinctively bent and picked it up. Adam looked at her like maybe she was a little crazy, which prompted her to explain the practice.

"I'm guessing this is a deal-breaker?" she said, half joking.

"Not at all." Around them, the autumn breeze picked up. "I'm not sure I believe in that stuff." He smiled. "But it's romantic that you do." Adam buried his hands in his coat pockets. "So what's that penny a sign of? Anything good?"

Grace squirted hand sanitizer into her palm. "I hope so."

Back in the living room, Jenny's voice chimes through the phone. "Look, you can't beat yourself up. Birdie knew you had your own life." She stops. "You know what I think she'd say if she were here?"

"Probably something maddeningly optimistic."

"Exactly. She'd tell you to stop being so hard on yourself. Clean yourself up. Go outside. Get some sun, and—" The baby wails. "Shoot. I'm sorry. I've got to call you—"

"It's fine," Grace assures her. "Really." She bites an unpolished nail, thinking. "Before you go, can I ask you something?"

"The secret to perfect pancakes is a smidge of ricotta and—"

"Cute," Grace notes, picking up the Magic 8 Ball again. "Granted, your kids are young, but out of curiosity, have you started to put boxes like these together for them yet?"

"There is currently a plastic bag in my underwear drawer filled with locks of hair and baby teeth," Jenny admits. "I'm like a sentimental serial killer when it comes to my kids."

"What do you plan to do with it? Other than store it with your underpants for eternity?"

"Hard to say." She consoles the baby with hushed *Shhh* sounds. "I just can't get rid of it."

Grace shakes the toy. *Will life get easier? Will I ever get through all this?* She turns it, watches the purple triangle float to the viewer's surface. *Reply hazy,* it reads. *Try again.*

"When will I feel like myself again, Jenny?" she asks, sounding newly desperate. "Like the old me. The one who had life figured out." Tears sting her eyes. "Tell me. Give me a date."

Jenny exhales. "I don't know, Grace. I wish I could."

"Nothing's helping. Not therapy. Not my silly keeled-over plants. Not time."

"Things will get better." Jenny's tone is soft and motherly, but firm. "You'll see. You'll find your way. Maybe not today. Or tomorrow. Or next week. But eventually, you will."

Grace lets out a heavy breath.

"What?"

"Nothing." Grace wipes her cheek. "It's just that Birdie used to say that, too."

~

Grace wakes to the sound of her phone ringing—a sharp, electronic trill.

She jolts, tugged mercilessly from a dream she feels but doesn't totally recall. Pulling herself up from the couch cushions, she rolls out her neck. It comes to her in pieces. Warm air. Golden sunlight refracting on the water. A sense of weightlessness, as if she's floating. The sound of a voice that feels familiar—comforting—but which, in her present state, she can't quite place.

Ring, ring.

The device beeps and vibrates on the coffee table, exactly where Grace left it after she and Jenny ended their call. Groggy, she tries to gauge the time based on the way the light hits the room. How long has she been asleep? Minutes? Hours? A whole day? Until recently, Grace wasn't a napper. Now? She finds herself nodding off constantly, like a tuckered-out toddler. Too much emotion or activity in one sitting and she zonks out. Just one more consequence of grief.

Who's even calling? she wonders. Not Adam (who rarely calls, typically texts). Maybe Jenny (prepared with a list of additional reasons why Grace should come stay). Not Mollie (likely already embarked on her own getaway).

Birdie used to call at the same times every day. 7:00 a.m. (*Morning, love! What's on the agenda?*) 3:30 p.m. (*Just left the high school and going for groceries. Should I pick up those cookies you like for when I visit this weekend?*) 8:00 p.m. (*Just checking in, my girl. What'd you have for dinner? Tell me about the chapters you wrote this afternoon.*) Birdie wasn't the sort to text. She preferred a real conversation—to hear the emotions in a person's voice and to talk.

Ring, ring.

Grace wipes a line of drool from her chin, glances at the clock on her phone—4:16 p.m.—then finally answers the call before it goes to voicemail.

"Hello?" Her words are scratchy. She clears her throat, tries to sound like a person who wasn't just drooling on a throw pillow in the middle of the day. "Hi."

"Oh, hi there." A male voice she doesn't recognize. "I was getting ready to leave you a message. I'm glad you picked up." The person's tone is bright, cheerful—too personable to be spam. "Did I get you at a bad time?"

Is there such a thing as not a bad time these days? Grace privately ponders.

"N-no. It's fine." She quickly peers at the screen, noting the unfamiliar number, then presses it back to her head. "I-I'm sorry. Who is this?"

"Caleb. From Beach Coast Rentals." A pause. "How are you doing today?"

"I-I'm good," Grace lies. "Wh-where did you say you're calling from?"

"Beach Coast Rentals." He waits for his comment to land. "We handle most of the rental homes down on Sea Drift." Another pause, as if he's giving her time to catch up. "The island. Down the shore?"

Grace straightens, then looks around, like she's being pranked. "I-I'm confused."

"Right. So this is out of left field, but based on our website history, it looks like you may have been in the market to rent one of our properties this week." He stops, gauging the situation. "I apologize. Maybe I have the wrong number." Through the line, the sound of fingers tapping a keyboard. "Am I speaking with Grace Whittaker?"

"Y-yes." Her pulse picks up. "That's me."

"Oh. Okay. That's great." Caleb's intonation lifts. "In that case, and this is obviously spur-of-the-moment, but we have some last-minute availability for a listing you were browsing earlier: 116 Surf Street. Ring a bell?"

Her stomach flips. This morning. Her desk. Had that only been a few hours ago, when she'd mindlessly browsed the page? "I'm familiar." Whatever dreamlike feelings previously blurred her thoughts are gone, everything suddenly in razor-sharp focus. "I know the address."

"Well, it's a bit of a long story, but things fell through with the original renter for this week. Since you plugged in the dates earlier, I thought I'd give you a ring, see if it'd be of interest. Saturday-to-Saturday rental. Check-in's tomorrow at two."

Grace blinks. Her heart flutters. Already, she's shaking her head. Going back to Sea Drift now—at any point—is an awful idea. "No." Her pulse drums in her ears. "I—I can't."

"Oh," Caleb says, dejected, as if he'd been banking on this. "All right."

"I appreciate the call," Grace adds, trying to buff away some of her rudeness. "But to be honest, I was only poking around for . . . *fun*." A knot forms in her throat, dry and burning. "My mom used to rent that property for us every year." She swallows hard, but the feeling stays. "I haven't been down to the island in a long time."

"Well, the good news is that nothing's changed," he teases. "Unless that's bad news."

She exhales a quiet, reluctant laugh.

"Water's warm right now," Caleb continues, waiting to see if he's hooked her, like bait to a fish. "No jellyfish. Tide pools have been gorgeous every afternoon."

Grace glances at her open laptop, still on the coffee table from earlier. With a fast swipe, she summons the blank page, praying the story has magically appeared.

"I wish I could, but I . . ." She stumbles, reaching for a reason, knowing there are several options. The boxes. Her deadline. "I'm just . . ." Her palms sweat. "I'm really busy and bogged down with work at the moment. I'm tied up all weekend—"

"I can give you a decent discount," Caleb interjects. "I hate to see the house sit empty. It's older, a bit rough around the edges. Even so, it's always been one of my favorites."

She sighs. Lets down her guard. "Mine, too."

As soon as the words fall from her lips, Grace hears it. A sound at the front window. She swivels her head. And there it is, looking back at her through the glass: a bright-red cardinal, perched on a branch amid a canvas of vibrant green leaves, its head tilted as if in question. Her chest tightens, some invisible force pulling it from both ends.

"Well, if that's the case, and you plan on staying there again, now's probably your chance," Caleb explains. "Seeing as it might not be an option much longer."

"What?" Grace squints at the glass, half expecting that the bird is a trick of the light. But it's not. It's there. Its feathers as bright as Birdie's favorite lipstick. "What do you mean?"

"The sign," Caleb continues. "It'll be up by mid-September," he adds, making her breath hitch. "The house goes up for sale this fall."

The sign.

A sign.

And that's what finally gets her.

FOUR

Saturday

There's only one way to get to the island.

No charming ferry slicing through waves. No tiny airport with a lone runway and a rickety passenger staircase wheeled up to the plane. Just two lanes of narrow asphalt stretched like a tightrope over the vast mouth of an endless, shimmering bay. One way in. One way out. That's it. Birdie used to joke that once they made it onto the causeway, there was no turning back. From where Grace currently sits—car shifted to Park, boxed in by midday traffic—it's hard not to understand what her mother meant. She's literally stuck in the middle of it.

"You're kidding me?" Jenny's voice flickers in and out from the bad reception—one of Sea Drift's many charms. "You're actually down there? Right now? This very minute?"

"Technically, I'm on the bridge," Grace clarifies, her phone in the cup holder and set to speaker mode. Behind her, a car strapped with boogie boards and beach chairs honks in quick succession, like the driver's impatience will move things right along. "If we're being official, I still have time to change my mind." Grace dips her fingers into a bag of pretzels she picked up at a rest stop—the only thing she's eaten all day. "For all intents and purposes, I'm not there yet."

Late yesterday afternoon, after she reluctantly agreed to the offer (*I guess. But probably only for a long weekend. I doubt I'll stay all week.*) and then gave Caleb her credit card information, Grace spent hours convincing herself she was a fool. *Of course* she couldn't go back to Sea Drift. Not now. Not ever. Despite the water and sand selling the illusion, it wouldn't feel like a vacation. Not one bit.

When her alarm blared at seven this morning (not that she'd slept), she swore she'd call Caleb and cancel. She told herself the same lie while she stuffed an assortment of faded tees into a bag. And again, shortly after nine, while she backed Birdie's Jeep—which Grace hadn't sold yet and had chosen over her own newer SUV at the last minute—out of the driveway. Grace navigated through town—a place that never felt like hers so much as a convenient zip code for Adam's commute—still playing chicken (*Just pick up the phone!*) with herself. As she drove over the bridge into New Jersey, then sat in traffic for three hours on the Parkway South, Grace kept saying it: *Next exit, I'll pull off, make a U-turn, and place the call.*

Only, she never did.

Deep down, something tugged at her—a question she wasn't ready to answer, one she'd been putting off for a long time. She didn't want to go back to Sea Drift—to write, to grieve, to plot out her next steps. But she wasn't ready to completely let it go, either. Which is how she ended up at her current coordinates—trapped between two shores, the wreckage of her present behind her, the ghosts of her past up ahead.

"Well, I'm impressed you made it that far," Jenny states, competing with the sound of her children. "It's a good step."

"Really?" Grace fumbles with the older car's knobs, still trying to remember how to operate the temperature panel. Birdie wasn't impressed by technological advancements. Bluetooth. Satellite radio. Even so, there's comfort in being in the Jeep. "Because right now," she adds, and glances at her laptop and her mother's photo album on the passenger seat, "it mostly feels like a mistake."

In the past, Grace cried on the drive home every summer, devastated when their week in Sea Drift was over. The only time she didn't was the year she brought Adam, the first summer they were dating. He aired small grievances about the house all week. No central air. No fancy coffee machine. It was nothing like the lake house, the one they'd visited together earlier that June and which he'd described as *rustic*, though it was professionally decorated to look as if it'd been torn from the pages of *Architectural Digest*.

"He has a lot of . . . opinions," Birdie noted to Grace one morning on that trip. They were having coffee on the patio while Adam—hoping to work out the kinks in his muscles caused by the home's springy mattress—was out on a run.

"A little bit." Grace laughed, still in that phase of a relationship where everything about a person—even his flaws—seems endearing. "Lucky for him, he has a lot of good traits, too."

Prior to that week, Birdie had met Adam twice on visits into the city. She liked him; there was much to like. He was steady. Reliable. Successful. Driven. He brought Birdie flowers the first time the three of them had dinner and always held doors open.

"He doesn't care for it here," Birdie said, her words framed as a fact.

"That's not true!" Grace exclaimed, as if offended by the remark. "Of course he does."

Birdie didn't respond, just gave her daughter a look.

"Fine," Grace huffed. "It might not be his favorite place on earth."

"But it's yours," Birdie said.

Near the street, the sound of footsteps on the pea gravel driveway signaled Adam's return.

"You laugh different when you're around him," Birdie said, eyeing a seagull overhead.

"What?" Grace swatted her mother's hand. "No, I don't."

"You do. It's more subdued. Restrained." Birdie stood and, without asking, took Grace's empty mug. "Just make sure you're letting him see you. The real you. The one who's always loved nothing more than being here."

The next few days, Grace tried to disregard her mother's comments, even as Birdie's words echoed in her head.

"So did you enjoy yourself?" she asked Adam as they drove over the bridge.

"Sure." Adam's fingers curled around the steering wheel as he navigated them back in the direction of their life in the city. "The house is . . . cute."

"I know," she said, as if she needed to apologize for the property, though it wasn't technically theirs. "It hasn't been updated in a long time." She forced a laugh. "Maybe ever."

"It was nice," he said as they crossed the causeway, the highway entrance up ahead. "I can see why you were inspired to write about the setting—well, a *fictional* version of it, as you keep insisting—for your book." He cleared his throat, offered a side-eye. "Speaking of which, think you'll ever let me read it?"

At that point, Grace had been working with her editor on *The Tides* for months. Even so, she'd yet to let Adam skim a single page. Grace said she wanted him to wait until it was perfect—no more revisions or copyedits—then privately told herself she was being foolish whenever she wondered if there were other reasons she kept putting it off.

"Of course." She summoned a bright, flirtatious smile. "But not until it's officially done."

"Well, in the meantime, I get why you love it there." Adam glanced in the rearview mirror, perhaps to confirm that the island was indeed behind them. "Though it might be more of a you-and-Birdie thing." Adam laughed. "Or a fiction-research thing." He reached over, squeezed Grace's thigh. "If only for the sake of my back. That bed was a doozy."

Grace laughed, but it wasn't real.

Now brake lights blink out one by one, a slow-motion domino effect. Grace taps the gas, cautiously at first, then with more certainty as the knot of vehicles unravels, like a tangled necklace finally shaking loose.

"Traffic's moving, so I'd better go," Grace explains to Jenny. "I just wanted to tell you my whereabouts—116 Surf Street—in case I go missing or something." Her eyes lower to her fingers, knuckle-white from gripping the steering wheel, and the permanent line of pale skin where her wedding band previously hugged her—a once silent, sparkling promise. "I thought at least someone should know where I'm at."

"Noted," Jenny states. "So what's the plan for once you're down there?"

"No clue," Grace admits. "Probably cry on the beach for a few days."

"Better than crying inside at home."

"Maybe," Grace adds, not certain yet if she agrees.

"Well, you know how to reach me." Jenny's presence—even though she's not physically there in the car with her—is certain and reassuring. "I can be there in two hours if you need anything. Just say the word. I might have three tiny people in tow, but—"

"Thank you, Jenny. I'm sure I'll be all right."

Before Grace has a chance to say goodbye and hang up, Jenny speaks again. "Grace?"

"Here we go."

Jenny laughs. "Look, I know my family never vacationed down there, but from what you've told me about the island over the years, as well as what I remember from the way you described the setting in your book, it's a pretty small place." She pauses. "A lot of familiar faces." Another brief interlude. "A lot of . . . memories, you know? Not only of Birdie."

"I'll be fine," Grace reassures her, understanding her subtext. "I'm not still sixteen."

The call drops. There's no need to dial Jenny back. They've both said what was needed for the moment. Instead, Grace buzzes down the windows, welcoming in the distinct smell of salt and brine as the Jeep glides over the bridge's crest. For a moment, it's nothing but sea and sky. Sunlight dances on the water. Gulls coast in the breeze. Fishing boats bob in the bay like toys.

And then, like magic, it appears.

The island.

Rows of beach houses. The black-and-white lighthouse on the north end. The Ferris wheel toward the southern tip. The wide Atlantic unfurls beyond it—a glimmering invitation Grace isn't sure she wants to accept.

This was always Birdie's favorite part. Not the arrival, but the moment right before it.

"I'm sure this probably sounds silly, but I love this," she said once. Grace was a teenager, her bare feet pressed against the hot dash, a dog-eared magazine on her lap. "Right here, Cece," Birdie went on, the open windows welcoming in a rush of warm air. "Right this minute." Her mother's long silver hair flapped around her face. "When everything good is still in the future. When the magic of our week here hasn't quite started yet."

Back then, Grace—desperate to just *get there*—had laughed and rolled her eyes. But now, as the bridge slopes downward, she understands Birdie's point in a different way.

Grace inhales deeply, gaze set straight ahead.

The tires rush over the break between the bridge and the roadway as she tries to determine if the fluttery feeling in her chest is hope or something else.

Mostly, though, as she clicks on her blinker, preparing to leave the causeway and everything else behind it, she finds herself silently hoping that her mother was right.

FIVE

Grace makes it onto the island without sobbing, so that's something. *A step,* like Jenny said. After a summer of nonstop push-and-pull emotion—grieving and remembering, trying and failing, holding on and reluctantly letting go—perhaps she's finally reached her limit and is all cried out. Like those sad houseplants back on her desk, maybe she's simply dried up, too.

The Jeep rolls off the causeway and up to Sea Drift's only four-way traffic stop. Despite the congestion on the bridge, things have always had a way of evening themselves out down here. Ahead of her, cars peel off in both directions at a leisurely speed, their smooth, even-keel motion the vehicular equivalent of a contented exhale. As usual, Grace turns right onto the main boulevard—a two-lane artery that runs the length of the island from tip to tip. It takes about three seconds for her to see that Caleb was right.

Nothing's changed.

The same weathered surf shops, their windows cluttered with bathing-suit-clad mannequins. The same five-and-dimes, their bins of cheap towels and sand toys spilling onto the sidewalks. The miniature golf courses and ice cream stands, drawing what look like the same midday crowds. The bakery where Grace and Birdie walked to get crumb cake. The small bookstore, with its striped awning and dollar-paperback bins. The seafood shacks, their windows buzzing with neon signs. The one-theater cinema that shows summer classics as matinees. The pastel motels, so dated they feel new again.

Grace drives. The setting slides by, frozen as if in another era—Pompeii at the beach. Memories of her at varying points in her life outside every establishment appear in her mind like pages in a flip-book. Time blurs here. This feature once warmed her heart, made her feel like arriving back on this strip of land every August was a homecoming. Now it makes her feel a little sick.

Up ahead, a young mother lingers at a crosswalk, a chair strapped to her back and a child at her side. Grace slows to a stop. They hustle across the street, pulling their packed wagon. *That could have been me,* Grace thinks, like she always does when she sees this type of scene. A mother. A child. The life she thought she'd have. A feeling of envy and heartache she can never turn off.

Grace glances at her phone to check the time, something to fill the void. It's a little after one o'clock—another hour to kill before check-in. No point in driving past the house yet. She knows from experience that the cleaning crew will still be there, valiantly attempting to sweep away every last grain of sand. When she looks up, the duo is on the ocean side of the block. The mother waves, just as a hot breeze drifts through the Jeep's open windows, carrying a familiar fragrance with it. Charcoal. Fryer oil. A thick, golden scent Grace could recognize in her sleep.

Grace waves back, but the dull pain inside her remains. *Why—Why?—couldn't that have been me?* She taps the gas pedal, the smell tugging her like a leash. Her stomach aches. The vehicle moves forward as the woman and child disappear in the rearview mirror.

Suddenly, Grace feels impossibly empty.

~

Smitty's isn't fancy. A decades-old snack shack tucked between a bait shop and a marina on the bay side of the island, it boasts a walk-up window, splintered picnic tables, and a revolving staff of teenagers who offer about a 50 percent chance of getting your order right. It's perfect.

Grace parks, cuts the ignition, then sits. All the movement of the morning—the packing, the driving, the breezing in and out of rest stops, the incessant contemplation of her choice to return—finally slows to a halt.

"Well, I'm back," she says aloud and observes the snaking line. Dads in board shorts. Moms balancing trays of sodas. Sunburned kids chasing each other at the edge of the street. It's a scene she's been a part of dozens of times. Today, she feels like an outsider looking in. "Timing's a bit off. Guess I'm a little late."

She watches the crowd, recalling all the occasions she waited there with Birdie—her mother's lips red, even though they were at the beach, her long gray hair tumbling from beneath a wide-brimmed hat. Before they reached the window, Birdie always handed Grace her wallet and said, "You know what we like, Cece," then expertly lingered near a picnic table, schmoozing up other customers in her charming way so she could snag their seats the second they were done.

"Anyway," Grace says now, "I'm not entirely sure why you nudged me here." She sighs, finally acknowledging the fact she's tried to ignore. "Or if you didn't and I'm simply desperate and read too deeply into things." She fumbles with her necklace. "Regardless, here I am."

She inhales again, buying herself a second, then grabs her wallet and faded-blue baseball cap, swings open the door, and steps into the August heat. The sun burns bright and blazing—what Birdie would have called a real gem of a summer day. Perspiration instantly beads all over Grace's body, the heat pressing her forward like a guiding hand. In the near distance, the bay shimmers. Grace joins the line, scans the chalkboard menu—the one that's sat on the ledge for about a hundred years. *Today's Special: Old Bay "Dune" Fries*. Same as always.

"Next!" a young girl—tank top, puka-shell bracelet, glowing tan—calls from the window a few minutes later.

"Hi," Grace says. "Burger and a small bucket of fries." There. Simple. Classic. Reliable. The food equivalent of an old friend. "Oh, and a red birch beer. If you still serve them."

The girl lifts a judgmental brow, her response to Grace's obviously foolish question, the regional soda a longtime staple of this place. "That's it?"

"That's it," Grace confirms and hands over some cash. *Unless you have a piece of my past you're hanging on to somewhere in the back.*

"You're Number 17," the girl says. "Next!"

Grace walks across the crushed-seashell lot. The seating area is packed. Families. Pods of friends. Dozens of strangers, all engaged in a good time. Not sure what to do with herself—*Am I seriously the only person here alone?*—she leans against a weathered fence. Nearby, a group of preteens plays an old hook-and-ring game, the one she often enjoyed herself at their age. She watches them, recalling the satisfaction of the metal hook hitting its target, back when life felt simple. Uncomplicated. A guaranteed win. *Clink.* A girl in a rash guard and bathing suit bottoms makes her mark. Everyone cheers. Grace smiles at the achievement, remembering, then turns to look at the water, the mainland a faint sliver off in the distance.

"Grace?"

A voice calls out from behind her. Grace turns, blinking against the sun, assuming it's a coincidence—that some other person shares her name. It takes a minute for her to register a woman moving toward her, arms waving overhead. Grace observes her in pieces. Waves of strawberry-blond hair. Jade-green eyes. Long limbs. Freckled skin. The pieces slide into place—a lock twisting into position. Meg. Her old beach friend. The one Grace last saw when they were both twenty-five. The one she never expected to see again.

"I knew that was you the second you got out of your car!" Meg proclaims, her tone as bright and bubbly as ever as she draws closer. "Your hair is way darker—and shorter—than the last time I saw you, but it's no difference! No matter how many years pass, I'd recognize you from a mile away!"

"Meg?" Grace momentarily freezes. "Meg Murphy?" She adjusts the brim of her hat, wishing she'd grabbed her sunglasses, too, like a celebrity out in disguise. Jenny was right. Sea Drift is small. Grace assumed she'd see *someone* she knew at some point, just not within her first ten minutes back. "Is that really you?"

"Of course it's me!" Meg, dressed in a sleeveless cover-up and straw surfer hat, throws her arms around Grace's neck like it's a life preserver, her skin warm and scented with SPF. She lingers before pulling back. "Where else would I be?" Meg peers around, as if this is the only place in the world that exists. "August in Sea Drift is basically a nonnegotiable, right?" She shrugs, offers up a thousand-watt grin. "At least, it used to be."

Grace blinks sweat from her lashes, her vision momentarily blurred. "I definitely wasn't expecting to see you here," she manages.

"I know, I know. It's been, what? Ten, no"—Meg stops, calculating the time that's passed—"fifteen years?"

Grace's throat tightens as she remembers their last night together, the one her younger self had turned over countless times. "I think this week marks thirteen, actually."

"Huh." Meg's eyes narrow as she works to solve the equation. "Yeah. That sounds right." She laughs. "Good memory!"

Behind them, the distinct clink of metal on metal. A hook. The preteens erupt in a cheer.

"I thought your family stopped renting in Sea Drift years ago."

"We did." A pair of parenthesis-shaped curves hug Meg's mouth. "My parents have been back a couple times the last few years." A wistful expression forms across her face. "Not me, though. To be honest, I haven't been on the island in a long time."

"Me neither." Grace lets out a quiet puff of a laugh. "Truthfully, I'm still processing the fact that I'm here at all."

Although new families sometimes came and went, for much of Grace's upbringing, it was the same faces on the island year after year. It went without saying that everyone who rented houses within a few blocks of each other during the same week were cemented as friends. For seven glorious days, you claimed the same stretch of beach, swam in the same quarter mile of ocean, watched the sun set from the same vantage point every night. The kids played. The adults shared cocktails. When you waved goodbye, you knew you'd see each other the next season.

Meg was one of those friends to Grace. For years, the Murphys—Carol and Burt, Meg and her twin brother, Ray, and their Labrador, Sandy—who hailed from a suburb outside Philadelphia, rented a house two blocks from Surf Street, over on Dune Lane, the same week as Birdie and Grace. The Murphys and the Porter girls never stayed in touch during the offseason. Didn't call or write or visit. They didn't even have each other's phone numbers or addresses. That wasn't what you did with summer friends. But for one magical week every August, the two families unfolded their chairs side by side.

Until eventually, when life changed.

The Murphys came into some money, moved on, began to vacation someplace else. The year after Meg and Ray headed to college, Carol and Burt moved the family down south. They spent a few more seasons driving north to Sea Drift, their final trip the year the kids all turned twenty-five. The last Grace heard, they'd begun to rent a different house every August in the Outer Banks.

"So you're just checking in today, I assume?" Grace asks, sliding a foot from her sandal.

"Not this visit. For once, we booked a two-week stay. Today marks our halfway point."

Grace nods, taking in this information and considering Meg's use of "we." She peers at the tables beyond Meg's pinkened shoulders, wondering if Carol and Burt are sitting at one of them, squeezing hot ketchup onto paper plates. "So who are you here with? Is your—"

"Can we go back to the beach now, Mom?"

Grace twists and spots two elementary-aged kids dressed in swimsuits—a towheaded boy and a redheaded girl—barreling toward them.

"Ah! My brood!" Meg grins and tousles the boy's hair. "You'll have to excuse them. Any sense of manners goes straight out the window at the prospect of bodysurfing." She laughs, kisses the top of the girl's head. "Emma and Quinn, say hi to my old beach friend, Grace."

The kids mumble something halfway between "Hello" and "Can we go now," both eyeing the beach a few blocks east like it might disappear if they wait one more second.

"Grace and her mom used to rent a house a few streets over from ours when I was your age." A new look crosses Meg's face. She throws up her arms as if she's forgotten to ask the most apparent question. "Birdie! How is she? Is she down here with you?"

"Oh, um . . ." Grace stutters, not wanting to have to tell another person. "She's, uh . . . she's great," she lies, not having a clue why she's said it.

"Please, Mom," the girl, Emma, interrupts, a welcome distraction. "It's getting hot."

Meg opens her mouth, about to apologize for her daughter's remark.

"It's okay," Grace says, grateful for the conversation to be moving on from her foolish remark. "If I remember correctly, we were the same way at their age."

"Order Number 17!" a voice shouts from the takeout window.

"That's me," Grace announces, signaling at the teenage cashier.

"Well, I won't keep you from your food," Meg states, her arms loosely draped around her children's shoulders. "Everyone knows you have to eat Smitty's fries when they're burn-the-roof-of-your-mouth hot." She taps her kids' backs, points to a bicycle rack. They run toward it. "I didn't ask . . . Are you staying at your regular house?"

"Same as always." Grace walks to the window, grabs her red plastic tray. "Like nothing's changed." *Except for literally everything,* she thinks. "What about you?"

"Different house, same street. Just me, my parents, and the kids. My husband isn't here. He, well . . ." Meg flicks the air, batting away whatever details she's left out. "Just work and, you know . . . *life*." She smiles, then watches Emma and Quinn pull their pastel cruisers from the metal rail. "Hey, if you're interested, I'm going to the Beachcomber tonight for dinner. Seven-ish. Just me. My parents offered to take the kids to fly kites and out for ice cream to give me a little break. If you don't have plans, you should swing by."

"Oh, um. I need to get settled. I haven't even checked in to the house yet." Grace swallows, forcing herself to remember the reason—*all* the reasons—why she's here. "Plus, this sounds lame, but I need to get a lot of work done while I'm down here this week."

"No pressure." Meg laughs, but it feels forced. A hint sad. "It's your vacation." Something unnamed passes between them. "It's not like we're still teenagers, right?"

Time stops as Grace—in no small way—privately wishes they were.

"Well, it was good bumping into you." Meg gives Grace a fast hug. "It's a small island," she adds, stepping toward the bike rack. "Maybe we'll run into each other again." She hoists her bubble gum–pink cruiser onto the asphalt. "I can't wait to tell my parents I ran into you. They'll get a real kick out of hearing that, like us, you and Birdie are down here again for the week." Meg stops herself, squints into the sunshine. "I'm sure Ray will get a kick out of it, too."

"Ray?" His name hits Grace like a wave. Her stomach lurches as if she's missed a step. The smell of the food, which only a moment ago made her feel ravenous, suddenly makes her queasy. "Is he . . . here? I thought you said it was only you, your kids, and your parents at the house."

"Well, yeah. At the *rental* house. Ray's staying at his own place." Meg cruises toward the corner. "He lives here now." Her strawberry hair brushes her back as she looks both ways before she pedals off. "That's part of why we finally came back."

Grace stands—stunned—and watches Meg melt into the orange glare of sunlight. *Clink.* Behind her, another win. Grace turns to look out of habit, then twists back toward the street.

But just as quickly as her old friend appeared, she's gone.

SIX

It's a little after four o'clock by the time Grace finally turns the Jeep onto Surf Street—two whole hours past her official check-in time. A crime, or so Birdie would have said.

She grips the steering wheel tighter than necessary as the car bumps over the familiar divot in the asphalt—the one that floods every time it so much as spits rain. Humid air, thick with salt and sunscreen, blows through the open windows as Grace takes in the view. Every detail of the oceanside block remains fully intact. Squat bungalows, some slightly updated but most untouched, their porches draped with towels. Surfboards leaning haphazardly against sheds. Barefoot kids, feet probably burning, racing toward the dune—the one that once looked mountain-size to Grace. It's all exactly as she left it.

Except, of course, that it isn't.

After her run-in at Smitty's, Grace sat at a picnic table—miraculously snagging a free seat—and picked at her food, her appetite gone. A few bites in, she tossed the rest, then drove the length of the boulevard twice. The whole time, the information Meg revealed sat in her chest like an unopened text message she couldn't quite bring herself to read.

Now, as she pulls up to the third bungalow in from the beach, she tells herself to mentally delete it. Not important. Not now. For the moment, her only focus is on surviving what lies straight ahead.

The house.

It feels more like a photograph than a real place. Chipped turquoise door. Cedar shingles. Blue hydrangeas flanking the steps. A white shutter that hangs slightly askew, as if the home is offering Grace a conspiratorial wink.

"Take a breath." Grace shifts the car into Park. "You can do this." She inhales deeply, steadying herself. "It's only a house. Wood. Concrete. Brick." She exhales, slow and measured. "It's not like it's a person. It's just a place."

She pulls Birdie's key chain from the ignition, drops it in her bag. She was freshly thirty-two the last time she sat here, two months from her autumn wedding in Manhattan, her debut set for publication the following June. The starting line of what she'd believed was her real life. She forces the memories away, then lets her eyes drift closed while a different set of recollections pours in. If she listens closely, she can almost hear her mother's voice in the breeze. Asking Grace to run around back to get the key. Rattling off a list of leisurely ways for them to fill the day. *What do you think, Cece? Bike ride to the lighthouse? Straight to the beach? Midafternoon ice cream?* The sound of it is so clear—so achingly familiar—that for half a second, she believes Birdie is there, dropping her woven tote near the door.

Grace's lids dart open. She unclicks her seat belt and twists toward the passenger seat to gather her things. Her hand hovers over the photo album. With a sigh, she gives in and opens it. The plastic sleeves are warped from age, but not enough to tarnish the memories they preserve. Elementary-aged Grace and Birdie, eating Popsicles on the lopsided front steps. Teenage Grace and Birdie, cracking through a bushel of blue crabs at the patio table. Early-thirties Grace and Birdie that final summer, standing at the end of the flooded street after a storm, their arms thrown up toward a rainbow, like they could catch the whole season in their hands.

She snaps the album shut.

With a quiet sigh, she gathers her things, pushes open the car door, and steps onto the pea gravel driveway, the stones shifting beneath her flip-flops. She sets her belongings down on the warped stairs, then takes off around the side of the lot. Despite modern advancements, according to Caleb, the home's antiquated security features have—like everything else—remained in place.

Out back, past the patio and threadbare hammock, Grace swings open the splintered door of the outdoor shower and reaches for the bottle of Suave strawberry-scented shampoo—the one the owners replace every season from the five-and-dime—revealing a single silver key. The metal is cool against her palm. It feels like a gift meant exclusively for her, rather than an object set here for different renters every week. She nearly yells "Got it!" like she used to do before she stops herself and runs back out front.

Grace slides the key into the lock. The door sticks—years of salt air having eaten away at the hardware—but then, with a quiet creak, it gives way. Her heart thuds harder, nothing but cardiovascular somersaults. She takes a reluctant step.

And just like that, she's inside.

There's no grandiose entryway, only a rectangle of cracked tiles where Grace slides off her sandals. The interior, although small, is bright with sunlight, like always, thanks to the fact that the brick fireplace and wood-paneled walls are all painted a crisp white. The couches are new—a practical beige microfiber, a minor upgrade—though the many beach tchotchkes are not. Everything—*everything*—has a seashell on it. Art. Throw pillows. Side tables cluttered with decorative trinkets. When it comes to coastal vibes, subtlety has never been the home's strength.

Barefoot, Grace takes a step, tries to wipe the inevitable graininess from her feet. She moves into the living room, clicks on the window air-conditioning unit, then heads for the kitchen, where she notes the same blue drinking cups and speckled coffee mugs in the glass cabinets. On the scratched wood table—a petite round thing with only two chairs—sits a basket that contains beach badges, a map, a printout of emergency contacts and restaurant recommendations, a tube of complimentary sunscreen, and a handwritten note from Caleb.

Welcome to 116 Surf Street—a classic slice of the Jersey Shore! Everything you need should be in the basket. Quick reminder that trash goes out on Tuesday night. Oh, and you probably remember this from your past stays, but the indoor plumbing is . . . fickle. Best to use the outdoor shower when you can. Hope you catch a sunny week!—Caleb

Grace sets the letter back in the basket—one more reminder that she's merely another guest here—then pulls out a glass and fills it at the tap, the island's questionable water quality the least of her concerns. She gulps it down too fast, instantly making herself queasy, then presses her hands against the scuffed butcher-block counter, giving herself a minute. After a second, the seasick feeling passes—a ship finally steadying in port. Grace stays in place anyway, peering out the window, trying to decide what to do next. Her focus lands on an old pair of wooden Adirondack chairs out back. So many summer nights, Grace lounged in one of them, writing her heart out in a marbled notebook, her dreams for her words as vast as the sky.

"It's perfect, darling," Birdie said the night she sat out there with Grace, reading the final chapters of what ultimately became *The Tides*. "The setting is completely picturesque, and the love story is so real. So beautifully composed." She pulled away her candy-colored readers, set them on the chair's arm. "But are you sure you're ready to send this out into the world?" she asked, knowing Grace planned to query literary agents that fall.

"I know," Grace said, self-conscious. She was twenty-eight, her birthday two days away. "It still needs work. I plan to fill in a few plot gaps and do another round of line edits before I—"

"I don't mean in terms of editing," Birdie clarified, the air around them beginning to cool. "I mean that, well, it's obviously not all fiction." She bit her red-tinted lip. "Right?"

Grace tugged her sundress around her knees. "Certain parts, I guess."

Birdie's mouth curled into a knowing grin. "Kind of interesting that you chose to name your protagonist Cece, no?"

Grace picked at her cuticle. "Maybe."

Birdie was the one who came up with the nickname "Cece"—the only person who ever actually called Grace that. Looking back, Grace didn't remember when it started, only that it'd always been there, stitched like a fine thread into their shared history. According to Birdie, Grace had been a relentlessly curious child. Always pointing. Always noticing. "See! See!" she'd shout at every small wonder. A shiny stone. A feather on the sand. At some point, "see-see" turned into Cece, which Birdie said made sense, the nickname rooted in the letters of Grace's name.

"Grace," Birdie said, her voice—and the name she used—a touch more serious.

"Not now, Mom," Grace said, knowing the direction their conversation was heading.

"It's okay to admit that you made a mistake, sweetheart."

"Is that what you think?" Grace asked. Not urgent. Not begging. Just wanting to know. "That it was a mistake? That I should have—"

Birdie sighed. "It's not about what I think, darling."

Grace sank back in her chair. A question rose to the surface of her mind, but she was hesitant to pose it. "Did you ever think we were going to end up together?" she asked anyway, knowing there was no need for her to state a specific name. "For real, I mean."

Birdie inhaled, long and slow. "I did," she admitted. "Maybe not in the beginning when you were younger. But later, there was a long period when I thought maybe . . ." One side of her mouth lifted. "It became hard to ignore the way you used to light up when you were with him."

Grace swallowed. "Why didn't you ever come out and tell me that back then?"

"Because, love," Birdie said, wrapping up, "before you could really find him, I knew you needed to find yourself first instead."

Back in the kitchen, Grace winces at the memory, right as her phone dings inside her pocket. She pulls it out and sees a message from Jenny.

Holding up okay? Any dramatic crying jags on the beach yet?

Grace releases a hushed laugh. Though she's hours away, Jenny's voice is a comfort.

At the house, Grace types. The lifeguards haven't started doling out free therapy . . . yet.

She tries to send the text, but it's caught by a dreaded green line. Finally, the signal catches. Grace begins to draft a second message about her encounter with Meg, then backpedals, deletes it, and types out a different follow-up instead.

Anyway, going to change in a minute and go look at the water, Grace writes. Will likely bring a box of tissues just in case. Stubborn, the message fails to go through.

Grace sets the phone on the counter, grabs her bag, and moves down the single-story home's only hallway, walking past the small bathroom until she's faced by two open bedroom doors. Usually, she'd walk into the one on the left—*her* room—but moves into the one on the right instead. The space is simple. A queen-size bed with a beach-motif comforter. A rattan nightstand. One dresser that's at least as old as Grace. Before she roots through her duffel bag for her bathing suit, she sits on the edge of the mattress.

"I'm here, Mom," she whispers. "I made it to the house." Her sight falls on the window, her fingers fumbling with her necklace. "Now what? Any plans in place for me this afternoon?"

She waits for a sign, but her request is met with only silence.

Grace pulls herself up and clicks on the window AC unit, not only to cool the too-warm space but also to fill it with noise. It's so quiet. No kitchen cabinets smacking shut. No screen door slapping closed. No voice calling out with promises of a joy-filled day. No anything.

"Oh, another thing," Grace adds. "It might have been nice if you'd found a clever way to give me a heads-up before I drove down." She presses her fingers against the glass. "You know, something to prepare me." Her reflection blends with the light. "Anything so I had some knowledge that Ray was also back."

SEVEN

The beach is breathtaking. Wide. Endless. Almost too perfect to be real.

Grace pauses at the top of the dune and takes it in. The ocean is a brilliant shade of blue green, so clear it could be mistaken for glass. Beyond it, the horizon line sits, as bold and crisp as an artist's brushstroke. Up and down the shoreline, white lifeguard stands dot the sand—silent, steady reminders that even in her absence, someone has been here watching over this place. She closes her eyes. For an instant, Grace just listens. The hush of the waves. Distant laughter. The whisper of dune grass. The melody of it all, once memorized, now almost forgotten.

Exhaling slowly, she kicks off her flip-flops, leaving them behind with the other scattered sandals—one of the many unspoken rules of this setting. She tromps down the dune, the hot grains sliding beneath her every step. It's late in the day, a little before five o'clock. The air is thick with heat but beginning to slip into that soft, golden-hour cool.

The magic hours.

Birdie's favorite times of day here, just before sunrise and sunset, when the sky softens into muted pastels, the world quiets, and everything feels like a dream.

Grace navigates toward the water, hauling an old chair she dragged out from the house's shed. She sees the beach is changing hands, like stepping into a restaurant between shifts. Families are packing up. Shaking out towels. Rinsing off toys. Stuffing food back into coolers. Brushing sand away from sticky legs. They're all preparing for the inevitable transition from day to night. Soon, the lifeguards will pull their warning flags, leaving this place ruleless. That's when it belongs to the stragglers—the ones who linger to watch the sun melt into the water, to swim out too far, to set up fishing poles in the fading light. And then, there are those like Grace. The people who've come to sit at the edge of the world and just think.

Down by the coastline, tide pools shimmer. Sea Drift is known for them. At certain times of day, the ocean folds in on itself, creating vast sandbars and shallow playgrounds. Grace settles by one. It's only a few inches deep before it gives way to the open sea. She wrestles the chair open—its metal rusted from saltwater and time—then sinks into it. Her toes press into the damp sand. She drags her fingers through the wet grains.

And then, not sure what she expects to happen, she stares out at the scene before her, takes a breath, and waits.

~

"Hey!" a voice calls out behind Grace, yanking her from a deep, dreamy sleep, the sort that makes you forget where you are. "You okay out there?"

Grace's head jerks up. Her eyes fly open. She gasps. Panic—instant and disorienting—pricks at her newly sunburned skin. Her pulse spikes. How long has she been asleep? Ten minutes? Two hours? She blinks and the scene sharpens. Wide-open ocean. Everywhere. *No, no, no*. Her stomach lurches. The water, previously lapping at her feet, swirls halfway up her calves.

"Oh my God," she stammers and scrambles upright, spinning to look back at the coast.

The beach, which had been directly behind Grace when she sat, is several yards away, separated by a pool of deep water. She scans left to right—*oh no*—her heart its own percussion instrument as she realizes she's stranded. Alone. On an increasingly narrow stretch of sandbar. Her own private island.

"The tides shifted," the voice yells out, as if Grace can't see this most obvious fact.

Back on the shore, the lifeguard stands are empty, the beach mostly deserted. There's only one man beside a fishing pole dug into the sand. He waves. And laughs. Not a restrained chuckle. A full body chortle. The kind that makes you hunch over and slap a knee.

"So I see!" Grace shouts back.

The man pulls himself upright, looking entertained. "Are you all right out there?"

"Uh, yeah, I'm okay!" Grace calls back, hoping to sound like a competent adult and not a woman who just marooned herself in the ocean. She eyes the distance between the shoreline and where she stands, gauging if she ought to abandon her chair, try swimming back with it, or possibly sink into the sea and disappear. "I think!" she adds, mostly for her own benefit.

"Hang on!" He steps away from his tackle box, pulls off his T-shirt, and wades into the water. "Let me give you a hand!"

"O-oh, you don't have to do . . ."

Before Grace can completely object, he dips beneath the surface.

"Guess you were having a pretty good dream," he states through an amused grin a moment later as he steps onto the sandbar.

"I'm mortified," Grace admits.

"Don't be." Tiny droplets of water glint on his tanned shoulders. "You're not the first person I've watched get stuck out here." He laughs. Two shallow dimples form in his cheeks. "Last week, a mom dozed off with a toddler asleep on her chest."

"Well, that's . . . comforting?" Grace shrugs, her shoulders pink and burning. "At least it's not only me."

"Pretty soon I may have to start charging," he jokes. "Here." He reaches for the chair and forces it closed. "Let me take that."

"Thank you." Grace squeezes water from the bottom of her cover-up. "I appreciate it."

"Not a problem." He hoists the chair under his arm. "You *can* swim, right?" he asks, walking to the edge of the sandbar. "I had to prop the toddler up on my shoulders."

Grace snorts. "I think I'll manage."

"If you say so," he says, already knee-deep in the surf. "Fair warning that my prices go up with a client's age." He dunks under, then reemerges, his head bobbing like a buoy. "If you change your mind, be sure to splash around and give me a sign that you need help, all right?"

Back on the shore, he tosses her a dry towel from his pile of belongings. He takes one for himself, twisting it around his waist, then slides his T-shirt back on. Grace tugs off her drenched cover-up—which, in her frazzled state, she foolishly kept on for her swim—and quickly wraps herself up so she'll feel less exposed.

"Beer?" he asks, reaching down into a soft-sided cooler bag.

"Oh, um." Grace hesitates, like a teenager at a beach party, though doing so is ridiculous. She's been legally allowed to drink for almost two decades. Still, her brain does the old mental tally. Caffeine. Alcohol. Sushi. All the things she trained herself to limit, carefully ration out, and avoid, just in case. A habit that outlived the dream. One that outlived her marriage, too. "Sure."

"No pressure." He raises an eyebrow. "I have waters if you'd rather—"

"N-no, I'll take one. A beer sounds good right now, honestly." She looks out at the ocean. The water where she'd been sitting is significantly deeper than it was moments ago. "I think after that public display of humiliation, I earned it."

"Agreed." He passes her an ice-cold can. "Cheers."

"Cheers." She enjoys a long, carbonated sip, the first she's had in ages. "I'm Grace, by the way. You know, in case you need that information for your rescue log."

"Caleb. Good to meet you."

"Wait." The puzzle pieces click into place. "Caleb." Her thoughts flip back to yesterday. The easy charm. The way he helped convince her to come here in the first place. "From the rental agency?"

"That's me." He squints as a thought assembles in his mind. "Oh, hang on. Grace." He nods toward the dune. "Number 116, right?"

"Guilty as charged."

"Boy." He laughs. "You really *haven't* been down here in a while, huh?" He enjoys another sip. "Seeing as you forgot how fast those tide pools can disappear."

"Trust me." She sets her can down in the sand. "I will be reliving—and cringing at—that little mishap for the rest of my life." Grace finger-combs her wet hair. "Dare I ask how long I was asleep out there?"

"I'd say I stood here and laughed for a solid half hour." Caleb grins. "Maybe more."

She covers her face with a hand.

"Don't worry." He smirks. "I wouldn't have let you get washed away out there."

A breeze blows off the water, sending goose bumps across Grace's skin. "So do you live down here or something?"

"Unfortunately for me, I live inland and go back and forth a lot for work. Bridge traffic's a real treat." His fishing rod curves, the line tightening. "My folks own the agency. I've been helping them out the last few months, though I haven't made any big moves to make this my permanent zip code yet." He winds the spool. "This week, though, I'm a renter, same as you." With a tug, his line emerges from the darkening water. "I'm the pink house on the dune." He narrows his eyes, investigating the bare hook as it swoops over the sand. "Lucky me. Looks like I caught another ghost fish."

Grace laughs, takes a fast peek around. The sky is changing, the light settling into dusk. "Well, thanks for the help." She pulls away her towel, prepared to fold it up and pass it back.

"Don't be silly." Caleb stops her. "Hang on to it."

"Are you sure?"

"I know where you're staying." His smile lingers. "I suspect we'll cross paths again."

Grateful not to walk back in her bikini, Grace drapes herself up in the warm terrycloth, then squeezes dampness from her hair. As she does, her hands absently trail past her ear, down her neck, and—

She freezes. Then gasps. "Oh no."

Frantic, her fingers fly to her throat. *No, no*. She pats her bare collarbone, willing it to be there. Hoping she missed it. *Please. Please*. But it isn't. A sharp, sick panic swells inside her, tightening like a clenched fist in her core. Her necklace. Birdie's birthday gift to Grace when she was a teenager. Her name, shaped in delicate gold. The nameplate she almost never took off. She presses her chest harder, as if she's able to will it to return. But it's too late. It's already gone.

"What?" Caleb releases his fishing line, instantly back in rescue mode. "What is it?"

"My necklace." Her stomach plummets as if she might get sick. "I lost it!" She drops to her knees and sifts through the sand, desperate for a quick glint of metal. "I can't believe this!" Grace smacks at her sternum, like she's mistaken things, as if maybe she's imagined it. "I *knew* I shouldn't have come here." Her fingers continue to pat her salt-marked skin, the space achingly empty, as though an actual piece of her body has been taken. "I should have listened to my gut and stayed home." Emotion burns her throat. "This trip. I knew it was a mistake."

"It's okay." Caleb, fueled by a new sense of urgency, crouches next to her. "We'll find it."

But there's nothing.

After a few more frantic minutes, Grace officially calls off the search.

"You're *sure* you had it on when you walked down here?" Caleb asks, still looking.

"I'm certain. I almost never take it off." Tears cling to her bottom lashes. "I must have lost it out there." She looks at the place that was previously a sandbar, the water now nothing but rolling waves. "And if that's the case—which I'm sure it is—I'll never find it."

Caleb continues to dig. "I'm assuming it was something special?"

Grace bites her lip to stop it from quivering. "It wasn't expensive, if that's what you mean," she explains, trying not to cry. "I-I've just had it forever. It was important to me."

Caleb stands, claps sand from his hands. "You'll find it," he states, like it's a fact.

"Thanks." Grace sighs, already accepting that it's gone for good. "But I doubt it."

"You'd be surprised." Caleb's tone, previously playful, softens. "A few summers ago, I lost a pair of brand-new sunglasses out there. Three days later, they washed right up at my feet."

"That's not a real story."

"It sure is," Caleb insists.

Grace turns to him, her brows arching in question. "Really?"

"Really," he confirms, and nods to prove that he means it. "Sea Drift is funny that way." He lifts his chin by a degree. When he does, their eyes meet in the dimming light. "There's something about this place," he adds, a sense of wistfulness in his tone. "For whatever reason, things on this island don't tend to stay lost for very long."

EIGHT

It's officially dusk by the time Grace stumbles into the outdoor shower—tired, embarrassed, devastated, like a contestant voted off a reality show she didn't know she was on. She hangs a too-small bath towel over the doorframe, wrestles with her bathing suit—the damp fabric clinging to her like a story she'd rather forget—then hangs it on a rusted hook and twists the ancient plumbing to life.

"Oh my God!" she squeals, her breath catching in a gasp, the water unbearably freezing right before it turns excruciatingly hot. "Are you *kidding* me?"

She hops on the planks, fumbling with the knobs, desperate for something between arctic blast and molten lava. After a brief battle, the temperature evens out, just as her foot slides across the slippery wood flooring, inviting a sharp, foreign object into her heel.

"Come on!" With a huff, she bites back an obscenity, bends, and spots the splinter. It's small. A nothing. Still, after today's events, she's so frustrated she could cry. "You're fine, Grace. It's a splinter, not a knife wound." The water runs down her face and trickles over her lips. "You're thirty-seven, almost thirty-eight. Not five."

Through the opening at the top of the shower, the steam curls into the fading light. Out there, the world hums with August. Seagulls squawk. Up the street, kids shout. Music plays. The water rushes over her, though she can still hear the distant pulse of the ocean—certain and steady—like a white-noise machine she can't click off. Even so, every cell inside her feels tense.

She lets the stream pound against her back, hoping it'll wash away the last few hours. It doesn't. With a heavy exhale, she rummages through the simple toiletry bag she threw together this morning—shampoo, a bar of soap, just the basics. Her fingers trail her skin while she works herself into a foamy lather and tries to ignore the new, unwanted vacancy on her chest. Impossible. Such a minor thing, yet the void it's left behind feels vast.

"It's not a big deal," she whispers, hoping to calm herself. "It's *only* a necklace," she adds, which, of course, isn't true. The bubbles wash away, slipping down her arms, over her flat torso—another empty space—and through the slats at her feet. "Not in the grand scheme of things." Still, that doesn't make it feel like less of a loss.

Grace sets down the soap and presses her hands against the slatted wall, trying to believe her lie. A cool breeze blows in, a contrast to the warm water. Suddenly, her ears perk up.

"Hello?" she calls out, thinking she's heard footsteps on the crushed-seashell lot. A trail of residual shampoo stings her eyes. She squints, peers through the cracks in the wood. "Is someone out there!"

But it's only wishful thinking. She's alone. No one here but her.

Grace straightens, rinses her face, then reaches for the soap again. Instead, her hand gravitates to the bottle of strawberry shampoo. She flips the lid, squeezes out a dollop of pink, telling herself it's only her imagination, that she hasn't just heard that noise, which sounds like footsteps—again. The gel turns into a mountain of suds as she rubs her palms together, bringing them to her nose.

She stays there, lost in a memory, until the water runs cold.

~

Back inside—dressed in sweats and a stretched-out tee, her wet hair twisted up—Grace sinks into the comfortable new sofa. She inspects her foot, pressing her thumb against her heel to see whether the splinter is close enough to the surface to easily slide out, but it's in too deep. The irritation is mild enough for her to momentarily ignore it—something to deal with later. She abandons the task and clicks on the home's sole television, a years-old thing set on a wobbly stand. There are no streaming services. No movies on demand. She flips—news, a reality series, renovation shows—in search of background noise. Finally, she lands on a Hallmark movie, the type of silly, predictable story she's always loathed (*terrible writing, so clichéd*) but her mother loved.

She shuts it off, pulls her laptop onto her knees. By force of habit, she clicks open her email. Her inbox doesn't load right away. The signal flickers—a lone black bar holding on for dear life. Her account opens. She scrolls through digital piles of junk, barely registering them. Not-so-new news alerts. Stores already pushing sweaters and pumpkin-spice everything. She doesn't expect to find a message from Mollie, sent late last night.

> Subject: Re: Checking in!
> Sender: Mollie Grey, Chapter One Literary Agency
> Hi Grace,
> Touching base again! Turns out the Wi-Fi up on the Cape isn't too bad. Knowing me, I'll likely check in on my emails from time to time in case you want to send the manuscript along now (even if it's still messy!).
> I don't want to put any pressure on you, but as you know, this next delivery date is pretty crucial in keeping your contract and the terms of your advance in place. When you have a minute, will you let me know where things stand? I'm rooting for you.
> xx,
> M

Grace exhales. Hard. The deadline. The contract. The advance. A different kind of drowning. Quickly, she closes the tab—something to deal with later—and clicks open her book document. That's part of why she came here, right? To embrace a fresh perspective. To at least *try* to find her voice again. The file appears. She swipes, though it's practically blank, same as the last time she looked at it. Some scattered notes. A handful of incoherent and unfinished paragraphs. The sad, unspecific words "Book Three" staring back at her on the first page.

The day Grace finished writing *The Tides*—the *real* version, the one that'd been edited and cross-checked by everyone on her team dozens of times—the first thing she did (after calling Birdie to squeal about the fact that it was complete) was print out a copy for Adam. Three days after she gave it to him, he called her at lunchtime and asked if they could meet for dinner.

By the time Grace walked into the restaurant that evening, she'd convinced herself she was minutes away from Adam ending their roughly yearlong relationship.

"Hi," she said when she entered the dining room and noted her manuscript on the table like a piece of incriminating evidence. "I guess that means you finished reading it."

"I did," Adam said, his voice not doing much to reveal any emotion. "Late last night."

Grace took a seat and instantly sipped from her water glass. "Okay," she said, waiting.

"And, well, I don't think it's very fair that you've been keeping such a big secret from me," Adam said and folded his hands.

She set down her glass, but her fingers stayed cold. "Wh-what do you mean?"

Adam leaned across the table, making sure their eyes met. "The fact that you're an incredibly prolific writer and have been downplaying your talent to me since the day we met."

"Oh." Her posture quickly straightened as her heartbeat settled. "Um . . . thanks."

For the rest of the meal, Adam rattled off his favorite scenes. "It's wonderful, Grace," he concluded as their waiter set down their dessert. "Or should I say . . . Cece." His lips lifted into a teasing smile. "It's cute that you used your mom's nickname for you for your protagonist," he noted, not reading into it any further. "But truly, the book is so enjoyable. It's going to be a huge success." He took a bite of his lava cake. "The whole plot feels so . . . real. Like something you pulled out of your life."

A pit formed in Grace's stomach, knowing it was her chance to tell him about the parts of her story—her past—she hadn't talked to him about yet. To explain the truth behind the fiction. She pulled in a deep breath and parted her lips. "Thanks" was what came out instead.

The next week, while at a wine bar near her downtown studio apartment, Adam asked Grace if she'd move in with him. She breathed a sigh of relief, glad she hadn't said anything.

Now, alone in the beach house, Grace wills herself to push the memory away.

"Stop daydreaming and just write something," she says, so angry and agitated to have found herself—*put* herself—in this position. "Anything." She rolls out her wrists. "Describe the weather. Set the scene. *Any* scene. When in doubt, sprinkle in some verbs for action." She stares at the screen as if it's a crystal ball. *Please—please—tell me what to do.* "Just *start.*"

She types a few lines, deletes them, tries again. But there's no point. She's so far removed from this manuscript—this whole story—she doesn't even remember her original vision for it.

Grace slams the laptop shut, drops it on the coffee table, and heads for the kitchen—half hungry, half looking for an excuse to quit. A feeling in her stomach—hollow and sour—suddenly reminds her that she hasn't consumed a real meal all day. She opens and closes cabinets, hoping to find something—a bag of chips, a rogue box of dry pasta—left behind by past renters. But there's nothing.

Not so much as a morsel or a crumb of anything to inspire or nourish her here.

"Don't even think about it," Grace tells herself, remembering Meg's offer. The Beachcomber. Dinner. Although the vintage motel's waterfront restaurant was once one of Grace's favorite spots to catch a late meal, there's no way. A casual run-in was one thing, but having to sit face-to-face for an extended period? There's too much history she'll be forced to cover, too many life updates she doesn't want to give or hear. "Absolutely not." She pulls open a drawer, only to find chopsticks and a ketchup packet. "You're better off starving."

In the living room, her phone rings, ripping through the quiet. Grace jumps at the sound, then slams the drawer shut. She moves to the sofa and grabs her device, not sure whose number she expects to find flashing across her screen.

"Adam?" She says his name like it's a question. "Hi." Her pulse picks up, her mind conjuring up potential reasons for his call, their days of casual check-ins long behind them. "What's going on?" she asks, already assuming the worst. "Is everything okay?"

"Do you remember the first time we came up here together?" Adam asks, a complete curveball. "To the lake?"

"What?" Her heartbeat settles, then lifts in a different way. "Uh, yeah." Realizing he's fine, Grace heads back into the kitchen and rummages through a cabinet, though all that's there is a box of baking soda. She shakes it, like a slice of pizza might fall out. "It was our first summer together, right? A few weeks before my thirtieth."

"It was." His tone is uncharacteristically nostalgic. "We sat out on the dock one night and talked about the future. If we both wanted to stay in the city forever. Where we saw ourselves in five years." He clears his throat. "We were so young—too young to realize all our plans might not work out." A quiet beat passes. "It's not fair that they didn't."

Grace sets the box back on the shelf as memories of that night flicker to life, reel by reel, in her mind. The moonlight on the lake. The warm glow of the house behind them. Adam's hand wrapped around hers. It was a version of herself—her whole life—she was sure would last.

"Wh-why are you bringing this up right now?" she asks, confused and caught off guard.

"Ready to laugh?"

"I don't know." Grace is cautious. "Am I?"

"I'm out on the dock, having a drink," he explains. "I was thinking about you. About us." He stops himself, like he's embarrassed to go on. "Anyway, I felt something on my hand. When I looked down, I saw a ladybug—completely random—sitting on my knuckle." He chuckles, soft and melancholy and forced. "A sign, you know?" His voice is laced with uncertainty, as if he's feeling out how this will land. "Thought it meant I should give you a quick call."

Grace's pulse stutters again. Her fingers fumble for her lost necklace—a phantom comfort—though, of course, it's not there. For a second, her thoughts drift. The two of them, their feet flirting with the water's surface. The conversation. Grace admitting that maybe she wanted to leave Manhattan soon, then ever so hesitantly adding that perhaps she'd like to get married one day, try her hand at being a mom.

"Well, look at that," Adam had joked that night, shortly after Grace divulged these things. "I found a sign." He reached into his pocket, set something between them. "A penny. Guess that means it'll all work out, right?"

"Very funny." Grace laughed. "Coming from a guy who's too logical to believe in those sorts of things."

Adam picked up the coin and flicked it into the lake. One *plop* and it disappeared. "I believe I'd like to be with you for a long time," he said, his eyes on the water. Grace ignored the fact that he didn't mention whether he wanted to be a parent, too. "Does that count?"

Back then, it did.

At the beginning, things between them felt ideal, like a hard-to-put-down story—the pacing, the ways the characters interacted, all of it just right. It was the middle—the part that followed the courtship and dreamy honeymoon phase—when everything began to feel so hard.

"I don't even know you lately, Grace!" Adam had shouted one summer night two years earlier. "You've completely lost yourself—your whole identity—to this process!"

They were home, eating Chinese takeout. Though *eating* was a generous term. Grace hardly took a bite, instead carefully extracting every mung bean sprout from her meal, after an article she'd read claimed they were detrimental to early pregnancies if not properly cooked.

"Look what you're doing!" Adam continued, their dinner apparently done. "You're picking your meal apart like it's a crime scene and you're not even pregnant right now."

He was right. Grace wasn't pregnant. She'd taken a test two weeks prior to confirm as much. Still, she often found herself caught up in fertility math (this cycle, plus this day, added to this many weeks *could* mean . . .). Grace couldn't help it. She always wondered *what if.*

"You never know." She didn't want to tell him about the dream she'd had the night before. A baby boy. The sound of coos. Or about the ladybug she saw on her nightstand the second she woke up. He'd roll his eyes, say it was irrelevant. "I could be really early or—"

"Look at this." Adam gestured to a dozen vitamin bottles on the counter. "You've bought every possible supplement." He pointed to a calendar on the fridge, the dates marked with red circles and X's, like a strange game of tic-tac-toe. "You've plotted out our entire life based on your ovulation dates." He raked his fingers through his hair. "Is this what we want? You? Me?" He gripped the counter. "Our entire life has become so tangled up in this. I don't want this." Adam met her eyes, and Grace saw it: an early shift in his gaze, one that looked like two train cars starting to head in different directions on the tracks. "Do you?"

Grace looked down. She didn't answer. What was the point?

"You've heard the doctor," Adam said, releasing an exasperated sigh. "There's nothing clinically wrong." It was true. She'd had every test, only to learn she was fine. "You have to stop obsessing and trying to force it. It's a matter of chance. When it's supposed to happen—"

"It will," she said, though it never did.

Now, back inside the beach house, Grace's tone quiets. "So . . . a ladybug, huh?" she questions as though she's testing him. "I thought you didn't believe in signs. Too woo-woo."

"It's been a long few months." Adam sighs. "I'm not sure what I believe anymore."

"I need to go," Grace states, confused and not wanting to fall into this rabbit hole. "The market up the street closes soon, and I haven't even had dinner yet."

"The market?" he asks, sounding confused. "Isn't Whole Foods in town open until ten?"

"I'm not at home," she states, recalling that he's unaware she left. "I'm in Sea Drift."

"Sea Drift?" Adam echoes, like he hasn't heard her right. Or like he hopes he hasn't. "Since when?" His voice tightens, as if he's trying to squeeze some thought tight enough that it won't come out. "With *who*?"

Grace lets his question hang in the air. "Since today," she finally says. "And I'm not *here* with anyone, Adam," she says, understanding his subtext. "It's just me. I got a call late yesterday. An opportunity for me to come down just sort of presented itself out of the blue."

"Huh," he says, almost to himself, still working something out. "You haven't been there in years," he adds, his statement coming out slower this time.

"I know," she says, wondering if that, in and of itself, is why she came.

A silence forms between them, one that nearly stretches too long.

"Well, then, I'm sorry for bothering you." Adam swallows, as though he's trying to push something that's risen to the surface back down into him. "I hope you enjoy yourself." His tone evens out, but his words don't quite ring authentic. "How long are you staying?"

"I don't know," she admits, not even sure why she's telling him. "Still undecided."

Adam breathes. "Well, if you need anything, you know how to reach me."

~

By the time Grace arrives at the market a few streets away, it's night. She leans the seafoam beach cruiser, one of the two that come with the house, against the building's chipped white clapboard siding and hurries up the steps two at a time, knowing from her many past visits that the place never stays open late.

A bell jingles as she pulls the door wide and steps inside. The market is less of a grocer and more of a vacation-inspired hodgepodge of things. Wine displays and imported oils. A barrel of pool floats. Baskets of overpriced fruit. Bottles of bright-green aloe vera gel. A freezer full of ice cream bars, but not a single loaf of decent bread.

Grace wanders, gathering assorted odds and ends in a basket. Crackers. Gummy candy. A box of sugary cereal she loved as a kid. At the last minute, she takes a few items out and puts them back, telling herself she's buying too much. She's still not sure how long she plans to stay.

A moment later, she finds the register and sets the basket on the counter. Just as the front bells chime again, she shifts her weight and bends to check her heel. The splinter is tiny, almost invisible, but still the skin around it gently throbs. Just another quiet, buried ache for her to carry.

"One second. I forgot something," she tells the cashier, an older man who just nods, like he's watched this scene unfold a thousand times. She spins, prepared to go find a pair of cheap tweezers.

But she turns too fast.

Her sandaled foot catches, sending her off-balance. She stumbles and crashes softly into the patron behind her in line. Her face collides with his warm, solid chest.

"O-oh, my gosh." Grace trips over her words, trying to redeem herself. She takes a breath but quickly realizes that doing so was a mistake. The scent hits her nose, then travels through her whole body. The fragrance fills her like helium—an invisible chemical capable of making her feel like she's physically lost contact with the ground. Slowly, she pulls her face off his body, telling herself she's wrong. "I-I'm so sorry." The words continue to fall from her mouth. "I didn't mean to . . ."

She steps back and tilts up her chin. Time halts. Her body registers the moment before her brain. A flash of heat overwhelms her as her hands gently shake.

"Ray," she says through a gasp, the first time his name—once like a song she couldn't stop singing—has touched her lips in years. She should say something else. Or move. Maybe blink. Instead, she just studies him, as if she's working to see if her mind is tricking her. Her sight follows the line of his jaw, the shape of his face, the curve of his mouth. Everything feels familiar. He's still him.

"Hi, Grace." His dark eyes fall in line with hers, like he never stopped looking at her.

I like your eyes, she told him that first summer when things between them started to change. Thirteen. A summer crush. A shared soda. A bench on the bay. *They're . . . cool,* she said, still too young to have more grown-up words to articulate what she meant. *They shine gold around the rims.*

I didn't realize you were looking that closely, he said, only half joking.

The truth was, until that moment, neither did she.

"I—I . . ." Grace's eyelids flutter. She reaches for a coherent thought but can hardly speak.

Ray lets her unfinished sentence hang there, like an old photograph nailed to a wall. His chest—still sturdy from all those youthful years spent surfing—rises and falls beneath his black T-shirt like a wave. He adjusts his backward baseball hat, a near replica of the one he's worn practically his whole life. His gaze stays on her while they both stand, just inches from each other, and wait.

"Did you forget something?" he finally asks. "Looked like you were running off to search for something else."

If Grace once knew how to breathe, she no longer remembers how. Her lungs, as well as every other part of her, tenses up. "Ray, I—"

"Your basket, Grace." He gestures down at her provisions. "Thought I overheard you mention you had to grab something else before you checked out."

She shakes her head, as if such a simple movement might help the feelings that now pulse inside her to go away. "I, um, I have a splinter." She licks her lips, which have gone dry. "I was going to see if they had anything to help me get it out."

"Tweezers." He nods. "Aisle three," he tells her, clearly knowing this place. Knowing her and what she needs. "Bottom peg."

The man at the register clears his throat. "Actually, we're all out." The bells chime once more, another customer walking in. "Delivery delay. I've got a shipment of things coming from the mainland early next week."

His eyes still locked on Grace, Ray slowly lifts a brow. "Guess you'll have to deal with it the old-fashioned way," he says through a subtle smirk.

A memory. The two of them. Sixteen. The boardwalk. A three-inch shard of wood in her foot.

Who walks barefoot on the boardwalk? he said, smiling, her leg in his lap like it belonged there.

I can't watch, she said, twisting to look toward the Ferris wheel when he pulled out the small pocketknife he always carried for fishing and surfing emergencies. *Please don't hurt me.*

I'd never hurt you, Grace, he said, and before she even had a chance to realize what was happening, the splinter was out, his word—like always—kept.

The recollection fades away just as quickly as it flowed in.

"Well, good luck with that," Ray says now. "And with everything else, I guess."

Grace swallows, her insides still quivering. "Thanks."

Ray takes a step toward an aisle to go find whatever it is that he needs. Before he gets too far, he turns back. "It's funny." Some hard-to-read emotion passes over his face. "I've never been one to believe in rumors." He shrugs. "Turns out, one of them was actually true."

"Wh-what do you mean?"

Ray bites his plump bottom lip, then waits, like he's deciding if he wants to state what comes next. "Nothing." He laughs, though it's hard for Grace to tell if the sound is rooted in amusement or something else. "It's just, well, a little birdie told me I might bump into you again this week."

NINE

Sunday

Morning.

At least, this is what Grace assumes based on the early hints of light. After the last forty-eight hours—Mollie's emails, Birdie's boxes, her out-of-the-blue return to Sea Drift, that bizarre call from Adam, then Ray—sleep felt more like a suggestion than a requirement, one that proved itself to be a complete and utter impossibility.

For a while, she paced. Back and forth in the living room, picking through a bag of gummy worms while her mother's Hallmark movies played on a loop. Through the kitchen, eating a bowl of marshmallow-flecked cereal while she moved. By the time she made it into Birdie's bedroom, still wearing sloppy sweats (*Did she really need to be dressed like a college kid when she saw him?*), her stomach swirled with sugar and memories she was in no shape to face. Beyond the point of exhaustion, she lay on the springy mattress, determined to turn off her brain.

But that never happened. Instead, she stared at the ceiling while her mind raced. Grace tossed and turned, tugging at the seashell-motif comforter as though the two were engaged in an unruly wrestling match. It didn't help. The hours—stubborn as ever—refused to pass.

Now it's shortly after 6:00 a.m. Grace sits straight up and presses her back against the wall, indulgences like headboards not something the beach house provides. Through the window, the sky is webbed with the traces of sun. It's her first official morning back on the island in five years. And for better or worse, her last.

How can she possibly stay here? Alone. Lost. Practically drowning in her past. It's time to leave. To turn around, go home, and figure out a plan. There's nothing left to dispute or second-guess. This trip—this hiccup of disillusion—was a mistake. A series of coincidences—the phone call, the cardinal—that, in all her desperation, she convinced herself were signs. It's only now, in the early light of a new day, that she sees they weren't. Sometimes a bird is just a bird, and a call is just a call. Birdie, if she had any say from the afterlife, would never have sent Grace here, not knowing what—*who*—was waiting.

Her head throbbing with fatigue, Grace throws aside the comforter and stands. When she does, something falls from the bed and hits the floor. She rubs her eyes and finds the old photo album, which she carried into the bedroom last night but never looked through, now sprawled out on the floor. Grace bends to pick it up but stops when she sees her sixteen-year-old self—faded-blue tank, hair wild and sun-streaked—staring back at her through time. Grace sits on the edge of the mattress and sets the album on her lap. She runs a finger over the page's plastic sleeve. Although the picture is 2D, the memory isn't. One look and she's lost in the sensory details of it. The warmth of the sun on her tanned skin. The water lapping her ankles as she searched for pearlescent treasures in the surf. The undeniable feeling that she was happy.

"No." Grace's words are the only sound in the house. "Don't do this to yourself." She slaps the album closed. "It's time to go."

Several minutes later, the few items Grace actually had time to remove from her bag the day before are folded and packed back up. The cereal and remaining snacks are sealed and stored in the kitchen cabinets, gifts for the home's next guests. Soon, she's dressed—shorts, a fresh T-shirt, the same faded-blue baseball cap she wore on the drive down—the bed neatly made, her duffel bag ready and waiting near the front door. Quickly, she breezes through the house, giving everything a once-over before she leaves.

For a beat, Grace stands in the entryway and takes it all in one final time.

"So long, house," she says, like it's an old friend.

She doesn't pull the door open yet. Instead, she waits another second, perhaps to see if anything will happen, some unexplainable something that will confirm this is the right path—or maybe the wrong one. But there's nothing.

"We had a good run together, didn't we?" She traces her fingers over the knob—a small, unconscious goodbye. "Thanks for all the memories." With a sigh, she twists it open and sets one foot outside. Before she's fully gone, Grace briefly looks back. "For everything, really, I guess."

After she drops her belongings—bag, phone, laptop, the album—inside the Jeep, Grace walks around back, collects her toiletries, and places the key beneath the bottle of strawberry shampoo. Once she's settled back at home (*Is that what I should call it? Is that what it feels like now?*), she'll call Caleb and explain.

But that's later.

For now, before she gets in her mother's car and heads to the bridge, Grace knows there's one final thing she needs to do before she drives away.

~

The beach is quiet. Empty. The breeze still cool with night. She kicks off her shoes, walks down the dune, and makes her way toward the wide, vacant stretch of sand. The lifeguard stands are empty—nothing for anyone to watch over yet. Up ahead, the water is a smooth sheet of blue that gives way to the gentle ebbs and flows of low tide. Above it, the sky has begun to soften into day. Muted yellows. Soft peaches. Bands of lavender and gray.

The magic hour.

Grace walks to the ocean and into the surf. The water is the ideal mix of cold and warm—a burst of refreshment, but in a welcome way. She twirls her toes through it, letting droplets splash up her calf. It's calming. Cleansing. The sound so timeless and full of peace.

Her eyes close. Grace gives herself a few minutes to experience it. If only everything in her life could feel this simple, this easy to wade into without the need to think about what comes next. Back inside the house, everything felt too tight, the air heavy with things she couldn't quite name. Out here, it's different. Open. Lighter. At least for this minute, easier to breathe.

This is how Grace and Birdie ended every trip to the island. Whether Grace was five or seventeen or twenty-eight, it was a tradition they refused to break. The last day of their rental week, before they climbed back in the Jeep—or separate cars as Grace got older—and headed back to the mainland, they'd wander to the beach together at sunrise to collect shells, share a few quiet moments, get a last glimpse of the ocean for the season, then say goodbye to this place.

Grace reopens her eyes, deciding to walk. The haze lingers, though behind it the sun has started to rise, its bold, bright light warming her face. In the far distance, a few figures take shape. Someone walks an unleashed dog. A person carries a surfboard.

She stops, not wanting to go too far, knowing she should hit the road early. Before she heads back, Grace bends down. She runs her hand left to right through the shallow water. Her fingers rake the cool grains of sand, tracing lazy circles before they curl around her first discovery of the morning—a half-moon of a clamshell, its edges worn smooth with time. She thumbs it, then tosses it back, knowing it's not the right find. Gentle waves roll in, bringing with them the usual suspects: fragile coquina shells, ridged whelk bits, the long narrow halves of razor clams. They're all broken, each piece a remnant of something larger, something that was once whole.

Grace sighs, lets a collection of fragmented shells slide off her palm and plop into the water. She turns at an angle, her back to the beach and her face tilted up toward the sky.

"Mom?" She adjusts her hat, tugs it down to block out the glare. "Are you there?" The tide pats the shoreline—a rhythmic hush that fails to provide any answers. "I wanted to tell you that I'm leaving now." With a subtle swivel, she scans the horizon, as if some sign or solution to her problems might be sailing out in the deeper water. "And to be honest, I don't ever plan on coming back. As much as I once loved it here, it doesn't feel right to me anymore."

She shakes her head, trying to shake it all away, to be okay with this decision. It's the right one. Still, a feeling of sadness lingers in her core. In no small way, this is grief. Learning not only to say goodbye to a person, or a relationship, or a version of yourself you once believed you'd be. But also about bidding farewell to certain places, too—ones that once filled you up but that ultimately transformed themselves into sources of pain.

"My whole life, I always felt as if you and I were a lot alike," Grace goes on. "It's only lately that I realize there's one big difference." She wipes a tear from her face. "You lost Dad, just like I've lost you. Only, you seemed to know what to do when you did." She tries to swallow down some of her feelings, but they're too big. "You knew how to turn lemons into lemonade, Mom. And it turns out I don't."

Grace cups water over her arms, then sits alone with her thoughts for a beat.

"Anyway, I thought coming here might give me some answers. Help me figure out my next steps. Point me down a path toward finding myself again, or at the very least, help me remember the person I used to be." She sighs. "But unfortunately, I can see that's not the case." She closes her eyes, the light suddenly too bright. "This would all be so much more manageable if I wasn't stuck doing it alone, you know?" Behind her, a splash—likely a fish, or a seagull swooping down. "I feel like my whole life right now would be so much easier if I had someone else here with me to talk to or to help me or to give me tips or advice or—"

"I found another one!" a voice shouts out.

Grace jumps—literally jumps—at the sound, the surprise of it making her feel as though someone has sucked out all her breath. Off-balance and newly disoriented, she tries to steady herself, but it's no use. She falls helplessly into the surf.

By the time Grace pulls herself up—her hair, her clothes, absolutely every part of her fully soaked—she's choking on water, her mouth full of salt. She manically blinks, her vision blurred from the droplets that cling to her lashes, as she swooshes her hands all around her, suddenly on a mad search for her hat. An instant later, she grabs it, along with a handful of brown seaweed. Grace rubs her eyes, slides her drenched cap back on, then squints.

At first, she thinks she's seeing things, that the sun is too bright and distorting her vision. But when she blinks again—slower, controlled this time—she sees more clearly. The person before her assembles in fragments, like a Cubist painting coming together piece by piece. The faded-blue tank top. The wild, sun-streaked hair. And then, the most inexplicable detail of all: a glint of gold at the girl's collarbone. A necklace, one Grace knows as well as her own reflection.

Another wave comes in, a bit stronger now, the tide officially starting to shift. Grace, feeling as though she's stepped outside her own body, like she's watching the scene unfold on an old VHS tape—grainy, surreal, a little slow—ignores it and lets it slam her side. All she can do is stare at the pendant—the familiar *Cece* charm—that sits on the girl's neck.

"I'm sorry I scared you!" the girl—a beautiful, bouncy teenager—finally says, her tone full of life and yet lighter than air. "I just got really excited!" She smiles, the expression taking up her whole face, then holds up her arm. There, pinched between her electric-pink-painted fingernails, is a whole, perfectly intact sand dollar, its circumference half the size of her palm. "I'm basically obsessed with these things. Sometimes I find a ton, and other times I can't find any." She lifts it toward the sky, taking in the shell's natural beauty. "Today must be my lucky day," she explains. "I've already found six."

Grace stands there, dripping. Her head tilts from left to right, like maybe if she sees things from a different angle she'll snap back into reality. *You're losing it,* she tells herself, even though the sight before her appears way too real for her to deny. *You're having a breakdown. Or you're drowning. Maybe you're in some strange mental limbo state while your body drifts out to sea.*

She opens her mouth, but the right words don't arrive. Instead, her heart races so hard it feels as though it might rip a hole through her chest. Grace points. A measly fragment falls from her lips, along with a gasp.

"T-the necklace," she stutters as her thoughts rewind to yesterday and the tide pools with Caleb. "Where did you get that?"

"What?" The girl taps the charm. "This?" Her freckled nose wrinkles in question. "It was a gift." Another smile, this one bigger. "My mom gave it to me last night. Early birthday surprise." She shrugs as if to say *All in the world is good.* Like nothing—anywhere—could possibly weigh her down. "We're here for my birthday. I turn sixteen this week."

Though she knows she won't find anything, Grace trails her fingers along her chest, only to discover her wet T-shirt and skin. In a rush, her mind floods with questions—too many for her to process, like a dam inside her brain has suddenly burst. Her vision travels from the sand dollar to the necklace and back again. "How did you find—"

"What, this?" She looks down at the shell, thinking that's what Grace means. "I'll be honest. I'm a little bit of an expert when it comes to sand-dollar hunting." Her eyes sparkle. "I come down here to search for them a lot of mornings," she says, her words like an invitation. "You know, if you're ever looking for advice." She bends down, rinses the shell in the glittering water. "I may be young, but when it comes to finding beach treasures, I've got *loads* of tips."

Grace stands still, the irony of the girl's words hitting her even harder than the rising tides.

"Welp, I'd better get going. I've had my face down looking for shells." The girl twists, peers back over her bronzed shoulder. "I didn't realize how far I wandered. I need to get back." Her smile subtly changes, both brightening and softening at once, the same as it was before, yet also something new. "I promised a friend I'd come out to meet him this morning," she adds, her expression as she mentions this person as easy and warm as summer itself. "We sort of have this thing the last few seasons where I hang out and watch him surf."

Without warning, something tugs at Grace's chest. A feeling. A memory. Hot days. Warm sand. Her eyes tracking one board—one *person*—slicing through the waves. On those long afternoons, she didn't worry about grades or how she looked or what came next. She was just there. Present. Happy. Her full self, without even trying. Without even realizing it.

Nearby, more people begin to appear through the lingering veil of mist. A man in running clothes. A mother and young child, both dressed in their pajamas.

"Here," the girl says to Grace right before she heads off. "You take this one." She extends a slender arm and hands over the sand dollar as though it's nothing. "It's the least I can do for scaring you and making you fall and get all wet."

Grace's fingers close around it, the shell's surface already dry and warm in her grip. Her lips stay parted, but no sound comes out.

"Anyway, I hope you like it!" the stranger says as Grace continues to take her in. Her perfect face. Her sparkling brown eyes. Her whole demeanor bright, carefree, and happy. "My mom says they're lucky—the whole, unbroken ones, at least."

With that, she turns, kicking through the water as she moves in the direction of whatever place she just came. Before she gets too far, she pivots and gazes back.

"It's so nice out today, isn't it?" she shouts. "It's supposed to stay like this, too." She tilts her chin toward the sky. "From what I hear, it's going to be a really great week!" The girl waves with all the enthusiasm of someone her age—a person who still believes in dreams and the future, an individual fueled by the relentless hope that nothing bad will ever happen and that every last thing she wants will miraculously work out in the end. "I'll see you around," she calls out, turning to leave, then spins back. "Oh, one other thing." She flashes an easy grin. "I'm Cece! Figured I'd mention it in case we run into each other again. You know how it is around here—no real strangers on the island, right?" she adds before she walks away.

Not having a clue what just happened, or how she could ever explain or make sense of it, Grace stands half paralyzed in the rising surf, the shell still inside her cupped palm.

"Cece?" she says, the word she's been trying to get out finally coming free from her throat.

And then alone, but not really, Grace watches as her almost-sixteen-year-old self walks away, into the fleeting curtain of morning mist, and disappears.

PART TWO

Yesterday

TEN

Grace sits, stunned, on the front stairs of the house, her mouth hanging open as if she's a gasping fish that's washed ashore. Despite her initial plan—one last beach visit, then get in the car, say goodbye to this place for good—her hands are too shaky to drive. She can hardly think straight, let alone safely navigate a speeding vehicle along five lanes of highway traffic. Her clothes—old T-shirt, jean shorts, baseball hat—remain soaked, her skin chafing at her thighs. She can't even bring herself to run around back and grab the key so she can change into something dry.

For the moment, all she can do is sit.

It's been at least a half hour, possibly longer, since her—her what? Encounter? Hallucination? Spiritual awakening? Complete emotional break? Her thoughts are still too muddled for her to even think clearly. She just keeps replaying the scene—over and over, around and around, like an amusement ride that never stops. The girl. The necklace. The impossibility of it. The unmistakable wave of déjà vu.

"Y-you're being foolish, Grace," she mumbles for the hundredth time. "You're exhausted. Probably dehydrated." She stares off into space. "You've hardly eaten or slept in days." As she talks to herself, Grace recalls a past therapy session when Dr. Anne explained the notion of visual distortions—how people deep in grief look for shadows or other things that aren't really there. "Of course," Grace decides and lets out a stunted laugh—short, breathless, possibly a touch deranged. "This is just a trauma response triggered by hunger and a heavy hit of nostalgia." She imagines Dr. Anne gently nodding from her upholstered chair. "Or heatstroke. Probably a lesser-known consequence of too much saltwater to the head."

While she listens to her own words, trying her best to believe them, Grace presses the sand dollar tighter in her palm. It's warm, familiar, and without a single crack. She swallows, hoping to steady the trembling feeling inside her, and makes a conscious effort to remind herself it's not a talisman, only a random organic object she discovered in the surf.

"Ten more minutes," she announces to the ground. "Catch your breath. Collect your thoughts. Put on dry clothes. Then get in the Jeep. Leave. Drive away."

"Enjoy another unplanned swim?" a voice interrupts.

Grace's face pans up. In her current state, it takes her a minute to realize a person has appeared. That he's looking at her. Speaking to her. Expecting her to react. She blinks, her lids quickly opening and closing like a camera shutter as her eyes work to relay the scene to her brain.

Caleb.

"I'm not one to judge." He casually tucks his hands into the pockets of his board shorts, his whole stance ripe with beachy ease. "And I, for one, know the ocean's temptation can be strong." A playful grin stretches over his face, long and thin. "But most people tend to wait until they're actually in their bathing suits—just their bathing suits—before diving in."

Although it's early, and in spite of Grace's temporary paralysis, she now sees that Surf Street has begun to come to life. A dad rounds the corner carrying a white bakery box, likely full of jelly doughnuts and crumb cake. A pair of kids, already dressed in bathing suits, ride in concentric circles on their bikes, like dogs chasing their own tails. A trio dashes out from another bungalow, the mom shouting at the two teens about SPF. Up on the boulevard, a sprinkling of cars breezes past. For everyone here, this is the start of another normal mid-August beach day.

Everyone, that is, except for Grace.

“Hi,” she manages, trying to bring herself back down to earth, and looks at her dripping-wet getup. “I fell in.”

Caleb waves to someone passing by in the street. “We ought to look into some water-safety classes for you,” he jokes, then gives Grace a good, hard stare. “You all right?”

“I-I’ve had a strange morning,” she admits, the correct mix of honest and vague.

Caleb gives her a fast once-over. “I sensed that.” His mouth curves, charming and welcoming. “Care to talk about it over breakfast?”

~

Sunny Side is about the size of a large shoebox, a vintage diner right on the bay. Paper menus. Greasy utensils. Huge platters. Burned coffee. Water views. Always a long wait.

Caleb sits across from Grace in a too-tight booth, peeling back the paper lid on a plastic creamer, his mouth curled in an amused grin. Following his invitation back at the house, Grace finally dragged her weekender bag from the Jeep, ran back inside, and changed. A fresh white tank top. A clean pair of cutoffs. In the home’s dollhouse-size bathroom, she splashed cold water on her face, doing her best to disregard the morning’s events. She remained set on leaving, though rationalized that a hot meal before she merged onto any highways was a smart idea for her stomach, her overall safety, and her mental state.

“What?” Grace asks now, still feeling uneasy as she settles into her vinyl seat. “Why are you grinning?”

“Hmm?” Caleb stirs his coffee. “Nothing.” He sets down his spoon. “It’s, well, I didn’t want to say it before but . . .” He reaches across the table and gently tugs a strand of Grace’s hair, still partially damp and hanging like limp string from beneath her salt-stained cap. “I just wasn’t sure if you were planning to save this clump of seaweed.”

Her cheeks flush pink as she considers how she'd failed to notice a web of kelp attached to her head. "I'd say thanks, though I'm not sure that's the right response." She watches him place it on the table, next to a lazy Susan full of jellies. "Maybe I should keep it, start a scrapbook of embarrassing moments you've witnessed of me on this trip."

Caleb chuckles and skims his paper menu. "I'll be honest, I was surprised to see you sitting out front before. I'd gathered that you were leaving today." He sips his coffee. "I was outside first thing, hosing off my fishing gear. Saw you loading up your Jeep." He sets down his mug and waves over their waitress. "Figured you'd had enough after the tide pool and were heading out early."

"I was." She grasps for a clear thought, sifts through the bowl of creamers. "I am. I think."

"Hunting for something other than decades-old dairy pods in there?"

Grace looks up, surprised to see him watching her, not even sure what she's searching for.

"This place is a bit stuck in time, but they've made some improvements." He lifts his fork and wipes away a smudge of grease, even though he's yet to use it, then looks at her in a conspiratorial way. "If you ask really nicely, they'll bring you sriracha or oat milk from the back."

Grace laughs. "I'm fine with plain old creamer. Sometimes I gravitate toward the fancy stuff, though it's purely a preference. Not a necessity."

Caleb nods, apparently making a mental note of this small fact.

"Well, it's a shame that you're leaving today," he states, just as the glass door behind him reopens. A gaggle of boisterous teenagers—loud, full of energy and flawless skin, all youthfully oblivious—wanders inside. "I get it, though. I remember you saying you were pretty weighed down with work at the moment."

Grace pours a splash of creamer into her mug, then takes a hot, caffeinated sip. As she does, she catches a flash of a girl in a pale-blue tank top with long blond-streaked hair flying by the window. The sight makes Grace's fingers go numb. She sets her mug down, hard. A puddle of coffee splashes across the table, splattering her menu and the front of her shirt.

"Shoot." Grace fumbles for a napkin and wipes up the spill. The door opens. Grace's eyes dart up. "Cece!" she blurts before she can stop herself, and waves a frantic arm, not even sure what she's doing. The girl turns, reveals her face—one Grace doesn't recognize. Of course. What did she expect? "Oh, wait . . ."

The girl meets Grace's stare and rolls a judgmental eye. She squeezes through the crowded diner, joins her friends at a table. They pull together for a huddle, whisper something, then break out in a collective laugh.

Caleb's brows rise in question. "Someone you know?" he asks as their waitress—a hardened woman Grace recognizes who's worked at Sunny Side since the dawn of time—appears.

"I mean, no. Or yes." Her face is on fire, teenage-level mortified. "She looked like . . . I thought . . ." In her mind, she contemplates if it'd be appropriate for her to slide down the booth and hide under the table. "I guess not."

Their waitress taps her pen on her notepad, unamused. "Ready to order?"

"Crab Benedict for me," Caleb jumps in, giving Grace a chance to collect herself. "And extra home fries," he adds. "Like usual, please, Toni."

Toni's lips tug sideways, clearly wooed by his unpretentious charm. "I'll tell them to make them extra crispy, Caleb." She turns, looks at Grace, her expression instantly fading. "You?"

"Um . . . uh." Grace picks up her sopping menu, too wet for her to read it. "Eggs. I guess?"

Toni blinks, unimpressed.

"She's had a long morning. Bring her the chocolate chip pancakes, Toni," Caleb interjects, but not before looking at Grace for her approval. She nods. "With a side of scrambled, to be safe."

Toni jots something on her notepad, reaches across the table, and picks up the seaweed. "Saving this for breakfast, sweetheart?"

Grace peers down at the tabletop—a scolded schoolgirl—and shakes her head.

"Toni's a bit of an acquired taste," Caleb says once she's gone. "Like a lot of things on this island, I guess." He finishes off his coffee, waves down a different waitress for a refill.

"I remember," Grace states. "Both about Toni, and, well, other things, too."

Caleb sits with this comment, letting it float for a beat before it vaporizes. "So," he begins a moment later, "you're bogged down with work at the end of the summer?" He leans back in the booth, but the movement is stilted—there isn't much room. "Isn't this typically the time everyone pumps the brakes, takes it easy, coasts to the end of the season?"

"I'm a writer," Grace explains. *For now, at least.* "A novelist. The only time I pump the brakes is the forty-eight hours after I submit a manuscript."

"A novelist, huh? That's pretty neat."

"Sometimes." Grace used to feel proud telling people this fact. Now, not knowing what her future career path has in store, it just leaves her with a pit in her stomach. "Depends on the day and which page you're currently stuck at, I guess." Behind her, the teenagers erupt in an explosive cackle. Grace can't help but wonder if she's the butt of their joke. "I'm on a deadline. A tight one. I thought I could work down here, that maybe the ocean air would give me the push I need to get my story down. So far, I've mostly found the change in scenery . . . distracting."

Though hardly any time has passed, Toni emerges from the kitchen, a tray balanced on her shoulder. Without a word, she sets down their plates. They're huge. Piled high. Stacked and dripping with everything delicious and unhealthy.

"What about you?" Grace asks, desperate to change the topic. She cuts a bite of pancake, the batter fluffy—even better than Jenny's—and perfectly studded with chocolate. "You work for the rental agency year-round?"

"For now." Caleb slices his knife through a smothered hunk of crab. "I've had some big life changes this year. I grew up right over the bridge, though I've been out on the West Coast for a long time." His tone drops, as if someone clicked down the volume on a remote. "Eventually, though, everything—even year-round sunshine—runs its course." He cuts another piece. "Moved back after the holidays last winter. Never been married. No kids. Had a pretty boring office job, which frankly, I was happy to leave. Fairly easy move, all in all." Caleb sets down his fork, wipes his mouth. "My folks still live out on the mainland, though during peak season they end up needing to be here on the island almost daily. A lot of times during the offseason, too. They've had the business since I was a kid, but they're getting older. They don't want to keep it much longer. It was time for me to come home, figure out my next steps."

A few moments of silence pass as they both work their way through their meals. Salt. Sugar. A perfect balance of protein and grease. As they do, Grace looks—*really* looks—around Sunny Side, as if for the first time since they walked in. The bustling counter. The marine-themed knickknacks on the walls. The sweeping views of the bay and wooden docks out back.

Birdie used to bring Grace here at least once during their annual visit. "Get anything you want," she'd say, waving at the air as if they were in the middle of a fancy department store buying every shoe from the display. "French toast. Bacon. Cinnamon rolls," Birdie would rattle off from her side of the booth. "If Dad were here, he'd laugh and tell us to tack on the chocolate chip pancakes as an appetizer," she'd add brightly, then look to the empty seat beside her. "He would've wanted you to enjoy this week to the fullest."

Although their shared life in Pennsylvania was comfortable, money, for the most part, was often tight. Birdie was a single parent. She clipped coupons. She knew how to stretch a meal. She budgeted all year for

Sea Drift so the week would feel like Christmas—not a detail missing. Except, of course, for one thing—one *person*—no amount of sugar or boardwalk rides could bring back. Maybe it was Birdie's way of trying to fill the invisible void that'd been left behind in her daughter's life when James died. Or maybe, to some degree, it was a way for Birdie to try to heal the void that'd been left behind in her own life, too.

"So what time are you hitting the road?" Caleb asks now, pulling Grace away from her memories. "It's Sunday. Sure you'll hit some pretty fun bridge traffic on your way out."

"Probably right after this." She pushes away her plate, a signal that she's done even though it's half full. "Figured I'd lock the house up—you know, for a second time—and leave the key in its usual spot for next week's tenants."

"And then?"

"And then what?" Grace asks.

"Do you think you'll ever come back?"

The question lingers. "I'm not sure," she admits, just as Toni sets a to-go box and their check on the table.

Before Grace can reach for the paper, Caleb grabs it, like a seagull making a quick dive.

"In that case, my treat," he insists. "Just in case it's your last visit."

~

Outside, the sun is on fire. The air hangs heavy and humid. There isn't a single cloud in the sky.

"Well, thanks for breakfast." Grace holds the take-out box filled with the rest of her meal, which Caleb encouraged her to pack up and take. (*A little car snack for later.*) "Also for the opportunity—the nudge, really—to come back to the house these last few days." Nearby, a line of other hungry visitors flocks at the diner's door, waiting to get in. "I'm sorry things didn't work out and that the place will end up empty anyway."

Caleb smiles, as though he wants to say something but is busy figuring it out. Before he has an opportunity to piece it together, his phone rings. He looks away, abruptly tugged from the moment, as he pulls his cell from the pocket of his board shorts.

"Dang it." He glances at the screen, looking annoyed. "I'm sorry." He toggles, glancing back and forth between Grace and the device, as if he's trying to decide who to root for in a Ping-Pong match. "I've gotta take this," he announces, having chosen his team. "It's another one of my renters." Something about the phrasing lands sideways in Grace's ears. "Their fridge broke last night. Or, at least, they think," he explains, sounding newly exasperated. "They reached out earlier, but the call kept dropping." He shrugs, lifting the phone to his ear. "It's a whole thing."

Grace nods her understanding, even while an unexpected feeling of disappointment blooms in her as Caleb turns, takes a few wide steps in the opposite direction, and answers the call. She stands on the curb and waits, unsure if she should stick around or if this is his way of saying goodbye. She tugs down her cap, runs her fingers through her hair to check for any more tangles of seaweed, and hangs out a minute just to see.

The next part happens so fast, Grace doesn't even realize what's occurred until it's over. A bump—a hard one—at her back. She falls, the take-out box arching overhead and flying wide open, launching out pancake pieces like confetti. It takes about two seconds for the crowd of waiting patrons to gather around and see if she's okay, and half that time for a flock of determined seagulls—already pecking at the sidewalk—to swoop in.

Quickly, Grace tries to collect herself, wondering how many more moments of mortification this short-lived trip will provide. The bystanders, recognizing that she's all right, inch backward, giving her space. Grace brushes off her knee, badly scraped as if she were a rambunctious child, and then stands.

"Wh-what happened?" she asks, half delirious.

"It was that girl!" A middle-aged father points to the street corner. "She smacked right into you! Didn't even stop to apologize!" He peers at his own adolescent offspring beside him, gives them a warning look. "Kids these days," he says by way of an explanation. "No respect!"

Grace twists her body. Her gaze drifts to the end of the block and the young girl with wild, unmistakable hair who glides on a longboard-style skateboard across the street.

"Oh, come on!" Grace shouts, throwing up her arms.

Then, before she can consider what she's doing, Grace bolts, and for reasons she doesn't fully understand, takes off, chasing some version of her past.

ELEVEN

The arcade is a sensory explosion. Flashing lights. Blaring music. Dinging bells. In every direction, sugar-fueled kids dart in frenetic zigzags. Even the carpet is loud, a geometric collision of primary colors masquerading as a pattern. In reality, like everything in here, it's mayhem.

Grace stands at the entrance, breathless. Her pulse kicks her ribs, erratic and urgent. Her previously fresh T-shirt clings to her like wet gauze. She ran five blocks to get here, weaving around beach-ready families, the midmorning heat searing her neck. The whole time, she kept her sight locked on the girl—until she disappeared into this neon vortex.

Once her airways settle, Grace steps fully past the doorway. The noise swells around her, a jarring contrast to the faint sound of waves outside. She blinks, letting her eyes adjust to the artificial light, and scans the crowd, but fails to spot the one person she hopes to find.

"What are you doing, Grace?" she asks herself as she wanders by a wall of claw machines. "You just chased a teenager—a stranger—across the island." A young boy races past, pausing long enough to shoot Grace—an adult, alone in a place meant for children, rambling to herself—a not-so-nice look. "You're following a doppelgänger. A fabricated figment of your imagination." She stops beside a giant Plinko game, her thoughts settling at last, like a snow globe someone stopped shaking long enough for an unobstructed view of the scene inside it to appear. "A strange, definitely questionable, probably diagnosable, response to too many forms of grief."

Maybe she'll call Dr. Anne. She'd have an explanation, some medical jargon to make sense of why Grace keeps convincing herself she's seeing things that aren't really there. She might have a mindfulness technique—a breathing exercise or visualization practice that will calm Grace and help her make sense of all these unexplainable things.

Grace shakes her head and pivots toward the arcade door, feeling foolish for so many reasons. For sprinting into the arcade. For thinking a weeklong return to her childhood vacation spot might heal her. For believing her marriage would last. For convincing herself her mother was immortal. For thinking her dream career might have some longevity.

But when she turns back toward the neon-lit entryway, her thoughts all fall away as one very specific sight stops her—physically, mentally, cardiovascularly—in her tracks.

The first thing Grace thinks is that she's beautiful. Strikingly so. Like a piece of coveted art come to life. Sinewy arms. Mile-long legs. A dozen mismatched accessories that somehow, on her, seem just right. She stands beside a bank of Skee-Ball machines, longboard propped against a wall, her face tilted down as she holds a smoothie and digs through her Boho-style crossbody with her free hand while she looks for something she can't seem to find.

Cece. In the flesh. Somehow, again. Only this time, younger, by at least a few years.

Grace proceeds cautiously, suddenly afraid to move too fast. She takes a step as everything inside the arcade slows. At first, Cece doesn't notice her—all her attention is focused exclusively on her current task. When she finally looks up—her face so perfect, so noticeably lineless—and sees Grace, a total stranger, standing a touch too close, her expression twists in surprise, just as she releases an alarming, high-pitched scream.

"Ahhh!" she shouts and leaps back, nearly dropping her cup but quickly recovering it.

"You're okay." Grace instantly jumps in and touches the young girl's arm to console her. "I didn't mean to scare you or—"

"*Eww.* Weird." Cece shakes away Grace's embrace. "Why are you touching me?"

"What?" Grace startles, suddenly aware of what she's doing. "Oh. Sorry. You—you seemed frightened and I—I don't know." She recoils, as if pulling herself out of a lingering dream. "I felt bad," she adds, half mortified that she just touched a stranger (Is *she a stranger?*) and half babbling as she struggles to work out the details of what she assumes is a full-fledged nervous breakdown. "I-it was an instinct or something."

Cece narrows her eyes—two sharp, judgy slivers. "Are you a mom?" she asks, too young to understand what questions she's really posing. *Are you happy? Has your life worked out the way you've wanted?* Even so, the words stab at Grace's chest like tiny phonetic knives.

"N-no," Grace says, wishing this wasn't her answer but not having the bandwidth right now to think too deeply about it. "I'm not. Wh-why do you—"

"Are you sure?" Cece adjusts the thick fabric strap of her bag—Grace's old bag, the one she adored in middle school and has since forgotten ever existed, but now suddenly remembers quite well. "Because that *definitely* seems like something a mom would do or say."

She pauses, eyeing Grace, who continues to stand awkwardly close, like someone who hasn't yet been versed in the rules of personal space. Finally, Grace gets the memo, takes two big steps back, and stares. Her head tips sideways as she tries to determine if what she's witnessing is magic or memory.

"I-is that really you?" Grace stammers, still erratically batting her lids as if there's something in her cornea she's desperate to blink away. Finding reasons to brush off her experience earlier on the beach felt borderline reasonable. The bright sun! The early hour! Who can see *anything* clearly that time of day? But having this experience happen twice, and in two completely different settings, feels harder to explain. "No, of course not." She wags her head like a dog—hard and inelegant.

"Or is it?" she asks, her focus falling on Cece again. "How? I mean, you're not real, are you? Wh-what are you doing here?"

"Well, first off, really strange opener." Cece clicks her tongue. "Also, I can totally be here. I'm not, like, a toddler, thanks." She sips her smoothie. "The last few seasons, I'm pretty much allowed to go anywhere I want on this island." Her chest—not yet curved with womanhood—shakes when she laughs. "Not that it's any of your business," she adds after another slurp.

Grace's mouth is dry, as if she just spent the morning licking sand. "This doesn't make sense." She rubs her temples hard, like they're stress balls—the kind a woman in her grief group sometimes brings to their meetings for all the members to knead—then notices one of the girl's bracelets—a thick, colorful band of braided string, into which her name is stitched. "I think I'm having a spasm or something, so I'm going to casually walk outside, and when I come back in, you're not going to be here, okay?"

"Do I know you?" Cece's perfect face tilts. "Did Birdie send you here or something? I know she's less than pleased with me right now because I bailed on the lighthouse to come here instead." She expels a quiet, annoyed huff. "She thinks I'm moving too fast with this guy I like and that I should slow down and just *be a kid*," she volunteers under her breath, even though no one asked. "Which is *ridiculous*, considering she married my dad—her high school sweetheart, might I add—when she was, like, twenty-five." A pause as she counts off on her fingers. "That's only, what, twelve years from now for me?"

Grace goes still, like someone has flipped an invisible switch in her body. Any doubts she's carried with her today—after her encounter on the beach, upon her arrival here in the arcade, and every spare moment in between—vanish as fast as curtains yanked open on a stage. Grace didn't know what to expect—not when she chased Cece into this arcade, not when she touched her uninvited. Did she think the teenager would announce she was a hologram? That Grace would wake up in her bed back home and realize the whole trip here had been a strange dream?

The last thing she expected to hear was Birdie's name.

"Birdie?" Grace repeats back, like the girl's words were a mistake. "How do you . . ." she stammers, feeling half drunk. "What do you . . ."

"I know." Cece's defenses slowly lift as it dawns on her that Grace isn't an immediate threat. "Funny, right?" She smiles. "It's a not-so-common nickname for Elizabeth. It's what my mom's gone by for years."

Grace blinks and everything clears.

Elizabeth Grace Porter. Birdie, to those who knew her best. To Grace, just . . . Mom.

"So let me get this straight," Cece continues, not realizing the gravity of what she's just said. "Do you know her or something?" She lifts a slender arm, her wrist wrapped up in a dozen friendship bracelets, and flips a section of golden hair from the left to the right side of her face. "You feel familiar." She gives Grace a quick once-over. "You seem like someone she'd befriend."

Nearby, an elementary-aged girl smacks a mallet at a Whac-A-Mole game. The machine erupts in a jingle, every light on it flashing. She might as well have used her rubber weapon and pummeled Grace square in her chest.

How is she supposed to respond? Does she know Birdie? Of course. She knows every detail of her, the same way she imagines the sun's likely memorized every square inch of the sky. The sound of her voice. The bright smell of her Clinique perfume. The exact dimensions of the heart-shaped sunspot on her hand.

"Wait. Exactly *how* old are you?" Grace poses, still absorbing all the details of their conversation. She takes a fast look at the girl's neck—no nameplate yet—then recalls her earlier comment. "You must be in middle school, right?" She calculates some fast mental math. "Which would make you about—"

"Thirteen," she announces, a sense of pride lifting her words. She straightens her posture, like she's trying to look a touch older. "Or, at least, I will be this week."

Thirteen. A teenager. The first real chapter in no longer being a mere kid.

"That's basically why I'm here." She sets her smoothie cup on the floor, then resumes searching in her bag. A moment later, she holds up a woven coin purse like a prize. "I knew I had it!" She pulls a candy wrapper from its side, unfazed. "Now it's only a matter of how many coins I have." She unzips it, invites a pile of loose change to cascade into her palm. "Cool." She takes a quick tally. "That should be plenty."

She bends down and begins to feed quarters into a metal slot. The Skee-Ball machine blares to life—bells, lights, contained electronic anarchy—then spits out a dozen brown balls. Cece tugs away her crossbody, dropping it in a heap on the dirty carpet, then lifts a ball.

"I used to love this game," Grace says, remembering the sounds of it in a partial daze.

"Well, good." Cece squares off her shoulders. "Then prepare to watch the absolute best!"

Cece bounces on her heels and positions herself in an athletic stance. While she does, Grace watches her, sifting through her memories and trying to remember if this exact scene ever happened. Skee-Ball. A middle-aged stranger. Nothing specific comes to mind. On this island, everything feels like a moment you might have lived once—some other year, some other version of you, some other time.

"Ugh!" Cece exclaims as her first ball misses the hundred-point target by a mile. "That was a terrible shot!" She shifts her weight, tosses another one down the smooth lane. A ten-pointer. Total waste. "It's fine," she states, mostly to herself, as if she's forgotten Grace is standing nearby. "You've done this before. Just concentrate." She stretches an arm over her torso, like a runner preparing for a long and important race. "You can totally do this again."

"You seem really determined," Grace states, trying to recall the feeling of being so young and of wanting something so arbitrary so very badly.

"Yeah, well, you would be, too, if you were me." Cece looks away from her game, points up at an electronic board, and pinches the air. "I was *this* close to beating the high score yesterday."

"Maybe you will today?" Grace gently offers.

"I'd better." Cece feeds more coins into the machine. "I'm running out of time to do it."

"Because you're leaving?" Grace tries, not clear on her urgency.

"No," she says, like it's the most obvious answer on the planet. She tosses another ball—gutter shot. "Because after this week, I'm *done* with kid games for good."

Grace's chest pulls tight at the certitude in her voice. Slowly, the memory begins to coalesce. Not the exact scene, but the feeling of it.

"Why are you done with kid games?" Grace asks her anyway, even though she knows the answer. She watches Cece wind back up, her whole body so focused and serious. "Especially this one. You love it." Cece gives her a look. Grace stops, backpedals. "At least, it seems like you do."

Cece takes another shot. This time, the ball swoops and drops right into the fifty-point slot.

"Because I'm not a kid anymore." Her tone is firm and a touch rehearsed. "What I *am* is a person—an almost-teenager—who's *in love*."

The declaration pulls Grace back—hard—into a place in her mind she's not sure she's ready to face. She watches Cece with a strange pang of recognition. *She wants proof,* Grace realizes. *That she hasn't outgrown who she used to be. That she's still good at something she loves before she lets it go.*

"At least, I'm pretty sure that's what it is," Cece continues, her tone softening. She doesn't look away from the game. "Love, I mean." She grabs another brown ball, tosses it down the smooth lane. "Ray," she adds, nearly under her breath. "He's a friend. From down here." Her lips break into a grin. "This trip, though, it feels . . . different."

Grace's heart flutters and drops as recollections of that summer week rise in her mind. The first time he reached for her hand. The first almost-kiss, his cheeks pink when he missed his mark. The way she felt like she was finding someone—something—important outside of her, while also discovering a new part of herself at the same time.

Come on, Porter, he teased her that year, playfully employing her last name every time she rolled a dud. *You missed that last one by a mile!* The arcade was garish, even back then. Swarms of kids. Blinking lights. But there, beside Ray, something in her always stilled. The world grew quiet. Like she could hear her own voice clearly, despite the noise. Some days, though she never told him, she missed on purpose. Not to lose. But just to stay there with him—with that feeling—for a few extra minutes.

"Darn it!" Cece blurts out now. She looks down at the machine, ready to grab another ball, but realizes the game is done. She begins to dig in her change purse again, then huffs.

"What's wrong?"

"I'm out of quarters." Cece frowns, all frustrated little kid. "Just nickels and dimes."

"Here." Grace reaches for her own purse strap, not wanting this moment to end. "I'm sure I have spare change in my . . ." She stops, looks around.

"What?"

"My purse." Grace sighs. "I must have left it outside the diner after you ran into me."

"Oh. Was that you? Sorry. I was racing to be one of the first people here when they opened so I could score my favorite machine." As if on cue, the game coughs out a belt of tickets. Cece gives them a quick yank and tugs them free. "Want these?" Without waiting for an answer, she hands them to Grace. "I think I've won everything this arcade has to offer the last few summers."

"Isn't that the point, though?" Grace asks, genuinely meaning it. "If you get the high score, then you get to take home a big prize?"

"Sure." Cece's tone drips with sarcasm. "Because what I *really* need at my age is to lug a giant six-foot stuffed panda up the boulevard." She grabs her bag and her cup, preparing to get on with her day.

"What happens if you win?" Grace asks, not remembering. "Do they display your name somewhere or something?"

"No." Cece looks around the arcade in case she's missed something. "I don't think so."

"Then why are you so invested in winning?"

"I don't know. I just really want to do it." Cece shrugs, slurps up the last sip of her fruity drink. "I think it'd be kind of fun. Isn't that enough?"

Maybe that's part of what I've been missing, Grace thinks. Not deadlines. Not discipline. Not goals crossed off, stories perfected, or expectations met. Just the thrill and the joy that come from liking to play, not because the advances you forward several steps.

"Probably." Grace thinks back to the feel of the ball coming free from her hand, the innocent pleasure of seeing it arc its way into the right hole. The way her writing used to make her feel this way, too. And other things. "To be honest, I don't really remember the last time I did something like that just for the fun of it."

"Oh." Cece winces so hard it's practically audible. "That's . . . sad."

"Yeah." Grace sighs, letting what Cece said sink in—the layers of scaffolded meaning beneath her statement. "Tell me about it."

"Well, I need to get out of here. Cool talking to you," Cece adds, walking the tightrope between pity and amusement, and makes her way toward the door. "I guess."

"Cece, hang on!" Grace calls out, not meaning to project so loudly. "Where are you—"

"Wait." She turns, squinting against the fluorescent lights. "How'd you know my nickname?"

A brief moment of panic.

"It's stitched into your friendship bracelet," Grace says, quickly recovering. *The one you bought at that souvenir shop last summer. The one you'll keep wearing every day until it breaks.*

"Huh," Cece notes. "Good vision for someone your age."

"Will I see you again?" Grace asks. Cece looks at her, like she's suddenly second-guessing this interaction once more. "You know, so I can find out if you get the high score," Grace clarifies.

"Oh." Cece's expression relaxes. "Right. Um, maybe." She pushes open the door, letting a stream of natural light filter inside. "I mean, I haven't hit it yet. So yeah, at some point this week, I'll probably be back."

The tickets dangle from Grace's fingers, a tangible souvenir of this bizarre meeting. As they do, she watches Cece—a different version of the girl she saw earlier—step outside, a tangle of bracelets and certitude fueled by the hopeful belief that not every missed shot is a loss.

"Hey." Cece pops her head back inside. "Were you any good when you were my age?"

"More than good," Grace says without thinking. "I was the best. A long time ago anyway."

"Cool." Cece nods, considering something. "In that case, if I see you in here again . . . want to play against me?" She pauses, finally revealing an ounce of her adolescent insecurities. "I haven't hit the high score yet, but I can probably give you some good tips." She shrugs. A smile spreads across her face, as big and bright as the arcade's many illuminated bulbs. "You know, if you're up for trying to get your game back."

TWELVE

Grace sits on the front steps of the beach house, her mother's photo album—retrieved from the Jeep, its windows still irresponsibly buzzed down from yesterday—sprawled open on her lap. For the last half hour or so, she's been here, baking in the late-morning heat, staring at one photo in particular—the slouchy surfer-girl bag, the stack of knotted bracelets—while trying to make sense of the impossible. It's so hot out that the sun's incessant rays are making her dizzy. Just like earlier, she still hasn't worked up the nerve to grab the key from the outdoor shower and reopen the door. After this most surreal day, she's too afraid of what—or *who*—she might discover inside.

"I see you're a fan of the slow-burn leave," someone says from a few feet away.

Grace looks up and finds Caleb standing at the curb, looking at her like she's lost it. Again.

"Don't ask," she says, her skin burning. "I don't know what I'm doing." The arcade tickets sit next to her in a perforated line. "It's a long, bizarre, borderline-unbelievable story."

"Says the fiction writer," he jokes, shifting his weight from one flip-flopped foot to the other. "Isn't that part of what you do?" His brows rise. "Make the unbelievable seem within reach?"

"In theory," Grace states as another renter from their block strolls past and waves. "Though this one is pretty far out there. Even for me." Grace timidly returns the gesture, wishing that, like this stranger, she was busy enjoying a carefree day in the sun, too, instead of what she's currently doing: sweating—both literally and figuratively—as she contemplates where the division line lands between the present and the past. "I'd planned to get on the road right after breakfast." She sighs, wipes a slick of perspiration from her neck. "Life, it seems, had other plans."

Caleb nods his understanding, even though he couldn't possibly comprehend an iota of what she actually means. "Here." He takes a few steps forward. "Assuming you'll need this in order to leave." He pulls his arm out from behind his back and passes over her purse, the one that also contains her wallet and car keys. "You left this at the diner earlier. Toni ran out and gave it to me right after you left."

"Thanks." Grace feels so out of sorts that she nearly forgot about it. "I swear I planned to walk back to Sunny Side any minute to go grab it," she fibs, and sets the bag down beside her, feeling embarrassed and like an utter mess. "I'm sorry," she adds, not sure who the apology is directed at—Caleb? Herself? Both of them? Nearby, a family moves up the block, carting enough coolers and towels to last them for a week. "My head's been a bit . . . in the clouds today." She stops, contemplating. "If I'm honest, it's been floating in the stratosphere all weekend, really."

"No judgment," Caleb states in his easygoing way. "We all go through days—weeks—like that." A reserved grin unfolds across his face. "Seems like those seagulls back at Sunny Side made out pretty well as a result, though."

Grace cringes, remembering the scene she caused when she toppled to the ground, as well as the fast-moving teenager at the center of it.

"You doing okay?" Caleb asks, his eyes narrowing with concern. "Really. All kidding aside." Behind him, another troop of beachgoers tromps up the street, wearing matching wide-brimmed hats. "I know you mentioned having a heavy workload on your plate, but it seems like you've had a bit of a rough go since you got down here yesterday."

Grace specializes in words, or used to. But right now, she can't think of a single one to say that will seem right. She can't exactly tell this charming and handsome stranger that she's been seeing people who maybe—probably—aren't real. That everything she once valued, everything that once made her feel like herself—her mother, her marriage, her career, even her necklace—is gone. That she's terrified she might be losing her mind, too.

"Let's just say that I have a lot of memories on this island," Grace explains. "Some that feel a little too real at the moment."

"I understand. I have a lot of history down here, too." He lifts an arm, scratches his fingers through his thick brunette hair. "Listen, I know we only just met, but if you ever want to talk . . ." He trails off, letting the ocean breeze fill in some of the gaps. "I'm just saying I know firsthand that life—even down here—isn't always as simple as it seems." He smiles. "You're welcome to unload on me."

In the near distance, the sound of an ice cream truck playing a familiar childhood song fills the air. "Can I ask you something, Caleb?" Grace looks down at the album and the smiling thirteen-year-old who stares back, then up at Caleb. "Though I should warn you—it's kind of out there."

"Of course." He gives her a playful wink. "So long as it's not about a broken fridge. I think I've filled my quota on those types of questions for the day."

"Do you believe in . . . signs?" She waits to see if he'll laugh or serve up a joke. He doesn't. She presses ahead. "Little unexplainable clues or coincidences, you know? Like someone, somewhere, is trying to point you down a certain path?"

"Honestly?" Caleb stretches his arms upward. "Yeah, I sort of do." He exhales, working out the second part of his reply. "I didn't always, though. It's a bit of a newer thing for me, I guess."

"What made you suddenly start?"

He tilts his chin up, as if searching for an answer in the bright-blue sky. She sees through his shirt that his inhalations deepen, his chest rising heavy and smooth.

"Someone I cared about believed in them." Caleb lowers his face, bites his bottom lip, as a look of sadness fills his eyes. "But I didn't start believing in them myself until after she was gone."

~

Grace passes the rest of the day asleep on the couch. After Caleb left to cater to more rental dramas (an ant issue over on Bay Road, a wonky AC unit out on Shore Drive), she closed the photo album and gave herself a dozen pep talks. (*It's easy, Grace! Just get in the Jeep, turn on the ignition, and drive!*) Still, she failed to force herself into action. Despite logic, possible mental breakdowns, and the pressing weight of her real life and responsibilities back on the mainland, after everything she encountered that morning, she couldn't bring herself to actually leave.

Instead, she dragged herself into the living room and, for the first time since arriving back on Sea Drift, let herself cry. A thousand tears, expelled like breath. At some point in the midst of it, everything caught up with her—the sun, the emotion, the sugary breakfast, Cece—and knocked her out with all the force of a tidal wave.

Now she pulls herself up from the comfortable new sectional following what she can only assume, based on the late-afternoon light that spills across the room, has been an epically long nap. Grace stretches, catlike, easing back into her body like a guest returning after a long absence.

"What time is it?" The inside of her mouth is stale with sleep. She pats around on the cushions for her phone, which rests next to the album, and sees it's already almost five o'clock. "Good job, Grace. You're officially a toddler." She wipes her chin. "You've more or less slept the whole day away."

Grace sets down her phone while her body begins to fully awaken. As it does, she turns her attention to her foot. The splinter, which she'd hoped might work itself out by now, is still there, suspended under her skin. It gently pulses, soft yet persistent, like a whisper beneath her flesh. She scratches the area with her fingernail, though the thin sliver of wood—this small, stubborn piece of the island lodged within her—doesn't budge.

Annoyed by her inability to force it out, Grace sighs. If Birdie were here, she'd know exactly what to do—the precise way to press and pull it away, a practice she perfected over years of tending to her daughter's wounds and scrapes. There were so many things Birdie innately knew how to do. Whip up a pot of perfect chicken soup with hardly any ingredients whenever Grace was sick. Determine, with just one look from across the room, whether her daughter had a fever. How to best heal all her child's small injuries. It was as if some important switch inside Birdie—one that triggered a specific set of instincts—had been clicked on the moment she became a mother, one that's never been activated for Grace.

Frustrated, Grace gives up now, choosing instead to ignore her heel and telling herself that the ache in it will eventually fade away.

She drops her feet to the floor and gives herself a minute. On the scuffed coffee table, the sand dollar and arcade tickets sit—two very real objects that feel impossible to dismiss or ignore—and she remembers what Caleb said about his newfound thoughts on these sorts of things.

Grace only ever asked Birdie about her belief in signs once. It wasn't something she ever questioned, but more something her mother—and in turn, Grace—fully trusted.

"Did you always believe in them?" Grace had asked one August night while they sat in the Adirondack chairs. "Signs, I mean." She was almost thirty and officially dating Adam, who—not a fan of outdoor nudity—was showering inside. She and Birdie were sipping iced tea and sorting through a pile of sand dollars they'd found that afternoon. "I know you've always talked about them. But when did you *really* start believing in them?"

Birdie held up a shell—one perfect circle. "Oh, I don't know, sweetie. Memories start to blur at my age." She paused, turning it in her palm. "But if forced to guess, I'd say it was right after your dad died." Birdie dropped her head back and looked up at the early-evening sky, all layers of lavender and gray. "When you lose someone that important—and that fast—you start searching for any way to keep talking."

Grace nodded, let a moment pass. "You've never had any desire to find someone else, have you?" Although she knew the answer—Birdie hadn't once, in Grace's whole life, gone on a date—she'd never directly asked. "I mean, because if you wanted to, you could easily have your pick of the good-looking fifty- to sixtysomething crop."

Birdie laughed, her silver hair billowing in the breeze. "Not for me, Cece." She tilted down her chin and looked at Grace, just as Adam opened the back door. "Sometimes your first love turns out to be the right one." She thumbed the shell, smiled. "Even when you can't be together in the way you want to be, that's still enough."

Now Grace leans forward and picks up the shell from earlier, trying to determine what, exactly, it is that she believes. About this house. About her mother's absence. About her whole life. Before she can get too deep into her thoughts, her stomach grumbles, the sound of it unapologetically loud, as if it's personally offended that she's neglected it for half the day.

She doesn't fully understand what's happening anymore. What she's supposed to do. Why she's even back on this island in the first place. What she saw this morning or didn't.

For the moment, all she knows is she needs a shower, a meal, and some time to recalibrate.

THIRTEEN

Birdie swore that eating out by yourself was something special—a privilege only enjoyed by a brave and confident few. She had plenty of friends—neighbors from her town house community and colleagues from the high school who felt like their own form of family. All she had to do was pick up the phone if she wanted some adult company. Once Grace, her longtime restaurant companion, left for college and set out on her adult life, Birdie—on the rare occasion she had extra splurge money—never placed those calls. When given the choice, she preferred to dine out alone.

"If you can't sit comfortably and enjoy a meal by yourself, then how can you expect anyone else to sit with you and have a nice time?" Birdie used to tell Grace whenever she pressed her mother about the practice. "One day, Cece, you'll understand," she'd explain. "The most important thing you should strive to be in life, my love, is your own best friend."

Now, as Grace sits alone at a corner table at the Beachcomber—her shoulders and thighs still scorched from her time baking on the porch—she's not so sure. The waterfront dining room is packed with parties of two and four and six, everyone engaged in conversation as they share appetizers, exchange banter, and laugh. For a beat, Grace tries to imagine Birdie sitting in the empty seat across from her, noshing on crab dip, and telling her to relax and order a drink.

"Good evening." A waitress approaches the table. "Welcome to the Beachcomber." She begins to expertly fill Grace's water glass. "Have you dined with us before?"

Grace looks up, ready to make eye contact with this person and engage in light conversation. Before she does, her body screeches to a halt when she notices a familiar glint of metal on the woman's wrist. Panic wraps itself around her as she zooms in on the silver charm bracelet—a near replica of the one Grace had when she was eighteen.

"No!" Grace blurts out, sharper than intended as she braces for the impossible . . . again.

"Oh, um . . ." The waitress, surprised, stumbles over her words. "O-okay," she says, regaining her footing. "Well, glad to have you joining us tonight." Her tone downshifts. "I guess."

Grace exhales. She realizes a moment too late that the voice isn't familiar. A second glance at the bracelet confirms it—different charms from those she once owned.

"I-I'm sorry." Grace's pulse settles. "Long day." She adjusts herself in her seat, hoping for a reset. "I meant to say *yes*. I've been here." She clears her throat. "Just not in a long time."

"Hmm," the waitress offers—less a response and more a judgment—as she starts to fill the second empty water glass on the table. "Assuming we're waiting for someone else to join us?"

Grace peers at the seat across from her.

Try to enjoy yourself, love, she hears Birdie say in her mind. *Tell her to bring bread.*

"Not tonight," Grace admits, hoping to sound cosmopolitan—an independent woman of the world—even though she feels like a child eating alone in the school cafeteria. "It's just me."

Earlier, after her shower, Grace threw on the nicest items she'd packed—a newer baby-blue T-shirt tucked into a pair of tattered jean shorts with an older lightweight sweater knotted at her shoulders in case it got cool. Casual, but cleaned up. It wasn't like she was spending a night out in the Hamptons; it was Sea Drift. At least she didn't have seaweed in her hair.

Too afraid to venture back to the market for provisions, and too tired to bike all the way to the island's real grocery store and then put in the effort to cook herself a proper meal, she got on the seafoam beach cruiser and started to ride. The daytime joints—places like Smitty's and Sunny Side—were closed by that point, the local restaurants beginning to open their doors with the promise of easy coastal dinners and drinks.

The Beachcomber was an institution on Sea Drift, an old oceanfront motel with a surprisingly decent glass-enclosed restaurant that looked onto the water, and a lively open-air bar out back. It'd been there for decades. Pale-pink exterior. A sign with lettering straight out of the sixties. There were still two tall standing ashtrays in the lobby—relics from another time. Some years, Birdie took Grace here for her birthday—a special meal to celebrate a special day. As she got older, Grace frequented this place with friends. Happy hours. Late nights out. Plenty of different occasions, but never alone.

"Just . . . you?" The waitress blinks as if caught off guard. The Beachcomber, a gathering place for sunburned vacationers, doesn't exactly scream *party of one*. "That's . . . fun." She does a poor job of hiding her disappointment, likely doing a mental tally of her smaller-than-hoped-for tip. "Why don't I give you a minute to look over the menu?" She gathers the additional place setting. "In the meantime, I'll just . . . get rid of these."

The waitress wanders away, but not before stopping off at the hostess stand to whisper something to a colleague. Grace sits by herself, shifting in her chair and trying to feel—or at least *look*—comfortable. It's hard. *Just act natural,* she tells herself, staring out at the water through the windows and feeling like she's been stood up on a date.

"We really need to stop running into each other like this," a new voice says. "People are going to start talking."

Grace swiftly turns away from the glass.

"Meg?" She's unable to hide her surprise. "Wh-what are you doing here?" Although Meg had referenced coming here during yesterday's run-in, Grace hadn't expected to find her—a mother to two young children—dining here for a second night in a row. "Weren't you just here last night?"

Meg shrugs. Her long red hair bounces on her shoulders. "Quinn spiked a fever as I was getting ready, so we spent half the night at the urgent care on the north end of the island." She flips up her hands. "Ear infection. Change of plans." She laughs. "Story of my life."

"Sorry to hear that." Grace's thoughts drift to Jenny, who often needs to cancel and reschedule plans due to these types of hiccups. "How's he feeling?"

"He's fine. Nothing a whole mess of antibiotics and Popsicles can't fix." She stops to smooth the front of her casual, creamy sundress. "Needless to say, my parents bumped back their offer to watch him and Emma to tonight." A look washes over Meg's face, turning some of her brightness into concern. "Oh, gosh. You didn't have a change of heart and come here to meet me last night, did you?" She slaps a palm to her face. When she does, Grace catches a glimpse of Meg's wedding jewelry—a tasteful, sparkling stack—on her finger. "I'm really sorry. I was so wrapped up with Quinn that I honestly didn't even think of that until right now."

No, Grace thinks. *I was too busy spiraling after I face-planted into your brother's chest.*

"Oh, hello." Grace's waitress reapproaches the table. She looks at Meg, then Grace, then the empty seat. "Will you be dining with us this evening?"

"O-oh. Oh, no. I . . ." Meg glances over her shoulder, as if searching for someone who isn't there. "I was just making my way back to my own table." She points at an empty two-top. "I have my own reservation." Meg holds up a single finger. "Another party of one."

The waitress's shoulders slump.

"D-do you want to sit with me?" Grace asks before she can second-guess her choice.

"Perfect!" The waitress claps, sealing the decision before Meg even responds. "I'll go get an extra utensil roll-up and a plate." A crooked grin breaks across her face as she waves down the hostess. "Be back in a jiff."

~

The conversation goes down easily, as does the wine, which Meg insisted on ordering. By the time their waitress—noticeably pleased by the turn of events—clears their dinner plates, full of sucked-dry oyster shells and picked-through crab legs, the two of them have collectively put down a bottle and a half of sauvignon blanc.

It's been so long since Grace has allowed herself to let go in this way. To fill a glass of alcohol with more than two fingers' worth, to enjoy something as innocent as seafood without the fear that some pregnancy-ending bacteria might be lurking. They were terrible, all those months and years of worry, the constant pressure of telling herself she could control something that was entirely out of her grasp. (*Just steer clear of deli meat and runny eggs . . . and no vigorous exercise . . . or parabens . . . or unpasteurized anything . . . or heavy lifting.*) Even after it was clear that Adam and her efforts to conceive were over—long before their marriage was over, too—she held on to most of those habits for ages (caffeine a newly reintroduced luxury, albeit necessity). Over time, they'd become not only practices but parts of her—parts she was still learning to let go.

Now Grace tips back her head and enjoys another crisp sip. Maybe it's the setting. Or the company. Or that certain chunks of this day still don't make an ounce of sense. Whatever the reason, she doesn't want to think of that part of her past tonight. For the moment, she just wants to be here, reliving happier times with her old friend, in the present.

"I seriously cannot believe you remember that, Meg." Grace's voice cracks with laughter. "We were, like, ten when that happened."

"Some memories fade with time." Meg swirls her glass by its stem. "However, seeing your friend bury her dead hermit crab and then watching three days later when that same crab crawled back out of the ground and walked right up to the porch steps of her summer rental is *not* the sort of recollection one ever forgets."

"A toast." Grace lifts her glass in mock-nostalgia. "To Mr. Crabby. He was a good pet." She finishes off the last sip of her wine. "Even if I only knew him less than a week."

For the first time since Meg joined her, there's a brief lull in their chatter. It feels like a ball dropping. Her thoughts a touch fuzzy, Grace mentally searches her mind for something to fill it with before it hits the ground.

"It's been a long time since those days," Meg says, beating Grace to the punch. "Though in some ways, it feels like yesterday, doesn't it?"

Their waitress reappears, offers them each a dessert menu. Neither woman pauses to look.

"Meg," Grace begins, her mind clearing. Sharpening. That last night they saw each other out on the beach the week of Grace's twenty-fifth birthday. The bonfire. A sky full of stars. Grace shouting things she wishes she could forget. "I'm sorry, I—"

"We were basically kids, Grace." Meg instantly cuts her off. "That was ages ago." She leans across the table to better emphasize her point. "Water under the bridge." She swats a hand. "We weren't even the same people then."

"So what'd we decide?" Their waitress comes back at exactly the right and wrong moment. "Are we in the mood for something sweet?"

"None for me," Meg says. "It's getting late. I should get back soon and check on the kids."

Their waitress nods and scoops up the dessert menus, promising to return with their check.

"We spent the whole night reminiscing," Grace points out, sinking back in her chair. Her entire body—not only her stomach—feels full in a way it hasn't in a long time. "I haven't even gotten to hear much about your life."

Meg leans back, too, sucks in a big inhale. "Well, you already know about the best parts. My little ones. Not that they're all that little anymore. They turned eight this year—twins, obviously, though you probably guessed that from their faces." She drums her fingers across the tablecloth. "Let's see. We live a little ways outside Philly—not far from where I grew up before we all moved south. My parents still live down there, though they've been back and forth a lot this year to visit with us in Pennsylvania." She softly bites her bottom lip. "Hmm. What else? I work in marketing, which is admittedly a bit boring, so nothing to write home about there."

"And you're married." Grace points to Meg's left hand, her rings glimmering beneath the restaurant's dimmed lights.

"Oh. Of course." Meg's face pinkens, like a schoolgirl admitting she's in love for the first time. "And I'm married." She closes her eyes, though her expression is warm. "Ben," she says when she reopens them. "We met in our late twenties. A not-so-original story, really. We were both in New Orleans for bachelor and bachelorette parties." Her face breaks into a hushed laugh. "We were in a bar, naturally. I was wearing some . . . oh, gosh . . . let's just say they were less-than-tasteful bachelorette accessories." Her sight drifts to the window, her gaze falling on the crashing waves out in the distance. "It sounds so corny, but it really was love at first sight." Meg smiles softly, lost in a memory she doesn't share. "But enough with my blabbering. How are you? How's your mom? She's down here with you this week, I assume?"

The question lands like a slap.

"S-she, um . . ." Any sort of good time Grace was having instantly disappears without so much as an apology. Her face grows hot while her mouth turns dry. "B-Birdie, well . . ."

"Oh, God," Meg interjects and reaches across the table to squeeze Grace's hand. "Don't even say it."

Grace looks down at the table and the last remnants of what had been—up until that point—an enjoyable evening. "February. Right after Valentine's Day." Around them, utensils clink. Voices chatter. "I don't know why I didn't tell you yesterday." She pinches her nose. "It's just been so hard." Inside her belly, the wine and seafood suddenly sit wrong. "Every time I tell someone new, it feels like a little piece of me dies."

"I'm so sorry, Grace. That kind of loss is . . ." She trails off, searching for the right turn of phrase, even though it doesn't exist. "It's just devastating. It changes everything. It rewires your whole identity. Alters your DNA."

"Yeah. It does," Grace admits, trailing her finger along the rim of her empty glass. "It's a big part of why I came down this week." She laughs, but not because anything about her story is funny; rather, because she's so drained that her emotions don't even know how to properly function anymore. "I'm in the midst of a separation." She gnaws her cheek, but the words pour out anyway. "We struggled for years to have kids, and it was just never meant to be." Grace keeps her focus on the table, each loss stacking in her mind, along with all the ways they broke her. Broke them. "Needless to say, I'm staying at the house solo. I have a work deadline that I'm utterly behind on and was hoping maybe a little sunshine might help clear my head."

Meg looks at her inquisitively, like she's both questioning something and understanding it. "That's one of the hardest parts of losing someone you love, isn't it?" she states, which makes Grace look up. "The fact that, even though your whole universe feels broken, the world just continues to turn."

Grace's gaze remains locked on Meg's face. Before she can ask her old friend if she's speaking from experience, their waitress walks back up and sets down their check.

"I'm buying." Meg grabs it. "It's the least I can do for horning in on your table."

"What? Absolutely not," Grace counters. "Y-you have kids. And urgent-care copays!"

"I'll make you a deal," Meg says, finding a middle ground. "I'll get the bill, and you get the tip. Good?"

"Thank you," Grace states, sensing this isn't a fight she's bound to win. She digs through her purse for her wallet. "For this and, well, for the company."

~

Grace excuses herself to go to the bathroom before she and Meg officially part ways and call it a night. Since she first sat down, the dining room has shifted—everything a little louder, the music from the Beachcomber's outdoor bar beginning to faintly hum just enough through the walls to subtly change the atmosphere. While Meg moves toward the lobby, Grace weaves through tables and down a hallway. In a miraculous twist for women everywhere, there's no line. She pushes the door open and heads inside.

"Surprise!" a voice shouts out, scaring Grace so badly that she physically jumps back and hits the door behind her.

"Jesus!" Grace yelps and instantly drops her face down to her knees while her heart beats so hard it feels like it might break one of her ribs. "Why would you do that?"

"I'm s-sorry!" the voice replies, the words slightly slurred at their edges and tangled up with a laugh. "I thought it'd be funny."

Grace lifts her face slowly and begins to straighten, already regretting that she didn't just hold her bladder and go straight outside with Meg. There, perched on the counter beside the sink, is a young woman—early twenties—wearing a black tube top, an all-too-recognizable gold necklace, and a few-too-many slicks of pearlescent gloss on her lips. One of her flip-flops is on the bathroom floor, while the other clings for dear life to her toe. An artificially colored pink drink sloshes in her grip.

Cece. *Surprise!* Again.

Grace says nothing at first, just waiting to see what might happen next. Cece slurps her cocktail, squints at Grace like she almost recognizes her, then, out of nowhere, starts to cry.

"Are you mad at me now?" Cece asks, tears plopping into her plastic cup.

"Oh, dear God," Grace mumbles, squeezing her lids shut. "Is there a cute toddler version of me around that I can hallucinate instead?" She brushes herself off, takes a deep breath, then turns (*Sorry, bladder!*), ready to open the door and exit. "Or maybe a future one who actually has her life together enough to not be experiencing whatever it is this is all about?"

"Right?" Cece shouts, her sudden enthusiasm so strong that she wobbles and nearly falls off the counter. "That's what I keep saying!"

"What?" Grace asks. "What are you talking about?"

Cece slides down, picks up her shoe, stumbles, then steadies herself against the wall. The hand dryer turns on and then off, which makes her start to laugh again. "That I just want to hurry up and get to the part where I have things figured out!"

Grace sighs, suddenly sensing that she's not leaving the restroom yet.

Cece turns, smoothing her long sun-kissed hair in the mirror. "Great, now I look terrible." She wipes the undersides of her eyes. "My mascara is everywhere."

Grace doesn't respond. She's too busy watching her: the uneven eyeliner, the too-sweet drink, the way she tugs at her tube top like she's just now realizing it's two sizes too small.

"I'm moving again," Cece announces, like she's picking up from a previous conversation. "Next week, after the beach." She catches Grace's reflection in the mirror. "Portland, Oregon. Don't ask me why." Still working to clean up her makeup, she accidentally knocks her drink into the sink. "I mean, I have a job lined up. It's a teaching gig. Not what I want to be doing, but for now, it's what I could get. One year. Maybe two, if I want it to be. It's this program. I did it up in Boston last year." Her face scrunches up from laughter. *"Baa-stun,"* she says, doing her best imitation of the region's accent. "God, it's so cold up there." She shivers, like she's still shaking off the chill. "Anyway, that's *why*. But I don't know why. Do you know what I mean?"

Grace remembers this version of herself clearly now, though in truth she hasn't thought about her in a long time. The one who felt so certain that being an adult meant she'd have everything neatly sorted out, even though she was still deep in the trenches and searching. It was a strange in-between time when it felt to Grace that her younger life no longer fit, while her present one didn't, either. All she wanted was the future—the next job, the next apartment, the next *thing*—not yet knowing that the feeling—the search—never actually ends.

Cece spins around, props herself up on the counter again. "Are you married?"

"What?" Grace asks, not having expected this question. *Jesus,* she thinks, her mind flicking back to the arcade and thirteen-year-old Cece's question about her fertility. *My younger selves really like to throw the diggers at me.* "Yes. I mean no. It's complicated."

"Interesting." Cece picks up her empty cup, tosses it in the trash. "I just feel like I'm behind already," she continues, even though no one has asked her anything. "I sort of thought I'd have a cute apartment and, like, all this IKEA furniture, and a whole sitcom-style life. Instead, ever since I graduated college two years ago, I just keep bouncing. Everything's kind of all over the place." She fluffs her hair and studies her reflection, as though she's not quite sure if she likes what she sees. "At least for now, I have someone who doesn't mind this mixed-up version of me. Even if it's only an annual week-long beach thing." She shrugs, perhaps more dramatically than she'd intended, the movement making her wobble. "It won't last forever. I know that, even though I sort of wish it would." Cece lifts her hands, clumsily points her fingers in opposing directions. "We want different things, you know? It's like, he wants roots or something, but I want *wings*." She explodes with laughter. "Oh my gosh, that was so cheesy!" She slaps a hand to her chest. "Don't blame me! I think I heard it in some stupid movie my mom had on last night!"

As Cece works to catch her breath, Grace lets herself remember. The way that time and perspective functioned. How you could be both young enough to cling to the idea that something impossible would work and just old enough to understand that it won't.

You're a disaster, Porter, Ray playfully shouted into her ear that summer. They were at the Beachcomber's outdoor bar, dancing and drinking under the stars and string lights. Adults, at least according to their IDs. *But a fun one,* he said. He twirled her, around and around on the splintery wood planks, even as she stole his backward hat and slipped it onto her head.

I'm so dizzy! she exclaimed, mouth wide, the air thick with citronella and salt. *I need to sit! I'm a disaster right now! Those drinks are lethal! We should go!*

She spun to leave, but he caught her wrist.

Not yet, he said. *One more song.* He drew her body closer. *Don't leave yet.*

Why? she asked, sensing even through her drunkenness that he was alluding to something more than just their bar date.

Because I like you when you're a mess.

Back in the present, the faint opening notes of a new song play through the bathroom walls.

"Ohh . . . I've got to go!" Cece announces, quickly changing gears. She jumps down, half trips on the perfectly even floor. "This is a hit!" She looks back at the mirror, adds another quick swipe of gloss. "Anyway, not that you asked about literally *any* of that." She laughs at herself once more. "Thanks for letting me be weird for a second."

"Can I ask you something?" Grace poses before her early-twenty-something self walks away. "Do you have any idea why we keep meeting like this?"

Cece looks at her, like maybe she's about to say something profound. Instead, she slaps her palm over her wide-open mouth. "Oh my gosh! Have we seriously already *met*?" she asks, cracking up. "I'm *really* sorry about that." She looks at the trash can. "I think that was already my third round of those drinks tonight." It takes a second for her to pull herself together. When she does, she digs in her bag—a too-small clutch with some designer logo printed on it. "Here." She passes Grace a neon-orange paper wristband. "I know one of the bartenders on the patio. He always gives me a few extras in case any of my friends have trouble getting in."

Grace takes it, not entirely sure of Cece's point. "Wh-why are you giving this to me?"

"In case that's why we keep meeting." Cece slides toward the door, shimmying her shoulders. "Because maybe we're just supposed to hang out together and dance."

~

"Long line?"

Outside, the sun has started to set over the boulevard. The sky is a spoil of colors. Deep reds bleeding into layers of orange that blend into streaks of lavender before softening into cool streaks of gray. Meg stands just beyond the hotel's lobby, taking it in.

"Epic," Grace states, not having a clue how else to explain why she took so long. "All the bargoers are starting to filter inside."

Just as she says it, a group of young twentysomethings—fueled on youthful enthusiasm, probably too many energy drinks, and the promise of a semi-reckless night—stroll past.

"Gosh, I feel old." Meg shakes her head and turns to watch them. "Their night's just starting, and here I am, ready to go throw on some leggings and put on a movie that I'll no doubt fall asleep watching halfway through."

"I can definitely relate," Grace admits. "This is way past curfew for me."

"Hard to believe that was ever us, right?" Meg cringes, recalling something. "Remember those drinks they served out there? The ones in mini beach buckets? What even *were* they?"

"Gasoline, I think. And a guaranteed headache."

"Speaking of which, this is your week, right? Your birthday, yeah?"

"Wednesday," Grace tells her through a hushed sigh, wishing it wasn't and knowing there's nothing for her to celebrate this year. "I'll be thirty-eight."

The twentysomething girls step inside, loud and tipsy.

"Listen, Grace," Meg says, "about Birdie . . ."

"I'm okay," Grace lies, and thinks of twentysomething Cece, the girl who ached to get ahead so she could get past the hard times, not yet knowing how many hard times still waited. "Or at least, I'm trying to be."

"You will be, Grace." A knowing glint flashes in Meg's eyes. "In due time." She holds out her arms, hugs Grace, then drifts to the sidewalk bike rack. "Sea Drift's a good place to heal."

Grace watches the last sliver of sun dip into the water. "I hope so."

Meg bunches up her sundress and slides onto the beach cruiser's slender seat. She pedals in a circle, briefly holding her arms in the air like a kid. *Look, Mom! No hands!*

"I didn't tell him," Meg calls back over her shoulder before she leaves.

Grace freezes in place, too stunned to look away from the sky, let alone speak.

"Ray," Meg clarifies, as if her subtext weren't clear. "About seeing you at Smitty's yesterday." She stops, plants her feet on the asphalt. "I considered it, but in the end thought it might be best that he doesn't know you're here."

Grace's thoughts race back to her encounter with him in the market. *I guess some rumors really are true,* he'd said. At the time, Grace assumed the leader of the rumor mill was Meg.

"What do you mean, you didn't tell him?"

"It's just, he's finally in a good place. I'm not sure it's the right time to reopen old wounds." Nearby, more partygoers wander past. "Sometimes I think it's best to leave the past in the past, you know?"

An ache forms in Grace's stomach, not because she doesn't understand but because she does. It's the reason she probably never should have come back here.

"But maybe that's me being an annoyingly protective sister," Meg continues. "Not that I even have full say." She places one foot back on a pedal. "It's a tiny island." Slowly, she starts to move forward, but not before she looks back. "If you two are meant to cross paths again down here, then I have to guess that, at some point, you probably will."

FOURTEEN

The streetlights are on by the time Grace turns her bicycle onto Surf Street, the asphalt dappled with orange islands of light. Shadows stretch long, the sun now almost fully set. The block is mostly quiet, save for a few kids up near the dune, their lit-up sparklers creating temporary illuminated arcs in the air. Grace watches them as she pedals, her skin sticky, hair tangled in knots from her ride. She wonders, briefly, how it would feel to be a kid again. Carefree. Lost in a world of play.

From somewhere nearby, a dog barks. Her eyes still on the children, it takes a second for Grace to fully register the sound. Before she does, a blur of golden fur darts across the blacktop. It barrels toward her, unleashed and at full speed. It all happens too fast—the running, the jumping, the unsolicited licking—like a strange sensory-rich dream. Grace stumbles, nearly loses control of the bike—but catches herself just in time.

And then, she pauses—*really* pauses—and sees.

"Wait," she whispers, her heart suddenly fluttering, wild and unexpected, like a dozen butterflies. The dog settles, but not before giving Grace one last round of inquisitive sniffs. Goose bumps ripple across her skin, her whole body reacting like she's just plunged into water that's ten degrees too cold. The dog continues to paw at her, as excited and rambunctious as a puppy, though it's clear she's not one. Grace pets the animal's head, patting around as if she's trying to feel out a memory. "Sandy?"

"Actually, that's Hooper," a voice—one that's all too familiar—says from the steps of house Number 116. "Sandy died ten years ago." Sadness paints the person's tone. "She was a good dog, though. Loyal right to the very end."

Grace turns in slow motion—an actor right before the big reveal. Not that she even needs to in order to understand what's happening. Already, she knows who she'll see in the shadows when her head makes it the full 180 degrees.

Ray.

Right there. Sitting on the steps. Looking at Grace. Holding a beer.

It's as if no time has passed. Yet, of course, it has. Years. Entire lifetimes. Whole relationships. Identities that came and went. But here they are. Here *he* is. The same gold-rimmed eyes. The same invisible pull. A thousand memories tightening like a piece of leather inside her chest.

"Hooper's friendly, though." Ray takes a sip. "She's just feeling you out, trying to determine if you're someone she knows." He sets his can down next to him. "Hoop! Come here, girl!" An obedient listener, the dog bolts. She licks Ray's arm, then settles in a heap at his feet.

"Hooper," Grace echoes, her fingers numb. She works to untangle her legs from the bike—clumsy, disoriented. "Richard Dreyfuss," she says once she's steady. "Like in *Jaws*."

"Some things change." Ray raises his shoulders slightly. "Some things don't." He pets Hooper's body. "It's still my favorite movie."

You'll love this place, he told her the summer she turned thirteen. *This movie*. The two of them, alone, in the island's cinema. *The story.* Hands inching closer on the armrest. *It's a perfect plot, Porter.* Staying long after the closing credits. Not needing to do anything. To be anything. *I bet you could write something like that one day.* Believing him.

Grace wheels the bike up onto the sidewalk, then sets it in the driveway in front of the Jeep. She stands there, everything inside her quivering, unsure how to proceed.

How many summers of her life has she walked into this same scene? Ray, there on the steps, waiting for her on that first day, knowing the precise time she and Birdie would arrive back after running their errands to finally settle in. Always, she ran to him—at fifteen, seventeen, twenty-three, and all the years in between—her arms wrapping around him as her body came back to life, as if the rest of the year it'd been in hibernation.

You're back, he'd say. No matter her age, or how much she grew, or the clothes she wore, he'd smile with his whole face. *You're still you.*

She's not the girl she was back then. Right now, her body doesn't care. Her skin flushes. She might as well be sixteen.

In the street, the kids—out of sparklers—sprint home, their laughter echoing behind them.

"Wh-what are you doing here?" she asks, trying to sound brave, though her voice subtly shakes. Even after all this time, he looks like he belongs here. Like he's part of this place. Of her.

Ray adjusts his backward baseball hat. A few longer strands of hair poke under its sides. "Thought I'd drop by, see if the owner ever fixed the front light." He glances up at the porch lantern, the glass still cracked all these decades later. "Remember that summer you freaked out when you saw the giant moth and smacked it with your sandal?"

"Ray . . ." She doesn't repeat her question. It's already there, lingering between them, thick and unanswered, like so many other things.

He positions his arms on his thighs, looks down at the steps, then up at her the way he always has, some secret in his eyes, like he can see something about her no one else can. "Maybe I could ask you the same thing," he says, the sound of his voice—the echo of it here on this street—enough to make her heart twist.

It was easy to say they'd loved each other for years, though that wasn't really the case. For every twelve months that passed, they only ever saw each other for seven sandy, salt-crusted days.

Summer friends.

A summer romance.

That was the rhythm of it, from the first time their families met the week Grace turned nine and staying that way long after their first kiss under the glow of boardwalk rides the year she turned thirteen. Up until that night, they were buddies. The two of them. Meg. A few other kids from neighboring families. They played Frisbee. Flew kites. Walked to the arcade. Went on long swims. Like most things on Sea Drift, their feelings were slow to start. A sideways glance. A too-long hug goodbye. A late-day walk on the beach, just the two of them.

In the beginning, Birdie told Grace to go slow and just enjoy her trips without getting boy crazy. But as the seasons pressed on, even she saw it was more than that. By the time Grace was eighteen and preparing for college, it wasn't just a summer crush anymore. It'd become a full-body ache. They never committed to a long-distance relationship, both knowing it'd never work. Ray would be down south for art school; Grace would be busy studying writing at Penn State. It was a dream. A cute movie plotline. It wasn't realistic.

Instead, they lived their lives, each of them evolving and finding themselves a little more with each month that passed. Every August—regardless of new friends or the spark of other romantic interests back home—they both ran to each other on that familiar stretch of coastline.

Until the year they both turned twenty-five.

That August—the Murphys' final trip to Sea Drift—a heavy fog hung over the week and refused to lift. Everyone knew it was an ending to more than a vacation. Despite the adults making promises to keep in touch, and Meg and Grace chatting about visits (*Seriously, though—let's plan something!*), deep down, they all knew it was just talk. Up until Friday night—the last before both families packed their cars and drove away—Grace and Ray didn't mention it. Not directly. But it was there, floating in every moment of silence, as quiet yet omnipresent as the waves.

"What if we didn't leave?" Ray said late that night out on the fishing pier. The adults were having margaritas on the Murphys' deck while the "kids"—all of whom were legal adults now—had one last bonfire on the beach. At some point, while everyone else was distracted by beer and music, Ray took Grace by the hand, and they walked off. "What if we just stayed here forever? Turned our annual vacations together into a real life?"

Since college, they'd both hovered in that strange limbo stage—grown-up, but not quite. Ray, doing graphic design down in Virginia and bartending to pay the bills. Grace, bouncing from place to place, scribbling down story ideas, trying to work up the courage to do the things she actually felt she should.

For the first time in her adult life, she had a plan. Not a yearlong Band-Aid, but a real one. In September, she'd move to Manhattan—had already signed a lease on a studio apartment and accepted a copywriting job at a small publisher—a way, she hoped, to plant one foot in the door of the industry. It was a step, a *real* one. An opportunity to get serious about turning her chaotic twenties into something steady.

"Ray, come on." Grace had laughed and leaned back on his chest. Out in front of them, the moon shone down on the ocean. "It's a beach town. People don't live here. Not for real."

"Some people do," he countered.

"Yes, but they're retirees," Grace pointed out. "Not twenty-five-year-olds trying to build their résumés and pay back student loans." Above them, the stars dotted the sky like glitter. "Maybe fifty years from now, after we've both actually done some stuff—*real* stuff—first."

Ray wrapped a strand of Grace's long hair around his finger, gave it a gentle tug. "Did you ever hear the story about the fisherman and the businessman?"

"Why do I feel like an impossible-to-solve riddle is incoming?"

"I'll give you the short version." He straightened his stance. "So this businessman is walking along the beach in a coastal village when he notices a fisherman sitting on the shoreline. The fisherman isn't doing a thing, just staring at the water while his boat is tied to a dock nearby. The businessman—always thinking about the future and how to gain more wealth—approaches the guy, asks why he's not out fishing and trying to make a bigger catch. So the fisherman says, 'Because I already caught enough fish. I'm done. Now I can enjoy the day.' Well, the businessman doesn't love this answer. 'But if you go out again now,' he explains, 'work harder, work longer, then you can probably expand your business, buy another boat, and make even more money.' And the fisherman asks, 'And then what?' To which the businessman replies, 'And then you could finally be content, just sit on the beach, and do nothing except enjoy your life.' The fisherman just laughed, looked at the guy, and said, 'But isn't that what I'm already doing right now?'"

"That's a nice story, Ray," Grace had said. "But it's just a story. It's not real life or—"

"Why not? Why can't it be?" He scooted back, pulled a local Realtor flyer from his pocket. "Look. There are apartments we can rent here for next to nothing. I can pick up a bartending gig in town. You can write and take on some odd jobs, and—"

"I'm moving to New York in a few weeks." Grace pulled herself up, standing. "I have goals. I need to start meeting people in my industry, taking my work more seriously, and—"

"When are we going to stop playing this game and pretending this is just a silly summer romance?" Ray bolted up. "I think about you constantly! For years, every night before I fall asleep, your face flashes through my mind!" He yanked off his hat, scraped his fingers through his hair. "We're both happy here. Why bother going to look for happiness someplace else?"

"Because it's a fantasy! And unrealistic!" Grace shouted. "You can't just be a bartender forever." Her voice cracked. "I'm not going to waste my degree working odd jobs and being a beach bum for the rest of my life."

"Why not?"

"Because, Ray!" Grace exclaimed. "Life isn't a clever parable!"

Ray walked to the far end of the dock. For a minute, Grace thought he was leaving. "Here," he said when he finally turned and headed back.

"I bought this for you today. A birthday gift, since I won't really get to see you on your actual birthday tomorrow, it being departure day and all." When he reached her, he held out his hand. "It's not fancy. But I thought you'd like it." He set a simple silver ring etched with a subtle wave motif in Grace's palm. "It's from that shop you love, the one with all the shells and wind chimes, where Birdie bought your necklace way back when."

"Ray, I—"

"It's not an engagement ring," Ray quickly clarified. "I'm well aware we're nowhere near ready for that." He paused. They both looked at the ring. "It's a promise." Time collapsed in on itself. All the years they'd known each other compressed inside that single fleeting moment. "If you're willing to make this something real, then I am, too. Because after tonight, there's no guarantee we'll see each other again. Not unless we really commit to it."

"Hey!" a voice called out from the beach. *Meg*. "Are you guys coming back? I'm going to walk to the market, grab more beer. You guys want anything specific, or—" Meg cut herself off. Like everyone, she knew about Ray and Grace's summer courtship. Even so, it was obvious she realized this was something private.

"We're fine for now, Meg," Ray said, not taking his sight off Grace. "We'll be back soon, all right?" In the distance, Meg ran off. "Grace. Please say something to me."

Every emotion she'd ever felt beat through her all at once. Love. Panic. Elation. Surprise. However, the one that came through the strongest was fear.

"I need to go," Grace said through a gasp and took off down the pier. "I can't do this. Not now. Not weeks before the whole next chapter of my life is about to begin."

"Grace, wait!" Ray called out, chasing after her.

But she kept running—so hard and fast that she accidentally smacked right into Meg.

"Come on, Grace." Ray was panting by the time he caught up with her. "I'm not a stranger! And this isn't a fantasy! I've known you forever!"

That was when the truth of it finally hit Grace, as hard and fast as a tidal wave.

"But not really," she said, looking back and forth between him and Meg, suddenly seeing them as strangers. "I've only ever known you for a few days every year."

"Oh, come on, Grace!" Ray retorted as Meg took a few hesitant steps back. "That's ridiculous, and you know it! Who cares how many days it's been! I've known practically every version of you that's ever set foot on this island! Isn't that enough?"

Grace studied his face, cast in silver moonlight. Ray. The boy she'd loved for so many years. The one she thought about every night before she fell asleep, too. She didn't know the answer to his question. *Was* it enough—him knowing these pieces of her past, the girl she used to be? Enough for her to give up on the future she was finally getting ready to build?

"No," she said, hating how much it hurt to say it.

Now, back in the present, Ray sits on the porch and looks at her, still waiting for answers.

"I read your book," he says as Hooper wags her tail, happy just to be next to him. "The first one," he clarifies. "*The Tides*. A few summers ago, back when it was released." He hesitates, then proceeds. "I didn't like the follow-up. What was it called? The one about a woman falling in love in New York. *One Night in October*, I think?" He winces at the title. "Didn't feel as authentic. Lacked heart." He drinks his beer. "I'm just one reader, though, so what do I know. Just felt like the storyline wasn't as good."

Grace stands in the driveway, hardly able to move while Ray's words—*lacked heart*—vibrate in her ears like a terrible song she wishes she could forget. It's not the first time this phrase, the one that once appeared in multiple reviews of her sophomore novel, rattled her.

"What do they know?" Adam said when the first of them rolled in from a well-respected trade review a few weeks before *One Night in October* was published, the third negative critique she received for the book that month. They were in the kitchen, where Grace had spent half the day crying and staring at her laptop screen in disbelief.

From the minute she wrote the first chapter—a young couple, a New York backdrop, a meet-cute in an elevator—she told Adam the novel was inspired by him. By *them*. And it was. But when Grace finished the first draft, her editor felt it was missing something she couldn't name. There were three more drafts spread across many months before her team felt enthusiastic enough to push it to the next editorial stage. Still, Grace had a hard time shaking the fact that the story—*their* story—had taken so much work.

"They're all just a bunch of grumpy old book nerds," Adam had continued, trying to sound sure of himself as his eyes skimmed the review yet again. However, his voice and the specific way it dipped gave away an important fact: Even though he didn't outright say it, like Grace, he'd been wondering if those reviews were somehow a critique of them, too.

Now, back on Surf Street, Grace's heart won't stop pounding inside her chest. "How'd you know about my book?" she asks, struggling to get the words out.

"Come on, Grace. It wasn't all that hard to find." His brows draw closer, like he's trying to determine if she's playing with him. "The cover was in the window of every bookstore in the country that season. All I had to do was flip to your author photo in the back." He stops, but his lips stay parted. "Plus, the protagonist's name was sort of a dead giveaway."

Grace opens her mouth, but her voice has vanished into the evening air. She wants to ask, *But did you go out looking for it?*

"You published it under your married name," he says, melancholy tracing his syllables. There's no follow-up. No accusation. Just this single fact. "I'll be honest. That part hurt."

A noise at the end of the street interrupts them. The kids from earlier are back outside and running just for the fun of it. Hooper springs to attention, barking into the night.

"I should go," he says, standing up. "I don't want to keep you."

He grabs a leash from next to him, clips it onto Hooper's collar, then steps forward. His feet crunch over the pea gravel driveway as he draws closer. Ray stops just a few inches from her, close enough for her to smell him and to see every small detail on his face—a tiny scar above one brow, a faded sunspot beneath his left eye. He waits, breathing, their eyes connected as if by magnets. When he swallows, Grace hears it.

"Before I do, though, I wanted to give you this." He reaches into his pocket, still so close to her. "You left it behind the last time I saw you." Ray opens his hand, revealing the silver ring—an artifact from another era. "I found it in the sand the next morning when I took a walk by myself before my family left." Without asking, he uncurls her fingers, sets the ring into the dip of her palm. "You must have dropped it that night when you were running away from me."

Every muscle in her body freezes. From his touch. From his statements. With hurt. With regret. With sentiments she's not sure she can even name.

The ring.

She always wondered what had happened to it. If it'd stayed buried. If a child discovered it weeks later while building a sandcastle. If it simply washed away with the tide. If someone stood looking at the horizon, saw its glint at just the right time and thought of it as a sign. She hadn't considered that Ray would have been the one to find it. That he'd still be the person who has it now.

"I saw someone earlier," he says, his hand still cupping hers. "A teenager. She looked like she could have been your younger self's twin."

"What do you mean?" Grace asks, uncertain if his comment is meant to be taken literally.

"Nothing." He holds her gaze for another long second, then slowly pulls away, steps back, and begins to walk out into the dark street. He stops beneath a streetlight. "She just reminded me of you."

Grace's stomach sours—the mix of seafood, wine, and this conversation not sitting right.

"I'll see you around," Ray tells her, his way of saying goodbye. "Enjoy your birthday Wednesday," he says, the sentiment sweet, even though it burns like an insect sting.

For a minute, Grace watches him, the person who once meant everything to her, walking away from her, just like she once walked—*sprinted*—away from him.

"Ray, wait!" Her mind flicks back to his comment at the market. "How did you know you'd find me here?" she calls out before he makes it to the corner, now knowing Meg didn't tell him. "At this house. Or on this island at all. For all you knew, I could have rented someplace different." She struggles to make sense of things. "I haven't come down here in ages. How did you even know I'd be back?"

Ray stops. His head tilts like a globe on its axis. "Really?" He lifts his arm—fingers wrapped up in the leash—and points at Birdie's Jeep. "I figured that part was obvious."

Something about his gesture makes everything stop. The seconds stretch out like a sunset.

"What are you talking about?" A new, uneasy feeling rises in her as she senses that whatever answer he's about to give won't make any sense. "What did you figure was obvious?"

Ray meets her eyes. Something in his expression shifts. He looks at her a beat too long, like he's deciding whether he should tell her the truth.

"The fact that your mother told me," he says.

FIFTEEN

Monday

Grace didn't sleep. Again.

Her skin burned, her stomach still bloated with seafood and wine, and her head pounding with information she hadn't been remotely prepared to hear, she lay on the springy mattress all night—physically uncomfortable in every possible way—rubbing the silver ring between her fingers and staring at the ceiling. Not a single thing in her life had made an ounce of sense these last few days. Not Caleb and his out-of-nowhere call. Not Adam and his vague wistfulness. Not the girl on the beach, the one at the arcade, or the one in the bathroom who shouted "Surprise!" and nearly gave Grace a heart attack. Not Ray and his confounding announcement, which—twist of all twists—might have actually been the most disconcerting item of them all. None of it.

What did Ray *mean* that Birdie told him Grace would be back on the island this week? Did he have a dream? Conjure up a memory that never happened? Or was he—just like her—grasping? For something. Anything. A sign. Some vague figment of imagination or hope?

And if so, why?

Early last August, a few weeks before the Maine trip, was the first time in several years that Birdie had brought up Sea Drift. She'd been staying with Grace and Adam for a few nights, keeping her daughter company and helping to care for her after yet another pregnancy loss.

Birdie knew what to do by that point. As soon as she arrived, she pulled the heating pad down from the linen closet. Lined Grace's nightstand with a fanned-out stack of gossip magazines, a bottle of Advil, and one too many bags of gummy candy. In a way, it was funny, like Birdie was setting Grace up for a sick day home from school. Except that it wasn't. What she was really doing was trying to comfort her as she once again said goodbye to a life she'd never get to have or to hold.

"So what should we watch, Cece?" Birdie had said on one of those nights and sidled up next to Grace in her spacious king-size bed. Adam was stuck late in the city (*Last-minute client meeting—I'm sorry!*), which had begun to happen more around that time. "I vote something incredibly mindless and yet completely addicting." She adjusted Grace's favorite weighted blanket, gave her a gentle nudge to encourage her to eat more of the homemade macaroni and cheese she'd prepared. "Any ideas?"

"Mom . . ." Grace said, not needing to utter another word, half of her and Birdie's conversations happening by way of telepathy.

"I know, darling," Birdie chimed in right away, scooting closer and extending her arms outward, like Grace was a little girl who needed to be held to feel safe. "It's awful. And it makes no sense. There's not a thing medically wrong with you to explain any of this. You're always so cautious and responsible, reading labels, avoiding all the things you're supposed to avoid." She gave her a tight squeeze. "It's not fair, my girl. You've done everything right. It'll happen in due time, Cece. Once you give yourself time to heal and talk to your doctor and you and Adam feel ready, you'll try again."

Grace was so tired. Enduring loss after loss for no diagnosable reason felt torturous, like being trapped in a *Groundhog Day* story and never knowing if or when the time loop would end.

For years, she'd been fighting an invisible burden—time, or maybe fate, or just the unrelenting villain that goes by the name of *Chance*. According to her physicians, it wasn't a clinical obstacle, seeing as her anatomy (and Adam's—they'd had him tested, too) worked fine.

Though it sounded awful, she almost wished something *were* wrong, just so a doctor could say, "Here's the problem," then prescribe a clear way to fix it. Instead, her trying-to-conceive experience had been like visiting her general practitioner when she was sick, hoping she had an ailment that necessitated an antibiotic versus a vague virus, the type of annoying and untreatable illness that required her to simply remain miserable while she waited to bounce back and feel like herself again.

"This wasn't the plan," Grace continued, and wept into her mother's shoulder.

"Oh, darling, of course not." Birdie pulled back, swept a strand of Grace's hair behind her ear. "This isn't anyone's plan. I never experienced it, love, but I know it's such an awful tragedy no person or couple should ever go through or—"

"It's breaking us," Grace said, the first time she ever admitted it, either out loud or to herself. "It shouldn't be, but it is. When we started dating, everything in both our lives was so neat and tidy. I'd just signed with Mollie. Adam was moving up in his career. We had the city and all that had to offer, and everything just felt so shiny. It was like we were both the best versions of ourselves back then." She looked down, dabbed away some tears with a corner of the sheet. "The problem is, I'm not sure we know how to be our worst selves with each other, too."

Birdie took her daughter's hand. "You'll figure out how to be," she assured her, though her tone wasn't entirely convincing.

"Will we?"

Birdie was quiet for a moment. It was no secret that she'd always been a bit skeptical of Adam. Birdie liked him, though early on had questioned Grace about whether the reasons *she* did were too rooted in his looks-good-on-paper ways. Birdie never outright said it, though she didn't need to. Deep down, Grace knew that, during moments like that one, her mother—just like her—privately wondered about a path not taken and *what if.*

"Did you and Dad need to figure out how to be that way with each other?" Grace finally asked through a sniffle and wiped her nose—a child in a grown-up's bed.

"Oh, things with Dad and I were just, well, different sometimes, Cece."

"How so?"

Birdie looked out the window. "We knew each other forever, honey. We grew up together, you know? He'd seen me at my best, my worst, and everything in between." A pair of birds flew past the glass. "In a lot of ways, you and Adam are still busy building your own history."

Grace set her half-full plate on the plush white comforter—the one she and Birdie had picked up together on a shopping trip at Bloomingdale's that spring. "This whole experience . . . it's changed me so much, Mom. And not necessarily in a good way." The words caught in her throat, like someone was trying to hold them down. "It's not even just the pain of what I can't have that's killing me, but what it's doing to my whole identity. It's all I think about, worry about, wonder about." She pressed the heels of her palms to her eyes, but the tears came anyway. "I'm supposed to be writing a book right now about a happy young family, and every time I try to churn out so much as a single page, the only thought that flashes through my mind is that I don't know these characters or understand their story at all." Grace paused, gave herself a second to catch her breath. "This just isn't the life I thought I'd have."

Birdie looked at her through kind eyes, an entire dialogue passing through their silence. "Well, love, unfortunately, as your old, widowed mother knows firsthand, we don't always get to choose the shape our lives will take." She rubbed Grace's leg through the blanket. "We make plans, Cece, and the universe—"

"Laughs," Grace said, finishing her mother's thought. "I wish it wouldn't, though."

A moment passed before Birdie conjured up a bright smile, her lips done up in her signature red, even then. "How about one of those silly Hallmark movies?" She grabbed the remote from the nightstand. "They're airing a new one tonight that takes place at the beach." She clicked, finally landing on the right channel. On the screen, a serious-looking businesswoman stood at a marina talking to an absurdly handsome fisherman type. "See! Told you!"

Grace chuckled, rested her head on Birdie's shoulder. She gave her mother the courtesy of a few nonjudgmental minutes before she offered up her opinions. "Oh my God, Mom, this is *so* bad! I can already predict every twist and tell you *exactly* how it'll end!"

"I know." Birdie laughed. "That's what makes it so good."

They kept watching it anyway.

"Do you miss it?" Birdie asked a little while later as the main characters collapsed into each other's arms and kissed. "The beach. *Our* beach. This month marks five years since we've been back."

Grace sighed, but it made her abdomen hurt more than it already did. "I do."

"I know, my girl." Birdie waited before she uttered anything else. Just one more conversation by way of telepathy. Finally, she lifted Grace's hand, pressed her crimson lips against it. "Me, too."

"Mom?" Grace asked, not taking her eyes off the television screen. "Do you think we'll be okay? In the long run? Me and Adam?"

Birdie breathed through her nose, her mouth shut tight. "I think sometimes life hands us hard things. But I also believe whatever it gives you, Cece, you'll come out okay on the other side of it," she said, never actually mentioning Adam or their marriage in her response. She nodded toward the TV. "And if all else fails, you can be like our leading lady here and run away to find yourself at the beach again," she added with a wink.

Later that month, the week of Grace's thirty-seventh birthday, while Birdie stayed home in Pennsylvania—their annual trips to Sea Drift a thing of the past—Grace and Adam sat outside having lunch at a coastal restaurant in Bar Harbor, Maine—a trip they'd planned late that spring, hoping it would serve as an early babymoon. Nearby, fishing boats with clever names bobbed in the marina, just like in that silly movie Grace and her mother had watched. Before the meal was over, Adam told Grace he wasn't ready—that he might not ever be ready—to try again.

His heart wasn't invested in it the same way anymore. At that point—all the losses they'd experienced together stacked up like a precarious tower of blocks—he wasn't sure if he even wanted a kid.

Now, back in Birdie's old bedroom in the beach house, it's light outside. After a long, solitary night spent trying to untangle a dozen unsolvable riddles, the first beams of sun stretch through the window, painting long yellow strips across the seashell comforter. Somewhere outside, a gull shrieks, a signal that the morning is officially underway.

Tired of being horizontal, Grace sits up. A wave of nausea washes over her, her body still processing last night's meal, the most food and alcohol she's consumed in ages. She clutches the comforter, steadying the feeling, sets the ring on the wobbly nightstand, then looks through the window, privately hoping that this new day will manage to shed light on things.

Beyond the glass, the other houses that separate hers from the beach sit like toys. At the end of them is the pink house—Caleb's rental—right next to the dune. Is that where he was when he called her on Friday? Sitting on the deck, casually poking around on his computer, when he told her that Number 116—a house that, for years, was steadily booked every week of the summer—was newly available and free for the taking?

A thought enters Grace's mind, one she hadn't once considered all night. Other than Jenny, Caleb is the only person in Grace's life—the only one on the planet—who had *any* knowledge that she planned to return here, to this setting, this house, and on a last-minute whim. Was it possible he and Ray knew each other? That this whole week was some elaborate game?

"Just go talk to him, Grace," she says aloud. "Throw on some clothes, walk over there, knock on the door, and ask."

However, she instantly shuts herself down. What would she even say? *Hello, attractive and charming neighbor whom I've already embarrassed myself in front of multiple times. By chance, do you know my teenage crush, and if so, are you two in cahoots to make me think my mother is communicating with him from the afterlife?*

"Sure," she tells herself. "That'd go over great."

She needs to tell someone. This information all feels too heavy for her to hold alone. It's early—too early to contact most people—though Grace knows one person who, like her, though for completely different reasons, will be wide awake.

I saw him, Grace types, and hits send. It takes a minute of battling the Wi-Fi for it to go through. Technically, twice, she types as a follow-up. He said he talked to Birdie. That she told him I'd be back on the island this week.

Three dots quickly appear on the screen.

What does that mean? Jenny responds. Like . . . through a medium or something?

I have no idea, Grace replies. I'm not even sure he knows that she's gone. He just showed up at the house last night, dropped that bomb, and left.

A moment passes before another message comes through. Whether it's because of a weak connection or Jenny's hesitation is hard to say. Jenny knew about Ray. For years, she'd seen the way Grace's face lit up whenever she spoke about him. Still, when Grace fell headfirst into a relationship with Adam—the steadier, more grown-up choice—Jenny never pressed her. It was clear Grace had already made her decision. Sometimes being a good friend meant giving someone the grace to rewrite their story, even though they still held the first draft of it close to their heart.

So, Jenny types, am I allowed to ask the obvious? She follows her message up with a half dozen winky-face emojis.

Grace hesitates, pushes away a strand of hair, then picks a flake of sunburned skin from her shoulder. She turns, quickly glances at the ring again, then swings her feet to the sandy floor.

He looked great, she admits.

~

Grace rinses off in the outdoor shower, then throws on fresh clothes, hoping these simple rituals—rise, lather, dress—might help inspire a feeling of normalcy. In the bedroom, she rubs lotion on her sunburned shoulders, combs her strawberry-scented hair, and slides on her sandals—the splinter and its dull ache still annoyingly present, much like the one in her head, compliments of her ongoing fatigue.

After a half-hearted attempt to make the bed—no sheet tucking, just smoothing the comforter a bit—Grace pauses in front of the room's sole dresser and looks in the scratched-up seashell-framed mirror above it. Why did she really come back here? To this island? This house? Was it to sit in the sun and photosynthesize? To heal and find perspective on the parts of her life that felt unclear? To write a story she has no real experience with—a narrative that once felt like a blueprint but that she's no longer sure she believes in?

No, Grace thinks. She grabs her journal and purse, as well as the neon bracelet from Cece to add to the pile of other objects—sand dollar, arcade tickets—out on the coffee table, then slides on her sunglasses and hat. *That's not really why I'm here.* What she came for was answers. The kind that might get her to stop spiraling and remember how to put one foot in front of the other. The sort that eventually might help her remember how to be Grace.

Before she steps into the hallway, Grace moves to the window—the same one she was looking out earlier while still in bed.

"Mom?"

It's the first time she's tried to talk to her—this person she can no longer see or hear or touch or smell and yet still feels everywhere she goes—since yesterday on the beach.

"I need to know if you told him I'd be here." Her fingers trail along the chipped white trim work. "And if so, how. And why. And when." She waits for a sign, but there aren't any. "Why did you really send me down here?" Grace leans forward. "Was it to find *me* again?" The tip of her nose presses against the glass, her mind swirling with more questions than she has time to pose. "Or was it to find him?"

~

A little while later, Grace stands at the counter of the local coffee shop, where a chipped-away coastal mural hangs on the wall beside her. It took her ten minutes to bicycle up here, then another ten as she waited on the curb for the sleepy-eyed teenage employees to arrive twenty minutes past opening. While they slowly eased into their routine, Grace looked around. Even in her pre-coffee-drinking days, she often came here, always on the hunt for a tropical early-morning or post-beach smoothie (mango, pineapple, and banana every time) or some other vacation-worthy treat.

"Iced coconut-milk coffee," a shaggy-haired staffer mumbles, and slides Grace her drink. He looks at her, his whole demeanor groggy, and tilts his head. "Didn't I make you a smoothie yesterday?"

Only half listening, Grace grabs her beverage and investigates the creamer-to-coffee ratio, which leans too heavily white. "Sorry." She moves to the garbage can, dumps a bit out. "Not me."

"Yes, it was," he insists, his tone perking up. "Remember? Right when we opened. I had to go in the back and cut up the pineapple because we didn't have any prepped yet."

Grace freezes mid-action, while drips of her beverage continue to spill out into the trash bin. "Remind me. What was the order, exactly?"

"It was that one." He points at a handwritten sign. "Mango. Pineapple. And—"

"Cece," Grace says sharply under her breath.

"What?" he poses, still gazing at the sign. "No. No seeds-seeds. Just fruit."

"Dude, *what* are you talking about?" Another boy, still wearing sunglasses, steps through a swinging wooden door in the back. "That girl yesterday was, like, *our* age."

"Was she?" boy number one states, then bursts out laughing. "I don't know, man. Beach bonfire last night, you know? I was up *suuuper* late." He turns, gives Grace another once-over. "You definitely *look* like her, though. Honestly, you could be her mom or something."

Finally, Grace swivels and levels off her cup—now half empty. "Might I ask *why* this young girl who somehow resembled me was so memorable?"

"Because she ran off without paying me!" he exclaims, or as close to an exclamation as his chill-guy demeanor allows. "Said she didn't realize till after she took a sip that all she had were coins and she needed them for the Skee-Ball machines." He shakes hair out of his face. "Swore she'd swing by today to pay me before my boss gets here and realizes my register is off." He stops, stares at the mural. "Gotta be honest, I sort of respect her commitment to the game."

Grace gnaws her lip. No amount of caffeine will wake her up enough for whatever this day has in store. She pulls a ten from her wallet. "That cover what she owes you?"

The boy nods. "Sweet."

Ready to walk away and determine where to go from here, Grace heads for the door and finally takes a sip of her drink. Instantly, her mouth turns sour. She spits it out, forcing it back down into the cup through her straw, her face twisted into a sickened expression. "Oh my God!" She dashes for the trash, tosses it. "Check your coconut milk! That one went bad!"

"What? No way! It was brand new. I just opened it."

"Well, look again." She pulls a water bottle from a cooler. "Because something about it sure isn't right."

Just like the rest of the island this week, she thinks.

SIXTEEN

Grace exits the coffee shop in a hurry, a new sense of urgency pushing her along while an acrid taste—part spoiled creamer, part disbelief—lingers in her mouth.

Outside on the sidewalk, she tugs down her hat, slides on her sunglasses, then wrestles her bike from a metal rack while the surfer boys' voices still rattle around like pinballs inside her brain. Cece. The smoothie. The one her younger self apparently *stole*. (Had Grace ever actually been brazen enough to do such a thing?) It was impossible. And yet, it was also proof. Maybe whatever Grace had been experiencing since arriving back on Sea Drift wasn't only happening in her mind. Which possibly made it worse.

In one ungraceful swoop, she throws a leg over the bike's hot plastic seat, drops her belongings into the woven basket, and starts to ride. The landscape blurs past—pastel houses, slices of water. It's been ages since she's pedaled this hard—beach cruisers are more typically used for, well, *cruising*. But she can't stop. Even though she's surrounded by a setting where people come to get away, Grace feels an innate need to escape.

Eventually, she reaches the northern tip of the island—a place where the boulevard comes to a dead end and all that's left other than water and a parking lot is a pine-tree-lined path. The muscles in her legs burn as she parks her bike, grabs her things, and sets off down the trail.

On certain days, the path is packed. Families posing for pictures. Kids off-roading while their mothers shout about poison ivy. Today, it's quiet. For many people, coming here is a rainy-day activity, something you do when the beach isn't an option. Which is maybe why Grace came. Because even though she'll technically be out in public, she's confident she'll be alone here so she can think.

Another few paces and Grace sees it, its black-and-white body taking shape through the dense green brush. The lighthouse. As stoic and certain as ever. A structure historically meant to safely guide people back into port. Grace and Birdie used to come here together to collect pieces of driftwood, look through the old-fashioned viewers at the ocean, then climb the lighthouse, walking the 216 narrow steps all the way to its top. Sometimes, when Grace was older, she'd come here for an hour or two by herself, often when Birdie was out getting more groceries or meeting up with Carol Murphy to enjoy baskets of clam strips for lunch.

Back then, Grace liked to be alone sometimes—not *lonely*, there was a difference—because doing so often meant carving out extra time to write. She'd bring an old composition notebook or journal, a few pens, and her thoughts, then plop down someplace and try to puzzle through whatever thoughts were taking up space in her head. And now here she is, thirty-seven, traversing the same worn path and preparing to do the same thing.

The trail splits. Most visitors veer left toward the main attraction and designated photo spots. Grace veers right instead and follows a narrower, more overgrown path, the one she knows opens up to the jetty. She steps off it, over to the long line of dark rocks that stretch out into the sea like an arm, and picks her way across them, careful not to slip on their slick surfaces. There's a danger to it—visitors aren't technically supposed to walk out this far—but it's a risk that's always felt worth taking. Once she reaches the last rock, Grace sits, kicks off her sandals, and inspects her heel, newly sore from her long bike ride in flimsy flip-flops. She twists her leg and picks at it, but it's no use. The skin around it blooms red, not in an urgent or dramatic way, but enough for her to notice. *Probably the early signs of an infection, love,* she hears Birdie say. *If you ignore it, Cece, it'll only get worse.*

She shifts her weight, trying to settle in and figure out what, precisely, to do next. She unscrews her water and pulls her journal and a pen onto her lap. Maybe it's the silence out here. Or the fact that sitting this far out in the sea has always made Grace feel both full of wonder and also infinitely small. Whatever the reason, she decides to just stare.

In two days, Grace will be thirty-eight. It's a nothing birthday. Not a new decade or milestone worthy of a special party. It was just supposed to be a day. A nice one, but simple. That's how she imagined her whole life would feel at this stage, too. Easy. All the questions that once haunted her—*Who am I? Where am I going? What do I want? When will I figure things out?*—tucked neatly away in her past. And wasn't that the kicker? The fact that they'd all moved back into her mind, like time had merely been an illusion and the years—the ones that'd felt so long sometimes—had never actually passed.

"Wh-what is that?" Grace suddenly stutters to herself, her sight trained on the water.

Something strange catches her eye. From beneath her dark sunglasses and the shadow of her baseball cap, she squints and tries to interpret the sight. Five—no, six—not-quite-right objects float past. At first, from her elevated spot up on the rocks, she thinks they're some unusual school of fish, a lesser-known species of bird, or a collection of small, discarded bags.

"Wait." She strains her neck forward, her whole face scrunched up in a question. "Are those . . . papers?"

"Yes," a voice—one full of drama that Grace instantly recognizes but really wishes she didn't—announces from behind her. "And that's exactly where they belong. In the water, where they'll disintegrate and no one will ever be subjected to reading the awful half attempts at prose written on them."

Grace turns slowly, not quite wanting to look but aware that—other than catapulting herself into a dangerously deep part of the ocean—there's no clear path for her to run away.

"Also, you don't need to remind me," the late-twentysomething girl who stands a little way back on the jetty states. She holds an oversize bright-pink journal—the words Be Calm and Carry On . . . with Your Story stamped in bold typography across its front. Without a word, she whips it back open, tears out another sheet, crumples it into a tight ball, and tosses it. "I'm well aware that what I'm doing is bad for the environment." She flings it. The paper catches in the wind before it touches the water's surface. "Selfish, I know. But honestly, not to sound terrible, that's the least of my problems at the moment."

Instantly, Grace's heart starts to do backflips, while her palms become coated with sweat. She blinks, as if one of the sheets of torn paper has somehow flown straight into her cornea, inhibiting her ability to clearly see. But of course, just like all her other recent unexplainable encounters on this island, her vision is not the problem.

It's her.

The wild hair, still golden but pulled up in a messy-yet-trying-too-hard high bun. The designer-distressed jean shorts (which cost her half a month's rent). The black T-shirt, which for reasons she couldn't articulate, made her feel a touch edgy. The oversize beaded bib necklace she wore everywhere that year, hoping to look . . . what? More stylish? More grown-up? More *New York*? Just above, her more garish jewelry choice, the glint of gold metal—the nameplate necklace—shines on her chest.

Cece. Ten years earlier. Freshly twenty-seven. Not yet knowing this would be one of her last weeklong visits here, or that the life she'd been pining for—the one that would ultimately crash a few short years later—waits just ahead.

"What are you doing?" Grace asks, pulling her hat down farther to better conceal her face. "Why are you throwing papers in the ocean?"

While she waits for a response, Grace flips through her mental Rolodex of memories in an effort to remember this day. But she can't. The older you get, the more specific instances from your past begin to dim. It's like your mind starts to run out of storage and begins to purge files to free up space. Some moments—the big ones—stay. But others, the in-between scenes that unfold in the quieter pockets of our days—words we said, small things we did—fade.

"Dear God, would you stop!" Grace shouts as Cece rips out another page and sacrifices it to the sea. "I don't remember why—I mean, I don't *understand* why you're throwing them into the water like that." A pair of seagulls swoop down, thinking they've found an early lunch. After a brief investigation, they fly away, disappointed. "Is this symbolic or—"

"You wouldn't." Cece smacks her journal—the one Grace distinctly recalls buying on a visit to the Strand—shut. She slides it into her canvas *New Yorker* tote bag, then crouches and takes a seat on the rocks. "That's part of the problem. No one does." She sniffles and tries to hide the fact that she's crying. "Also, lighting them on fire felt too on the nose, you know? Fire. Creative burnout." She quickly wipes her eyes. "It's bad enough that my writing feels entirely clichéd. I don't need the ways I reject it to feel trite, too." She lifts a hand to her chest. "God, I hate this thing," she announces, and unhooks her clunky necklace. "It's so heavy." Cece holds it out, looking at it from all angles, like she might chuck it into the tides, too.

"Wait!" Grace almost bolts up, but realizes she doesn't know all the rules of this most uncanny game. (*Does she know me? Do I tell her who I am?*) "Please don't throw that!"

Cece raises a well-manicured brow, her tears already drying up. "I'm not." She drops it in a pile next to her. "Though I probably should. I don't even like it. I only got it because every girl in my office has one just like it." She looks at Grace. "Why? Do you like it or something?"

"I don't mind it." Grace recalls the time she wasted in that too-big fast-fashion shop in Union Square, deliberating over it. Was it the right color? Would it make her look more stylish or in the know? Was it worth it to pay fifty bucks for a piece of costume jewelry—something that so obviously wasn't real—especially when she could hardly afford her rent? "It looks like something I might've picked out at your age, too."

A fishing boat cruises through the inlet, its wake causing a ripple of rough water to hit the rocks. The driver waves. Both Grace and Cece—as if on cue—wave back in precisely the same way. Once the boat is out of view, Grace glances over both sunburned shoulders, checking to see if anyone else might be nearby and witnessing this moment.

Unlike her previous encounters—at the beach, the arcade, and the Beachcomber—Grace has been afforded more physical distance this time. For a quiet minute, she watches Cece and allows herself permission to fully recall this time in her life. Not loving where she was living—New York a relentless experiment in claustrophobia. Always weighed down by worry . . . Was there enough money in her account? Did she have room on her credit card to go out with friends? Wondering if the right amount of silly accessories—if she wore enough uncomfortable shoes or wrapped herself up in trendy oversize scarves—could ever manage to transform her into the version of herself she'd moved there to be. And yet, beyond all those fears, there lived a quiet, if not somewhat delusional, sense of hope. If she stayed, toughed it out, kept trying and faking and fumbling and picking herself back up, it'd all work out.

"So," Grace asks, her tone tender for this version of herself who's trying so hard at everything, "what's with all the abandoned pages?" She points to the water, though most of them have sunk or floated away. Grace can't remember having done this, though it seems like exactly the sort of poetic gesture she might have made at that age. "You're working on something?"

"Trying." Cece lies back on the rocks. "And failing." She looks up at the sky. "It's a book. Or at least, I'd like it to be one day. It's about a city girl who falls in love with her childhood crush when she bumps into him again at the beach." She covers her face with her fingers. "Original, I know. It might as well be a Hallmark movie."

A gull glides overhead, its easy movements as beautiful as a poem.

"I wrote the first draft really fast," Cece continues. "I'm not even kidding when I say the story poured out of me in a few weeks. That probably should have been my first clue that it was stupid—the fact that it came so easily." She runs her fingers over the rocks, like she's looking for something just out of reach. "Anyway, I've been trying all morning to brainstorm a more unique spin on an ending. So far, everything

I've come up with feels impossibly contrived." She squints at the sun. "Probably because my heart's not really in it."

"That's the hardest part, isn't it?" Grace picks up a black pebble, rubs it like a worry stone. "Trying to force the words onto the page when you don't really feel them."

Cece rolls onto her side, like a college roommate ready for a gossip session. "Are you a writer or something?"

"I am," Grace admits. "Or I used to be." She sets down the stone, picks at a corner of her journal still sitting in her lap. "I'm not sure what I am right now, honestly."

"A writer?" Cece props her face in one hand. "A real one?" She studies Grace, trying to gauge her credibility. "Or, like, you have a blog?"

Grace laughs, privately recalling when these things mattered. It wasn't only about the writing but also the validation—to have a *real* book, a *real* agent, tangible ways to prove the dream she'd been chasing was real, too.

"No blog. Just books. Two, so far." Grace looks out at the water—blue and sparkling. "The third one is . . . let's say a work in progress." She picks up the stone again, tosses it, and watches it disappear. "To be honest, it's giving me ulcers at the moment."

"Wow." Cece sounds genuinely impressed. "That's amazing." She sits up. "I go to author readings *all* the time. I live in New York, so there are always a ton." Something about her tone lifts slightly. "I don't even necessarily care who the author is, you know? I just like to hear them talk about their process, how they finally got things to work."

It feels like yesterday. Sitting in folding chairs at bookstores across the city. Listening to every author speak, not as if they were people but Jedi Masters—people who knew the way forward in a way Grace did not. Even though it made her nervous to speak in public, she always made a point to ask at least one question during the final Q and A: *What advice would you give to your younger self?*

"Well, seeing as you're the real deal," Cece says, "I'm going to assume you've never wanted to throw your journal into the ocean."

"Ha!" Grace literally laughs out loud. "Trust me. You have no idea how wrong you are." Her mind drifts back to her home office—the crumpled sticky notes, the collection of dying plants. "There've been multiple times this summer that I've been *very* tempted to fling open my second-story window and chuck my whole laptop right out of it."

Cece looks down at the rocks and laughs. "At least it's not only me."

While they talk, Grace opens her journal and quietly flips. The first few pages are scribbles of notes she jotted down back at home—half attempts at outlines, scene ideas she thought might be important. Ultimately, they amounted to nothing.

"So what's the problem with your ending?" Grace asks, even though she recalls this part.

"I don't know." Cece smooths back some strands of hair that have come loose from her bun in the breeze. "My goal was for it to seem literary, you know? So people might actually take it seriously." She shrugs. "Right now, the whole story just feels predictable. A girl. A boy. A one-week rental. The ocean. A few heavy make-out scenes." Cece shakes her head. "Honestly, I'm mortified even thinking about the simplicity of it." She closes her eyes. "Like anything *real* could ever be that simple, right?"

Grace waits before she says anything, giving Cece the space she needs to think and talk.

"It's a love story." Cece rests her chin on her knees. "In case you didn't pick up on that." She huffs, annoyed with herself. "Right now, the two characters ultimately end up with each other, which every person I know who understands anything at all about books has told me isn't fresh enough to sell. It's too obvious. Too tidy. No real hook or twist." She tosses up her palms. "Two young people fall for each other in some beautiful setting. Blah, blah, blah. They decide to spend their lives together, like nothing else in the world matters. The end." She rubs her hands over her face. "It's sort of inspired by someone I used to know," she admits, her eyes half closed as she says it. "Our story wasn't quite that straightforward." Her voice drops just as the breeze picks up. "Though sometimes I wish it had been." Her words are so quiet it's as if she didn't really speak them. She turns, giving Grace a glance. "My writing group keeps telling me the protagonist needs to do something unexpected. Leave! Run away!" She inhales a big breath of ocean air. "But I don't want to write that story," she says.

Of course, Grace thinks. *Because you've already lived it.*

But that was the version she finally wrote. Not the first draft, the one twenty-seven-year-old Cece was presently reflecting on. Not the second, which she'd write that fall, even though certain parts of the story still made her flinch. But the one that came after it that winter, when the world felt cold enough to crack her open and the truth flowed out onto the page.

The Tides—the version that went to print—was a love story, one stretched across fifteen summers, a narrative set on a quiet strip of coastline where the tides kept carrying two people back to each other, even as they grew up and apart and no longer fit into the mold they'd hoped they were creating together. It was part love letter, part elegy. A romance marked not by grand gestures—no fireworks or long monologues or airport chases. Rather, it was about a pair of characters who loved each other deeply but chose different lives. A heartbreaking narrative about wanting to hold on but letting go instead. Until the final twist, when the protagonist had a change of heart, gave up everything she thought she wanted, and ran back. "A romantic triumph," as noted in more than one book review. *Fiction,* as Grace often reminded herself when she read it.

"Can I ask you something?" Cece's vision is cast out on the water—both here and somewhere far away. "You're a writer, right? So maybe you'll understand."

"Sure," Grace offers, uncertain what comes next. "What's your question?"

"How do you know if you're creating the right ending for a story?" Cece asks. "There are infinite possibilities to choose from. How are you ever certain that the one you choose is right?"

It's hard, looking back, to really remember. How bad something hurt. How much you wanted things you couldn't have. Right now, as Grace watches this version of Cece, she tries. She's not the bubbly teenager on the beach, the determined preteen in the arcade, or the searching-but-still-fun person she left behind at the Beachcomber. This version is wounded in a way the others haven't been yet.

"You don't."

Cece's expression is curious. "Then how do you choose?"

The breeze picks up, creating ripples in the shallow puddles along the tops of the rocks.

"Sometimes you need to stop and ask yourself hard questions," Grace explains, knowing she's not exclusively talking about the craft of fiction anymore. "Most of the time, though, the best stories come from the parts of us that hurt."

Cece nods, absorbing this information as she stands and brushes pebbles from the backs of her calves. "I need to get going." She gathers the rest of her belongings. "It was really good talking to you, though."

"You, too."

Before she leaves, Cece shields her eyes. "It's funny. I've been coming to this island my whole life. I used to live for this place." She takes in the wide-open view. "I must be getting too used to all that big-city noise. The last few seasons, something about being down here makes me feel sort of sad."

A memory. Grace and Ray, the summer she turned eighteen. The next week, they'd both leave for their respective colleges, everything about their lives just days away from changing.

Are you scared? she asked him, her head on his chest. The sky was bruised with clouds, the wind suggesting a storm was rolling in. *You know, about leaving?*

A little, he said, tossing a rock into the rough waves. *I don't really love change.*

Me neither. Grace picked at the frayed hem of her shorts, then cleared her throat. *So, Mr. Murphy,* she said, putting on her best authoritative and grown-up voice, *what is it that you want to be when you grow up?*

In the months leading up to that moment, it was the only question anyone asked Grace. What's next? Who do you want to become? The constant implication that change wasn't a suggestion but a requirement.

Happy, Ray said, his arms draped over her torso.

I don't think that's a job, she joked.

It's not. His finger tangled itself up in her hair. *It doesn't matter anyway, Porter. I'm already happy right here—right now—with you.*

The truth was that so was she.

"Anyway," Cece says now, "we're supposed to get some overcast mornings later this week." She gives a timid wave. "Maybe I'll see you here if you come back to write or something." Cece moves up the jetty. Before she gets too far, she turns back. "By the way, do you want this?" She holds up the chunky beaded necklace. "I totally lied to you before. If you hadn't been sitting there, I absolutely would have chucked it straight into the water."

Before Grace answers, Cece tosses it. The necklace lands in a heap on the rocks.

"Thanks?"

Cece smiles. "I promise I won't judge you if you toss it." Up in the distance, people appear on the path. "You know, if I were you—already having multiple books published—no matter what questions I had, I'd probably be so happy that I got to write at that level that I'd never stop." Her shoulders rise to her ears. "But maybe that's just the dreamer in me."

Cece waves again, then makes her way toward the trail. Grace watches until the pine trees swallow her whole. For a short while, she lets all the questions she has roll in. About Ray. About Birdie. About Caleb. She doesn't have the answers. Not yet.

And maybe that's the point.

Because the question, she begins to realize for the first time since driving over the bridge, isn't about the future or the present.

It's about her past.

And whether she's finally ready to really remember it.

SEVENTEEN

Grace doesn't immediately return to the house.

Once she finally walks off the jetty—pausing for a while at the lighthouse, remembering the days when all she longed to do was climb to its top and look out as far as she could see—instead of jumping right back on her bike and pedaling hard beneath the early-afternoon sun, she decides to walk, noting that her foot, irritated from too much activity, has started to ache. Wheeling the cruiser beside her, Grace meanders south along the boulevard's narrow sidewalk, feeling more confused and exhausted with each new step.

She stops off at a few familiar spots, not just to reminisce but also to give herself short breaks from the heat. First is the saltwater-taffy shop, a place Grace hasn't visited in years. It still smells like her childhood. Sugar. Humidity. Artificial fruit flavoring. She gathers pieces from the bins—root beer, orange sherbet, peanut butter swirl—dropping them into a white paper bag before she pays. Outside, she sits on a sunbaked bench, unwraps a piece of chocolate mint taffy, and takes a chewy bite. But it's not the same. It's too sweet. Too sticky. The memory of it better than the real thing.

"I like the strawberry ones, Cece," Birdie used to say, always insisting on stuffing the bag with way too many candies. "They taste terrible—nothing like actual strawberries—but I love them anyway!"

On their last trip, the one they took a few weeks before Grace's autumn wedding, the summer before *The Tides* was released, she and

Birdie stayed up late one night, talking and laughing on the patio and eating taffy until they nearly made themselves sick.

"You know, in another few years, we may need to rent a bigger place," Birdie said as she unwrapped another piece. "What's that old saying? First comes love, then comes marriage, then comes . . ."

"A hefty mortgage payment out in the suburbs, probably," Grace joked, even though she was daydreaming about her and Adam starting a family, too.

"I'm just teasing you, sweetheart." Birdie smiled, finally pushing the paper bag aside. "You'll cross that bridge—if that's what you decide you want to do—whenever you feel ready."

Grace leaned back in the Adirondack chair, looked up at the clear, star-speckled sky. "So can you believe it? The fact that I'm actually getting married soon?"

"No," Birdie admitted. "I can't." Her voice caught, snagged by her emotion. "My girl," she said, turning to look at Grace. "All grown up already."

"Already?" Grace laughed. "I'm thirty-two."

"I know it," Birdie said. "But you're still my Cece." She reached over and squeezed her daughter's thigh. "Speaking of which . . ."

"Mom," Grace droned, already sensing the direction in which their conversation was heading. "Again?" Birdie, in no subtle way, had already broached the topic several times that week. "I think you're making way too much out of this."

"Sweetheart, you're getting married in a few weeks, and you still haven't told your fiancé that the book you're preparing to publish next summer is about your first love."

"That's because it's incredibly awkward! And also, not really a big deal. Sure, there are parallels to what happened between Ray and me, but at the end of the day, it's fiction. I made the story up. There's even one of those little disclaimers on the copyright page—'This is a work of fiction'—to prove as much."

Birdie's brows arched upward. "Darling, what have I *always* told you is the first lesson about literature that I teach my students at the start of every school year?"

Grace slouched in her chair and closed her eyes, her version of a response.

"The best fiction," Birdie said, "is always built on a foundation of truth."

The next week, once she was back in the city, Grace—with her mother's voice pestering her in her mind—finally decided to tell Adam the story. Or at least a watered-down version of it.

They were up on the High Line after dinner one night and had stopped off at an artisanal Popsicle stand for a boozy-infused treat before they trekked to their apartment.

"I need to tell you something," Grace said between prosecco-flavored licks. They'd been walking in comfortable silence, looking at the stretches of gardens and the pink early-autumn sky, the type they hoped to have the night of their wedding. "It's about my book."

"Oh?" Adam looked at her in question, his Popsicle hovering near his mouth. "Big movie deal in the works?" he joked. It was no secret that Adam loved *The Tides* and was rooting for Grace's success. He told everyone he encountered about it. For weeks, he'd kept his advance copy on his nightstand, skimming it in bed, then smiling at her, as if he'd been gifted with an insider's view of her mind. "You're not going to run away with some hotshot producer, right?"

"Not quite." Grace gestured to a vacant bench, and they sat. "It's just . . ." Her heart beat harder. "When I first started to write it—back before we ever met—the original idea for the story was, well, loosely inspired by someone I used to know."

"Okay," Adam said, lowering his hand.

"It was sort of based on this guy I dated," she said and rolled her eyes, like she could convince them both that it was nothing. "Down in Sea Drift."

Adam's head tilted. "So, like, a one-time-summer-hookup sort of thing?"

Grace sighed. "Not entirely." Her shoulders dropped. "It was a bit more than that."

For the next half hour, she told him about Ray. About growing up with him on that strip of beach. About their ongoing romance that stretched from one summer into the next. She told him nearly everything, except for details about that final night Ray gave her the ring. Part of her thought he might laugh and find the whole thing endearing—everyone had experienced young love—or that Adam, being such a mature, levelheaded person, would simply shrug it off.

"Why didn't you tell me sooner?" His eyes narrowed. "Don't you think you should have told me that the first time I read it?"

"I—I—" Grace stuttered, Adam's tone—the seriousness of it—throwing her off. "I didn't think it was that big a deal."

"Of course it is," he said, tossing his melting Popsicle into a trash can beside him. "You wrote a story about the man you loved right before me, and in a few months it'll be available everywhere for everyone to read, both here and in six other countries."

"Adam," she said, "don't you think you're overreacting?"

Lines formed around his eyes. "I guess that explains the Cece bit, then, no?"

"What! No. It's just a name," Grace said. "I could have called her *anything*."

"But you didn't."

"It's fiction, Adam." Grace felt as if her throat was tightening. "The whole story's made up." She licked the edges of her pop to avoid it dripping all over her hand. "And the few parts that aren't, well, what does it really matter? It's all in the past."

"But it's not, Grace. It's here. In our present." He pinched the bridge of his nose. "I'm ready to head home. I need to be in the office early tomorrow," he said, already taking a step away from her.

Grace stood. When she did, the ground beneath her felt unsteady, like something had shifted, though she blamed it on the alcohol in the ice pop. "Adam?" she said to his back.

He turned, took a breath. "It's fine, Grace," he told her. "It's just a book."

That night, when Adam thought Grace was asleep, she saw him slide his early copy of the novel into his nightstand drawer. To her knowledge, he never pulled it out again.

Now, back on Sea Drift's main boulevard, Grace keeps walking. More beachy blocks pass her by—weathered rental homes, decades-old surf shops, souvenir stores selling tchotchkes. It's all so familiar, like a postcard preserved in time.

A little while later, the bag of taffy rolled up in the bicycle's basket, the old bookshop with the striped awning appears on her right. In the front window, a splashy new summer romance is on display, its cover an illustration of two happy people clinking cocktails in the sand. Grace wonders if either of her books ever sat here—something passersby might've stopped to consider, the way she's considering this one now. But more, she wonders about the person who wrote this new novel. If she wrestled with every word, straining to find the story.

Finally, a long while after she left this morning, Grace maneuvers the bike back onto Surf Street. It's midday now, the whole world a touch too bright, like it's trying its best to shine a light on things, even though it isn't. She's so distracted by her thoughts that she almost doesn't see it at first. Once she does, her steps quicken. She drops the bike on the curb, not even bothering with the kickstand, then stops. There, staked into the crushed-seashell lot, it stands.

The sign.

For Sale.

Grace stares at it for at least a minute, hardly able to move. All the air drains from her, like her body is being deflated. When she finally springs into action again, she turns, and without even thinking, marches to the end of the block. A melting pot of mixed-up emotions—anger, sadness, uncertainty—bubbles inside her. A few feet ahead, other renters trickle down the dune, sunburned and sandy. But Grace isn't heading to the dune, not waltzing off to pass a casual few hours. Instead, she stops right before it at the pink house on the right.

"Grace?" Caleb answers the door, surprised and maybe annoyed to see her standing there. "Um, hi." He looks over his shoulder at something—or perhaps someone—inside. His breezy, at times flirtatious, demeanor is gone. "Wh-what are you doing here?"

Grace felt confident on her way over here, though now Caleb's tone throws her off. "D-did you tell someone that I was coming here? Back to Sea Drift, I mean. This week."

"What are you talking about?" Caleb's brows furrow. "Is something wrong with the house or—"

"Caleb?" a voice—a female one—calls out from inside. The sound of it makes something inside Grace shift, her cells pulsing with regret. "Sweetheart," the woman continues, "is everything okay?"

A woman—older, closer in age to Birdie than Grace—appears behind him in the entryway. Grace blinks, momentarily caught off guard. It's not her, obviously. But for a second, something about her hair and breezy dress is enough to make Grace look away.

"Yeah, Mom." Caleb's brows settle. "I'll be back inside in a minute."

He steps out onto the porch, gently closing the door behind him.

"I-I'm sorry," Grace says. "I didn't mean to interrupt."

"It's fine," Caleb assures her. "Really." A hint of his usual brightness sneaks back into his tone, though it sounds less natural this time. "So what's going on? Why did you ask if I told someone you're down here?" He strains his neck, maybe to see if something is noticeably wrong at his rental property. "Which—to be clear—I didn't. I mean, legally all my renters' agreements are confidential. Not that I'm even sure who I'd tell."

Of course, he didn't. Because he's right. Who *would* he tell? What would he even tell them (*Hey—I rented a house to someone . . . because, you know, that's what I do for a living.*)? And also, why would he divulge Grace's whereabouts? They don't know each other. Not really. They've had a few conversations. A casual meal. Maybe a hint of something—flirtation, perhaps, or at least she'd thought.

But now she sees it for what it's really been. Pity. Mortification after mortification, stacked on top of each other like blocks. The tide pool. The seaweed. Even Caleb's initial call, which she was still second-guessing just a moment earlier (*Did he know something? Did he tell Ray?*), was one, too. The fact that Grace had been available to come back here at the last minute. No weekend plans. No end-of-season getaways already on the calendar. Just Grace. Alone. Stuck at home, surrounded by boxes of memories, putzing around a house that has become its own form of grief, trying her hardest to draft a story she'll probably never have the chance to truly understand.

And now this: showing up on her landlord's porch (because, technically, that's what he is—*all* that he is—to her), looking like a sweaty mess, running on sugar and limited sleep and hoping maybe he—a near stranger—can help her make sense of anything.

"I-I'm confused. I thought the house wasn't going up for sale until the fall," Grace says now, subtly shifting gears and realizing how foolish she must sound. What did it matter when it went up? Now? A few weeks from now? Today? Never? What difference did it really make in her life? It didn't. Yet seeing it there made something in her ache. "Why'd the sign go up today? Are the owners really anxious to get rid of it?"

Caleb squeezes the back of his neck, tense with something he needs to work out. He looks behind him at the door, then back at Grace. "Give me a half hour. I need to finish up some things with my folks." His eyes fall in line with hers. "You up for grabbing a midday drink?"

Unlike their first meeting on the beach, when Grace's initial reaction was to turn down his offer for a beer—old habits, old hopes, still guiding her small choices—this time, the answer comes to her right away.

"Without a doubt," Grace states, no hesitation in her voice. "I definitely am."

EIGHTEEN

"What's your poison?"

Grace looks up from the bar top and sees Caleb, who's just returned from the restroom, taking a seat on the stool next to her. It's the middle of the afternoon on what, weather-wise, is a perfect beach day. Even so, the Dive, Sea Drift's one and only classic dive bar (hence the clever, ocean-inspired name), buzzes with at least a dozen customers. There are a few older men at pub tables, sipping cheap beer and laughing about something. A trio of early-twentysomethings—just barely old enough to be in here—dance near the jukebox in their flimsy cover-ups and damp bathing suits.

"Whatever's cold," Grace says, feeling impossibly parched from her long walk down the island. "And maybe a snack."

Caleb laughs, waves down a bartender—a college-aged guy who wears a T-shirt printed with a new, updated logo for the bar on its front. "A bowl of pretzels and two Miller High Lifes." He looks to Grace for her approval. "It's the Dive," he adds. "I'm not sure they've advanced to artisanal cocktails just yet."

Unlike every other establishment here—all boasting water views, coastal knickknacks, and a light, airy feel that matches the setting—the Dive is unapologetically dark. Only two windows, both covered with broken slatted blinds. Wood-paneled walls. Countless framed maps of the island hung at uneven angles. Multicolored Christmas lights. A scratched-up shuffleboard game and decades-old pool table in the back.

Grace used to come here in her younger years—first with a bad fake ID, then later with the real thing. She was never alone, always walking in with Meg or Ray or other summer friends and stumbling out in a tipsy and giggling group. It was a place of fun times and bad decisions, of dollar drafts and late-night dancing. The August she brought Adam to Sea Drift, they popped by after dinner one night. It was packed. Drunk kids everywhere. People smoking cigarettes just outside the doors, the smell wafting in. They sat at the bar, its surface sticky from other people's good times, and each ordered a bottle of beer.

"This place is pretty vintage, huh?" Adam joked. "Straight out of the seventies."

"I know." Grace laughed. "It's a total time stamp." She noshed on peanuts like a circus elephant. "Honestly, it's sort of a mess."

Back in New York, Adam was a regular at a rotation of Midtown establishments—places with white table linens and multiple forks for different parts of a meal—where he took clients to talk about their futures, make sure they were prepared and had solid plans.

"This place is prime real estate, though." Adam sipped from his beer bottle. "A few lots in from the beach. Decent square footage." He looked around, lost in a daydream. "If they gutted it, opened it up, added a bunch of big windows, they could make a killing," he pointed out, even though the line to order drinks behind them was three people deep.

"Seems to me like they're already doing all right," Grace countered as someone sloshed part of their drink down her back.

"Yeah, but . . ." Adam trailed off, considering something. "They could turn it into something even better, you know?" He finished his drink, signaled for another. "That is, if the owners were just willing to clean it up."

Now the bartender walks back, sets down coasters marked with a clever anchor design and the bar's name, as well as bottles of golden beer and a bowl of salty pretzel nubs. Caleb slides a bottle to Grace, picks his up, and clinks it against hers. "Cheers."

They sit quietly as they both enjoy a long, refreshing sip.

"I'm sorry about earlier," Caleb states a beat later, just as a classic rock ballad steeped in memories starts to play. "I didn't mean to be rude when you knocked." He turns, their shoulders close. "I was just in the middle of dealing with some things inside that I sort of wished that I wasn't." The song plays on, the vocalist crooning away about the ups and downs of love and time. "My sister died," Caleb says, plain and simple. "That's why my parents dropped by."

"Oh my God," Grace gasps, feeling like a fool for interrupting their family gathering. She sets down her bottle, her eyes instantly flooding with tears. "I'm so sorry. I don't know what to say."

"It's okay. It was last year," he clarifies. "I probably should have led with that." He drinks again. "This month is the one-year anniversary. We're doing a little memorial for her on the beach next week."

Grace's mind floods with questions. She wants to ask him what happened. If it was sudden, like Birdie's passing, or something longer and more drawn out—and if he had any time to emotionally prepare. She wants to ask how he's coping. If time has made his loss easier, the way people—Dr. Anne, the authors of her self-help books, the women in her grief group—keep telling her it will. Does he feel better and more like himself one year after the loss, versus at the six-month mark? Or are the things that people tell individuals who are drowning in grief to cling on to—time and hope and faith, all the abstract life preservers they swear will help—just myths?

"Anyway," Caleb continues, picking at the paper label on his beer, "that's why I moved back to the East Coast a few months ago. My folks, as you can imagine, are still reeling. My dad could barely run the agency anymore. He was forgetting things, misplacing contracts, not following up with renters for payments. It's all been a mess."

The song ends. A newer one comes on, a track the twentysomething girls picked.

"I understand. I lost my mom back in February." She trails her fingertip across the bar. "My entire life's been turned upside down ever since. Sea Drift was always our place."

Nearby, the girls break out in a drunken dance, singing and twirling like it's late at night, even though it's the middle of the day. They don't care. Time is still on their side. The future is only as real as a daydream. They're all too young to realize that one day, the party they believe lasts forever will eventually come to a screeching end.

"Oh, Grace." Caleb briefly closes his eyes and shakes his head. "That's terrible," he adds, reopening them. When he does, a new thought settles over his face. "That's why you were hesitant at first—when I called you on Friday—about coming back."

She shrugs, such a simple gesture to express so many complicated feelings. "Part of it."

Their bartender reapproaches. "Another round?"

"Not for me, unfortunately." Caleb pulls a twenty from his wallet. He slaps it on the bar and signals that it's for both their drinks. The bartender nods, takes the bill, then walks away to help someone else. "I'm on curfew," Caleb says. "I promised my folks I'd be back in a bit so we can finish talking through things." He polishes off his last sip. "My mom ordered candles. She wants me to put together something to say." He sighs, long and quiet. "It's all just . . . a lot."

The young bartender walks back up, passes Caleb his change. Caleb holds up a hand, a way to tell the kid to keep it.

"I'm really sorry about your sister, Caleb," Grace says, suddenly seeing him—this charming, cheery, breezy man—in such a different way.

"I'm sorry about your loss, too." Caleb's phone rings. His breath deepens as he reaches into his shorts pocket to pull it out. "Ahh, the lady of the hour." He flashes Grace his device. Her name—*Mom*—glows on the screen.

As Caleb grabs a fistful of pretzels, getting ready to go back outside, Grace remembers their first conversation on the beach, right after she realized her necklace was gone.

"Did you mean what you said?" Grace asks, not getting up yet, just wanting to sit a little longer and finish her drink. "On the beach. About things on this island not staying lost."

He laughs. "Well, I wasn't lying about my sunglasses, if that's what you mean."

Grace lifts her brows. "It's not."

Caleb waits before he responds, like he really wants to answer the right way. "I did mean it, Grace. This place. There's something about it." He pauses again. "That's part of why I didn't want to list the house yet," he adds quietly. "The 'For Sale' sign," he clarifies. "That's why you stopped by earlier, right?"

Something occurs to Grace now that didn't then, when she was overheated and marching over to Caleb's rental. At the time, she thought maybe he had inside intel about the sign—why it was there earlier than it was supposed to be—simply because he knew a lot about different properties on Sea Drift. But now a new thought rushes in.

"Do you . . . Do *you* own it?" she asks, the light beer suddenly hitting her in a different way. "My house." A nauseous feeling, faint but newly present. "Well, my rental house. Is it yours?"

"Not me. But my parents do," he explains. "Since I was a kid. They've always rented it out, save for the two weeks our family stayed there every July." Behind him, the door opens. A quick peek of sunlight spills into the bar. "They just don't want to have to hold on to it anymore."

Grace swallows, but the feeling stays. The house. All this time, it had felt weighed down by her own loss. She hadn't considered that it might be haunted by someone else's grief, too.

"By the way," Caleb calls out to the bartender, his tone lifting, "where's the big guy today? He's usually here by now. Skipping out on work to catch some midday waves?" he jokes.

"Probably," the young employee states, matching Caleb's friendly tone. "Can't keep that one away from the water." He finishes pouring a drink for another patron. "Either that or he's still over at the Beachcomber having his usual pre-shift beer before coming here." He laughs. "Not as fun to have a drink at your own bar, I guess, knowing you've got work to do." He smiles. "He'll be in later. I'll let him know you were here."

Caleb looks back at Grace. "I go fishing now and again with the owner. Nice guy," he explains, filling her in. "He was friendly with my sister. She liked to pop in here whenever she came up to the island to see my folks. They surfed together a bunch last summer before she . . ." His voice trails off. The words disappear. There's nothing left to say. "Anyway, I'd better get moving." Caleb pushes in his chair, takes a step, then stops. "About your question." He bites his lip. "In my experience, I've found that being back in a place steeped in memories of the person you lost can hurt like hell."

He looks at the ground, like he's suddenly talking more to himself. It takes a second for Grace to see that he's observing something. A stray penny. He crouches, picks it up, puts it in his pocket.

"But slowly, in time," Caleb continues, rising, "I've also found that being immersed in those memories—not just remembering who you lost but also who you were when you were with that person . . ." He makes eye contact with her again. "Well, it can start to help, too."

Caleb leaves, the door swinging shut behind him.

"Here." The bartender sets another beer down in front of Grace. "This one's on the house." He twists off the cap. "I overheard your conversation. Thought maybe you needed it."

"Oh," Grace says, surprised by the gesture, but also not turning it down. "Thanks."

He nods, walks off to help someone else.

Grace remains seated, takes a sip—the liquid cold, carbonated, crisp—then another, deciding to stay for this next round by herself. Alone, yes, but no longer quite as lonely. For the first time since arriving, not only to the Dive, but to Sea Drift, Grace isn't in a rush to leave.

On the jukebox, an old Bruce Springsteen song she and Birdie always loved comes on. Grace listens, the lyrics reintroducing themselves into her thoughts. She looks down at her bottle, already half empty, thinking about the house and all the memories—not only hers—that live inside its walls.

"I'll do one more," she tells the bartender as he walks past, wondering if Caleb is right.

Maybe not everything on this island stays lost forever after all.

NINETEEN

Tuesday

Morning. Again. Only this time, Grace wakes up refreshed. For the first time in ages, she actually slept. After Caleb left the Dive, Grace stayed for a few more beers. She grabbed a sandwich on the walk back, ate quietly while one of Birdie's Hallmark movies played in the background—the sand dollar, the arcade tickets, the paper bracelet, and the clunky necklace piled on the coffee table like a makeshift shrine—then curled up on the not-so-comfortable bed and passed out. She didn't stir all night. If she dreamed, she doesn't remember it.

Now Grace pulls herself up, sitting. Her limbs are still heavy with slumber, though her mind feels a bit clearer than it did yesterday. She stretches, rolls out her neck, then reaches toward the nightstand and pulls her journal—the one she had with her out on the jetty—onto her lap. The room, cast in slices of golden light, feels calm. She tries not to think too much about the final product. Instead, she just writes. Not a story—certainly not the one she's supposed to be finalizing for Mollie—but a mishmash of her thoughts. Questions. Little scenes that pop into her head. Bits of characters. Memories she puts back together with a fictional edge.

This is how it starts, Grace remembers. A story. Not at the end when everything is neat and tidy, when every problem's already been cleverly solved. Not on the computer, where the pressure to get each line perfect and polished glows back at you from the screen. A good narrative never starts from a clean place. It begins when it's messy. When the end feels so uncertain and far away that you're not sure it'll ever come.

When she's done, Grace closes the journal, knowing she's nowhere near finished with the work that's still ahead or even what it might become.

But for now, at least it feels like something.

A step.

~

Once she's dressed in a fresh tank and shorts, Grace bikes a few blocks to the bakery, eats a too-big jelly doughnut, and downs a coffee. When she's finished, she moves north again, though not with any intentions of traveling as far up the island as she did yesterday. This time, there's a different place she knows she needs to stop by, and not just loiter, but actually walk in.

Ten minutes later, she parks the cruiser in front of the shop and goes inside. It's a small spot, overstuffed but welcoming in a no-frills sort of way. Every square inch of the space is in use. Floor-to-ceiling shelves, stacked with paperbacks. Bins of books—old, slightly tattered secondhand choices—line the floor. Unlike some of the bookstores Grace came to love over her years in the city, all offering little cafés in the back or of-the-moment aesthetic choices—moody paint, themed reading nooks, strategic lighting—this beach bookshop is just the basics. The whole place smells like dust and old pages. There's not even a soft soundtrack of jazz or lo-fi playing. It's just shelved stories and silence.

Grace smiles at the older woman at the counter, then wanders into the stacks and pretends to browse, even though she knows she's here to find one specific thing.

It's not out on a front table like it might have been all those years ago when the cover was arranged in artful pyramids in bookshop windows across the country. It's not even out on a summer reading or "staff picks" table display. Grace has to walk to the back to find it, searching alphabetically through all the spines until she reaches the *W* section and lands on it.

There's only one copy. Grace's sophomore novel isn't in stock at all. She pulls *The Tides* from the shelf, runs her fingers over its cover—a transportive photograph of a sunset over the ocean filtered with hues of pinks to lightly suggest the novel's romantic themes. Grace opens it, flipping through all the pages she once worked so hard to create and get just right. It's like seeing the inner workings of her heart in print. Before she carries it to the register—paying, in part, to remember certain parts of her past—she turns back to the dedication page at the beginning.

For Birdie—we'll always have our beach.

Now Grace blinks away tears, closes the cover, and takes a step, turning past the next endcap, just to see what else is out.

That's when she sees her.

At the end of the aisle, sitting cross-legged on the floor, wearing too many turquoise rings, the nameplate necklace, cutoffs, and a faded college hoodie. She holds an opened copy of Virginia Woolf's *To the Lighthouse*—a seaside novel about time, relationships, and the quest for meaning—in her lap.

Cece. Nineteen. Midway through college and on the cusp of a new decade.

She's not the lovestruck girl in the arcade. Not a breezy teen, a half-tipsy twentysomething, or a trying-too-hard adult, either. This version looks a little sleep deprived, sort of overcaffeinated, and completely engrossed. She doesn't see Grace; she doesn't seem to see anything, actually, outside of the pages she's reading, except maybe her pile of writing utensils and journal, where she keeps jotting down notes. Grace recalls reading the book a half dozen times that summer. Not for an upcoming fall class, but because a former professor told her she should. He'd said she might be too young to understand it, but that if she read and reread it and kept returning to it, eventually the true meaning would set in.

Grace considers speaking up, maybe calling out her name just to see how she'll respond. Instead, she decides to watch this version from afar. Cece's focus is intense and yet relaxed—completely absorbed in what she's reading, not because she has to read it for a deadline or an exam, but because she wants to understand it, as if some secret she longs to comprehend—something about love or life—might be hidden within the language.

She spent every day with Ray that summer week. Things between them were the same, but not. They talked about different topics, not just the beach and whether they wanted to take a bike ride or go play miniature golf, but *real* things. Their future. Where they eventually envisioned they'd each end up. The lives they both saw for themselves—hers off in a big city, his someplace quiet, like Sea Drift. They wanted opposing things. Still, they were young and hopeful enough to ignore these early cracks.

You liked it, huh? he asked her that week. The two of them. A bench outside the bookshop. A bag of taffy. Heat rising off the asphalt. *Not just the internship, but all of it.*

Two weeks earlier, Grace finished her first internship at a small regional magazine in Philly. A nice office. A tall building. A few small bylines. A desk with her name.

I did. She still buzzed from the experience. It was all she talked about—not just the unpaid job but the feeling of it. Like she was doing something. Becoming something. Like not only she but also the things she wanted really mattered. *I hope I get a chance like that again. Maybe not the office, but the writing part, anyway.*

You will, Porter, he said, a quiet sadness tracing his words. *Of course you will.*

What makes you so confident? Their hands dipped into the bag at the same time, fingers tangling.

Because I know you. He handed her a green piece of candy. Mint. Her favorite. *And because I know you can.*

Grace didn't respond, just chewed a sticky bite for a long time. It thrilled her, the way he believed in her when she wasn't so sure she even believed in herself. But it was also terrifying.

Even though he hadn't directly said it, they both knew he didn't want that same life.

That just like a perfect vacation, some things—even ones we love—are only temporary.

Back in the bookshop, Grace remains where she is for a few minutes, standing in the stillness, studying Cece as she studies the classic text. Every couple of pages, she pauses, writes something down. An observation. Or a question. A brief note about something she doesn't comprehend. Not giving up on it because it's confusing or rushing to reach the end, just content to be working her way through the middle of it.

"Can I help anyone with anything?"

They both turn to look at the same time. To the right of them, the woman from the register has left her post to restock shelves. For a second so brief it's as if it doesn't even happen, Grace's and Cece's eyes meet. Grace freezes, not sure how to react, deciding instead to let Cece lead. The girl's lids narrow, something confusing or maybe very clear, washing over her face. She sits with it for a moment, then dismisses it as she closes her book.

"Actually, I'm ready to check out now. I'm already running late to meet a friend." Cece quickly gathers her things, still half looking at Grace. "I need to pay for this one, plus the stack I already left up front."

The woman nods, shelves the titles she's holding, then makes her way back to the counter. Cece follows in her footsteps. Before she disappears into a new aisle, she turns back.

"You look familiar." Cece gives her nameplate necklace a gentle tug. "Do I know you?"

How could she ever explain it? The fact that she doesn't know Grace, but that Grace does, in fact, know her. That they're the same and yet so different, too.

"No." Grace smiles and takes her in. "I don't think so."

At least, she thinks, *not yet.*

Cece turns to go. As she does, one of her many highlighters falls from the pile she clumsily holds and rolls across the floor. She keeps walking, not even noticing. Grace grabs it, ready to catch up to Cece and give it back. Instead, she slips it inside her own bag.

One more piece. One more small reminder.

Of the person Grace once was. The one who, in time, she might be able to become again.

TWENTY

Grace spends the rest of the day the same way her younger self often spent days in Sea Drift—out in one of the Adirondack chairs beneath the shade of a tree, her legs tucked into her chest, with a glass of iced tea balanced on the armrest and a good book in her hands. But not just any book. *Her* book. *The Tides*. The copy she bought from the island's bookshop before she left.

It's been so long since she's read it. There was a period—back when she was writing, revising, and rewriting again—when she had entire chapters nearly committed to memory. She could hear words and sentences coming, knew exactly how every scene would end. That was one of the hard parts about writing. You spent so much time with a story, hoping to get it right, that you became immune to it. Try as you might, you'd never have the opportunity to read it and experience it in the way your readers did.

Today, though, she finds that she's finally spent enough time separated from it to come close. There are whole scenes she's forgotten about, some passages that even make her laugh. For maybe the first time ever since those weekends back in her Manhattan studio when she cranked out the first draft, Grace is able to really get lost in it.

Her body aching from sitting like this for hours—save for the occasional bathroom or snack break—Grace finally puts the book down and wipes her bottom lashes. Overhead, the sun has shifted. It's late afternoon, almost dinnertime—that hour of the day when the beach transitions from one shift to the next. She goes into the outdoor shower and slips on her bathing suit for the first time since the tide-pool catastrophe. The fabric clings uncomfortably on her chest, not sitting quite right and still warped from drying on the wood planks in a heap. Before she leaves, Grace moves back inside, slides on a cover-up, and checks her phone before she heads out. There's one text from Adam, received hours ago.

Thought I'd check in, see how you're doing, his message reads. Assuming you're still down in Sea Drift? Alone?

She almost ignores it, then decides to send a fast reply, suddenly wanting him to know that she's okay.

I'm fine, Adam, she writes, grabbing her sunglasses from the counter, not overthinking her reply. Doesn't edit it. Doesn't offer further explanation. And, yes, I'm still here.

~

Grace walks down the dune barefoot, her flip-flops—as usual—left with the few pairs piled up at the top. The breeze is warm but no longer hot, a welcome feeling after sitting outside in the heat reading all day. Out on the beach, the lifeguards are gone, their white stands empty. A few families linger near umbrellas while their children skim-board through the shallow sheet of surf. Once she's on the sand, rather than taking a seat, she walks south past neighboring Dune Street to a part of the beach where the waves have always had a habit of rolling in just right.

She doesn't bother with a chair this time. Instead, she just carries down an old striped towel from the shed. Grace rolls it out, takes a seat near someone's small pile of belongings, cups warm sand in her palms, scans the water, then just watches and waits.

Even though he's far off in the distance—well past the buoys meant to keep everyone at safe depths—she knows it's him. The ways his arms move. The shape of his body. He's just a speck out there, a single figure in the water—a body on a surfboard, floating and waiting for just the right crest to form and carry him back in.

Grace used to love sitting here, watching him floating. He wasn't hers, and vice versa, their feelings for each other strong, though apparently not strong enough for them to ever take the next step to formal titles. Still, there was always something, even in moments like these when there was distance between them—whole bodies of water—that made them feel connected.

Now she turns away from the waves as something up the shore catches her eye. A blur of fur running along the wet sand and chasing a flock of seagulls like they're her old friends. *Hooper*. The dog spots Grace just as the birds fly away. She runs over, tail wagging, her body wet and sandy.

"Hey, girl," Grace whispers, patting Hooper's head as she playfully licks and jumps, inadvertently rumpling the towel. "It's good to see you again."

After a minute, Hooper settles, curling up next to Grace and resting her snout in her lap. Together, they watch Ray catch a wave. Her heart both flutters and calms—like old times—while she watches as he pulls himself up to standing. Her eyes, nearly against her will, track his body like it's the only thing here. He cuts a clean line through the surf and rides it until the swell runs its course and goes flat again. When he looks up at the beach, Grace gives him a timid wave. Slowly, he makes his way out of the water, his board tucked under his arm. This late in the season, the ocean's far too warm to require a wetsuit. Instead, he wears his bathing suit and nothing else. Water beads on his body—shoulders, chest, all tanned and tight. She looks down, aware now that she's staring. Still, her cheeks flush, the image of him that way imprinted in her mind.

"Hey," Ray says as he moves up the sand. Hooper, loyal as ever, springs up and runs to him as if she hasn't seen him in years. "I thought that was you." He drops his board, grabs a towel from his small pile of belongings, then shakes out his hair, the movement somehow both nostalgic and new all at once. "You're still here."

"You sound surprised," Grace says, proceeding carefully as she tries not to read too deeply into his words. *Why? Were you out there looking for me?* "Like maybe you hoped I wouldn't be."

He rubs the towel over his head, then ties it around his hips, the motion casual but familiar enough to make a knot form in her stomach. "I never said that, Grace."

On the shoreline, an older couple walks through the ankle-deep water, hand in hand. Hooper, ears perked, runs off in pursuit of more gulls.

"Why did you say that about my mother the other night?" Grace asks, not in a demanding or angry way. Just flat. Straightforward. Direct. "You said Birdie told you I'd be here—in Sea Drift, at the house, this week." A breeze picks up, blowing around sand. "Did you mean that literally? Or, like, you had a dream or—"

"Is that why you walked down here?" he asks, his tone reaching for tension despite the way he looks at her. "To ask me about your mom?"

I love when you come here to watch me, he told her so many times. *Knowing I have the water and you there, it's like there's nothing else in the world I want or need.*

"Maybe," she says, not entirely sure. "I don't really know."

"Look, I'm sorry your life hasn't quite worked out the way you'd hoped," Ray states, not directly answering her question. "Really, I am." A swoop of wet hair hangs over his forehead—one that in the past she would have reached out and touched. "Trust me, I know firsthand that it's not fun when things don't go the way you planned." He runs a finger over his head, brushing the strand back. "But I have my own life now." Ray looks down, trying to figure something out. When he tilts his face back up, his posture shifts, like something inside him aches. "Whatever's going on between you and Birdie, I think it's best that I don't get involved."

A feeling rises in her, a sour, burning sensation that makes her mouth watery.

"What is it you think you know about my life?" Her eyes swell with tears that don't fall.

Ray takes a step, suddenly close enough that she can almost feel the warmth of his solid frame. For a beat, she can't tell if he'll move again, continue to close the space that still separates them. Whether she wants him to. Either way, he doesn't.

"Enough to know that you're not happy," Ray says instead.

Near the water, Hooper runs too far down the coastline. Ray shouts for her to come back.

"Why'd you keep it?" she asks hesitantly, while her fingers trace circles in the sand. "The ring. All these years later. You never got rid of it."

He doesn't answer immediately. Still, the burn of whatever he's thinking shows on his face. "Just in case, I guess."

See you next year, Porter, he always said on their final day, riding his beach cruiser over to their block and giving her and Birdie one last big wave. *In the meantime, don't change too much, all right?* he'd joke as the Jeep pulled onto the boulevard and away.

Except for the year Grace turned twenty-five. She never gave him a chance.

"Why do you keep bringing up my mom?" Grace asks, shifting their conversation backward by a few degrees. "I don't understand." The coastal air, as well as the topic, casts her skin in goose bumps.

"Why are you asking me, Grace? Just ask her." He gestures toward the dunes and all that exists beyond them. "I've walked past your house every night this week, and each time, her Jeep's been sitting in the driveway." He runs his hands through his thick hair, like she used to love to do when he emerged from the water soaking wet. "Knowing Birdie, I'm sure she's sitting out back right now, drinking an iced tea and reading a book or something."

It hits her now. The fact that Ray's words are not part of some game he's playing. He simply doesn't know. Of course he doesn't. Meg hadn't talked to Ray about Grace. Caleb doesn't even know him; plus, even if he did, he'd have had no reason to tell him anything.

"I can't ask her, Ray."

Grace forces herself to swallow the sick feeling that creeps with increasing speed up her throat. She doesn't want to say it. Doesn't want to have to admit it for the thousandth time. She closes her eyes, like a child too young to understand the rules of hide-and-seek, wishing that by shutting her lids, she could just disappear. That the whole story she's about to tell by way of only a few brief words would disappear, too. The fact forms in her mind, like a sign she'd like to speed past. These last six months, she's told so many people. Her mother's teaching colleagues. The teller at Birdie's bank. Mr. Sam.

Briefly, Grace thinks back to one of her first sessions with Dr. Anne. On that day, Grace started crying the minute she entered the office and didn't stop until she left. She apologized for her blubbering emotions, like they were a silly character trait she hoped to edit out. At that meeting—Grace seated on a worn sofa, looking at the office's many potted plants—Dr. Anne explained that in the beginning, one tends to cognitively register loss, but the emotional recognition often comes later, after the services, after the initial shock, after the sympathy cards stop coming, when life settles down. That's usually when your heart catches up with your mind.

Now it hits her. Not just the loss but all it really means. Maybe it's the setting. Or something in the air. Or that she's finally been away from home long enough to think. But she can't deny the truth. It's none of these things.

It's him.

His presence. His energy. This person who knows so many layers of her history, like a nesting doll that contains years of her past. There was something about him that would always let her put down her guard. To be present. To be her most authentic self in countless ways.

"Because, Ray." Grace reopens her eyes. The words take their time coming out. Before she speaks, they feel truer than any other time she's said them out loud. "Birdie's gone."

"What?" A look of genuine bewilderment molds Ray's expression. "What are you talking about?" Behind him, Hooper continues to explore the farther stretches of the coast. "When?"

"This winter," she explains, looking out at the horizon. "February. It was sudden. I had absolutely zero warning or time to prepare."

Absorbing this information, Ray closes his eyes. His bare chest rises and falls out of cadence. "Jesus, Grace. I don't know what to say." He reopens them. "I saw her car and, well . . ." He trails off while he tries to wrap his mind around it. "I had no idea."

Tears fall down Grace's face. Not a heavy sob or a dramatic downpour. Just a few sad lines of salt tracking down her cheeks.

"I told Meg," Grace admits, too wrapped up in her emotions to really think about what she's saying. "I ran into her at Smitty's the day I got on the island. We had dinner at the Beachcomber the other night, before you showed up on my porch."

"You had dinner with Meg? She knows you're here?" He looks up and down the beach, like his sister might suddenly appear out of thin air. "She didn't tell me that."

Grace sighs. "She said she thought it was best to leave the past in the past." Her fingers trail across broken bits of shells. "She said you're finally in a good place." Grace redirects her gaze upward, locking eyes with him. "She didn't expand on what that meant. Did something happen?" she asks, wanting to know and yet not sure she does. "Is that why you moved here?"

A new wave rolls in, its foamy cap creeping farther up the beach.

Another breath. Another long sigh. "I was engaged," Ray says, his words flat of feeling. "Down in Virginia. We never made it to the aisle, though. She broke it off a month before our date without any real explanation." Hooper finally runs back over. "I needed a reset after that. I came up here a few weeks later, rented an apartment for a couple months. Thought it was a good place to be while I figured out my next steps." The dog shakes off her golden coat, releasing a spray of water. "Turns out I'm not all that different than I was at twenty-five." His head pans from left to right as he takes in the setting. "October marks two years that I've been back."

"I'm really sorry," Grace says, meaning it. Wishing he hadn't experienced heartache. Wishing no one ever did. "About your engagement," she adds, even as something inside her burns with anger and jealousy for this unnamed person who left him, despite the fact that she once did the same thing.

"It's fine. At least, now it is," Ray tells her, his voice soft. He pets Hooper's soaking-wet head. "Life happens in funny ways. It ended up being a blessing in disguise for Meg, you know? Me moving here and being a few hours closer than I was before. My parents come up from down south for long stretches as much as they can, but they're getting older. It's hard." He takes a breath. "Me living in Sea Drift has made things a lot easier for everyone. Traffic's a nightmare, but if I time it right, I can head up to her place in Pennsylvania once or twice a week to give her a hand." A small smile molds his lips. "Hooper here keeps me company on the long drives. She's a good copilot."

"It's been a blessing for Meg?" Grace asks, confused. "What do you mean?" She thinks of their conversation—Meg glowing as she talked about her simple but perfect life. "What have you needed to give her a hand with?"

Ray's face changes then, his expression forming into a hybrid of frustration and sadness. "Let me guess." He sighs, long and loud. "Meg told you she's staying at the beach house with the kids and my folks, yeah?" He pinches the bridge of his nose, then releases it. "Ben's stuck at work for the week, right?"

"Well . . . yeah," Grace says, still replaying their dinner together, as well as their run-in at Smitty's, in order to determine if there was some detail she missed. "Is that not the case?"

Nearby, a family—dressed in coordinating blues—poses near the water for a photo, their arms wrapped around each other, their hair billowing just so in the evening breeze.

"Meg's a widow," Ray states. "Ben died in an accident last May."

The nauseous feeling returns to Grace, stronger this time, less like a ripple and more like a tsunami. Her fingers shake. She opens her mouth, but her vocal cords are paralyzed. Not that it matters. Not that she'd have a clue what to say.

"My sister's a mess, Grace," Ray continues. "She puts on a good act, but that's all it is. The last few months, whenever she sees someone she used to know or meets someone new, she just pretends it didn't happen. That her whole life worked out perfectly, according to plan." He reaches for the rest of his belongings. "I guess that just feels easier to her than having to relay the story of what actually happened over and over again." He clips Hooper's leash to her collar. "It's funny. I used to think people came to this island for different reasons, you know? To relax. To get away. Since moving here full-time, though? I'm starting to believe that it's just a pretty place where people like to come and grieve."

The family, having captured the perfect shot, unlocks arms and begins to walk away.

"How do I find her?" Grace asks. "What's their rental address? I want to talk to her."

"Don't go to the house," Ray insists, unwrapping his towel from his waist and tossing it over his shoulder. "Not with Emma and Quinn around. It's only recently that they're happy again and settling back into a normal routine." He slides his dry T-shirt over his head. Grace's eyes instinctively follow as the fabric slides over the lines of his chest. He slips on his hat backward, just like when they were teens. "But you can find my sister pretty much every night over at my place after the kids fall asleep."

"O-okay," Grace stammers, reaching for something to jot down his address, but realizing she doesn't have anything—no phone, no pen. "Where do you live?"

Ray's shoulders shake with a quiet laugh. "Not at my house, Grace," he clarifies. "At my bar. The Dive." He closes his eyes, a whole story unfolding in his mind. When he opens them again, he looks right at her, locking in her gaze before she can turn away. "I got a gig there a few nights a week when I first moved here. Something to hold me over. But then I remembered someone told me a long time ago that wasn't a very grown-up plan." The breeze blows, and it feels cooler than it should.

"An opportunity presented itself early last spring, a few months before we lost Ben. Maybe in some ways I owe it to you."

"Owe what to me?"

"The fact that I followed the signs, took a chance, and bought it."

"Wait." Grace's thoughts filter back to yesterday. Caleb. Cold beers. The conversation. "You own the Dive?"

Ray doesn't respond with words, only a head nod.

"Then you know Caleb," she says, the facts stacking up like a building, stories upon stories. "My landlord." Her breath shortens. "And his sister. The one who . . ."

She doesn't complete her sentence. There's no need.

A new sense of quiet settles over them, as if the landscape—picking up on this emotional shift—has turned everything down by a notch.

"I do," he says, his voice traced with a faint ache. "And for a short while, at least, I did."

"Ray, I—"

"There's nothing to say, Grace. You don't have to scramble and try." The dog starts to run, her leash tugging Ray's arm. "She was just a new friend." A soft sound escapes him—one caught between a sigh and a laugh. "There was a minute there when I thought maybe there was the potential for something more, but—" Ray stops, cutting himself short. "Well, until I realized . . ." He trails off, his thought hanging unfinished.

"What?" Grace asks, sensing there's something else he needs to say.

"The last time I saw her, she asked me to help her with something. Her parents own a rental on the island. I knew that; I just didn't know which one. Her folks had a new couch being delivered. She wanted me to hang at the house with her, wait for the truck to arrive, then give her a hand making sure they positioned it in just the right place." He shakes his head, waiting before he speaks again. "Like I said before, Grace, life really does happen in funny ways."

Another beat of silence. Another memory. Another sign.

"She literally led me to your doorstep," Ray says.

TWENTY-ONE

Grace walks alone up the coastline. Ray and Hooper are gone now, off to the Dive for a night shift, apparently. Most of the other stragglers who were still down here—posing for pictures, flying kites—have packed up and left. In the sky, the light has softened. All around, the air has cooled. The day is winding down. Deep inside her, so many thoughts and emotions feel like they're starting to settle, too.

Although she can't see them, Grace knows that beyond the dunes, inside the many rental homes, people are moving on. Children are being coaxed into bathtubs. Families are gathering around outdoor tables to eat. There are conversations. Maybe music. Laughter. The bittersweet hope that life stays like this forever, that these sorts of nights never actually end.

Maybe what Ray said was right. Perhaps this place was never just a vacation spot—a stretch of tide-smoothed sand a little ways out in the Atlantic where one could get away for a few precious days and forget. In reality, maybe it was a place people came to remember. The things they'd lost. The versions of themselves they used to be.

Grace keeps going, watching as the water ebbs and flows over her feet. It recedes. Then returns. Recedes again. The waves try so hard to reach farther ahead but always get pulled back. While she moves, Grace periodically stops and picks up broken bits of shells—the many fractured pieces of what were once full stories that have washed up on this shoreline. She rubs some pieces between her fingers and wonders how many people on this island—beneath the layers of sunscreen and rash guards, behind the sunburned cheeks and easy smiles—are also grieving, whether they say it out loud or not. Meg. Caleb. Ray. What do they all believe they'll find here? A recollection they can reach out and hold? A reminder of the people they were before their plans got derailed and grief became their guiding force? Or is it both these things?

Grace examines a shard of clamshell. She runs her fingers over its grooves and the chips along its edge. They're smooth. Grace drops it back in the surf, wondering how many years of tumbling around in rough water it took for it to finally become that way.

Maybe the truth is that Grace didn't drive all those hours back here on a whim to rediscover something about her writing. Maybe it wasn't to seek out some magical elixir in the coastal air that would help her heal. Perhaps the real answer is because she hoped that when she did return, in some small way, it might all feel like it did before. Before the miscarriages. Before she lost her voice. Before Birdie died. Before Adam left. Back when she still had a sense not only of who she was but also of who she wanted to be—where she was heading in the world. Back when she felt less like a ghost of herself and more just like . . . Grace.

A little way up, she sees someone else wading through the water—a teenager. Grace's heart skips, then stumbles. She's not even sure she wants to see her again. That happy girl—the one who still believed the future was a bright, beautiful promise. The one who still believed in anything at all.

The person turns, and Grace sees it's a stranger.

Of course it is, she thinks. *Because that carefree girl I used to be is gone.*

~

When Grace reaches the top of the dune—her back to the ocean and her face looking out toward the bay—she doesn't immediately realize that anything is different. The air smells like charcoal. Children bike up and down the street. A couple sits on their rental home's front porch, talking and having a drink. It's all the same except for one subtle, but noticeable, change.

A car in the driveway of Number 116, parked behind Birdie's Jeep. A newer, black SUV. Sleek lines. Flashy brand. New York plates.

Grace picks up her pace but only slightly, not sure yet whether she hopes this is one more thing she might be imagining. She doesn't even stop to pick up her flip-flops. Instead, she just keeps moving, steady and forward, down the sandy decline. The dune grass sways on either side of her, a quiet and peaceful melody. Its tune doesn't match the sounds inside her. Pulse thumping. Lungs working overtime. Heart beating too hard.

She reaches the street and steps onto the asphalt. The surface is no longer hot, though it's undeniably jagged. What feels like a dozen pebbles lodge themselves into her feet, a larger one—indisputably sharper than the rest—jabs itself into her heel, instantly intensifying the subtle ache she's tried to blow off the last few days. Even so, she presses forward, putting her weight on her toes while her gaze remains ahead.

Finally, she stops at the curb, right next to the For Sale sign. Although her mind is a jumble of words—thoughts and questions, a million fragments she's not sure will add up to anything—Grace doesn't say any of them. Instead, she just stands and waits for him to begin.

"I brought you a cupcake," Adam says from his place on the front steps. "You know, for your birthday." He holds up a small white box as proof. "And an iced coffee. Regular. With coconut milk." He smiles, but it's small. "I got it right this time." He gestures at the plastic cup beside him. "I've been sitting here for a while, though, so the ice mostly melted. It might be a little watered down at this point."

"What are you doing here?" Grace asks, the queasy feeling she experienced on the sand returning.

"In my defense, I did call," Adam explains. "About an hour ago. Right after I got off the parkway, before I reached the bridge."

"My phone's inside." Her mouth becomes watery again. "I was up at the beach."

"Alone?"

"What?" Grace's eyes snap shut. She shakes her head, reopens them. "What does that mean?"

Adam's posture straightens by an inch. "Nothing."

Out on the street, a young family—probably on their way out for ice cream—pushes a stroller while a toddler runs next to them.

"How was the water?" Adam asks, brushing past his previous question. "Your clothes are dry. Did you not swim?"

"You didn't answer me. Why are you sitting here right now? You said you were at the lake house. In New Hampshire. Seven hours away."

"It just seemed foolish," he explains. "Me, alone on the water up there. You, by yourself down here." He sighs. "I thought maybe we could both use some company." Adam doesn't move, though his sight shifts to a spot just beyond where Grace stands. "Hey, buddy," he says suddenly, sounding cordial, like he's just some guy exchanging pleasantries with other people on vacation. "How's it going? Nice night, right?"

Grace turns to look back slowly, though she already senses who's there.

"Caleb," she says when she sees him. He's still relaxed, as usual, though dressed a touch nicer—a short-sleeved button-down, flip-flops. Beachy, but slightly elevated. "Hi."

A flash of confusion crosses his face. He licks his lips while his eyes taper. Before they have a chance to stay that way too long, he looks up at the dune, then down at the bayside of the street. "How's the house working out, Grace?"

"What?" A shiver runs through her, the flimsy cover-up she still wears doing nothing to keep her warm. "What are you talking about?"

"Number 116," Caleb states, his signature warm smile returning. "An oldie but a goodie, even if the plumbing's not the best. Hope you're enjoying it." Caleb points at the sign. "Turns out there's already a prospective buyer potentially lined up. From the sounds of it, it'll probably become a year-round property. No more summer rentals after this season."

"Sounds like a good investment," Adam, always in business-mode, pipes up from the steps. "Turn it into something nice. This place has needed a good gut-job for a long time."

Caleb nods. "Anyway, didn't mean to interrupt. Enjoy your evening." He rolls back on his heels. "If you need anything—for the house, I mean—my number's in the welcome basket," he says, then moves up the street.

"Landlord, I take it?" Adam asks when they're alone again.

Grace tries to catch her breath, but it doesn't work. Her chest shudders as she struggles to get the right amount of air down. "The last time I saw you, you were collecting items from our house—the one we don't share anymore because you left it. And then, out of the blue, you called me the other night to reminisce. Now you're . . . here?" She crosses her arms over her chest, wishing she had additional layers covering her body. "Why? What did I miss?"

"How's your writing going?" Adam asks, not the first time he's disregarded her inquiries since he arrived. "Have you found any . . . inspiration?" Somehow, his question comes across as both sincere and suspicious. "You know, since you've been back down here?"

Her thoughts filter back several days to their last in-person interaction. The kitchen. The pages Adam accidentally knocked off the table. The way his brows knit and his expression—one that flirted with accusation—reshaped the look on his face.

"Is that why you're here?" The jealousy had always been there, ever since that night on the High Line. They never talked about it. Instead, it remained quiet and invisible, something that always hummed beneath the surface. "To ask about my . . . writing?"

"No. It isn't." Adam's intonation isn't entirely convincing. He sets down the bakery box, kneads his hands together. He doesn't say anything else just yet, instead taking a minute to look at the ground. "It was to tell you that

I had a dream about you the other night," he admits. "The night I got to New Hampshire. The day I stopped by and saw you at the house."

It's hard for Grace to pinpoint what she feels in this moment. Anger? Regret? Sadness? Nostalgia? Relief? Or is it all of these things, the emotions twisted up like adjacent plants whose roots have grown into each other, the sentiments intertwined and tangled up?

"Don't you want to know what it was about?" Adam asks.

"I'm not sure," Grace admits.

He keeps his hands folded, slowly looks up. "It was about us," he states. "That first autumn we were dating back in the city." Adam stops, presses his thumbs together. "You were so happy. All these heartaches of the last few years weren't so much as a thought yet." He picks at his fingernail. "It made me miss you. That version of you. That version of us, maybe."

Before Grace can speak—to shout or spew a litany of questions or something in between—Adam stands.

"Here." He hands her the bakery box, the iced coffee still perspiring on the step. "I wasn't sure if you'd want me to stay or not, so I booked myself a room at one of the old motels a few blocks south." He doesn't try to hug Grace or kiss her or touch her in any way. Instead, he meets her eyes. "If you want me to come back—if you need anything—all you have to do is say the word." Adam moves to his SUV, opens the driver's-side door. "Grace?" he says before he gets in.

She looks at him, not sure she wants to hear what comes next.

"I know your second book didn't sell nearly as well as your first one," Adam says. "Even so, I wish the draft you'd been looking at the other day had been the one inspired by us instead."

~

Back inside the house, the evening lasts forever.

The hours refuse to speed up and pass. Grace attempts to eat—cereal, leftover candy, nothing with actual substance—but her stomach is too much of a mess. She sits at the kitchen table, then tries and fails to process all that's transpired these last few hours in her journal, though none of her thoughts come out right. By the time it's dark, she clicks on the television and watches one of Birdie's Hallmark movies all the way through.

Nothing helps.

The feeling inside her, it isn't just grief anymore.

Grief implies a deep feeling of sorrow over something you've lost—something that, despite all your longing and bargaining and wishing, you can't ever get back. A piece of your past that's gone forever. A picture of your future that won't come to be. What happened this evening out on the steps was something different—having something, someone, she thought she'd lost turn up out of nowhere and make her question everything all over again.

Now it's the middle of the night. The credits for another movie roll across the screen, the next one already queued up behind it—another charming story where everything works itself out.

Grace mutes the TV but doesn't turn it off. The glow feels comforting. For a few minutes, she watches it without any sound and thinks about Adam, his comments about her creative work, his dream, that first season they spent together and the many seasons that came after it, all of which landed them here.

Grace looks at the items she's collected this week, laid out on the coffee table. The sand dollar. The arcade tickets. The paper bracelet. The chunky necklace. The highlighter. Her copy of *The Tides*, the cover curled back. The unopened bakery box sits next to it.

Slowly, she peels back the lid. Inside is a perfect pink confection, just like the ones she and Adam enjoyed together the first birthday of hers they were together. The night of her actual birthday, they celebrated with Birdie in Sea Drift—blue crabs on the patio, swirl cones on the boardwalk. The following week, Adam planned a fancier evening. Dinner in the city. A champagne toast. Cupcakes at some of-the-moment bakery. Cocktails and dancing with friends.

It hits Grace now. All of it. Their past, cut short. Their future, potentially still ahead. Not knowing if she's meant to go forward or backward. If she should begin again or let it all go.

Grace tosses down the cupcake box and runs toward the bathroom, her hand pressed against her mouth until she makes it inside, all the feelings she's been processing but unable to put into words finally finding a way to come out.

She gargles and splashes cold water on her face, her body empty of nearly everything. From the living room, she grabs her phone, too tired to click off the TV, then heads to bed.

Before she shuts her eyes, Grace taps her device to life, then opens her message screen.

I changed my mind, she types. I need you. At the beach house. I don't want to be alone.

She doesn't wait to see if the signal catches.

Grace is dreaming by the time the message finally goes through.

PART THREE

Now

TWENTY-TWO

Wednesday

Grace wakes to the smell of something warm and sweet.

For a minute, her eyes still closed, she thinks she's dreaming. Imagining. That she's remembering all those summers of her childhood, when Birdie would rise early, get started on preparing a delicious breakfast, never wanting to waste one vacation minute. Her lids blink open. Sunlight filters into the bedroom at slanted angles. The scent becomes stronger. Vanilla, maybe. Something cakey. A cabinet slams shut, followed by clattering. A pan sizzling. She pulls herself upright, realizes her senses aren't caught in a memory. They're experiencing these things now.

"Good morning, birthday girl," a woman's voice announces when Grace pads down the hallway in her pajamas, her heel still raw from her sand-scraped walk back from the dune. "I burned a few because this pan is absolutely garbage—half the Teflon's scratched off." She turns, offers a conspiratorial smile. "Also, I'm guessing people don't lock their front doors in Sea Drift?" Her head tilts as her eyes narrow with curiosity. "Why are you limping?"

Jenny.

Grace rubs away some remaining sleep and fully takes in the scene. A plate of bacon cools on the counter. Two glasses of juice are already poured. A colorful gift bag stuffed with bright tissue sits on the table beside Caleb's welcome basket. The house, which had been practically silent all week, newly full of life.

"Wh-what are you doing here?" Grace asks, ignoring Jenny's question and instead choosing to look around the room for more clues. "What time is it?"

Jenny, dressed in chino shorts, a PTA T-shirt, and a purple party hat, glances at her watch, the one she uses for every imaginable thing—scheduling playdates, counting her steps, probably navigating her way down here and figuring out how to fix things. "A little after ten." She flips a pancake. "At this point, we'll consider this brunch."

With a wave of her spatula, Jenny instructs Grace to sit, then brings her one of the home's old blue cups and a piled-high plate. Grace, still feeling woozy, takes a seat. The pancakes, like always, look perfect. Golden. Fluffy. She picks a crispy bit off one of the edges, nibbles it.

"Also, I take it you've been on a hunger strike since you got down here?" Jenny slides bacon onto Grace's plate. "The cabinets are basically barren. You didn't even have cooking spray." She leans down, kisses the top of Grace's head. "I've already been to that cute but sort of hodgepodge market down the street twice." She moves back toward the stove. "In case you were wondering, they stock every variety of Popsicle known to man, but not a single piece of bread."

Grace takes another small bite—cautious in case her body doesn't react the right way—thinking back to last night and the text she sent before she fell asleep.

"I didn't think you'd come so fast," she admits, cautiously swallowing. "I figured you'd call me when you woke up, maybe we'd come up with a plan."

Jenny rests a hand on her hip, uses her free one to adjust her pointy party hat. "I have three children under the age of six, Grace. I *was* up when your message came through." She smiles. "Lucky for you, Eric is able to work remotely today and tomorrow. Not sure how much he'll actually accomplish with the baby's sleep schedule, as well as the other two sprinting laps through the house, but he'll figure it out." She rinses some things in the sink. "He has a meeting in his office early Friday afternoon, but other than that, we're good to go, my friend." She clicks off the range, makes herself a plate. "Turns out when I only have to pack for myself and don't need to worry about grabbing eight hundred articles of tiny clothing, a dozen different granola bars, and an entire pharmacy's worth of just-in-case medical supplies, I can do it incredibly fast." Jenny slides onto a seat, tucks one leg up against her chest like they're teenagers. "Now dish and tell me why I'm here."

Grace's thoughts rewind back to last night. The iced coffee. The cupcake. Little details that once would have made her happy now a source of confusion and pain. She tries for another bite of pancake, but the feeling in her stomach returns.

"Adam's on the island." She sets down her fork. "I was out on the beach last night, trying to make sense of things with Ray, and when I walked back, Adam was just sitting on the porch, waiting for me." She crosses one leg, folding her ankle over her knee. "He said he got himself a hotel room a few blocks south of here."

"I'm confused." Jenny sips her juice, then without a word, grabs Grace's foot and inspects it while they talk. "I figured your text had something to do with Ray," she says, her maternal impulses—instincts Grace, despite her longing to be a mother, doesn't seem to intrinsically have—quickly turning up by several notches. She twists Grace's now noticeably red heel in her hand. "Or Birdie. Or I don't know, just . . . you." She rubs the tips of her fingers together, sharpening her nails like they're knives. "How did he even know you were here?"

Grace pushes away her plate. "He called the other night from the lake house. He was reminiscing . . . or something." She thinks back to their conversation and the wistfulness in his tone. "I think he's having second thoughts." She winces as Jenny uses her fingernails to expertly pluck the splinter straight out of Grace's skin with the ease and precision of a surgeon. "You know, if you'd given me *five* minutes to actually process the fact that you're here, I would have gone ahead and actually *asked* you for your help with that."

"Would you have?" Jenny's brows lift. "It's out, but you definitely have a little infection." She wipes the retrieved splinter on a napkin. "How long has that thing been in there?"

"Not long," Grace lies.

Jenny gives her a side-eye.

"Fine," Grace admits through a huff. "All week."

"Well, did you put anything on it?" Jenny asks.

"Umm."

"Grace," Jenny says, her voice sounding like a sigh, "why not?"

Grace peers at her foot. She notes how much redder it looks now than when she was out on the jetty and wonders if a day will ever come when she'll be equipped like Birdie and Jenny to take care of these sorts of things. "Will you yell at me if I say I was sort of hoping it'd just magically go away?"

"Come on." Jenny folds up the napkin. "You know you can't ignore stuff like that. The longer you let these things linger, the worse they get and the more time they take to heal."

Told you, love, Grace nearly hears Birdie whisper.

Jenny shakes her head. "Anyway, back to the topic." She gives Grace's foot a fast squeeze. "After what Adam pulled on you at the start of this summer, does he still have the right to indulge in things like second thoughts?"

"I don't know. I was up half the night trying to wrap my head around it."

Jenny stands, grabs the syrup from the counter, then tops off both their plates, like a bartender realizing her customers are in need of a heavier pour. When she puts it back next to the stove, she lifts something else in its place. "Meanwhile, I read back through the first two chapters while you were asleep." In her hands, Jenny holds Grace's folded-back copy of *The Tides*. "It was on the coffee table when I got here."

Jenny knew the story—both the fictionalized account and the real one. How many nights of their youth had they curled up together during sleepovers while Grace went on and on about the boy from the beach? How many times had they visited each other during college with Jenny catching Grace "accidentally" calling other guys on her campus *Ray*? How many phone calls in their late twenties had Jenny listened through as Grace gave bullet-pointed reasons why Adam was such a great catch, as if she needed to rationalize her choice?

Jenny smiles, sets down Grace's book. "Having second thoughts of your own?"

"I'm not sure," Grace admits.

Jenny pulls off her hat, revealing an indentation along her chin from the too-tight elastic band, and rejoins Grace at the table. "How about we change gears for a minute?" She nudges the gift bag closer to Grace. "Open it."

"You really didn't have to bring me something. You leaving your family and driving down here first thing this morning is *more* than a sufficient birthday gift."

"I promise it's nothing," Jenny assures her. "Didn't cost me a dime."

Grace removes the pastel tissue and pulls out a picture frame, its edges decorated with glittery flowers and hearts. Inside it is a faded photograph of sixteen-year-old Grace and Jenny on junior prom night—their hair twisted into fancy updos, Jenny's still dyed blue thanks to her "Niffer" stage, way too much glitter on their eyes, colorful corsages at their wrists.

"You made me nostalgic the other day when we were on the phone and you were going through Birdie's boxes," Jenny explains.

Grace examines the picture, suddenly remembering that night as if it were yesterday.

"I like to think maybe we're still a bit like those girls." Jenny laughs. "Just a touch less flexible, and with better makeup application skills." She takes another bite of her breakfast, then pushes her plate away. "So other than all *that* news, and the fact that you've self-elected to mildly infect your own foot, what else have I missed since you came back down here?"

Grace's vision drifts to the coffee table and the strange little shrine that's taken shape there throughout the week—the girl from the prom photo existing somewhere among the pile.

"Honestly?" Grace sighs. "More than I can logically explain right now," she says.

TWENTY-THREE

After breakfast, Jenny—pleased to be child-free for forty-eight hours—insists on cleaning up the kitchen and then driving herself to the real grocery store on the far end of the island to pick up snacks, fruit, and a few cases of seltzer (*Based on that little bombshell, sounds like we'll need wine, too!*) so they're well stocked for the next few days. Using her most stern and motherly tone, she instructs Grace to stay put (*It's your vacation; you don't need to be running errands. That's what I'm here for now.*), take a hot shower, give her foot a good scrub (*The* one *time I don't have the kids' first aid kit in my purse!*), then get out in the fresh air for a little while to relax, think, and take care of herself until Jenny gets back.

Grace, happy to have someone else take charge, grabs a towel and heads out back. Once the water temperature from the scaly showerhead evens out, she steps into the stream, hoping to rinse away at least some of her mixed-up feelings. She washes her body and does her best to clean her heel. For the first time this week, she pauses long enough to look—*really* look—at it. She can't recall the exact moment it transformed from a dull ache into something that truly hurt, or how long she managed to ignore it. Now, though, she sees she's put too much pressure on it, shifting her weight while she convinced herself it wasn't so bad, telling herself it would work itself out, only for it to turn out worse.

Once the area is clean, she flicks open the lid on the strawberry shampoo bottle and lathers her hair in the comforting artificial scent. All those years, she never wondered about who owned the house, but now she can't stop thinking about Caleb's parents going to the five-and-dime every few weeks to replace the bottle, creating the illusion that the same one was always there. Maybe the memories the fragrance conjured provoked certain feelings—old times they wished they could reclaim, old wounds they were trying to heal—inside them, too.

Once she's dressed in what's become her uniform this week—shorts, a tee, a salt-stained hat, and a pair of sunglasses to cover her puffy eyes—she goes out front, pulls the cruiser upright, and starts to ride, knowing in which direction to head. Jenny was right. You can't let certain things fester. Doing so only extends the pain. She heads south, past the market, beyond Dune Street and the amusement pier, until she reaches the small pharmacy a little ways past it.

Grace pushes open the glass door and is instantly greeted by a vaguely medicinal smell paired with sunscreen and citronella candles, compliments of the end-of-summer display right up front. The store is mostly quiet—a teenager stocking allergy medications, a woman squinting next to a tower of reading glasses. Grace grabs a basket. She breezes through the aisles—shampoos, baby items, dental products—then slows as she rounds the corner into the greeting card section. For a second, Grace pauses, imagining Birdie—a lover of handwritten notes, sentiments that one could hold on to and read over the years—standing there, deliberating between something heartfelt or funny, then ultimately buying both.

"You'll miss all my silly notes someday," Birdie always said when Grace laughed at the fact that her mother gave her multiple cards for her birthday, each one inscribed with a whole paragraph of wishes.

"I'm sure you're right," Grace would shoot back, then squeeze her mother's hand. "But not today, because you're still right here."

How foolish Grace had been to think they had so much time.

Now she walks away from the aisle and turns again. Naturally, the items she needs—Band-Aids, hydrogen peroxide—are organized immediately beside the family-planning products. Pregnancy tests. Ovulation kits. Things she once required with such regular frequency that she had them set up on a monthly delivery subscription.

She always chose the "good" brands, those that promised the earliest detection and clearest lines, like certainty and dreams were things you could buy. She reaches out, lifts one of the boxes, the false promises printed all over it branded into her memory.

"Grace?" A voice rings out from the end of the aisle. "Sweetheart? Is that you?"

Her face instantly hot, Grace shoves the box back on the shelf like it's contraband, her fingers quickly working to grab a tube of antibiotic ointment to toss into her basket instead. She turns. Carol Murphy stands at the endcap. She holds a box of Popsicles and some children's Motrin. Her strawberry-blond bob is brushed back beneath her visor. A pair of sunglasses hangs from the front of her preppy cover-up.

"I was hoping I'd run into you at some point," Carol says, already making her way toward Grace. "Meg told me you two had dinner together the other night." She folds her arms around Grace and gives her a tight squeeze, the ice-cold Popsicle box pressing against her back. "I'm so, so sorry about Birdie," she whispers into Grace's neck. "Meg told me about that, too." She pulls back, a trace of wetness in her eyes. "Burt and I had no idea."

"Thank you," Grace says, not able to get much else out.

Carol pulls back, loosens her grip on the Motrin, and wipes a tear from her eye. For a moment, she just stands there, staring at Grace with a familiar look of pity. Carol inhales, collecting herself, though it's clear her mind's been flooded by a million memories. For so long, their two families spent their favorite week of the season together—separate houses, yes, but so many shared moments from those coming-of-age years.

"I have such fond memories of sitting by the tide pools with your mother, the two of us having a cocktail and laughing while we watched you kids all play." Carol's lids briefly close, like someone pulling down window shades, before she opens them back up again. "We were just reminiscing about those times when we had lunch together here on the island last year."

In an instant, the whole world stops.

"What?" Grace asks. "When did you see my mom?"

As far as Grace knew, Birdie hadn't been back to Sea Drift since their last visit together, the summer before Grace was married. It was their tradition, one they'd enjoyed together over the years, and one they'd let go together, too. Or so Grace thought.

"Last August, sweetheart. You were up in New England. I think that's what Birdie said, at least. For your birthday. We bumped into each other up at the lighthouse, then got clam strips over at that little spot we used to love near the inlet." Carol wipes the bottom of the Popsicle box, the corner of it dripping. "Burt and I spent most of last summer staying with Meg and the kids in Pennsylvania to help them with—" She stops herself, waves a hand. "Just with *everything*." She quickly sniffles, trying to get past the emotions embedded in that single word. "Anyway, I was only on the island for the day to help Ray with some things." She stops, one brow lifting in question. "I'm sure Birdie mentioned to you after our run-in that he lives in Sea Drift full-time now."

Grace doesn't answer, instead just forcing herself to smile while her heartbeat thuds.

"Anyway," Carol continues, "he'd rented an apartment up on the north end of the island the first year he was here, but he finally bought the most *adorable* little house on the bay late last spring, not long after he bought the bar." She grins, proud to tell her this, but it fades fast, this one point of happiness quickly overshadowed by the other life-changing event that unfolded for their family around the same time. "After everything that happened with Ben, it took him a few months before he really started to make it into a proper home." She rolls her eyes, but in a loving way. "My son is great at a lot of things, but picking out curtains and bath linens is *not* one of them."

While Carol talks, Grace thinks back to her trip to Maine last August. She and Adam sitting on the water. Adam telling her he wasn't sure he shared her dream for a family anymore and that he needed a long—maybe permanent—break from the topic before he could consider whether he wanted to try again. They were just sentences, but they carried such weight. The future they envisioned together, the one they were clinging to with relentless hope in countless waiting rooms and on endless examination tables for years, just . . . gone. Throughout that trip, Grace snuck off a dozen times to call her mother. To talk. To cry. To fill her in.

Birdie was home that week. She told Grace that fact plenty of times. Making lesson plans for the upcoming school year, the last she planned to work before retiring, something she kept putting off until she had a grandchild to spoil and regularly visit. Working in her little vegetable garden in the back of the town house. Meeting friends in the nearby park for walks.

Was she here, alone, back at the beach—*their* beach—and never said it? And if so, why? Was she looking for something? Or someone? Was there a reason she didn't tell Grace?

"Grace, honey?" Carol says now. "Are you okay? You look a little . . . off." Her lips curl with worry. "I hope I didn't say the wrong thing or . . ."

"It's fine," Grace states, even though her mind is a swirl of new, even more complicated questions than those she had when she first woke up. "I'm still just . . . processing."

Carol nods just as another customer walks down their aisle. "Well, I'd better get going." She holds up the items in her hands. "I'm sure Meg told you the other night about Quinn's ear infection. Naturally, now Emma's fighting one, too." She shakes her head at the ludicrous nature of motherhood. "I should probably swap out these Popsicles and get a fresh box. They're likely half melted at this point." They embrace again. "I'm glad I saw you, sweetie."

When Carol finally lets go, she steps back and offers Grace one last smile before she walks away. Grace, too shaken by Carol's news to concentrate, begins to toss a random assortment of first aid items from the shelf into her basket, her fingers moving on autopilot as she hardly even looks to see what she's throwing in.

"You know," Carol says an instant later, popping back around the endcap, "Meg told me a little bit about your conversation at dinner the other night." She looks down at the ground, like she's uncomfortable stating this next part. "Not just about Birdie." Slowly, she raises her face again. "I understand you're staying at the house by yourself. If you don't have plans tomorrow night, you ought to drop by Ray's bar, the Dive. All of us Murphys will be there, even the kids, so long as Emma's antibiotics kick in."

"Um, maybe," Grace states, struggling to get in enough air.

"It's just a little get-together," Carol explains. "For Ray." She swallows, a brief moment of hesitation. "Life's been so hectic and unpredictable lately that, as a family, we never even had a chance to celebrate the bar's one-year anniversary a few months back." Behind Carol, another customer appears, excusing herself as she reaches for something on the shelf. "We're all getting together there around six if you'd like to join us."

Grace tries to swallow, but it gets caught in her throat. "Thank you," she says, fighting the urge to cry. "I'll . . . think about it."

Carol nods, choosing not to press Grace any further. "Well, I'm happy I ran into you, Grace. I'm happy I had the chance to run into your mother one more time last summer, too." She waves, shaking the bottle of Motrin in the process, and turns out of the aisle again.

This time, she doesn't come back.

Grace stays put so they don't bump into each other in the checkout line.

For what feels like forever, she just stands there, beneath the glow of fluorescent lights, contemplating how anything stocked on these shelves could begin to help her.

She wonders how anyone can ever really heal.

TWENTY-FOUR

Grace steps out of the pharmacy and into the heat. Everything feels too hot. Too bright. Too much. Despite her attempts to breathe through her feelings, her heart isn't beating right. How could it? Too many opposing emotions have shown up all at once for it to know what to do.

She slides on her sunglasses, pulls her hat down to block out the light, then takes a seat on the curb, the asphalt warm on the back sides of her thighs. Grace fumbles through the brown paper bag in her lap, not even bothering to look into it. Instead, her fingers blindly dig down and pull out a box of Band-Aids. She tears one open and slaps it on her heel, knowing that at this point it'll hardly do a thing.

Why didn't Birdie tell her? All those calls from Maine. The brief early-morning conversations. The late-night check-ins. Not a single word. Never so much as a hint.

A few moments later, and with her thoughts racing, Grace hardly even remembers getting back on the bike. All she knows is that she's moving and pedaling again. Up the boulevard, past blue hydrangeas and shuttered porches and little shops she's been in a hundred times. By the time she reaches the amusement pier, her stomach queasy from all the motion of the morning, she's not even really sure why she's there.

Grace hops off the cruiser and walks with it. The tires clunk over the old wooden slats as she moves. The boardwalk always feels abandoned during the daytime—the ring toss and big wheel games shuttered until evening, the snack stands that sell buckets of fries and funnel cakes preparing for a busy night, the Ferris wheel and other rides all turned off.

Up ahead, Grace sees her.

She's alone, just like every other time they've crossed paths this week, sitting outside the old fortune teller booth and staring at the ocean. This time, Grace doesn't question if she's really there. She doesn't tell herself she's hallucinating or dreaming or imagining. While so many of her memories on this island have blurred, this moment she remembers almost perfectly.

Cece. Thirty-one years old. What was, up until this present week, her last visit to Sea Drift. A few weeks later, she'd be married and moving on.

Although Grace walked past this booth dozens of times, always intrigued by the wooden sign that swayed above the entrance—MADAME MERMAID: SEE YOUR FUTURE AND PLAN FOR IT!—and the beaded curtains that concealed the one small window and glass door, she'd only ever stopped at it one time.

"That's a silly waste of money, Cece," Birdie used to say as the two of them strolled past, licking ice cream cones on their way to the rides, little-kid Grace asking a million questions. *Can she really see the future? Maybe she can tell us a winning lottery number! Can we go in so I can find out which teacher I'll get in the fall?* "She's just a fake, love," Birdie always explained. "For better or worse, no one really knows what life has in store for them."

Cece doesn't seem to notice Grace at first, her gaze locked on the waves. This version is more polished than the others. Her hair is still sun-kissed from a week at the beach, but it's brushed back into a smooth, loose twist. She wears a nice linen shirt and leather sandals—simple, stylish, grown-up. The nameplate necklace hangs between her collarbones, the gold plating catching the light. On her left hand, a diamond engagement ring hugs her finger, which she keeps touching and twisting, like maybe she's afraid it'll disappear if she doesn't.

"There's a bit of a wait," Cece says when Grace slides onto an empty chair on the opposite side of the door from where she sits. "Someone just went in."

"Are you waiting, too?" Grace asks and looks out at the water, both of them studying the horizon.

"I already went." Cece rubs her ring. "A little bit ago."

Out on the boardwalk, seagulls peck at French fries smashed between the wooden planks.

"How'd it go?" Grace asks, cautious not to say too much. Although she doesn't recall whether she talked to another potential customer in this moment (*Maybe? Possibly? Is that even how this all works?*), she remembers with crystal-clear clarity why her thirty-one-year-old self came here. "Did you get the answers you wanted?"

"Hard to say," Cece admits. She crosses her legs. Her linen top rises as she indulges in a long inhale. "I'm not entirely sure what answers I was hoping to get."

A moment passes. Cece doesn't say anything else. Rather, she gazes ahead while lost in a thought she hasn't shared. Grace waits and then almost gets up to leave, wondering if this is it, that the point of this particular encounter is not to talk or to learn some lesson, but to simply see this version of herself again. The one who was standing on the edge of everything, the whole future she'd been plotting so close that she could touch it with her hands.

"I'm getting married," Cece suddenly says out of nowhere. "In October. The venue's gorgeous. It's this rooftop, all glass-enclosed, in Lower Manhattan. You can see the Hudson River and Jersey City. It's beautiful." While she talks, she never turns her face. "Adam." Her lips break into a smile. "That's who I'm marrying. He's great. Kind. A gentleman. Good job. Stable. He even folds laundry." She laughs. "We're going to start looking at houses in the suburbs in the spring."

"That all sounds . . . nice," Grace tells her.

"I know. That's why I'm completely terrified." She twists the ring again, slower this time. "I have absolutely everything I ever wanted. At least, I'm about to, anyway. And instead of bubbling with happiness, I've just been a nervous wreck that it won't work out. That someone will pull the rug out from under me. That it's all just one big trick."

"Why do you feel that way?" Grace asks, even though she already knows the answer. Remembers those worries like they were blooming in her mind just yesterday.

"Because I don't know what I'd do!" Cece exclaims, loud enough to scare off the gulls. She rubs her face, laughing, but obviously also a bit embarrassed. "This is my big happy ending, you know?" Her voice is lower this time so she doesn't frighten any more wildlife. "What if it all doesn't pan out the way I've envisioned? I think I'd just completely break, turn into a puddle or something."

The warm breeze picks up, bringing with it a new thought for Grace. What if she just tells her? Not only who she is but also what she knows. Encourage her to get up and run away. Warn her that all her perfect plans will shatter, and that in a not-so-far-off future, she'll be forced to start her whole life all over again.

Before Grace can say any of this, though, Cece begins to speak. "I asked Madame Mermaid the dumbest question," she admits. "As if coming here wasn't the dumb part, right?"

"What'd you ask?" Grace remembers the feeling of this day, but not the semantics.

"She was reading my tarot cards, and before she pulled one, she told me to ask something, and that the card she picked would provide the answer." Cece waits, like she's still absorbing some of what Madame Mermaid said. "I asked whether I'd be happy. In the future, you know? If she saw a version of me that was just . . . content."

"What'd she say?" Grace asks, looking at this once polished version of herself. "What card did she pick?"

Cece bites her bottom lip before she responds. "The Fool."

Grace remembers the card now. The way Madame Mermaid traced her finger across its illustration—a man dressed like a court jester who stood on the edge of a cliff, a knapsack tossed over his shoulder.

"She said it marks new beginnings," Cece continues. "That the person who pulls it is at the start of a long journey, one they're equipped for but that they need to travel alone." She stops, thinking about Madame Mermaid's words and quietly laughs. "And then she gave me this." Cece pulls a small blue card from her pocket. "It's a twenty-percent-off coupon for my next reading. Apparently, if I want to know more about the *long journey*, I'll need to come back." Cece reaches out her arm and passes the coupon to Grace. "Here. You can use it for your reading," she tells her. "I doubt I'll ever find myself here a second time."

Grace accepts it, one more small token of where and who she's been. Right after she does, the door between them swings open. The cluster of bells hanging from it jangles. Another patron walks out, looking satisfied to have had someone tell her, even if it's a lie or just pretend, that her future will turn out as bright as she believes.

"Perfect timing." Cece points to the door. "Looks like you're up." She stands then, ready to walk toward the life she's so hoping will work out. "I'll see you around," she says, and starts to move up the boardwalk.

"You won't," Grace shouts before she gets too far.

Cece turns and looks over her shoulder, her face tilted at an angle. "I won't what?"

"Turn into a puddle," Grace clarifies. "If things don't work out. You'll survive it." She lifts her leg, crossing her ankle over her knee, and smooths the curling edges of the Band-Aid over her foot. "You might be a mess along the way, but you'll find your way through."

Cece shakes her head. "You say it like you know me."

"Maybe I do in my own way." Grace shrugs. "I remember that time in my life, too."

Behind Cece, a young couple appears, strolling along and taking in the summer view.

"Were you scared?" she asks Grace, and when she does, loops her finger around her necklace chain. "Back when you were in my shoes." Her cheeks lift. "Metaphorically, I mean."

Grace lets herself remember. Adam. Her first book. The life she always wanted, the one she gave up so much along the way to find.

"I was," Grace tells Cece. "I was afraid, just like you."

The couple walks past, arms linked, their faces happy.

"Good to know I'm not the only one, then." Cece stuffs a hand in her shorts pocket, turns to take another quick look at the water. "It's funny," she says, shifting their conversation. "I've been coming to this island my whole life." She laughs at something private. "I used to be in love with this boy I knew down here." A pause. "Ray." She laughs softly. "Every summer, it felt like it was just me and him."

"What happened?" Grace asks, though she already knows, has already lived it.

"He knew my past," Cece says, her gaze still set on the sea. "Eventually, we reached a point where I needed someone who wanted to know my future. My *real* future, the one that involved more than just a few days spent lounging in the sand."

"Do you feel like you found it, then? Your future?"

Cece pulls in a big breath and looks down at her shimmering ring. "I do," she says, not yet knowing that Adam would only know a piece of it, and that finding love was not always the same thing as finding yourself.

I hate winter, Ray said one summer night. The two of them. This boardwalk. The scent of funnel cake. Laughter from the rides. Neon lights. Both of them weeks away from their senior year of college. One last twelve-month stretch before real life began.

Grace laughed. *Lucky for you, it's currently ninety degrees.*

I'm serious, Porter. Ray set down the bucket of fries they were sharing, took her hand, threaded his fingers through hers. *I'll miss you this year.*

It was something they never said, just quietly felt, like a heartbeat you knew was there but didn't acknowledge each time it pulsed. The fact that, every year, the moment they drove west over the bridge and then off in the opposing directions of their real lives, something inside both of them broke and didn't feel repaired until the sun shone warm again.

I'll miss you this year, too, she said. *But it'll go fast. We'll blink and be back here.*

Grace looked at him then. The boy she'd known forever, now broader, taller, with a voice so deep it still sometimes surprised her that it belonged to him. She often wondered if he thought those things about her. If he could see the ways she'd changed, even as they continued to return to this place. If he cared. Or if, like her, he just carried the years with him like souvenirs.

Things will be different when we come back here next August, he'd said. *Life will be different, you know?*

She did.

But for the rest of the night, as they enjoyed each other's company beneath the distant glow of the Ferris wheel, she tried not to think about it. Instead, she just kept telling herself that no matter what happened—no matter who either of them became—they'd continue to return to each other, to this place, as inevitably and constantly as the seasons.

Back in the present moment, the breeze shifts off the water, the air suddenly warm and cool at once.

"So what are you going to ask?" Cece poses, circling back on their conversation.

Grace looks at her, confused.

"Madame Mermaid," Cece clarifies. "For your reading."

"Oh." Grace laughs. "Right." She sets her foot back down, the wound on her heel still there but at least covered for now. "Same as you, I guess."

Cece nods. "Makes sense." She shrugs. "Sort of a universal question, right?"

The door opens again. A woman wearing too many scarves and far too much thick blue eyeliner steps out and looks around. "Anyone else ready to hear what life has planned?"

Cece turns to Madame Mermaid and then to Grace. "Good luck," she tells her. "Hopefully she'll pull a better card for you."

TWENTY-FIVE

Grace doesn't even bother pretending she's surprised when she turns onto Surf Street and spots him on the steps. At this point, Sea Drift seems set on scripting out her life like a bad stage play—same setting, rotating cast, new emotional unraveling at every beat.

"I'm starting to associate these stairs with existential crises," she says when she pulls up to the house. "Either I'm sitting on them completely mortified with myself or someone else is waiting there ready to tell me the world is falling apart."

Caleb shrugs. "At least, unlike you, I'm not soaking wet," he points out.

Grace wheels the bike past the For Sale sign and up the driveway.

"You know, per your rental agreement, you're technically only allowed two visitors whose names aren't listed on the lease," he deadpans. "You've hit your quota."

"Don't tell the landlord." Grace balances the cruiser against the side of the house.

"I'm sorry if I was rude last night." Caleb meets her gaze. "To be honest, I'd gotten used to seeing you out here by yourself all week." His mouth lifts right before he looks down at his feet. "If I'm honest, it sort of threw me when I saw you out here with someone else."

"Adam," Grace says, his name somehow heavy on her tongue. "My almost ex." She sighs. "I think." She grabs the pharmacy bag from the cruiser's basket. "He just showed up here out of the blue last night. I'm still trying to figure out why."

Caleb nods, like he's already been privy to the full story. "So I heard." He folds his hands over his thighs. "Jenny told me."

Grace's eyebrows lift, a silent question.

"She was heading out when I knocked on the door," Caleb explains. "Told me she forgot wine and was running out to pick some up, then managed to explain your entire life to me in the time it took her to walk to her car." He smirks. "She has a lot of opinions on Adam, huh?"

Grace closes her eyes, the weight of it all feeling like too much right now. "He kind of announced that he didn't want to be married any longer at literally the worst moment of my life."

Behind Grace, a car hums down the block, windows down, music drifting out.

"So did you mean it?" Grace asks and turns to look at the sign stabbed into the crushed seashells. "Someone's already interested in buying it?"

"Seems that way," Caleb admits. "If things go the way I hope they do, it should be a quick sale." He twists to look back at the house, like he's checking to make sure it's still there, at least for now. When he turns back to Grace, he waits a minute before speaking again. "Kelly," he states, plain and simple. "That was my sister's name. She was a few years younger than me. She lived in Delaware, a runner. At least six miles every morning." Caleb shakes his head at this, half somber and half laughing. "One of those 'I run a marathon every year' nuts." He looks up at the sky, not a cloud in it, everything bright and clear. "It was her heart. Incredibly sudden. None of us had a chance to say goodbye."

Quiet falls between them, a soft kind that fills the space between two people who have more than they maybe initially realized in common.

"This house reminds you of her," Grace says, not as a question but a fact.

"It does," Caleb admits. "Two weeks every July. We shared the bed in the front room. Ate dinner barefoot out back every night." He rubs his thumbs over each other. "Funny how a place you only ever stayed in for a few days every year can feel so much like home."

At the end of the block, the faint sound of a song fills the air as the ice cream truck turns onto Surf Street. Like clockwork, a sea of children swarm it from every direction.

"Can I ask you something?" Grace poses and watches the kids, so happy to receive something so small. "Are you able to view past rental records? See if someone named Elizabeth Porter stayed in the house this same week last year?"

"No need to check," he responds. "House was empty. My parents canceled all reservations for the remainder of August after Kelly passed, paid everyone back. They didn't want to deal with any landlord emergencies in the wake of everything." Caleb's gaze narrows, like he's thinking about something. "Why do you ask?"

Grace shifts the pharmacy bag to her other hand. "Just trying to figure something out."

Caleb nods, then stands. "Anyway, I won't keep you." A small, teasing smile forms on his face. "Seeing as you have so many unauthorized visitors and all." He makes it a few steps toward the street before he turns back. "I'm sure I don't need to tell you how much loss changes a person." He holds his palm to his forehead, squints. "If I was the old me—the one I was before I lost Kelly—I'd be pretty jealous of Adam. You seem like someone I'd be very interested in."

"And now?"

"Right now," Caleb tells her, "I'm still trying to figure out which version of myself I am."

~

Back inside the house, Grace puts the pharmacy bag in the bathroom, then sits on the couch to wait for Jenny to return. While she does, she adds the Madame Mermaid coupon to her pile of strange souvenirs, the growing museum exhibit of all her past selves right there on display.

She sinks into the couch, kicks off her sandals, and grabs Birdie's old *Summer Memories* album, which still rests on a cushion from the other day. She flips, past photos of her and her mother from every era of her life, now viewing each picture a little differently than she did just a few nights ago. Grace holds the album close to her face, examining the images, like maybe the answer she's looking for will appear, as if Birdie's expression is a Magic Eye illustration: If she just stares at it long enough, some secret will be revealed.

"Why did you come here?" Grace asks the air, the first time she's spoken aloud to her mother in days. "What were you doing or looking for that you couldn't tell me about?"

The phone rings, the intrusion of it enough to make Grace jump. She drops the album, fumbles in her pocket for her phone, and quickly presses it to her ear.

"Grace," the voice says through the line. "Hi. I'm just checking in to see if you're okay. It's Dr. Anne. You missed your weekly appointment yesterday."

"Shoot," Grace says through a sigh. "Dr. Anne. I'm so sorry." She rubs her forehead, embarrassed to have stood up her therapist. "I'm fine. Honestly, I just completely forgot to call and cancel." For a moment, Grace thinks back to last week, sitting in Dr. Anne's office, talking about breath work and breakthroughs. How much has changed—not just her location but so many things—since then. "I ended up taking a very last-minute trip down to the beach," she explains. "I've been here since Saturday and am still sort of wrapping my mind around the fact that I'm even here at all. I'm sorry that I flaked."

"It's okay," Dr. Anne assures her in her typical kind and professional way. "I just wanted to be sure you were all right. It was out of character for you." She lets her comment sit there, like they're in session, giving Grace a minute to process and then reply.

"It's the place my mom and I used to come every August," Grace says. "Our old rental house became available at the last minute. I hesitated, but then gave in."

"That's . . . interesting," Dr. Anne states, always leaving a syntactical door open.

Grace lets a few long seconds pass, deciding whether she wants to proceed with the questions running through her mind. "Do you remember that session we had earlier this summer?" she finally asks. "The one where you told me to try to remember what I was like when I was younger?"

"I do," Dr. Anne says, willing to listen even though this isn't their scheduled time slot.

At the time of that meeting, Grace had been seeing Dr. Anne for a few months, mostly to help her work through Birdie's loss. But by that session in June, so many other parts of her life had started to crack. Trying to think about the past felt like purposefully placing her hands on hot coals, an excruciating pain that did nothing but make her hurt.

"I've been . . . seeing myself," Grace says, cautious to phrase things in a metaphorical—not a literal—sense. "Past versions of me, all over this island." She glances at the photo album, the one full of images of them. "Everywhere I go, it's like there's a new one waiting for me, like my memories are staging an intervention or something."

Dr. Anne doesn't laugh. She never laughs. "What have they all been like?"

Grace looks down at the assorted objects on the coffee table and runs through a mental roster of them all. "Happy. Determined. Messy. Full of doubt. Thoughtful. Confused."

"And how did you feel toward each of them?"

Grace exhales softly. "Tender, I think."

"Interesting," Dr. Anne states again. "Well, maybe you ought to turn that observation into a question," she suggests. "How do you think a future version of yourself might view present-day Grace, the one you've been awfully hard on the last few months?"

Grace picks up the sand dollar, turning it in her fingers. "The same way, I hope."

~

Grace is half asleep on the couch when Jenny bursts through the door, wearing a wide-brim hat and holding a bottle of wine in each hand.

"I've got good news and bad news!" she announces and steps into the living room. "Also, are you asleep?"

"Not anymore," Grace jokes.

"Perfect. Because the good news is that I found this amazing hat at the five-and-dime on the boulevard, and it's possible that it's now my entire identity."

Grace can't help it. She snorts. "Is that also the bad news?"

"Very funny." Jenny moves into the kitchen, sets her car keys and the wine bottles on the table. "How was your morning, birthday girl? Did you take a little time for yourself?"

Grace pulls herself up on the cushion. "I found out my mother was down here last August and never told me." She massages her fingers over her face. "Apparently, the entire Murphy family knew, and I didn't."

Jenny nods, the hat's wide brim shaking with her movements. Without a word, she picks her car keys back up and heads toward the door.

"What are you doing?" Grace asks. "You haven't even told me the bad news."

"It's on the counter." She points toward the kitchen. "Adam stopped by earlier and dropped off a birthday card, then made me promise I'd tell you he's hoping you'll meet him for dinner tonight at the hotel where he's staying." She adjusts her hat. "Apparently, all the details are written down."

Grace lets herself melt into the cushions, frowning. "I don't understand. Where are you going?"

Jenny pushes open the screen door. "I think wine might have been the wrong choice." She looks at Grace, then the counter, then back at her friend. "I'm going back to the store. I thought Adam's card would be the bomb, though after your news, I'm thinking we might need something stronger on deck instead."

TWENTY-SIX

It was high school all over again.

Grace and Jenny spent the rest of the day deliberating. Making pro/con lists. Talking. Crying. Laughing. Trying to figure out whether Grace should accept the invitation outlined in her birthday card—*Dinner? Tonight? Just us? 8:00 p.m.? The restaurant at my hotel, the Beachcomber.*—and go on a date with a handsome boy. Only unlike in high school, the boy in question isn't some cute crush from geometry class. It's Grace's husband. Or almost-ex-husband. Or whatever he is to her at the moment.

"It doesn't fit," Grace says, standing in front of the beach house's small bathroom mirror, tugging at the neckline of her dress. Jenny's dress—a simple white linen maxi she threw in her duffel bag, just in case—which she insisted Grace wear, telling her she'd feel better about things if she is confident in the way she looks. "It doesn't sit right on my chest. It's pinching my rib cage." Grace pulls and twists the fabric to get it to lie right. "I feel like I can't breathe in it."

"That's impossible," Jenny insists, sitting on the edge of the bathtub and picking on a leftover pancake. "For one, we're practically the same size. And second, it's designed to be loose-fitting." She takes another nibble, wipes her fingers on the front of her PTA tee. "Pretty sure the shortness-of-breath thing has more to do with the situation you're about to walk into than it does with hemlines."

Grace huffs, takes another look at her reflection. "What am I doing?"

Jenny stands, smooths a strand of Grace's hair. "I think that's what you're about to go try and figure out."

"You're sure you don't care that I'm ditching you to go meet him?" Grace asks.

Jenny smiles at her in the mirror. "I didn't come to be entertained." She blends an uneven patch of makeup on Grace's cheek. "I came to make sure you're okay."

~

Adam stands when he sees her. He wears a collared shirt, the sleeves rolled to his elbows, and a pair of khaki shorts—casual dressy. Grace makes her way through the dining room, still pulling on the neckline of the dress. The restaurant is busy—families having early dinners, couples getting a head start on the night, the space buzzing with conversation and the clink of glasses.

"I wasn't certain you'd come," Adam says when Grace arrives at their table.

"Neither was I," she admits.

"Well, I'm glad you did." He pulls out her chair. "You look very nice."

They both sit and fidget, smoothing napkins over their laps, taking sips of water, neither of them sure what to do or say next. Nearby, laughter rises from another table. Just as their silence begins to feel awkward, their waitress appears, sets down two wineglasses, and tells them she'll return in a few minutes.

"I hope it's okay that I ordered for you." Adam gestures to the stemware. "I noticed on the menu that they have that rosé you used to like. The dry one that the Italian place near our old apartment used to stock." His smile is so small it's almost not even there. "Remember?"

Of course she did. They used to go every Wednesday night, Adam meeting her after he left his office, Grace just emerging from the library or a coffee shop or whatever her chosen writing cave was that day.

They'd drink wine and talk and eat off each other's plates. It felt so grown-up, like something from a good sitcom. Except that it wasn't. It was real life.

"I do," she says, not able to lie and pretend those memories have faded.

Adam nods, happy to hear this. He holds up his glass, gently taps it against hers. They both take small sips. Grace can't ignore the fact that it does taste like that old place, that whole era in their relationship. Their sixth-floor apartment with the tiny kitchen and the radiator that made too much noise. How the light filtered into their bedroom. The way their shared future felt as big and beautiful as the city's skyscrapers.

"I drove the whole island today," he tells her. "Back and forth a few times." He takes a drink of his blush beverage, like he needs it to calm his nerves. "Stopped off at the lighthouse for a bit. Went down to the boardwalk. Took a walk on the beach."

Grace doesn't say anything. Instead, she listens, her fingers trailing the stem of her glass, and tries to gauge what he's getting at.

"I tried to imagine you at every different place," Adam says. "This week. In the past when you used to come here."

Grace swallows, but it doesn't go down smoothly. "And what did you find?"

He pushes his glass away, leans in a little closer. "Someone I missed."

Grace feels it then. It's gentle, but there. A quiet tug, like a current pulling her out to sea. She thinks about fighting it, swimming against the tide and getting herself back to shore. Instead, his words floating there in the space between them, Grace lets herself drift in it.

"I haven't been able to shake that dream for days, Grace," Adam states. His words quiver. It's subtle, but enough for her to notice. "I miss the people we were back then so much." He licks his bottom lip, delaying his next statement. "Things felt so easy then, you know?" he says without listing everything that's happened since then. Her books. Her successes. Her losses. All the ways life smashes down on a relationship to figure out if it's a diamond or a rock. "It was just you and me." His eyes softly close while he indulges in a long breath. "We can go back," he says, sounding desperate. "We can be those happy, easy people again."

Could they? Could *she*? Was it possible for someone to revert and become the person she used to be? Our experiences. Our emotions. Could they ever be wiped away, the slate made clean?

"People change, Adam," Grace says. "Love is supposed to change and evolve along with them. Otherwise you find yourself stuck living in the past."

"The past?" He bites his cheek, and without him even saying it, Grace can read his thoughts. Those papers. Her early draft on the table. "Maybe I'm not the only one who's been thinking about that a lot lately."

A long, quiet beat, one that pulses with anger and sadness and jealousy and regret, falls over them like a gauzy veil, one that's transparent and yet hard to see through. Is that why he's here? Because he's been thinking about their past? The one they shared? Or because he senses that she's been thinking about her own, the one she experienced before she met him? Who could say. Time and feelings—they're such confusing things.

"I bought you something," he says, his tone curling upward like a leaf, as if he's trying to make amends for their last exchange. "It's a little birthday gift." Adam pulls a small gift bag from beneath the table. "It's nothing fancy. Just something I saw in my travels today that I thought you'd like."

Whether it's the dress or the inner workings of her body, Grace can't be sure. All she knows as she removes the crinkled pieces of tissue, lifts the petite box inside it, and pulls away the lid, is that her lungs no longer work right.

"It's just a tchotchke," Adam states, trying to sound casual. "From this little shop I wandered into earlier. I didn't realize until I was inside and saw the baskets of shells and beachy wind chimes that you and Birdie took me there one rainy morning the week I came down."

Her fingers tingling, Grace lifts the ring and examines it between her fingers. A tchotchke, yes, but also more than that. A simple band of silver etched with a subtle wave motif. A piece of jewelry, and yet years' worth of memories, too.

"I was browsing to see if they had anything a bit nicer. Maybe something with a real stone in it." Adam quietly laughs, amused by something. "The closest they had were earrings made of sea glass." Their waitress sets down a breadbasket, then walks away. "When I saw that ring in the display, I remembered you telling me you had one just like it when you were younger, but that you'd lost it."

Grace can't speak. Instead, she just places the ring in the dip of her palm and looks at it.

"Anyway," he says, not having a clue of the weight his gift actually carries, "I thought maybe it'd make you happy to finally have it back."

Her hand moves before her mind has a chance to stop it—slowly, cautiously, like she's not even entirely aware of what she's doing until it's done. The ring slides easily onto her finger, covering the faint white line of skin where her sparkly wedding jewelry once sat.

"You don't have to actually wear it. I know it's a bit young looking, not quite your style these days." He looks at the way it sits on her finger. "It was more about the memory, I guess."

Even though Grace's face is tilted down, she senses it. A prickle. A shift in the air. Something inside her turns, as if toward a magnet. A sensation that she's swum out too far and gotten caught in a current—a pull—she can't outswim. Someone, somewhere in this room, is looking at her. An invisible energy she feels in every cell, too strong for her to dismiss.

Her chin lifts slowly, her breath so off-kilter she's scared to move too fast, as if anything sudden might make the moment shatter. The restaurant narrows into a tunnel. The other tables. The ocean views. The waitstaff and other diners. Even Adam. They all fall away. The ring, still snug on her finger like a promise, fades, too. It's as if she's underwater, everything newly muffled and distant. In this moment, there's only one thing Grace clearly sees.

Ray.

He sits, motionless, at the casual indoor bar just off the main dining room, a pint of untouched golden beer before him. Their eyes meet, like a key sliding into a lock. He doesn't need to say anything. Doesn't need to make any dramatic movements. She knows. The only thing in this space he's been looking at is her.

Time collapses.

The memories all rush in at once.

Thirteen. Ray laughing as she tried again and again to get the high score on her favorite game, his voice rising with hers when she finally did. The first flutters of something new.

Sixteen. Warm sun on her shoulders. Lying on her towel and watching him slice through the waves. Listening for his laughter through the breeze. Feeling like it was the only place on earth she was meant to be.

Nineteen. Bike rides and sunsets. Quiet afternoons on the dunes, reading and telling him about her dreams, and him smiling at her like they were already real.

Twenty-two. Late nights. Strong drinks. Ocean breezes. Dancing in his arms and knowing that, even if the rest of her life was messy, that one part—one moment—was right.

Twenty-five. The pier. The ring. The request. Her leaving to go find her way, not realizing that she was never more herself than she was right there with him on that coastline.

Thirty-one. Almost married. Being back on the island and knowing he was someplace else far away. Telling herself the search was over—for love, for the person she was supposed to be—not knowing that in a short time it would all circle back in on her again.

"Grace?" Adam asks now, noticing her sudden change. "Are you okay?"

"I—I . . ." Grace stammers. Her throat tightens. She grasps for words. Meaning. They're not there. Adam. The ring. Ray. This moment. The impossibility of sitting between two lives she once thought were real. How easily in just one glance she could remember so much. Love. Time. The girl she used to be.

A frantic, unsteady heat rises in her chest. In her stomach, panic works itself into knots. "I need a minute." She pushes out her chair too fast. A dizzy feeling wraps itself around her. She grabs the edge of the table, steadying herself, then looks from Ray to Adam, not sure where her focus should land. Finally, she straightens, takes a breath. "I-I'll be back."

~

Grace pulls open the bathroom door, half expecting to find someone waiting for her inside. Maybe the Cece she saw in here the other night, propped up on the counter, sipping a sugary cocktail, on the verge of accidentally saying something profound. Maybe some other version of herself she hasn't met yet this week.

All she knows is that for the first time since arriving in Sea Drift, she hopes she crosses paths with someone—anyone—who can tell her what to do. Who can show her which way is forward when her heart keeps tugging her backward into different parts of her past.

But there's no one here.

She peeks into each stall to double-check and confirms the room is empty. No hidden message. No meaningful sign. Just Grace, her erratic pulse, and her spinning thoughts.

She moves to the sink, cups water in her hands, and splashes it against her neck. It doesn't help the feeling inside her go away. Adam—the man she loved and who left her, now asking for a second chance. Ray—the person she loved and ran away from for reasons that, right now, don't fully make sense. She holds her hands beneath the faucet, trying to cool herself down, but it's no use. Not when the only thing she can focus on is the ring.

She needs air.

Grace slips out of the bathroom, slides through a back door, steps out onto the Beachcomber's patio bar, weaves through the forming crowd, then down a short ramp and onto the sand. It's dark, the whole beach empty. Grace kicks off her shoes, pulls up the bottom hem of her dress, and walks toward the water, hoping to find a stronger breeze. Standing on the shoreline and looking out at the ocean at night is a different experience than staring out at it during the day, the clear horizon and translucent water becoming an endless sheet of black.

The night breeze brushes Grace's skin, but it's not nearly as cooling as she'd hoped. She steps a bit farther, past the dry part and down to the firmer stretch of sand. The water rises up over her feet, providing her with a momentary feeling of relief.

Until she hears it.

Footsteps. Fast ones. Barreling up the beach.

Grace turns. A silhouette charges through the moonlight—ripped shorts, baggy sweatshirt, wild hair whipping in the warm breeze.

Cece.

One day shy of twenty-five.

And sobbing.

"Hey!" Grace calls out as Cece gets closer. She drops her dress hem, the fabric trailing through the water, and rushes to her. "Slow down!"

Cece stumbles to a stop at the sound of another person, drops her palms to her knees, her breath ragged. She gasps once, then again, like she's trying to put herself back together before she falls apart.

"What happened?" Grace asks when she reaches her, though she already knows. Despite the darkness, the memory of this night remains painfully clear. "What are you running from?"

Cece keeps her tear-streaked face tilted down. "I just left the most important part of my life behind," she says, still half gasping for air. "The person I love, the one I've always loved! I threw one dream away to chase another." She wipes her cheeks on her sweatshirt sleeve. "And the truth is that I don't even know why I did it."

Grace stands beside her. This version of herself, the one who gave up on something because she thought maybe she'd find something better, only to find that *better* didn't last. The one who still believed every choice she made would lead her somewhere brighter.

"The truth is, he only knows a part of me," Cece says, panting. "The part he's always seen down here. He doesn't know the one who has a life and dreams outside of this place."

Her inhalations and exhalations evening out, Cece stands, looks out at the dark water, and wraps her arms around herself so tightly it's as if she's trying to keep her body from unraveling.

"Maybe you should go back," Grace says, her words as quiet as the air, not sure that she should be saying this, but feeling so confused about everything that she's not certain she cares. "Maybe you should go back to the thing you ran from and pick it instead."

Something changes then. The air or the energy. Whatever it is, Grace can't ignore it. There's a shift.

Cece turns toward Grace slowly, their gazes locking into place. A flash of recognition shapes Cece's expression. It's only then that Grace realizes that for the first time this week, there's nothing there to conceal who she is. No hat or sunglasses. No drunken veil to make the encounter seem fuzzy. Here, in the dark of night, everything is suddenly clear.

"Don't you see?" Tears continue to fall down Cece's face. "Don't you understand by now that this isn't how it all works?"

"How what works?" Grace asks, though the flush of goose bumps all over her body suggest her mind already knows.

"This." Cece waves her hands at her sides. "Whatever it is that keeps happening here."

Around them, the breeze picks up, making everything feel momentarily suspended.

"Wh-what do you mean?" Grace rubs her thumb against the cool metal of the ring.

"Everything," Cece says. "You can't change the outcome of any of this. You can't reshape history just because you're confused and sad."

Grace flinches, Cece's words—*her* words—hitting her as hard as a rogue wave. "I don't know what I'm supposed to do," Grace admits to herself, her voice cracking.

"Neither do I," Cece says. "Because I'm not you yet."

She's right. None of them have been her—present-day her. But they've all been something. A girl who believed the world was full of small treasures. The one who, even when she lost the game, was willing to try again and win. The young woman who, despite all her messy, inebriated confusion, carried so much hope beneath her doubt. The individual who was willing to study and understand something, not for an accolade or a deadline but just for herself. The one who wondered whether her story was worth telling but believed in herself enough to tell it anyway. The woman who was terrified that her happiness was only temporary but was still brave enough to chase it.

Grace blinks. "Then what's the point?" she asks, her thoughts heavy with all that's transpired this week. "Why are you—all of you—here?"

Cece opens her fist, which she's had clutched tight since she arrived. Inside it is a near replica of the ring she was gifted back on the fishing pier. She takes one long look at it, and then, even though her expression looks pained, lets it fall into the sand.

"It's not about us," Cece states. "It's about the next one."

"The next what?" Grace asks, confused.

Cece takes a step away from her, then another. "The next version. The one that comes after all this." Cece quietly laughs, like this is the most obvious fact of them all. "Her story's the one that hasn't been written yet."

~

Back inside the Beachcomber, the dining room is busier. Silverware scrapes. Banter fills the air like a song.

"Grace?" Adam rises as soon as he sees her. "Where have you been?" He looks both ruffled and relieved. "I had our waitress go into the ladies' room three times. You weren't there."

Grace peers down at their table, full of untouched appetizer platters, which Adam must have ordered in her absence. "I went outside," she says and looks over at the bar and sees that Ray is gone. "I needed some air."

Adam's face pans down. "The bottom of your dress is soaking wet," he points out, accusation carrying his words like a raft. "Were you with someone?" he asks, unable to hide the jealousy in his inquiry. He quickly backtracks. "I mean, wh-what were you doing?"

"I don't think I can do this tonight."

"Grace, come on. Sit. Please." A sense of urgency creeps into his tone, lifting each syllable up like waves. "This is important. We need to finish our conversation."

Grace looks through the window at the beach and lets herself remember that feeling. Of being twenty-five, running away from the familiar and toward something new and better—something that, up until a few months ago, she believed she'd found.

Something that, tonight, she lets herself accept she hasn't landed on just yet.

"I think we already did, Adam," she says, taking her purse from the back of her chair. "Back in June. When you left."

In reality, Grace walks calmly to the door.

But in her mind, she's in the sand, barefoot and sprinting.

TWENTY-SEVEN

Thursday

"Good morning, sunshine," Jenny says.

Grace wakes the next day to the sight of Jenny perched on the edge of her mattress. The bedroom is flooded with golden sunlight. Her mind still foggy with the lingering fragments of a dream she doesn't quite recall, Grace pulls herself upright. When she does, an achy, heavy feeling blooms in her chest, as if she pulled a muscle or bruised her body from her erratic breathing while wearing Jenny's too-tight dress.

"How are you feeling?" Jenny asks, already aware from their conversation when Grace got home from the Beachcomber of how she saw Ray from across the room and how the dinner with Adam ended.

"I'm okay." Grace's gaze lands on the nightstand and the pair of nearly identical silver rings—two different promises from two different people at two wholly different points in her life. "I think."

"Here." Jenny passes Grace a plate. "No pancakes today. I made you toast, though. The good seedy kind, with some jam. And I picked up coffees from that little place up the street. They're in the kitchen." Jenny stands, lingers in the doorway. "Oh, one other thing. Clean yourself up a bit before you come out. Your cute landlord—the one I met on my way to the store yesterday—is on the porch. He knocked a few minutes ago. Said he needs to talk to you."

~

"I found something," Caleb states as soon as Grace pushes open the screen door and moves onto the top step. He stands on the walkway. "Last night. I didn't want to knock too late."

Grace—dressed in a tee and shorts—pushes a strand of loose hair out of her eyes. "What is it?" For the first time in days, her fingers drift to her collarbone to search for her old necklace chain—something familiar for them to tangle themselves up in. "What did you find?"

Caleb pulls a folded-up sheet of paper from his shorts pocket, though he doesn't unfold it just yet. "You said your mother's last name was Porter, right?"

Her lungs freeze, everything in her chest instantly becoming tight. "Yes." Barefoot, she steps down the remaining stairs. "Why?"

"Well, in that case, she definitely didn't rent the house last year," Caleb confirms. "It was a totally different family who rented it. At least, before my folks canceled on them."

His comment both instantly deflates Grace and simultaneously fills her up. "Oh," she says, not sure what answer she hoped to hear. That, yes, her mother was here last summer while Grace was in Maine. Or that, no, she wasn't, and the Murphys were all caught up in some elaborate misunderstanding. "Okay." She shifts her weight on her feet, yesterday's Band-Aid curling off her heel. "That makes sense."

Caleb smiles, pleased to share this information. His expression calms Grace, makes her believe that, at least for now, this one point of confusion in her life can be put to rest.

"Grace?" he says before the feeling has a chance to sink in. "Do you remember when I called you last Friday and said things fell through with the original renter for *this* week?"

"Y-yes. Why?"

"My dad, well, I told you, he's been a mess since Kelly passed. He didn't realize until the other day that this week's renter never sent a deposit; half was due back in February, and half at the start of this month. I called, but the number I had on file was disconnected. I finally just figured they decided to bail on it." He pinches the bridge of his nose, like he's trying to determine how to say the next part. "By chance, did your mom go by a nickname or anything like that?" He steps forward, passes her the sheet. "Because if so, then I think it's possible she was the person I was trying to reach one final time last Friday, right before I called you."

Grace unfolds the paper slowly, afraid any sudden movement might make it detonate in her grip. There, printed at the top of the lease for 116 Surf Street, is her mother's name: *Birdie Porter*. A few lines below it, in the section indicating any additional occupants, the words *Grace Elizabeth Porter*—her daughter's maiden name—appears. Her eyes quickly skim over the blocks of text—rules and regulations and fine-print legalese—until they land on the most pertinent details of the agreement. The dates. A one-week rental set to begin at two o'clock last Saturday, the same day Grace checked in.

"Everything okay?" Jenny pushes the screen door open. Grace looks back, her expression revealing everything. Jenny steps outside and, without a word, takes the paper from her friend. She gives herself a minute to skim it, then looks up, her eyes bouncing back and forth between Caleb and Grace. "Your mother booked the house for the two of you when she was on the island the day of your birthday last year?" She pauses, letting the puzzle pieces click together in her mind. "For you to come down together *this* year?" Jenny looks at Grace, then at Caleb, then at Grace again. "As in, right now? This current week?" She takes another glance at the sheet, trying to make sense of something, then passes it back. "I don't understand. She never mentioned it to you, Grace? Why wouldn't she have told you she planned to do that?"

Grace looks at the paper, flipping it over as if some hidden message might appear. "I don't know." Her sight falls to the bottom of the agreement and the boldfaced word—SIGN—just beneath her mother's name. "Maybe she was planning a surprise for my birthday?" Grace suggests, though she's not sure this makes sense. Birdie wouldn't book something like that—a full week away—without running it past Grace and cross-checking her availability first. Would she? Just as she thinks this, her mind tumbles backward to last summer and the day Birdie came and watched Hallmark movies with her in bed—the afternoon she subtly hinted that she felt Grace's marriage might not last and the little joke she made about running away to the beach. "But I know someone who might have some insight." *Someone,* Grace considers, *who I think my mother wanted me to come down here and see*. She looks to Caleb, holds up the agreement. "Can I keep this?"

"Of course. It's just a copy. That's why I brought it."

Grace nods her appreciation, then turns to walk back inside. Before she makes it to the top step, she pivots back. "I understood what you meant yesterday. About how loss changes you." She tucks the sheet into her back pocket. "For the record, I'm still trying to figure out which version of myself I am these days, too."

~

Ray is nowhere.

For the last two hours, Grace has biked the full stretch of the island, hoping to find him and force him to tell her everything he knows. Back on her porch the other night, when Ray initially mentioned Birdie, her mind turned to the surreal—maybe a weird dream he'd had or the impossible fact that he was somehow seeing bits of the past everywhere on Sea Drift, too. Now, though, after bumping into Carol and hearing Caleb's news, she understands that he didn't mean his remarks in a metaphysical way. He saw her. Last summer. Talked to her. Knew something right now about Birdie that Grace didn't.

Even though Jenny insisted that she come (*Let's at least drive . . . in a car . . . with AC!*), Grace told her she wanted to be alone. She didn't know exactly what she was looking for or what she might end up learning, only that she wanted to be by herself when she finally found it.

Grace pedaled her way to every logical spot. She started at the Dive, hoping to find him working an early shift, but when she arrived, the lights were all clicked off and the door was locked. She rode over to Dune Street, walked her cruiser up and down the block three times while she studied every porch and window with the intent of catching a glimpse of Carol or Meg—someone to tell her something or point her in the right direction—but she had no luck. She pushed onward. Up to the lighthouse. Back to the boardwalk. Over to the old fishing pier. Down to the part of the beach where he liked to surf.

Nothing.

The whole time she rode, Grace thought of her mother. She tried to imagine Birdie driving over the bridge by herself last August—while Grace was hours away in Maine, stuck in a place and a part of her life where she didn't quite want to be—and finding Carol, then Ray, then . . . what? Did Birdie stay for the week in some other rental or hotel? Did she drive back home after going to the rental agency and signing a lease for Number 116 for this very week?

Grace had so many questions she might not ever be able to answer. So many things about her mother she felt desperate to know.

And that, she understood, was one of the hardest parts of losing someone you loved.

You couldn't pick up the phone anymore to call and ask a simple question—*Do you still have that recipe for those cookies you made? Do you remember the name of that little place we went to that one time? Did you talk to my childhood crush, book our old vacation home, then never tell me about either thing?*

The absence hurt Grace in ways she couldn't explain. Her mother was nowhere. And everywhere. She saw her in everything, not just on this island but in every part of her life. But she couldn't talk to her. Hear her voice. Beg her for advice. Instead, Grace just clung on to her beliefs and told herself a bird in the window or a feeling in the breeze was Birdie.

Now, her search more or less over and feeling hot, tired, and completely wrung out, Grace slows her pedaling, looking for somewhere to stop.

It's lunch by the time she parks the bike in the rack outside Smitty's. As always, the lot is packed. The line from the takeout window already snakes halfway down the crushed-seashell lot. Sunburned kids dart in every direction. Moms balance trays of food. A group of preteens is gathered around the old hook-and-ring game, cheering with every bit of enthusiasm they have each time one of them lands a shot.

"Anyone sitting here?" Grace asks a few minutes after she orders. She stands next to one of the picnic tables holding a plastic tray—red birch beer, small bucket of fries—and waits for the woman in question to respond.

"Nope," the woman says, her gaze focused on her food. "My kids are off running somewhere." She waves to the empty seat across from her. "It's just me."

"Your brother told me what happened," Grace says when Meg finally looks up from her paper plate. "We've run into each other a few times down here this week."

"I know." She looks exasperated—the bright grin she's worn during all their previous encounters currently extinguished. "He stopped by our rental the other night after he saw you down at the beach." Beyond her shoulder, Emma and Quinn—their antibiotics having apparently kicked in—chase each other near the fence. "We sat on the porch together, talking for a while," she explains. "He told me he gave you back the ring from that night out on the pier."

At the take-out window, the teenage employee calls out some other person's order.

"I should have told you," Meg says. "Especially when you told me about Birdie at dinner. I should have told you I'd lost someone, too." She absently picks at her hamburger bun. "But the truth is, I just didn't want to say it again. It's easier sometimes to pretend with people I don't regularly see, you know? To let myself imagine, just for a minute, that I actually got the life I thought I was building instead of the one I really have."

It'd be easy for Grace to tell her. Tell her, yes, of course, she understands. Tell her, no, her current life isn't the one she thought she'd have, either. But sometimes silence says more than words do, a sort of camaraderie that blooms in quiet. For a few minutes, each of them privately seeming to understand this fact, they both just sit in it.

"Ray knows something about my mom, Meg," Grace says then, just as the preteens erupt in another round of applause. "And I need to figure out what it is. Do you know where I can find him? Today, preferably. I've looked everywhere."

Meg sighs while a piece of strawberry hair blows around her face. She understands what it means. To get one last message. To have one final answer solved. To feel like maybe there's one more conversation you can still have with the person you've lost.

"You're not going to find him anywhere around here today, Grace," she states. "He left the island hours ago."

"Left the island?" Grace asks, confused. "What do you mean? I thought your whole family was going to the Dive tonight for a celebration for him."

"We were," Meg states as Emma and Quinn, their faces flushed, barrel toward the table. "Until last night. He showed up at our rental after his shift to say something came up and he needed to get away. That his manager was going to cover things at the bar for the rest of the week. He hasn't answered our calls since."

Grace's chest tightens. "Wh-where do you think he went?"

Meg shrugs. "No idea. He didn't give us much detail about anything." She rises to standing and gathers her things. "Grace?"

The way she says it makes Grace's breath shorten. "Yeah, Meg?"

"Am I right to assume that something happened between you and Ray last night?" Meg asks. "That you spoke or saw each other or something of the sort?"

Grace's thoughts pulse with an image. The Beachcomber's bar. The untouched beer. The way he looked at her, there with Adam. The stories his mind must have been creating.

"I mean, I saw him," Grace stammers. "Just for a minute. At dinner. I was at the Beachcomber. My ex showed up on the island kind of out of nowhere, and I saw Ray across the dining room, and then—"

"And then he left," Meg says.

TWENTY-EIGHT

"He's gone," Jenny announces.

Grace, still at the doorway of the beach house, takes another step inside, the screen door slapping closed behind her. She blinks away a series of sunspots that swirl in her line of vision and fully views the scene. Jenny sits on the couch, Grace's copy of *The Tides* on her lap, as well as a plate full of snacks. The TV is turned on, right on the station where Grace last left it, another silly Hallmark movie filling the space with white noise and made-up stories about love.

"How do you already know?" Grace asks, thinking she's referring to Ray.

Jenny sets the book and her plate on the coffee table, moves into the kitchen, and gets Grace a can of seltzer from the fridge. "Adam," she clarifies, suddenly realizing this is necessary, then encourages Grace to sit down and drink. "He stopped by about an hour ago, said he didn't want to call you. We talked for a minute. He just wanted you to know he was leaving."

Her body more exhausted and lethargic than she can ever remember, Grace chugs a few significant gulps from the can, then nearly collapses onto the sofa.

"Grace?" Jenny sidles up beside her. "Are you okay?" A look of concern stretches over her face. "No offense, but you don't look so great."

"Ray left, too," Grace says, which is not an answer, but an explanation. "Apparently after he saw Adam and me at dinner last night, he left the island. So as far as whatever my mother was doing here last summer, it doesn't seem like it's in the cards for me to find out."

She reaches into her shorts pocket, pulls out the crinkled-up lease agreement, and sets it on the coffee table with all the other oddities she's collected since arriving here last weekend. She picks up each item, feeling it in her fingers, then places it back down, trying to remember how she got here. Not just to Sea Drift or this week but to this whole part of her life. The one where the script isn't working and nearly everyone she's ever loved is gone, as is the person Grace believed—that *all* the past versions of herself once believed—she'd be by now.

Jenny just sits, watching her, a sense of maternal patience practically radiating off her. While she does, Grace sifts through more items, her fingers ultimately landing on her book. She thumbs through the pages. They flutter like a deck of cards in a magician's hands. And maybe that's what writing was, too. A form of magic. A story you knew wasn't real but that you wanted to be so badly that your heart found a way to bring it to life on the page.

"I haven't written a word." Grace's eyes remain on the book, the one she once felt inside every cell in her body and that she only now truly realizes a quiet part of her privately hoped might someday—somehow—come true. "For my new novel. Not since I turned in the original draft back in January."

"You don't mean that." Jenny scoots closer. "You're just always so hard on yourself. Every line has to be perfect before you'll—"

"No," Grace admits, the first time she's really said it out loud. "That's not it this time." She closes her copy of *The Tides*, effectively closing the story—the real one that once inspired it—too. "There's not a single salvageable sentence there."

For the first time in days, she reaches for her laptop—still on the coffee table from the other night—and opens it. The screen illuminates. Without a word, Grace scrolls through her document, past the "Book Three" title page, then the few pages of bullet points and jumbled notes.

"I've had my agent bump back the deadline three times," Grace points out, even though, of course, Jenny already knows this. They've talked about it dozens of times. "Everyone has been more than accommodating and understanding."

"Grace, what if we pull out one of your journals. We can sit, look over all your early notes for the book, brainstorm some new ideas together, and—"

"It's too late for all that," she acknowledges. "Even if I started tonight—really sat down, focused, forced myself to write a crazy amount of pages every day—I won't be able to do it."

"Then just ask them for a few more weeks, Grace," Jenny suggests. "Nothing dramatic. Even a couple of spare days might help give you the space you need to—"

"It's not about time anymore." Grace closes her computer. "It's about me." She sets it on the arm of the couch, rubs her face. "I used to write to find answers to my problems. If I felt lost about something, I wrote until I stumbled upon a conclusion. If something hurt, I wrote until some of the pain went away. But this book, I can't even get the first real sentence down." Her words begin to quiver, but she pushes through anyway. "It's supposed to be about a happy young family. A couple. A baby. A house full of laughter and light. But every time I sit down to write about them, there's just . . . nothing. I can't see them. Hear them. I'm so far removed from their world that they don't even feel real. I'm just faking it. I hardly even remember the person I was—where my heart was at—when I came up with the concept."

She feels it then, a sensation forming in her belly, then swelling and moving up her throat. A tidal wave of emotions—a whole, unforgiving spectrum of them—rises in her. Every loss she's felt—this week, these last six months, the past few years—comes out in a heavy, guttural sob.

"What do I do, Jenny?" Grace begs. "Please just tell me what I'm supposed to do."

"You do in real life what you haven't been able to do on the page," Jenny says and wraps her arms around Grace's body, pulling her in close and letting her cry against her chest. She hugs her friend tighter. "You contact your agent, and you tell her the truth."

~

Grace wakes up on the couch, even though she doesn't remember closing her eyes. She bats her lids open slowly and sees that the light in the living room has dimmed. The TV is still on but muted now, Jenny's snack plate and Grace's empty seltzer can cleared away.

"I ordered dinner," Jenny says from the kitchen as she uncorks a wine bottle. "I looked through some of the stuff in the welcome basket and called a pizza place up the street." She pulls two of the old blue drinking cups from the cabinets and pours. "In the meantime, how about some wine?"

Grace rubs her face and sits up, though a bit too fast. A wave of nausea washes over her, the weight of the whole day crashing back in. She nods, twists her body, and drops her feet to the floor. Jenny passes her the glass. Grace takes a sip, but it doesn't go down quite right. She sets it on the table, then grips the edge of the couch cushion, like she needs it to steady herself.

"I admit it's not the best quality," Jenny says, thinking that Grace's reaction is meant as a joke about the wine's too-sweet taste. "Though I probably should have assumed that when I grabbed a bottle sitting on a table along with a sunscreen display."

Grace blinks and pulls herself to standing. "Sorry." She does her best to swallow the feeling down. "I think I'm just kind of dehydrated from the last few days."

Jenny quickly moves back to the kitchen. "I'll get you water. And a fresh seltzer. Come sit. I'll bring you both."

"I will," Grace states, already moving toward the hallway. "I think I'm just going to go wash my face."

Inside the bathroom, Grace lets the water run cold over her wrists, then cups some in her palms and splashes it over her cheeks. Although the queasy feeling doesn't disappear, in time, it starts to settle into something tolerable. From inside the small under-the-sink vanity, she pulls out a washcloth, wets it, then takes a seat on the closed toilet and lays it on the back of her neck. For a moment, she lets the dampness work its way into her skin.

Her gaze shifts down. The Band-Aid barely hangs on to her skin. She peels it off and sees that her heel is still red. She takes the washcloth from her neck and places it on her foot, then reaches into the narrow nook beside the toilet and the sink for the pharmacy bag from yesterday.

She unfolds the brown paper, hardly even remembering what she bought, and places each item on the sink ledge. A box of Band-Aids, already opened. Alcohol wipes. A tube of ointment. She almost stops there, unscrews the cap, and dabs the gel on her raw skin. Instead, her hand dips back into the bag, aware from the weight of it that something else still lingers at the bottom.

Initially, when she pulls it out and sets it with her other purchases, Grace hardly even thinks twice. She's removed nearly this exact box—soft blue with bits of pink in the design and a clean white font—countless times these last few years. It takes a minute for it to hit her. That in her overwhelmed state from seeing Carol and hearing her news about Birdie in the pharmacy aisle, she inadvertently tossed a pregnancy test into her basket.

Once she realizes that it's there, Grace freezes. She just sits, looking at it, trying to retrace her steps and remember how it ended up in her bag. She reaches for it slowly, as if her hands are moving through water, and unwraps the protective plastic layer, then peels one end open, wondering if this was truly a mistake on her part—a random slip—or if it was a most unusual and blatant sign. If maybe a quiet voice deep inside her on some level already knew.

"Grace?" Jenny says through the door. "Are you all right?"

"I'm fine." She slides the plastic tester out from the packaging. "I'll be out in a minute."

Everything that comes next is muscle memory. The right angle to hold it. The way to carefully lay it down flat, never shaking it or moving it too much. The correct amount of time to wait, which isn't long but feels like an eternity—the reason her impatience always wins and she looks too soon.

Even though it's only been a minute, the timing seems to be just right. The answer Grace has waited for is there. Not faded. Not uncertain. Not metaphor. Not memory. Not maybe.

It's present.

Two lines, as strong and blue as the ocean.

A new story.

A new future.

A new version of herself that, until right this instant, she had no idea she was already in the process of becoming.

TWENTY-NINE

Friday

Rain taps the bedroom window. It's a drizzle, not a storm, but it's enough to wake Grace up. After what happened last night, it's a miracle she slept at all. She pulls herself upright, slowly so as not to instigate any unpleasant feelings in her stomach, then sits for a few minutes and looks outside. For the first time all week, the sunlight is blocked by blotches of gray clouds. It's not a beach day, but something else entirely. The memory of that test and those two crossed blue lines weighing down on her—she's not really sure what it is.

"I'm officially the most terrible friend in all of history," Jenny announces when Grace pads into the living room. "This has to go down as the worst imaginable time ever for me to have to leave."

Grace pans her face from left to right. The kitchen is fully cleaned. The throw pillows on the couch are nicely fluffed. Jenny's weekender bag sits, already packed and zipped up, beside the front door.

"You have to get home to your kids. Eric has his meeting later today. I know," Grace says. "It's okay."

Last night, after Grace finally stumbled out of the bathroom holding the slender plastic test, she and Jenny sat on the couch together for half the night. Initially, Grace was stunned and speechless as she stared at it there on the coffee table among the Madame Mermaid coupon, the crumpled lease agreement, and her smorgasbord of other unlikely belongings. It wasn't until the initial shock wore off that she became consumed by panic.

Up until the last few months, she'd spent five years monitoring and rationing out her life. Limiting alcohol and certain seafoods. Turning her nose up at caffeine. Since arriving here, she'd done the opposite. She couldn't even recall the last time she took a prenatal vitamin. Jenny assured her it was okay. That these things, as Grace certainly understood, don't always happen according to a finely orchestrated plan.

They did the math. Grace counted backward like she had so many times, all the way to her and Adam's last intimate moment in mid-June, the day after her lunch in the city with Mollie. Of course it was—always had been—a possibility. Grace knew how bodies worked. But after all the years of losses, hers barely seemed to function right. Cycles happened whenever they felt like it—no rhythm, no reason, no real regularity—her hormones constantly all over the place from the many losses, like they were confused and trying to figure out what they were meant to do.

The signs had been there. Of course they had. But it was only then, last night on the couch with Jenny, that Grace realized she'd chosen to ignore them. The nausea. The fatigue and constant napping. The achy, heavy feeling in her chest. In her mind, she kept gathering them all up and spinning them into a different narrative, telling herself they were the result of loss and grief, when really they were all pointing instead to life.

"I made you a little something for breakfast," Jenny says now and gestures to the table, where a plate of toast and scrambled eggs sits. "No coffee, though," she adds. "I didn't have a reason when I went to the store the other day to pick up any decaf."

She steps forward, pulls Grace in for a tight hug.

"I can't believe this is happening," Grace whispers into Jenny's neck.

Jenny pulls back. "I can." She squeezes Grace's shoulders. "Life can be full of surprises. Not only bad ones. Now and again, the universe throws us good curveballs, too."

~

Everything is quiet. Rainy days are always like this here. There are no families pulling overstuffed carts, trying to cross the boulevard to get to the beach. No kids running around barefoot in the street. It's a reset day to hang inside, finally wash some sandy towels, start to clean out the fridge, spend the afternoon picking on leftovers and playing gin rummy.

Grace drives. She has no real plan. Right now, she just needs to feel like she's in forward motion, that she's moving—although slowly—toward something. After she cruises the full length of the island once, she navigates back to the south side, then decides to make all her stops. She doesn't visit them in any particular pattern or order, but rather whichever place happens to pop up along the way.

Everywhere she looks, she finds absence. Inside the arcade, with its flashing lights and chaotic carpet, Cece's favorite Skee-Ball machine is left vacant. Up on the boardwalk, both plastic chairs outside Madame Mermaid's booth remain empty. Inside the Beachcomber's bathroom, the only people Grace stumbles upon are a few women her age who are freshening up after a rainy morning brunch. Down on the beach, on the stretch between the old motel and the fishing pier, no one is there. In the bookshop, a few unfamiliar shoppers browse the aisles, pulling spines from the shelves and heading on their way, though that's it. Out at the lighthouse, there's no figure standing on the jetty, searching for the right ending.

When she climbs back in Birdie's Jeep, Grace can't quite say where they've all gone. All she knows is that for the first time this whole year, the loss doesn't feel like a void or an emptiness.

It feels more like a clearing.

~

Grace doesn't plan to stop until she sees it.

A white facade with blue trim hugging its edges. Bold red letters—Sea Drift Movie House—on its front and the words Today's Showing: JAWS up on the old-fashioned marquee.

She parks the Jeep, pays for a ticket, then walks inside, through the hallway of faded movie posters, buys a snack, then goes into the practically empty theater to sit.

Even though, over the course of her life, she's seen it dozens of times, she watches the film all the way through. In the past, she'd always watched the movie for fun, the few times she and Ray came here on rainy days just like this one to watch it, or the countless occasions back home on cold winter nights when it popped up at random on a cable channel. Back then, it was always about the shark, the scary thing that lurked just beneath the surface.

But today, as Grace sits by herself, sipping water and nibbling on unbuttered popcorn, she realizes the shark isn't entirely the point. In many ways, the film is about pretending. The tourists on Amity Island, all wide smiles and golden tans, acting like everything is all right. That there's no real threat. No reason to be afraid or believe that everything will crash. That the plans they've carefully laid out—to enjoy the sun and bask in all the joy of the Fourth of July holiday—will, despite the warnings and signs posted up and down the beach, go off without a hitch.

"Hooper's always been my favorite character," a voice says when Grace steps back outside onto the sidewalk. "He's the one who's willing to stick around and face the thing everyone else on Amity is too afraid to name."

Ray sits on a white concrete bench just beside the cinema's entryway. Same worn-out hat. Same steady presence. Same him.

"I thought you left," Grace says as the other moviegoers filter out behind her. "I saw Meg yesterday. She filled me in."

"I did."

"Where did you go?" she asks, her tone hesitant.

"Nowhere," Ray admits. "Once I got over the bridge, I just . . . drove. This island's pretty small sometimes, Grace. I just needed to get away for a minute."

"But you came back," she points out.

Ray pulls off his backward hat. "I did." He rubs his head, then slides it back on. "I got stuck in traffic somewhere in Delaware and followed a detour. Almost an hour passed before I realized I took a wrong turn and was heading back in this direction the whole time." He sighs, long and heavy. "I thought about backtracking, but then I remembered that an old friend used to say the signs are always there in life if you pay attention."

Overhead, the sky spits a light drizzle, but in the distance, the clouds are beginning to break.

"How'd you know I was here?" she asks.

"I saw Birdie's Jeep." He points to the parked vehicle. "Took a lucky guess."

He scoots over on the bench.

"Thanks," she says and accepts his invitation.

There's space between them, yet their thighs brush, barely a touch. A tingling sensation vibrates through her body, like when they were young. A bolt of electricity every time their fingers touched. Even the softest, shortest-lived graze enough to steal her breath.

They stay silent like this for a few minutes as more people exit the theater. With grief, Grace has come to learn quiet often feels scary, something empty you long to fill back up. But not this. The quiet feels familiar. Full. It's like settling back into a cherished memory.

"She ran into my mom at the lighthouse that morning," Ray says, knowing it's unnecessary for him to use names. "It was a total coincidence, the fact that either of them were on the island and standing in the same place at the same time."

Grace doesn't say anything. Doesn't ask a question. She just listens and lets him talk.

"Naturally, my mother insisted they go for lunch." He leans back against the wall. "She called me, said I had to stop by to say hi." Ahead of them, a few cars coast smoothly up the boulevard. "I popped by at the end of their meal." Ray takes his hat off again, sets it on his knee. "My mom was going to a store on the mainland that afternoon." He rolls his eyes. "She kept insisting that she needed to buy me better sheets." In the sky, one of the larger clouds drifts, giving way to a crack of sunlight. "I told your mom to come by the Dive later if she was free. She mentioned that, like my mom, she was only on the island for the day. I didn't think she'd take me up on my offer. But she did."

"And then what?" Grace asks, trying her best to fill in the gaps. "What did she talk about?"

"You," he says. "The only thing she talked about the whole time was you." Ray leans forward. "I made her a few Shirley Temples. She told me she was worried." He presses his forearms against his thighs. "She said some things had been happening in your life that made her think you might need a place to land or—I don't know—reset, maybe. Like she planned to book the house for the two of you for this week because she anticipated that you'd need to be down here for some reason."

"Why did she tell you all this?" Grace asks, her question half directed at Ray and half at herself, even though she already senses the answer—*has* sensed it for a long time but tried to ignore it. Her mother dropped so many clues over the years, always nudging her daughter back to this place.

"I can't say for sure, Grace," Ray admits. "I only know she said it felt like a sign that she ran into my mother, and then me, while she was down here for the day. That she'd been thinking about my family—about old vacation memories—a lot in recent months." He pauses, clears his throat. "And that, at some point this week while you were both down here together again, she hoped to bring you to my bar for a drink so that the two of us—me and you—could find a time to say hello."

Grace softly exhales as recognition settles over her. Of course Birdie had orchestrated this trip. Not overtly, but in her own gentle way. Knowing that, in doing so, she'd nudge Grace back toward him.

While her mind processes all this, Grace's thoughts drift back to February and the night of their last conversation, though neither of them knew that's what it was at the time. Birdie called shortly before bedtime while she watched one of her silly movies, just like always, to check in. Grace wasn't having a great day. She'd sat at her desk all afternoon, staring at her computer screen, though it'd been like trying to squeeze water from a rock. Adam was working late in the city again. Earlier, she'd received a catalog in the mail from a children's clothing company, page after page of other people's infants dressed in ruffles and pastels.

"You know what I think we need, Cece?" Birdie said, sounding perfectly healthy and happy and like herself. "A trip to the beach. Just me and you. We'll get crumb cake and clam strips and sit out in the fresh air and reset."

"It's February, Mom," Grace pointed out through a quiet laugh. "There's a half foot of snow outside right now."

"I know it, my girl," Birdie said, and even through the line it was easy for Grace to tell that her mother was smiling. "But let's both promise to dream about it tonight anyway."

Now, back on the bench outside the cinema, Ray continues with his story.

"Anyway," he goes on, "she told me that after she left my place, she planned to go to the rental agency and book the house for this year during your birthday week. She said she wanted to surprise you. That it was a gift. That some voice inside her kept telling her that you'd need it."

Grace thinks of the lease agreement from Caleb, currently sitting on the coffee table. The one on which Birdie wrote out her daughter's maiden name. Like maybe she knew which way things were going. Or like maybe she hoped it'd serve as a small way of reminding her of the person she used to be. That none of it—booking the house, getting Grace back on the island—was about pastries or fried seafood. It was an instruction manual. A map.

"She said the past few years you'd been working so hard to try and be everything," Ray continues. "A writer. A mother. A wife." Slowly—hesitantly—his hand drifts an inch. His pinkie touches hers, followed by the rest of his fingers, then his whole hand. "She was worried you'd become so busy trying to hold everything together, striving for the person you thought you were supposed to be, that you'd started to forget how to just be yourself."

Grace blinks away the tears. "She always saw me for who I really was," she says, thinking of all the moving boxes back at home, the ones filled with reminders of all her phases and desires, milestones and ill decisions—every piece of it, according to Birdie, worth preserving. "Not just in a moment. Not just one version. But all of it. Every part of me." She lifts her free hand, wipes her eye, then tilts her face toward him, this man who, through the years, always loved and accepted her at every stage. Whichever version of her showed up on the island each August, she was enough. "Just like you."

Ray squeezes her fingers. Together, they sit this way, hands locked together, the sound of waves in the distance, breathing in the salt air, just like at so many other points in time.

"I'd better get going," Ray says at last, the goodbye just one more part of their tradition. He rubs his thumb over her pointer finger, letting his touch linger, neither of them ready to let go just yet. "I haven't even told my folks I'm back yet."

Grace nods. It's time for her to move on as well. To go back to the beach house and pack up her things before her check-out time in the morning. To call Adam and tell him the news and then try to figure out what it means for them. To finally email Mollie back and ask her to meet in the city next week and explain the real story—that sometimes, even when you try, even when you want something so badly, the only way forward is to walk away.

"Me too," she says. "Today's my last full day here."

Somewhere in the distance, the melody from an ice cream truck fills the air.

"You think you'll be back?" Ray asks.

"Undecided for the moment," Grace admits and subtly looks down at her belly. "I don't have a clue what the next few months are going to bring."

Behind them, a few people trickle into the cinema in advance of the next showing.

"Well, whatever life brings, Porter," he says, the first time he's called her by her old nickname in years, "I hope you do come back." Finally, he lets her hand go. "Whenever you feel ready." He smiles, and it feels like a sort of homecoming. "It's a small island," he tells her, as if she needs the reminder. "Whenever you decide to cross that bridge again, you'll know where to find me."

THIRTY

Saturday

It's time.

Although it's early, the sun not yet even fully up, Grace is awake. Showered. Dressed. The trash tied up. The bed linens stripped. Caleb's beach towel, which she forgot to give back, neatly folded on the kitchen table. Her bag's already packed and in the Jeep. Once again, just like when she first stepped inside here one week ago, the house is still.

After seeing Ray at the cinema yesterday, Grace returned here, quietly began to close things up, then spent the rest of the day out back in one of the Adirondack chairs. She didn't read. Didn't write. Didn't do anything productive.

Instead, she just let herself sit and think.

About her mother and their memories here together. About the strange tenderness of being known so intimately by a place. About how, now and again, a setting can come to remember you in ways you forgot to remember yourself. The versions you loved. The versions you lost. The versions you're only now learning to forgive.

She thought about how some people—if you're lucky—can see you that way, too. Not as chapters, but as a whole story with twists and turns and messy parts you've at times wished you could rewrite.

How sometimes you had to go backward in order to go forward again. And how, on other occasions, life hands you circumstances that force you to go forward alone.

How the ones we love—the people who shape us—don't really vanish when they go. Not really. Instead, they turn into stars—distant and quiet and impossible to reach—but always there and still lighting the way.

Now Grace locks the house for quite possibly the last time in her life. She heads around back and leaves the key beneath the bottle of strawberry shampoo. Then, in the dim light of early morning, she walks slowly up the empty street and in the direction of the dune.

Before she leaves, she knows there's one thing left for her to do.

~

The beach is quiet. Hazy. Empty. The breeze cool with lingering hints of night.

Like always, Grace kicks off her shoes, then walks down the dune's incline. The cool grains shift beneath her bare feet. All around her, the grasses whisper a quiet lullaby. She makes her way past the vacant lifeguard stands and across the wide stretch of sand. She moves toward the water, as still as a canvas. Above it, the sky is a muted palette. Blots of gray. Hints of lavender. The first precocious webs of yellow and peach.

The magic hour.

That pocket of time when the world quiets and everything feels like a dream.

Which is what Grace tells herself is happening when the haze starts to clear down by the water and she sees her. Sitting just past the slope, not far from where the gentle ebb of waves hits. A woman in a classic one-piece, a breezy cover-up, and a straw bucket hat. A chubby toddler runs in circles at her side.

Grace takes a cautious step toward her, remembering what Cece said the last time they saw one another the other night. That it was time for Grace to stop thinking about the past and to instead begin to consider the next version of herself, the one who comes after all this. She touches the lower part of her stomach, assuming that's what this is. Not the girl she was at sixteen or nineteen or twenty-two, but the woman she's on the cusp of becoming.

Until the person in front of Grace turns around.

It takes her a minute for the details to assemble themselves in her mind. The way her shoulder-length hair that hangs from beneath her hat seems blond from a distance, but gray when the hints of sunlight peering through the clouds hit it just right. The way she holds her posture, strong and confident so that she can comfortably balance the weight of her loss on it. The hint of red still staining her lips even though she washed her makeup off the night before at bedtime.

Birdie.

Not as she was when Grace lost her. But as she was a long time ago.

"Oh, don't even look at me," she calls out and wipes her bottom lashes. Her face is the same, but younger, smoother, the skin taut with youth. And yet, still remarkably, impossibly, hers. "I thought I was alone down here. You're probably best to keep walking. The lifeguards ought to stab a bunch of warning flags around me when they arrive. I'm a mess."

"I-it's okay." Grace moves a little closer, her breath caught inside her throat. "To be honest," she continues, her fingers shaking, "I'm kind of a mess these days, too."

Birdie scooches over by a few inches, not because there's no space, but more as an invitation for this stranger who's appeared behind her to come sit. Grace lowers herself into the sand and stretches out her legs, her sight no longer cast on the water, but rather on the two people—the woman and her child—to her right.

"Sorry about all the crying," Birdie says, still dabbing the tears away like they're nothing, and not every feeling inside her. "You're supposed to be happy when you're at the beach." When she says this, she gestures at the setting as if to say, *Just look at this place.* "Unfortunately for me, our time down here this week hasn't just been a vacation." Her hair catches the breeze and billows across her shoulders. "For me, it's also been a time to grieve."

Beside them, the toddler—the youngest version of Cece that Grace has had the opportunity to see this week—digs for shells, clapping each time she discovers something new.

"Her father died," Birdie states and looks at the girl. "My husband. This winter." She turns back to the water. "A patch of black ice on the highway, and just like that, he was gone."

It's a version of her mother Grace never had the opportunity to see. At least not in any way she'd recall. Broken. Scared. Mourning not only her lost love but also the person she was when she was with him and the future she once imagined they'd build.

Grace's mind floods with questions she wants to ask her. *How are you here? What am I supposed to do?* Before she can pose any of them, Birdie starts to talk again.

"We came here for our honeymoon," she says and waves a hand at the air. "It was several years ago." She laughs at some private memory. "We had the best time. The two of us were like fish. Every afternoon when we finally pulled ourselves out of the ocean, our fingers were all wrinkled up, like we were kids." Birdie pulls in a big breath and then another, like she's been deflated and is trying to fill herself back up. "We promised each other before we left that if we ever had a child, the minute we had enough money saved up, we'd bring her here for a happy family vacation." With this comment, Birdie flips her hands up toward the sky. "So here we are. Me and my girl. Only without him."

Grace was so young when James died. Other than stories her mother shared and a few framed photos around the house, she had no real memory of him. In turn, she had no real memory of her mother this way, either—alone, her grief still so raw, crying to a stranger on the beach. She only knew her as the strong, independent, and fearless widow she ultimately became.

"She's so little." Birdie swallows hard, trying to keep her voice steady. "She'll never remember him." Her eyes close briefly. "I'm so worried for her," Birdie says. "And if I'm honest, for me, too." She casts her sight down on the sand. "A single mother," she says through a heavy sigh, like she's just realizing what the words mean. "This wasn't the plan. Not at all." She pinches the bridge of her nose, but the tears fall anyway. "I'm so terrified I won't be enough."

"You will be." Grace chokes up at this unexpected symmetry. "You'll be so much more than that."

Birdie slowly lifts her chin. "Thank you." Tears track down her cheeks. "Sometimes it helps just hearing that." Just as she says this, the toddler waddles over and gifts her mother with a gray clamshell, then plants a kiss on her cheek. "My girl. Always discovering something beautiful." Birdie clutches the shell tight in her palm. "It's perfect, love."

Above them, the sun pierces through the clouds, casting pockets of glitter on the water.

"Want to hear something very silly?" Birdie asks and turns to look at Grace. "Today's our last day here, and I haven't been out in the ocean once for a swim."

"You should go," Grace says, still in disbelief over what's happening, and yet impossibly calm. "Before you leave."

Birdie thumbs the shell. "Not this year." She looks over at her daughter, who's resumed her treasure hunt. "She's too little. She'll get scared if I bring her with me and go out too far."

The realization settles on Grace like warm rays of light.

"I'll take care of her for you," Grace says. "I promise. I'll sit right here. I won't move."

Birdie's eyes narrow in contemplation. She looks at Grace, then at the child, and then at Grace again—not having any way of knowing that she's looking at the same person. "Okay," she agrees, brushing some sand off her slender calves. "Maybe just for a quick dip."

She stands, kisses her daughter, then removes her timeless cover-up and her hat and sets them both down. When she reaches the water, she makes sure to look back to ensure all is okay back on the shoreline before she proceeds. Slowly, she steps in. The water rises past her ankles. Then her knees. Then her hips. She takes another look at them, then dips beneath the surface. A long moment passes before she pops back up, her whole body wet and cool and healthy.

"It's wonderful!" she shouts and waves an arm. A smile spreads across her face. "I'll just be one more minute."

While Birdie swims, the child moves closer and passes over another find: a petite purple-tinged scallop shell. Once she gifts it to Grace, she sidles up and, with no real hesitation or restraint, takes a seat on her lap. For a moment that feels like it both lasts forever and not nearly long enough, Grace holds her as together they watch Birdie float and indulge in a temporary feeling of peace.

"We'll be okay," Grace whispers into the child's ear. "Me. You. Her." More daylight begins to break through the haze. "We're all going to be all right."

A few minutes later, Birdie dips again and then swims back to shore. She stands in the shallow surf for a moment, allowing the gentle swells to make contact with her legs. A look of contentment on her face, she bends and scoops her hand through the water, picking up a palmful of finds. From her place on the beach, Grace watches her sift through her discoveries.

"Huh," Birdie says, her silver hair wet against her neck. "Look at this."

At first, Grace squints, certain she's not seeing things right. But as Birdie steps out of the water and back onto the sand, any sense of doubt fades away.

The necklace dangles from Birdie's fingers, as if they'd always held it.

"Someone must have lost it while they were out there." She draws closer, the glint of metal unmistakable. "Lucky I found it." Her skin dripping with beads of water, Birdie holds it out for Grace to see. "Cece." She taps the delicate pendant. "What an adorable name."

Before Grace can react, the child—so happy to see that her mother is back—stands and runs into Birdie's arms. She lifts her up, quickly twirls her around.

"Thank you so much for watching her." Birdie sets the girl back down and then reaches for her belongings. "Getting to go out there like that lifted me up in ways I can't describe."

"Of course," Grace states, not wanting this moment to end but knowing deep down that it must. "Don't even think about it."

Birdie nods her appreciation. She slides on her hat, then her cover-up, the fabric clinging to her wet swimsuit.

"I guess it's time for us to get going," she says. "Me and the little one still have a long drive." She takes the child by her hand. "I'm going to leave the necklace up on one of the fence posts at the top of the dune, just in case someone comes looking for it."

The hard thing about life is that no matter how bad you want to, you can never stop time. You can't live inside a moment. Try as you might, you can't bend and stretch the hours or minutes. All you can do is be in it. Appreciate it. Knowing it means even more because of the fact that it will pass.

"Maybe I'll see you here again next year," Birdie says. "I think this might be our new tradition." She looks down at her daughter with all the love in the world. "The two of us. A few days down here every summer. A chance to step away from some of the other stuff I have to deal with back home."

"I'll look for you," Grace says, realizing then that tears have begun to fill her eyes.

"Well, in that case, I suppose this isn't goodbye." Birdie smiles again—warm and bright and comforting. "I'll be sure to look for you, too."

With that, Birdie and Cece—who isn't quite Cece just yet—begin to walk up the sand.

Grace twists her body and watches them, not sure where they're heading but knowing it's not her job to follow them.

That wherever it is they're going, they'll be fine.

That goodbye doesn't always mean forever.

That no matter how you change, or life changes, one thing is always certain.

The months slip away.

New days start. Hard ones end.

Eventually, despite everything, summer—beautiful summer—always comes again.

PART FOUR

Tomorrow

THIRTY-ONE

The boxes are right where she left them, stacked up like toy blocks across the living room floor. Some open, some still sealed, many of them labeled in Birdie's handwriting. *Baby years—Don't Toss! Elementary—Art Projects! Journals & Notebooks—Important!* Reminders—some big, some small—of all the different people her daughter ever was.

After a long day of driving, Grace gives herself time to settle before she rushes back into anything. She makes a few trips out to the Jeep, careful not to lift too much at once, and sets her belongings just inside the front door.

Upstairs in her bedroom, she drops her duffel bag onto the bed and begins to unpack. The last of the beach still clings to her clothing—grains of sand spilling onto the comforter and into the rug. When everything's sorted, she showers. For a long time, she stands under the water and inhales the steam. She scrubs away the salt and peeling, sunburned skin, lets it all swirl down the drain. When she's finished, after she slips on some comfortable clothes, she sifts through the linen closet, takes out some medical supplies, and properly bandages her foot so the wound she's carried with her all week can finally start to heal.

When she's done, Grace steps into her office. Of course, the room hasn't changed. It's as cluttered as ever. Crumpled notes. Abandoned plans. Neglected planters filled with plants that have long since gone dry. Grace pulls in a deep inhalation, filling herself with breath, finds the wastebasket, and starts to purge. Balled sticky notes. Her scribbled-up planner. The piles of crispy leaves. From the bathroom, she grabs some cleaning wipes and a cup of water. She gathers the ceramic pots and pours a little liquid into each one, just in case there's any hope in the dried-up stems coming back to life. When the desk surface is tidy, she wipes it all down, then reaches for the gold frame—the image of her and Birdie at the top of the dune, suspended together in a moment—and sets it on the corner of her workspace. Then, quietly, she sets down her laptop and plugs it in so that it's ready for her, whenever that day comes again when she needs it.

Back downstairs, she pulls some provisions from the pantry and makes herself something simple, but whole, to eat. She carries her plate into the living room, turns on the TV. For a moment, she clicks until she lands on her mother's favorite station. She watches it for a couple of minutes while she takes a few bites of her meal. And then, finally, not wanting to put it off any longer, Grace begins.

Item by item, she puts it all away. One thing at a time. The Magic 8 Ball. The folded-up notes from Jenny. Her old retainer. The rolled-up posters. The floppy disks. Every last thing: the remnants of a girl—*girls*—her mother once loved so fiercely she couldn't bear to throw any part of her—not a single memory—away.

Before she closes the boxes, Grace adds a few additions of her own—all the small things she's accumulated and saved herself these last few days: The sand dollar. The arcade tickets. The paper bracelet. The highlighter. The chunky necklace. The coupon for Madame Mermaid. The two nearly identical silver rings. And then, finally, the gold nameplate. The one she thought she had lost but that was always waiting for her, right there beneath the surface.

The moment she adds it in, Grace hears it.

A tapping. So soft at first that she assumes she must be imagining things. Grace reaches for the remote and mutes the television, though the sound remains, soft but present. She looks up and sees it. There, at the window, watching her pack up these final pieces of her past.

Tap, tap, tap.

Its orange beak pecks the glass.

Grace stands and crosses the room slowly, careful not to startle it and scare it off. The bird doesn't move, just remains perched on its branch, a beautiful burst of red set against a backdrop of green leaves.

Maybe it's a sign. Maybe it's just a bird. Either way, right now, Grace is glad it's there.

Her elbows propped on the top of one of the teetering cardboard stacks, she stays and studies it until eventually, it flaps its wings and is gone. Once it disappears into the sky, Grace turns back to the couch, her elbow accidentally knocking a pile of loose papers off one of the boxes in the process. They flutter, then scatter onto the floor. She kneels, gathering everything—an old high school talent-show flyer, a marked-up math test from junior year, a playbill from a small Bucks County theater production. She's halfway through the pile when her fingers land on the envelope, just another memory among many. She nearly shuffles past it, tucks it in with everything else, until she turns it over and sees that it's still sealed.

Back on the couch, Grace peels it open and discovers an old greeting card inside. The front is faded, yet still bright, a swirl of colorful flowers framing a glittery number sixteen. Somehow, despite the years that have passed, the paper carries a hint of her mother's perfume. With great care, she opens it and finds Birdie's penmanship marking both sides. A letter. Or a wish. One final note for her daughter before she officially moved into the new year ahead.

> Cece,
>
> Happy birthday, my beautiful girl! I'm writing this to you from a bench outside the pharmacy while you soak up a bit more sun at the beach. It's hard to blame you—what a gorgeous week we've had down here this year!

Sixteen. Can you believe it? Not quite a child anymore, but not quite a grown-up yet, either. Just . . . you. Which, if you ask me, is the most perfect thing for you to be. I hope that no matter what life hands you, my love, that you'll always remember the happy, curious, endlessly empathetic, and intuitive person you are today and try as best you can to keep her close. She's someone special and worth knowing. Someone who, even as you get older, is worth keeping around as a friend.

My wish for you this year is a simple one: that you always find a way to stay as happy as you are today. Not because life will always be kind to you (it won't be), but because you can always be kind to yourself . . . even on the hard days.

I hope you like your gift. It's small, nothing fancy. I had it made for you at that shop we love. You know the place, the one with all the shells and wind chimes. Just a little something for you to wear as a reminder of the individual you are today.

Happiest of birthdays, my girl. May all your dreams come true today, next year, and always.

My love forever,

Mom

Grace reads the letter a second and then a third time, letting the words echo in her mind until she's nearly committed them to memory. When she's ready, instead of sliding it back into the envelope and putting it inside a box, she keeps it out, leaving it propped open on an end table, just like she would have if Birdie were here to give her a new birthday card this year.

She's done enough for today. Grace picks up the remote and allows herself to sink deeper into the couch. She clicks up the volume and then watches the movie, even though it's already halfway through. On the screen, two people kiss on a snowy street, the town twinkling, like the world dressed itself up just for them.

As always, Grace already knows the ending. There'll be a fight. A big obstacle. A crossroads. A bakery or a town fundraiser or a Christmas tree farm in peril. A necessary choice. Before the final credits roll onto the screen, they'll figure out a way to make things work. The whole plot will tie up neat and tidy. The actors will all wear smiles on their faces in the final scene. Grace laughs softly to herself as she watches it, not because the movie is any good, but because it's familiar.

The music swells. There's a big, dramatic moment.

Don't worry. They'll find their happily ever after, she can almost hear her mother say. *Just wait and watch until the end.*

And even though there's no one else here in this house with her—at least, no one that she can see—for the first time in as long as she can remember, Grace is alone but not lonely.

She's content just to sit in the quiet of it.

THIRTY-TWO

One Week Later

The restaurant is flooded with sunlight. Pools of it pour through the large industrial windows that look out onto Manhattan's Chelsea neighborhood and cast shapes across the tiled floor. It's midday on a Wednesday, though most of the tables are empty. Tomorrow marks the start of the long holiday weekend, the last leisurely stretch of summer before a new season begins.

"I don't understand." Mollie's lips are tight. "Are we talking a few pages?" She tilts her face. "A couple chapters?" She holds her water glass, like she needs to physically touch something cold to cool herself down. "How much do you still need to write?"

"All of it." Grace's tone is neither emotional nor smug. For once, she just states it for what it is: the truth. "The whole thing."

Mollie sets down her glass. "This is bad, Grace," she states, as if this fact needs to be stated, like her comment is a nice wine that requires a bit of time out in the air so it can breathe. "You're under contract. There are production schedules. I'm sure I don't need to remind you that you've already been paid. They were pretty clear the last time around that they couldn't just keep pushing the deadline back."

"I know," Grace says as their waiter approaches the table and offers them each a leatherbound menu. "I'm fully aware of the consequences."

"Then I'm confused." Mollie sets down her menu, not even bothering to open it. "What are you asking for? Do you need more time or—"

"Nothing," Grace admits. "I'm genuinely not asking for anything." She smooths the front of her maxi dress, the fabric noticeably a bit tighter near her waist than it was a few seasons ago. "I'm going to walk away from the contract. Start over. I'll pay everything back."

Mollie pinches the bridge of her nose, then briefly closes and reopens her eyes. "Grace, you know if you do this, they're not going to work with you again in the future, right?"

Grace nods. Over the last few days, she's reminded herself of this most important detail numerous times. "I do." She sets her palms on her thighs like they're anchors. "And I also understand that, after a move like this, it's more than likely that you'll choose to part ways with me, too."

Mollie sighs heavily. "Look. I know the past year hasn't been kind to you—these last few months especially. But business is business. Once I put the wheels on this in motion, Grace, I'm not going to be able to go back."

"I know." Grace straightens her posture, sure to say this next part with all the certainty and confidence she feels surrounding it. "But even if they gave me another extension—gave me another year or all the time in the world—I still wouldn't be able to write it for them." The waiter sets down a breadbasket no one will touch, Grace already aware that their meal is coming to an end before it's had a chance to start. "I'm not the same person I was the day I signed that contract, Mollie. The story I wanted to tell back then, it just doesn't work anymore."

"Well, what story is it you want to write today?" Mollie asks, her expression suggesting that she's genuinely interested in Grace's response. "Do you have something else in mind that you can put together quickly and maybe we can try to spin into—"

"I don't," Grace tells her, the thought both scary and freeing. To not have a plan. A vision. A mental blueprint. A neat and tidy picture in mind for how everything's supposed to go. "I'm not sure that I will for a little while."

Their waiter walks back up and pulls a notepad and pen from his apron. Grace looks at Mollie. A whole conversation unfolds in their silence.

"I'm sorry," Grace tells the man. "I don't think we're going to stay. There's been a change of plans."

With this, Mollie pushes out her chair, stands, then glances at her watch. "I'd better get back to the office and make some calls before everyone heads out of town for the holiday." She reaches for her purse and turns to walk away. Before she takes a step, she pivots back. "And Grace. You were wrong." Her expression softens. "When you do come up with your next story idea—whenever that might be—make sure you give me a call."

~

Grace walks. All through the city, up and down the blocks she once navigated daily, so busy chasing a dream she'd only later realize was temporary. The soles of her sandals slap against the sidewalk as she moves, the sound swallowed up by the symphony of metropolitan noise. Horns blaring. The hiss of steam from the subway grates. The song of thousands of people all reaching for something so big.

She doesn't mean to intentionally walk past it, but she finds herself standing in front of it anyway. Her once favorite bookshop, the one she used to frequent on weekends when she lived here, browsing in and out of the aisles, her fingers trailing over the rainbow of book spines.

Now she stops.

Her eyes linger on one of the shop windows and the display inside it.

A little more than five years ago, Grace walked into this establishment on a warm June night to celebrate the launch of her book and first-ever tour. She smiled while sitting at the front of the shop, looking out at the filled-up rows of folding chairs, proudly holding a hardback copy of her debut, her whole future opened up to what, at the time, felt like exactly the right page. How fast things change, and with so little warning. How much we grow, and in so short a time.

What advice would you give your younger self?

That night, she was asked the question for the very first time. A young woman, probably fresh out of college, was the one to pose it. Grace gave what she believed was the right response.

Keep going. Don't give up. You'll get there soon.

It's only today, standing on the other side of the glass and looking in, that Grace realizes her reply wasn't correct at all.

The real answer is that getting there is only one piece of the story. That even when you do, it's not always the victory you imagined. Sometimes the dream changes shape after you've caught it. Things you thought would be yours forever slip away.

But none of it has to do with age. Being older. Or younger. Where you happen to fall on the timeline.

For better or worse, it's just life.

~

Grace sits on a stool beside the window of the coffee shop on Amsterdam Avenue, the one she often came to when she and Adam lived up the street. She'd work here sometimes when she felt like she needed to get out of their apartment, nibbling on croissants and sipping espresso drinks while her fingers clacked away on her laptop keyboard like she was a pianist.

Outside the glass, the Upper West Side pulses with life. A few women push strollers. Bursts of cars race past. People in summer work attire—eyelet shift dresses, tucked-in golf shirts—emerge from the subway. A thirtysomething couple wheels carry-on luggage up the block, then slides into a car, likely ready to venture to the Hamptons or Fire Island or whatever place they're going to unplug and reset for these last few summer days.

"Sorry I'm late," Adam states when he walks in. He's dressed in his normal work attire, droplets of sweat dotting his hairline. "My last call of the day ran longer than I expected."

"It's fine," Grace assures him, then watches as he takes a seat. She gestures to the iced Americano she ordered for him in advance. "Really."

It didn't make sense for them to come all the way up here, more than a hop, skip, and a jump from Grand Central and Adam's office. Still, when they texted about it two days earlier, Grace thought that meeting in their old neighborhood just felt right. To end where they had their beginning. For their story to feel like a circle, something round and whole.

"You look . . . great," Adam stammers, like maybe he's not sure if he's still allowed to make comments like this. "How are you feeling?"

"I'm okay," she tells him, which is true. "Now that I'm back home and settled into a routine and eating more than just seafood and French fries, the nausea and fatigue haven't been quite as bad."

"Good." He wipes his forehead, even though he's now settled in the air-conditioning. It's hard to say if he's sweating from the heat or the circumstances of this meeting. "That's great to hear."

Grace twists then, reaches into her purse on the back of her chair and produces a medium-size white envelope. She turns back toward Adam, opens it, and slides out a strip of glossy black-and-white ultrasound images, all connected like still frames on a film reel. Without a word, she passes it to him, then watches a smile spread over his lips as he takes in the tiny profile, the curve of the spine, the unreal nature of it all.

There was a time, back in the beginning, when it seemed that a family was something Adam did want. A period in their relationship when he'd get excited seeing the positive test sitting on the bathroom counter, his chin set on Grace's shoulder as he admired her in the mirror and traced his fingers along her stomach. But with every loss, that light—that hope—faded from his face like a film dissolve sliding off the screen. Now, though, seated across from him, Grace sees it—a faint flicker of something. A dream. An emotion. A glimpse of the person he used to be.

Adam dabs the corners of his eyes with the tip of his pinkie. Sweat, maybe. Or something else. "So I'm guessing this means things look okay?" A trace of hesitancy carries his words. "Things look all right?"

Grace sips her decaf coffee. "That's what the doctor tells me." She gives a small shrug. "Further along than I've ever made it before."

"It's amazing." Adam shakes his head in disbelief, takes another look at the images, then hands them back. "I'm speechless."

"Those are for you," she says. "I had the tech print out two copies. I thought you'd want to keep one at your apartment."

His shoulders rise as he inhales. "Thank you for that." His expression drops by a degree. "I appreciate it."

They sit in silence. Adam's gaze shifts toward the street and the world moving just outside. Grace wonders for a second what he's thinking about. If he's imagining their past selves walking out there hand in hand. Or if he's thinking instead about the future and how they'll raise this child together but separate. If he's remembering all the moments that got them here—the good ones, the hard ones—and if they were all necessary in order for them to throw out their old plans and create space for this new dream.

"We'll make this work, Grace," Adam says, suddenly sitting up straighter. "I know this situation isn't ideal—certainly not one we ever planned on. But we'll figure it out. Find our own version of normal. I plan to do my part. To be involved. I won't leave you alone to navigate all this." He clears his throat, evening out some of the emotion that made the last few words shake. "Things may not have worked out for the two of us," he says, referencing their relationship, "but we'll find a way to make it work for the three of us, okay?"

"Okay," she says and nods. "That's important. That all sounds good."

"A-and I want you to stay in the house," Adam says, jumping back in. "I've been thinking about this a lot. Once we speak to the attorney and have the papers drawn up, I plan to have that put in writing. I want you and the baby to be settled. I know you're taking some time off from writing, but I'll help and do whatever I need to do to make sure the two of you are—"

"I don't want to stay there, Adam," Grace tells him, grateful for his offer even though she knows it's not the right path. "But I've been thinking about that part of things a lot, too. And though it'd probably be the most convenient option, I'm not sure it's the right one. I need a fresh start."

"Well, where will you go?"

"For the long term?" she asks. "I don't know." She takes the final sip of her beverage, then pushes it to the side. "But once we sort things out with our lawyers and the house sells—which I imagine it will rather quickly—I have somewhere to go for the short term."

Adam's brows lift in question as he waits to hear more details.

Grace takes one last look through the window, at this setting she once worked so hard to chase. She squints, like she's looking for something. Or maybe someone. Some former version of herself out there, still searching on these streets. She takes a breath, then another, and fills her whole self up with air.

"I'm still working out the details." She rests a soft palm on her belly while she looks at her reflection blending with the cityscape just beyond it. "But for the time being, I'm in the process of putting together a plan."

AFTER

THIRTY-THREE

One Year Later . . .

Saturday

Before her eyes are even open, Grace smells it. The warm, comforting scent of vanilla and yellow batter, strong and enticing enough to tug her from her dream. She blinks herself fully awake, stretches, and pulls her body upright in the bed. The plush comforter still wrapped around her limbs, she straightens, presses her back against the upholstered headboard, and looks through the window. Outside, the sun shines with all the strength of August. A pod of children creates chalk drawings on the sidewalk. A woman walks a dog. A pleasantly predictable morning in their sleepy Pennsylvania neighborhood.

There's a quiet knock on the bedroom door, then a pause before it creaks open.

"Breakfast is ready." Jenny pops her face around the doorframe. "I should warn you, Charlie dumped half a container of rainbow sprinkles into the batter." She laughs. "I guess it's his version of a cake, since we won't see you on your actual birthday in a few days."

Grace rubs her face, smiles. "I'm sure they're delicious."

Jenny steps into the room, dressed in a pair of running shorts and sneakers, like she's already lived a whole life this morning. "You slept in," she says, not in a judgmental way, but just as a fact. "Late night?"

"A little." Grace leans over to look inside the bassinet that sits comfortably beside the bed. "He was a bit fussy," she says, just as the baby starts to stir. "I probably should have set an alarm and gotten on the road by now." She smiles down at her son as he opens his eyes. "I'll pay for it, sitting in bridge traffic this afternoon."

"It'll be worth it." Jenny peers lovingly at the baby, gently touches his wisps of soft blond hair. "You both need your rest."

Downstairs, the sounds of children playing, shouting, and laughing fill the house with a happy mayhem that Grace has been grateful to be part of these last six months.

"Eric plans to put the crib together while you're away." Jenny moves back toward the hallway. "When you get back, he'll put the bassinet back up in the attic after you're done using it this week."

"Thank you," Grace says, her heart so full of appreciation for her friend. For this life. For everything.

"Speaking of which, is Adam still planning to come again next Sunday?"

Grace nods. "That's the plan," she says. "He doesn't like to go more than two weeks without seeing the little guy. Plus, he mentioned that he picked up a bunch of fall clothes—a little jacket and stuff—that he wants to make sure to give me before the seasons turn."

"Great," Jenny says and smiles, pleased by this news.

For a moment, they're quiet, a whole story passing between them. Nearby, the baby softly coos.

"Oh, one other thing before I forget," Jenny states. "Those town houses, the new ones up the street. I saw on my run earlier that they're *finally* done with construction on the development. They had a sign posted that they're going to start renting them out later this fall." She leans against the wood trim. "Would you like me to call and make an appointment so we can go see them together after Labor Day?"

"Sure." Grace lifts her son and places him on her shoulder, his head warm and perfect against her neck. "That'd be great."

"No rush, though," Jenny insists, just as a clatter breaks out below them. She smiles, her expression warm and bright and comforting. "You two are more than welcome to stay here with us for as long as you both need."

THIRTY-FOUR

The Jeep tires crunch over the pea gravel driveway. Hours after they left Jenny's house, Grace finally shifts the gear into Park. Things take time now. Packing extra bags with diapers and soft clothes. Folding up the bassinet. Double-checking a half dozen times to be sure she has all the things she'll need.

The baby's asleep in the back seat. Careful not to wake him, Grace unclicks his five-point harness and then straps him into the carrier she's already positioned on her chest. As if by instinct, she walks to the patio and outdoor shower to grab the key, only to remember, just as she opens the door, that the new owner doesn't keep it there anymore.

"Breaking and entering?" Caleb teases when his face appears in the kitchen window. "See? This is exactly why I didn't want renters here." He smirks. "Give me a minute. I'll meet you around front."

A moment later, Caleb steps onto the front steps, holding a duffel bag at his side. He sets it down, then moves up the walkway and gives Grace a hug, careful not to disturb the baby.

"Congratulations," he says.

"On the baby?" Grace asks. "Or on being the only person you'll actually let rent out your home for a week?"

"A little of Column A, and a little of Column B," he jokes.

Grace inhales and takes a long look at the house. "Looks the same from the outside."

"Is that a good thing?"

"It is."

Caleb takes a few steps back and grabs his bag. "The extra-good news is that I gave it a bit of TLC on the inside. New furniture. Fresh paint. A little facelift in the kitchen. Plus, there's actual insulation in the walls now." He pretends to shiver. "Now *that* was a necessity. The ocean breeze makes winters down here a bit tough."

Out in the street, a family travels home from the beach, the parents' shoulders strapped with chairs and coolers and every other imaginable thing.

"So how do you like it?" Grace asks. "Being a full-time islander and all?"

Caleb waves to the passersby, then looks up and down the street, like he's just now really taking it all in.

"Good," he states. "Quiet. Familiar. But also sort of new."

Grace nods. In some ways, this is what her current life feels like, too. The comfort of Jenny's home. The newness of motherhood.

"Well, I guess I'll leave you to it," Caleb says, rolling back on his heels. He digs into his pocket, pulls out a silver key. "She's all yours." He hands it over. "Until Saturday at two o'clock, at least."

"Thanks, Caleb." Grace gently adjusts the baby's weight against her body. "I really appreciate you doing this for me."

"Enjoy it," Caleb says in his easygoing way. "I hope you catch a good week." He smiles warmly, like an old friend, or a new one. "And that you and the baby get to make some special new memories."

~

The beach is perfect. A wide swath of smooth sand. An endless sheet of gentle waves. The air an ideal mix of warm and cool.

Grace stands at the top of the dune, just as she's done on countless occasions, the baby secured in the carrier—everything the same and yet vastly different. As always, she slides off her sandals and then carefully traverses the decline. The reedy grasses whisper a quiet song as she moves. Up and down the wide stretch of sand, people are switching gears. A pair of children fly a kite. Families pack up. The lifeguards blow their whistles, letting everyone know their shift is complete. Ahead, the ocean sparkles with tide pools and pale sandbars, the sea a shimmering and brilliant blue.

The magic hour.

The best time of day here.

She walks out toward the water—not too close, but just enough to really be able to appreciate the view. The baby asleep on her chest, Grace sits on the warm sand, briefly closes her eyes, inhales the salty air, and lets herself relax after a long drive. Although the traffic wasn't as bad as she expected, it suddenly feels like it took her forever to get here. To this place. To this moment. To this stage of her life.

And maybe that was part of it. That she'd always been searching. Pushing forward. Always the next step. Trying to get to the next version of herself. Always wanting to arrive. But here, on this calm strip of sand, she could just be present. For one sweet week, she could just be Grace.

"You caught a nice first night," a familiar voice says from behind her.

Grace reopens her eyes and sees the shadow of a figure.

Ray.

"How was the drive?" he asks, taking a seat beside her in the sand, not enough to crowd her but closer than a stranger would venture.

"Long," Grace says. "But worth it now that we've arrived," she adds and looks down at her son, knowing that the timing of things—this trip, this moment, everything—feels exactly right.

Ray adjusts his hat, then tilts his face to get a good look at the baby. "So this is the big guy, huh?" He smiles, then gently touches his small, soft foot. When he does, Ray's finger swipes her hand, featherlight but still enough to make her breath briefly catch. "That's a good-looking kid right there."

Grace laughs. "Thank you. He is pretty cute, if I do say so myself."

Ray slowly drops his hand, cups some sand, lets it fall down on his calves. "So . . . August." He looks at the baby once again. "It's a solid name." He playfully winks. "Even if he *was* born in March."

She shrugs, feeling herself smile. "It felt like the right fit the first time I held him."

Out in the water, a few kids throw down skim boards in the shallow surf. They run to chase them, jumping on, then gliding as long as they can until they crash right where the waves break.

"So you're renting Caleb's place for the next couple days?" Ray asks, even though he already knows—Grace told him a few weeks ago when she called him at the Dive to say she'd be down during her normal week.

"I am," she says. "It'll be nice. He said he's cleaned a few things up inside, which I'm looking forward to seeing."

"It looks good in there," Ray says, to which Grace offers him a sideways glance. "I popped over to see it recently after we went fishing." One side of his mouth rises in a timid grin. "It's possible your name came up and that I finally filled him in on a couple things."

Ray is right about one thing: The island is small. A smudge on a map. A tiny dot out in the sea. And yet, tucked among its white-sand shores, weathered houses, and old landmarks is enough space for it to hold a lifetime's worth of memories.

"Well, I'd better be going. I just wanted to pop by and say hello." Ray pulls himself up to standing. "I gave one of my managers the day off, so I'm up for night shift." He brushes sand from his legs, delaying a minute while he looks down at his old summer friend. "Motherhood looks good on you, Grace. You seem happy. Content."

"Thanks, Ray." She smiles up at him. "I am."

He reaches out a hand. She takes it and lets him help pull her up. They stay this way for a beat longer than is necessary, their palms cupped together, their eyes cast in a line.

Nearby, the kids all splash into the water and emerge from it laughing. Their youthful sounds are enough to make Grace and Ray both turn, breaking their gaze, before they both laugh, too.

"Meg says hi, by the way," Ray says. "I told her you called me at the bar to let me know you were coming down for the week, that we were hoping to get together while you're here."

"How's she doing?" Grace asks.

"She's getting there," Ray assures her. "My folks spent the first half of the summer in Pennsylvania to give her a hand once school let out. After they left, she and the kids came down to stay with me at my place for two weeks." He lifts his palms toward the sky. "Uncle Ray equals free vacation house," he jokes. "Lucky them."

He leans in then, gives Grace a hug and a soft kiss on her cheek. Time slows. His face lingers next to hers—one second, then two, three—their skin just barely touching. Ray pulls in a long inhalation, like he wants to remember this moment. Breathe it in. Finally, he exhales and pulls back.

"Can I give you two a hand walking up the dune?"

Grace shakes her head, still feeling the heat of him on her neck. "We're okay," she tells him. "We're going to stay down here a bit longer, watch the first part of the sunset."

Ray stuffs his hands into his pockets. He begins to walk backward. One slow step. Then another. It's like he knows he needs to go but doesn't want to leave yet.

She watches his silhouette becoming smaller, a shape she's known in every season of her life—the pull still there, gentle but certain, like the tide.

Maybe next summer, she hears a voice inside her say.

"I'm glad you came back down, Grace," he calls out before he makes it too far. "It's nice knowing you're here."

On her chest, the baby starts to wiggle and wake up.

"It's nice knowing you're here, too," she says, the late-day sun like honey on her shoulders. "It's good to be back."

Or maybe sooner, she thinks.

~

The water feels cool but refreshing. It splashes up Grace's ankles and onto her calves. The baby carrier in a pile on the sand, she holds her son with his face forward so he can see the water, too. Together, they look out at the horizon—that perfect line full of promise where the sea kisses the sky. Up above them, the sun has begun to settle, what was earlier a bold orange canvas now a wash of soft, muted pastels.

For a moment, Grace softly closes her eyes and lets herself feel her.

In the air. In the water.

She's everywhere here.

The memory of her outlines every surface. Her voice is a whisper in the breeze.

Grace bends down. She holds the baby tight and lets him splash his feet through the surf.

"Your grandmother used to love it here," Grace tells him and thinks of all their memories in this place—all the different women they'd *both* been while standing on this stretch of coastline. Birdie, the wide-eyed child. Birdie, the blushing newlywed. Birdie, the recent widow. Birdie, the young mother. Birdie, the strong and independent individual she eventually grew to become. "It was always her favorite place." Tears form in Grace's eyes, though they're not all sad ones. "I wish she could be here with us this week, though I like to think that maybe she is, just in a different way."

As she talks, the waves gently ebb forward, then retreat back and push forward again. Each time, they carry something new with them. Bits of shells. Tangles of seaweed. Fresh grains of sand. Although the water here sometimes looks the same, it never stays that way. The tides change. The currents shift. Each time you lay eyes on the sea's vastness, what you're really looking at is something brand new.

It's getting cooler. Time to head back, finally enter the house, and get settled in.

Grace lifts the baby. She dries his feet off on the front of her T-shirt, then wipes some sand from his chunky legs. Once he's propped back on her shoulder, Grace turns around in the direction of the dune.

And that's when she feels it.

The gentle touch of something brushing across her toes.

When she looks down, her breath catches at the sight.

There, right in front of her—a whole sand dollar.

She crouches, rinses it off, then stands. It's perfect. A brilliant circle. Not so much as a single crack in it.

Grace looks up at the sky and smiles for so many different reasons.

In her mind, she thinks of all the times in her life that she's stood on this exact stretch of coastline. The versions of herself she's been. The ones that, in the future, she might still become. But mostly, she just considers this moment. Right here. Today. And this version that she is, here in the present.

Grace sets the shell in her palm and holds it up so the baby can touch it. His fingers trace its surface and the smooth ridges that have formed on its edges during its long journey to washing up here.

Maybe it's a sign. Maybe it isn't.

But for today, just knowing that it's here and that it's found her feels like enough.

"It's beautiful, isn't it, love?" Grace whispers to her son. "Though I don't think this one is meant for me." She kisses the top of his head—soft and sweet and perfect. "In my heart, I just have a feeling this one is meant for you."

ACKNOWLEDGMENTS

I first dreamed up the idea for this book the summer I turned twenty-five. At the time, I was living on a stretch of New England coastline, having just walked away from one dream to chase what I believed was the right one (spoiler: It definitely was not). One afternoon, I swam alone at a small, quiet beach (yes, Mother, there was a lifeguard present), looked out at the horizon, cried my eyes out, and thought: *Please, please, let there be a future version of me out there who's figured her life out, someone who will look back on this whole year and laugh.*

Lucky for me, there was. And she did.

She even went ahead and wrote a story inspired by it.

To my agent, Eve Attermann, thank you for always believing in my work and for enthusiastically championing my writing at every step. Your support continues to mean so much to me.

To my editor, Carmen Johnson—I'm very fortunate to work with someone who so genuinely appreciates the types of stories I love to tell, who always knows exactly how to make them even stronger, and who trusts in my ability to create them. Thank you for everything.

To Faith Black Ross, thank you, once again, for all your valuable insight and feedback and for the many ways you help to make my stories shine.

To everyone at William Morris Endeavor, including Rikki Bergman, thank you for the countless ways that you work to turn my story ideas into an actual career.

To the incredible team at Little A, I'm so appreciative of your collective talent and professionalism and the many steps you take to help my books find their way to the right audiences.

To my readers, I'm still left stunned each time I receive an email or a DM or read a review from one of you. Thank you so much for spending time with my words. It's something I'll never take for granted.

Writing is hard (end statement). Writing with kids is . . . something else. I wrote this book during what felt like a very different season in my life than my previous two novels. My big kid needed me in new ways. Our household calendar suddenly became a puzzle of sports and activity schedules. My little guy, who once liked to sleep beside me while I quietly edited pages, grew into a very active toddler, one who had zero interest in competing with a laptop for my attention. I'm grateful to my family—my husband, my two children, and both my parents—for the many ways everyone chipped in so that I could carve out additional hours in the days to focus on this project and give it the attention it deserved.

This was the first of my books in which I began to explore on the page some of my personal experiences with fertility struggles and pregnancy loss. If you're currently on that journey, my heart is with you.

I love to discover fun Easter eggs in films and books, and so I always try to include a few in my own work, if for no other reason than my personal amusement. As such, I owe a special thank-you this time around to my daughter, Hadley Grace, and my son, August Oliver, for letting me borrow their names for two of my characters in this novel.

Finally, to my mother, if you've read this far, I'm sorry. I lied. There definitely were not lifeguards on that beach. Literally ever.

I promise I never swam out too far.

xx

ABOUT THE AUTHOR

Photo © 2023 Sylvie Rosokoff

Angela Brown is the author of *Some Other Time* and *Olivia Strauss Is Running Out of Time*. In addition to her novels, Angela's writing has appeared in *The New York Times*, *Real Simple*, and other publications. She holds an MFA from Fairleigh Dickinson University. Angela lives in New Jersey with her husband and two children. For more information, visit www.angelabrownbooks.com.